P9-CRY-001

LIVE FREE OR DIE

ALSO BY ERNEST HEBERT

The Dogs of March
A Little More Than Kin
Whisper My Name
The Passion of Estelle Jordan

LIVE FREE OR DIE

Ernest Hebert

Viking

VIKING
Published by the Penguin Group
Viking Penguin, a division of Penguin Books USA Inc.,
375 Hudson Street, New York, New York 10014, U.S.A.
Penguin Books Ltd, 27 Wrights Lane, London W8 5TZ, England
Penguin Books Australia Ltd, Ringwood, Victoria, Australia
Penguin Books Canada Ltd, 2801 John Street,
Markham, Ontario, Canada L3R 1B4
Penguin Books (N.Z.) Ltd, 182–190 Wairau Road,
Auckland 10, New Zealand

Penguin Books Ltd, Registered Offices:
Harmondsworth, Middlesex, England

First published in 1990 by Viking Penguin,
a division of Penguin Books USA Inc.

1 3 5 7 9 10 8 6 4 2

Copyright © Ernest Hebert, 1990
All rights reserved

Library of Congress Cataloging in Publication Data
Hebert, Ernest.
Live free or die / Ernest Hebert.
p.   cm.
ISBN 0-670-83133-6
I. Title.
PS3558.E277L55   1990
813'.54—dc20   89-40795

Printed in the United States of America
Set in Primer

Without limiting the rights under copyright
reserved above, no part of this publication
may be reproduced, stored in or introduced into
a retrieval system, or transmitted, in any form
or by any means (electronic, mechanical, photo-
copying, recording or otherwise), without the
prior written permission of both the copyright
owner and the above publisher of this book.

Author's Note,
Acknowledgments
and Dedication

This is the fifth and final of a series of novels about the fictional town of Darby, New Hampshire. Some place names and other elements of the real world appear in the novels. The geography of Darby is a composite of Westmoreland and Sullivan, New Hampshire. But the characters and stories are fiction. I made it all up, and I'm proud to say so. I'm tempted to ramble on about what I set out to do, what I discovered and what I think this series means. But once books are in print, they belong to the readers, not the authors, so, as Howard Elman would say, I'll pipe down.

I'm not sure why, but through the writing of these novels I've been stingy with acknowledgments. It's time to give thanks. The most important person in my life and the greatest inspiration to my work has been my wife, Medora. Others who have contributed in some way to the writing and/or publication of the Darby novels include:

Delia Daniels, Dayton Duncan, Kathryn Harrison, Audrey Lyle, Mavis MacIntosh, Ted Parent, Nancy Pindell, Terry Pindell, Rita Scott, William Sullivan, Charles Verrill, Lael Wertenbaker, Alan Williams, my parents, my teachers, and many writers whose work I have drawn from and been sustained by, in particular: E. M. Forster and his novel *Howard's End,*

George Orwell and his novel *Coming Up for Air,* and John Gardner for a method of writing that worked for me.

A special thanks to those who helped with *Live Free or Die:* Ted Timreck, for his wise counsel and friendship; Sandra Bonneau, Jan Cohen, Dayton Duncan, Sharon Eason, Karen Gallup, Lynn Kochanek, Jackie Metivier, Terry Pindell, Lynn Simington, Stella Sise, Jeanette Uhlig and Jan Walker, who critiqued an early draft of the book; Wayne Scheeler, a Dartmouth College student whose writings on bears assisted with the bear sequences in this book; and Russell Banks, whose novel *Continental Drift* contributed alchemically to *Live Free or Die.*

To those whom I have inadvertently left off the list, please forgive me.

That said, I'm honored to dedicate this book to the people who helped make the Darby series possible.

Contents

PART I

1

The Bridge

"Freddy's *smaht,* but he ain't as *smaht* as he thinks he is," the dream father spoke from a pit he dug out in the barn to repair cars. The dream son watched as his father's words drew him apart, one self off to cruise the avenues of the U.S.A., the other self stalled in the shadows of Darby, New Hampshire.

Frederick Elman popped awake, a beefy young man with muddy eyes, full beard, sleeping bare-ass. The real world cleared out the dream, and he knew he was in the Live Free or Die, that rust-bucket camper pickup truck he called home, parked in an abandoned shopping center, just outside of the great city of New Orleans. He sat up in his bunk and reached for the first article of clothing of the day, the headband he'd impulsively bought at the K-Mart store. Eighty-nine cents, the receipt said. He had thought, Gotta be the cheapest thing in the store, and sprung for it. The headband was red and yellow, the ends tapering so they could be tied like a string. Since he'd started wearing the headband, the fellows on the paint crew called him Mohawk.

By the time he had fully awakened, and stood hunched over in the tight confines of his camper, the words "Grace Pond" broke the surface of his mind like trout jumping out of the water on that selfsame pond. Grace Pond was a small water

3

body high up on some private land where his father used to take him fishing.

He dressed in white cotton overalls, which were flecked here and there with the green paint with which he and two other men painted the steel frame of a magnificent bridge that crossed the great river.

He scanned his environs. Grass grew in cracks on the graying blacktop. The deserted shopping center had been so long neglected that even the graffiti on the plywood over the windows were drab and dated. Yet he liked it here. He could smell nature about to make a move and take over the territory. There was something about this day, a feeling he translated into a color. The day was green, forest-green, midsummer-green. It was never a color he had particularly liked, although at the moment the thought of it made him ache as one in love. He was sweetly nostalgic for something, he wasn't quite sure what. In fact, he felt an ache for home. A May morning in Louisiana was like a July morning in New Hampshire—warm, misty, pleasantly dank.

Frederick drove the Live Free or Die out of the lot to Joan Cotton's in the town of Algiers for his morning fare of sausage, grits, and runny eggs. He'd made Joan's little place his head-quarters. Here he ate every meal, drank, and socialized. Joan was a slender woman about fifty who had a cousin in the major leagues and a great-aunt who had sung the blues in a time when the blues really were the blues. Joan had skin like camp-fire embers, at once black and glowing. She surprised him that morning. "Telegram for you," she said.

He tried to read her eyes. It struck him that her ancestors had been slaves, people who display one emotion and feel another. He had no idea who his own ancestors were. His parents had both been "fosters," as the term went in his home-town of Darby, origins unknown.

"Somebody die?" He felt icy.

4

"Not exactly," Joan said.

Frederick read the telegram: "Howie hurt. Call home. Elenore." His father injured. He couldn't make heads or tails of the idea. What can I do for him? he thought.

He called collect from the pay phone in the restaurant.

"Ma, it's me, Frederick."

"No, it's Howie—he built a tree stand to hunt coyotes."

"So?"

"Freddy, he fell."

"Fell? My father. Fell?"

"His leg's busted. You gotta come home and run the Honeywagon."

"The Honeywagon! You want me to do the trash route?"

"Oh, Freddy—he needs you."

"Needs me? My father never needed anybody for anything."

His mother said nothing. Frederick listened to low static on the line.

"I don't know, Ma. I gotta go to work; I'll call you tonight." Frederick hung up the phone.

No way was he going to return to Darby to work on the Honeywagon. He wasn't about to give up a good job, a good life to get his father out of a business jam. Howard would survive, broken leg or not. His father would not approve of his son's coming home, so there was no point in the son's returning. His mother tended to be excitable and negative, like any good convert to Catholicism. Frederick was sure she'd exaggerated the situation. If he could get a hold of his father's friend Cooty Patterson, he could learn what was really going on. But how to do that? Cooty lived in a cabin with no electricity, no telephone.

As always, the sight of the bridge rising up over the waters of the great river and then falling back down into the city of New Orleans held Frederick Elman in awe. The bridge was a thing connecting two ideas. It was what God had in mind for the work of human beings. Although Frederick said nothing about his troubles at home to Eddie, his Native American work partner, or to the Cajun, the painting-crew foreman, he felt a desire to justify himself, argue his case. It's not that I hate my father and refuse to help him—I love him. I'll leap into freeway traffic for him. It's just that proximity to him diminishes me; a few months with a Howard on the mend and I might vanish altogether. Besides, I know, just know, he doesn't really need my help.

Eddie was already waiting in the paint shack in the shadow of the bridge. He used to say, "You're late," but he'd learned his words meant little to Frederick, so now he only smiled. The two men were intimate in an odd way. They were partners painting the bridge, and as such they were companionable and compatible on the job. But here, before the ascent, they were uncomfortable with one another. They solved this problem simply by saying as little as possible until they went up; there would be plenty of time for chitchat on the bridge. The business at hand was to prepare to ascend.

Frederick looked out of the shack window, and Eddie read his mind.

"The Cajun's not here, be back in a minute," Eddie said.

"I'll count my blessings," Frederick said.

The Indian grunted. Frederick and Eddie watched one another with intensity and seriousness as they slipped on their safety harnesses. As the Cajun had said time and time again, checking the harness, making sure it "secured the flesh to the steel," was part of staying alive on the bridge. "Your partner's equipment fails, his kin and me will curse your soul to hellfires," the Cajun had said. Frederick put on his harness quickly, then waited while Eddie finished up. Eddie was wiry but strong, his manner cautious but not fastidious. Eddie was only about thirty-five, but his sad, hairless, Indian face had

6

been burned by so many suns that it was deeply lined, and as far as Frederick was concerned he belonged to the ancients.

The harness was made of nylon, pulling up and around the crotch. Straps and buckles held it taut; at the front was a snap, dangling at belly level, that hooked onto a line set up on the staging for painting the bridge. Frederick and Eddie stood nose to nose, each man tugging the other man's metal snap, pulling his straps, testing his buckles.

When Frederick suggested to Eddie that this ritual the two of them went through every morning, gravely and in silence, making sure the other man was secure for the ascent, might have reminded Eddie of the Indian rites of his youth, Eddie had said, "I forget and I don't care." Eddie had separated himself from his heritage. He was, he said, going to be a success Anglo-style, because there was no other way in an Anglo world. Eddie regarded himself as an immigrant. He'd pointed out that Indians really were Asians, wanderers who had crossed a land bridge between Alaska and Siberia during the low water of the last ice age. Indian land, Indian culture belonged to another place, another time. Never mind that twenty thousand years had passed since his people had settled here; Eddie insisted he was not a native American.

The Cajun walked into the shack as Frederick was tying his headband.

"Hey, Mohawk, you going to behave yourself today?" the Cajun said.

"You want me kiss your wazoo, or what?" Frederick said.

"Young folk today got no humility." The Cajun turned his back on him and walked away.

Frederick know that what irritated the Cajun about him was his swagger. Young fellows weren't suppose to stomp around, treat their elders like gerbils. Frederick hadn't always been like this. Growing up, he'd been shy, sometimes sullen. In college, he'd been withdrawn. But there was something about

7

this job, high up on a great bridge, that made him cocky; he liked the feeling. The job took nerve; nerve came from bluffing God. Frederick made no effort to change. Swagger could get him through in place of true courage. And, too, he had a great role model for his behavior: Howard.

"Let's go," the Cajun said. The three painters left the shack. It was going to be a good day, sunny, warm, not too much wind, perfect weather to paint a bridge. Frederick and Eddie went first, and the Cajun followed.

The first time Frederick had seen the staging set up to paint the bridges, it had reminded him of equipment for mountain climbers, ropes and connectors everywhere, and procedures to follow to get from down to up and back again. In fact, it took more time to move the staging to a new location than actually to paint the section.

They began the ascent, first climbing metal ladders, then following a slender aluminum catwalk, their safety harnesses hooked to a rope, until they reached the section set aside for that day's work. The trip took twenty minutes; they were almost at the top of the bridge. From here they could not see the road below, because it was obscured by the metal gridwork of the bridge, but they could see the crescent of the river and Lake Pontchartrain shimmering in the sun.

The black girl was only about fifty feet above the pavement, well below the painters, and off to the side of them by several hundred feet. Because she was preoccupied with her own problems, she did not notice the painters; because the painters were preoccupied with each other, they did not notice her.

"Hey, Mohawk, *poot* on *thee* safety belt." The boss's words sailed up the steel beams of the bridge.

"The Cajun's on your ass again," said Eddie.

Frederick knew Eddie was entertained by the skirmishing between himself and the boss. Frederick himself might have remained indifferent to the Cajun, for he did not hate him but merely despised him, as young men despise bosses the world over, but he taunted the boss for the very reason that the boss taunted him. And, too, there was something in Frederick that wanted to get fired, so he could move on to another town, another bridge, without having to make the decision himself.

"Eddie?" Frederick called in a tone of mock intimacy. When he caught Eddie's eye, he added, "This is goodbye."

Frederick pretended to slip off the catwalk. Eddie quivered for a moment in horror, and then he grinned as Frederick hauled himself up, leaned forward, and saluted the Cajun below.

"Son of a *beech!*" The Cajun's outburst contained a spatter of fright.

Frederick snapped his harness to the lifeline. "There— hooked up to mamma bridge."

The black girl continued to climb the bridge. She had no lifeline. It was early in the day, but the girl was dressed in evening wear that made her look like a woman. In fact, she was very young, fifteen or sixteen, maybe younger; perhaps she herself did not know her own age. She seemed dazed, as if she'd suddenly awakened from a nightmare to find herself in this place of sea, sky, metal, and wind.

"Hey, Mohawk, you Indian? Or you phony Indian?" The boss's forced laughter followed his words up the bridgework.

"You might have some Indian in you, but I doubt it," Eddie said.

"Who knows? Who cares?" Frederick said to Eddie, then hollered down to the boss. "You're goddamn right I'm an Indian, and I'm going take that miserable Cajun scalp of yours."

"Hoodee, haaa-haaa, hoo." The air currents lent a spectral quality to the boss's laughter.

The black girl on the bridge stopped for a moment and looked down. The distance between herself and the world seemed to draw out, like the sound of a passing automobile. She moaned softly, and continued upward.

Below, Officer Conrad Haynes, who had immediately called for help when he had seen the subject in distress, drove his squad car to a point on the bridge road under the girl. The traffic zipped by unconcerned. He stepped out of the car and looked up, shading his eyes from the sun. The beam of his blue light circled, but he knew better than to run the siren. Jumpers got nervous at the sounds of sirens. Officer Haynes was about sixty, a calm, detached man who viewed his work life in much the same impersonal way that a TV camera frisks a crowd for images.

"Mohawk, know what your problem is?" Eddie paused for Frederick to answer.

"Problem? What problem?" Frederick grinned at the Indian.

"You got a problem. You may not be an Indian, but you think like an Indian. You got a chip on your shoulder; you got daring but no ambition. Underneath, you're chicken."

"And you, Eddie?" Frederick was amused by his friend's earnestness.

"Eddie's got ambition." Eddie held his paintbrush like an emblem and thumped his chest with his free hand. "Mohawk, the old lady and me went to the bank yesterday. We're going to open a restaurant."

"A restaurant? Eddie, a million people a year break their hearts opening restaurants."

10

"They don't have Eddie's formula."

"Oh, sure."

"Serve the best food, sell cheaper than anybody else, and hire good help. And here's the key: Italian restaurant. You ever hear of an Italian restaurant going down the tubes?" Eddie began to paint fast now.

"You're a genius, Eddie."

From below, the Cajun shouted an absurd question into the void, "Hey, Mohawk, any Indians up there in *Newwwww Hamp-shyre,* or only phony Indians?"

Frederick dipped his brush into the paint bucket, then flicked the brush at his side. A fine mist of bridge-green paint began to rain down.

"Mohawk—Frederick," Eddie addressed his young co-worker, "a young man like you who wants nothing, don't go after nothing, no dreams—there's no place for him in this country. You understand what I'm saying?"

Officer Haynes watched a panel truck skid to a stop behind his cruiser. A beautiful blond newswoman and a cameraman hopped out. The policeman blinked as the hot-blooded, cool-eyed newswoman approached him.

"This bridge your beat?" she asked.

"Thirty-one years."

"You must have seen a lot of jumpers."

"More jumpers than the L.A. Lakers."

The newswoman turned to her cameraman, a roly-poly fellow wearing glasses. "Get some footage of the jumper." Then she looked up at the girl and whispered to herself, "Poor thing."

The cameraman aimed his instrument upward; his neck hurt. The black girl had stopped, and she resembled a resting bird. The cameraman zoomed in on her. The wind parted her dress. Her vulnerability and his own sense of secretiveness behind the long lens filled him with desire.

11

The black girl struggled upward a few feet, stopped, then looked down. The sight of the water a thousand feet away, or so it seemed to her, froze her in place. She put a hand on her flat stomach, as pregnant women will to feel their babies kick.

A Volvo pulled to a stop. Behind the wheel was a dignified, somewhat overweight man with a meticulously trimmed beard that contrasted with Mohawk's free-form facial hair. Officer Haynes answered the newswoman's questioning glance: "The shrink."

The psychiatrist stepped out of the car, looked up. The sun was bright and it hurt his eyes.

"Holy smoke, she's awful high," he said, in the faint, snobby New England accent college students pick up going to schools in Cambridge, Massachusetts.

"You want the horn?" asked Officer Haynes.

"No, it'll scare her. Call the fire department. I need a bucket."

"Okay, cap'n," Officer Haynes said.

"No sirens," the psychiatrist said with an authoritarian edge that impressed the policeman.

"Aye, aye, cap'n," Officer Haynes said.

The newswoman, whose attention had been on the black girl, now turned to the psychiatrist. Before she could speak, the psychiatrist snapped, "And no interviews."

The newswoman wheeled from the psychiatrist to the policeman. "Want to be on TV? How about it? For the grandchildren."

Frederick unhitched himself from the safety line and moved a few feet. Then he heard the alarm in Eddie's voice: "Will ya look at that!"

Frederick's mind converted image into language: She's in

trouble; you could save her. He began to swing from beam to beam.

Below, a mist of bridge-green paint imperceptibly enveloped the Cajun. "He's free—free!" the Cajun said to himself in a jealous whisper, then shouted, "You don't buckle up, I'll send your ass to Slidell!"

But Frederick was headed for the black girl.

The newswoman addressed the lens of the camera. "They've sent for a bucket from the fire department, where psychiatrist Martin O'Brien will attempt to talk the girl down. We'll bring you that in minutes. Meanwhile, we're live with Bridge Officer Conrad Haynes.

"Officer Haynes, what is it about this particular bridge that leads so many unhappy people to leap from it to their deaths in the waters of the Mississippi?"

While she spoke, the camera browsed the river. There was no response from the policeman, who glanced at his watch like any bored workman waiting for his lunch hour.

"Is it the bridge itself? The river?" the newswoman pressed.

Officer Haynes did not speak.

"Live with Officer Haynes. Officer Haynes?" the newswoman said.

Officer Haynes mumbled a word that sounded like "Myrtle."

"Would you repeat that for our audience? We're live. The question: What is it about this bridge that leads people to jump from it?"

"Myrtle," said the policeman, deadpan as an aging comic.

The newswoman, for once in her life, was flabbergasted, speechless; then the policeman finally made himself clear.

"Myrtle," he said. "Most of 'em got myri-tal problems."

The cameraman swung his instrument upward. He rubbed his eyes under his glasses. Could this be real? A man coming into view, approaching the girl on the bridge?

Frederick was not six feet from the black girl. She was scrawny, a stranger to him, and yet she seemed familiar, someone he'd loved from another lifetime. She hugged the bridge for life. If he could say the right thing, hold her with a word, he could pluck her up and carry her down. It was with that thought that he came to an understanding about himself. He had no "right word"; nothing to say to this girl, nothing to say to anyone.

"Nothing to do but go up, and look around, because there's nothing below but nothing," he said.

The black girl cocked her head sideways, trying to figure him out. The sun made a halo around her blue-black skin. The paint on this side of the bridge had faded to a pale green that reminded Frederick of the cabbages his mother grew in the family garden.

"You have a hometown?" he asked. "A place called home? I know how it is. Nothing back there, nothing where you're at, nothing ahead. So, you say, I'll go on to the next place, I'll . . ." At that moment, in mid-sentence, it struck him: Now, now is the time. He reached out his hand to the girl.

Her eyes, full of suffering, met his and she jumped.

2

The Elmans

Through his brief time in college and all through the years of drifting, these rebellious years, Frederick Elman never quite dropped the look of his New Hampshire origins, and when he left for home that night of the day when he failed to save the black girl, he was, in his appearance, in blue jeans and scuffed work boots that had never been shined, halfway back. With his untrimmed beard and dusty, disheveled dark hair falling over his ears, he could have passed as a Center Darby construction worker, or a woodcutter, or a truck driver, or some guy unemployed, desperate, and running a bluff to hold on to his pride. When he was growing up, his father had criticized him for wearing his hair long, because workingmen didn't do that. Only rich college kids and fairies wore long hair. Today the college boys and the fairies were wearing their hair short while the working stiffs were wearing their hair long, and—as Frederick was soon to learn—even Howard himself, although he was almost bald on top, had let the hair curl up on the sides and back of his head.

Frederick wore the headband when he hit the road. It was part of his getaway gear. The headband might be accepted in some circles of New Hampshire workingmen—or might not. Didn't matter. What mattered was the whattahyahgonnadoaboutit challenge. The only garment on his back, the blue

T-shirt that bore lettering that said "Monkey Hill—New Orleans," would be inadequate dress for New Hampshire. It was just too skimpy for the season.

It was almost midnight when, without a goodbye to anyone (he hated the emotion of parting), he drove off "upriver." Frederick called whatever road he was on "the river." North was "upriver," south "downstream," east "to the ocean," and west "to the other ocean." The Live Free or Die was his craft. He drove two-lane roads, kept off the interstates to avoid the long-haulers; they made him vaguely jealous because of their big trucks, which slighted his own modest rig.

Just before dawn, he pushed on through sleepiness, but in the late morning he pulled off the road and catnapped, awakening out of a dreamless sleep with a taste in his mouth like sofa stuffing and a feeling he'd been cheated out of some hours of life and motion.

In Georgia he passed a catfish farm. A couple of disreputable shacks and a trailer hunkered down in the grim shade of pine trees too close together. Just beyond was a vegetable stand and an old man behind a crude wooden awning. Frederick hit the brakes, and the pickup screeched to a brave, awkward halt like a middle-aged man sliding into second base in a softball game.

Frederick stepped out of his rig and said to the old man, who obviously was the proprietor, "You the proprietor?"

"You want to look around, buy something—what?" The proprietor blinked in wonder at this bearded young buck.

"Peaches."

Frederick studied the old man while he put the peaches in a brown paper bag. He wore gray-blue cotton overalls, and his eyes were watery blue, and he looked as if he didn't know where he was going or where he had been, but here and now was okay.

"You look like a friend of mine," Frederick said.

16

"Is that so? This is Batesville. My name is Bates. Art Bates. 'Ay Bates,' they call me. In this town you have your Dee Bates and Ree Bates, and forty-five or fifty just-plain Bates, and a soul, ain't related to me, they call Master Bates."

"My friend goes by Cooty Patterson."

"Praise the Lord, but that's a funny name."

Frederick suddenly found himself with nothing to say. The old man looked at him quizzically—*Well, what do you want, chowderhead?*

"You run this place, do you?" Frederick said.

"You want to buy a gun?"

"A gun?"

"You got a look in your eye that says, I want to buy a gun."

"I don't want a gun. I'd probably put it to my head. You sell guns?"

"Nope, but an old gentleman I know, name of Mac Bates, sells guns. Good money in it."

"Money? That your interest?" Frederick looked at the vegetable stand and the catfish farm beyond. Sunlight shone on three small man-made ponds. The sight of water, not the mighty Mississippi but small water, made Frederick think of home. Tuckerman County was loaded with tiny glacial lakes and ponds. One good thing about returning to Darby, perhaps the only good thing, was that he'd get out in the woods, do some fishing, go hunting.

"I just want to keep busy. I am at an age, you see . . ." The old man let the sentence trail away, as one begging a meaning from his listener because his own meaning is so meager.

Frederick spent the night in a small town in southern Virginia. When he was traveling, he preferred to settle in for a night's rest on turnoffs on deserted two-lane roads, but towns were okay, too. For a one-night stand the safest place was always on a residential street in the nicest part of the community.

He woke in the first gray morning light, babbling in a dream about fishing. Before he opened his eyes, he saw a streak of yellow-green that he recognized as a perch from Grace Pond. He started the engine and headed north.

He knew he was within striking distance of New Hampshire when he saw diners instead of cafés. He'd been traveling a couple hours and he was hungry. He ate a huge breakfast of scrapple, eggs, and home fries. It would last him until he arrived in Darby.

There was a chill in the air when he reached Pennsylvania, and he was about to put on the sweatshirt he kept handy, but something made him stop the Live Free or Die and rummage through his things until he came up with a flannel shirt and Boston Celtics cap. He was getting in uniform for Center Darby.

He soon hit the East Coast megalopolis, where the charm of two-lane roads was swamped by traffic, strip development, and the general dreariness of the architecture of the age. Terrific radio, though. He pulled onto I-95. Trucks, toll roads, and toll bridges—they bugged him, but there was no other practical way for the out-of-town traveler to get from here to there on the East Coast. Worst place in America to drive. Soon as his father's leg healed, Frederick was going to get as far away from it as possible. But the New York skyline at night, as always, thrilled him and made him conscious of the awe/anger of his country-boy inferiority complex.

Somewhere just north of Springfield, Massachusetts, on I-91, the bright milky way of the megalopolis night faded into the starry lights of individual houses in the hills of rural New England. It was downright cold now, and Frederick completed his outfit with a down parka liner. He hadn't worn it since Colorado. Another hour passed and he turned off the interstate onto Route 21. It went to Darby. He was almost home.

There was a big moon out when Frederick pulled his pickup onto the dirt driveway of his parents' place. A light was on in the kitchen, which was odd, because it was well past his parents' bedtime and they were always stingy about using electricity. The mobile home depressed him for its lack of distinction. By contrast, the barn with its twelve-pitch gabled roof seemed full of nobility.

He was about to get out of the truck when he remembered he was wearing the headband. His father would not like it, but that was not why he ripped it off his head. The headband was courage and freedom and his identity as an individual; it was a self within a self. Now, home, he found a need to hide that deep-down self. So he stuffed it—self and headband—in the glove compartment of his truck.

The yard was littered with junk cars, which Howard used for spare parts to his various vehicles. The garden was plowed and rototilled, awaiting planting. One new touch: a shrine to the Virgin between the garden (Elenore's domain) and the fields littered with junk cars (Howard's domain). The concrete Virgin stood serenely in a long concrete gown, her concrete head bowed, her bare concrete feet on the body of a concrete snake. Frederick put his hands on those feet. They were cold. The air was cold—Darby was cold. Spring hadn't caught on here yet.

He walked among the junk cars until he came across the hulk of an old wringer-style washing machine. It was full of bullet holes, some put there by himself.

In the driveway, parked beside the barn, the trash-collection truck, with its battered red cylindrical body, reminded him of a prehistoric beast. On the body in bold, gold lettering, in two rows, standing at attention, were the words "Honeywagon Inc.—Howard Elman Proprietor."

Frederick walked to the barn. In anything but the worst weather, the wide door remained open, and Frederick knew right where to snap on the light. In the radiance that followed, his boyhood appeared before him: the pit where his father worked on cars, the clutter of machinery and tools, the dark barn wood, and the faint aroma left over from when farm animals were housed here. Nothing appeared to have changed. He rattled steel animal-traps hanging from a nail on a wall. They sounded like angry chimes.

He snapped off the light and turned away from the barn. It was late, and the light on in the kitchen of the mobile home disturbed him mildly and put him on alert. He entered through a whacked-together plywood mud-room—his father called it "the porch." Here Honeywagon Inc. uniforms hung on coat hooks; they smelled of the trash route and his father, or perhaps he only imagined that. He didn't knock, but opened the door and stepped into the mobile-home kitchen.

Here he was treated to the spectacle of his father, Howard Elman, splayed out on the floor on his back, his broken leg encased in plaster sticking up in the air at a strange angle, the wheelchair beside him tipped over.

"Pop?" said Frederick.

"I heard you drive up—hearing aid, see?" Howard pointed to his noggin. "You took your good time getting to the front door." Howard spoke in counterfeit outrage to mask his pain.

"How long you been on the floor?" Frederick was stunned; he didn't feel quite grounded in reality. Too many hours on the road.

"Midnight. Had a couple beers," Howard said.

"It's two A.M.," Frederick said.

"Got it in my head I could walk. Figured I'd change the oil in the Honeywagon. Couldn't even take a step. Jeez!"

"Why didn't you wake Ma?" Frederick was still a little knocked off his pins by this situation.

"Ah, she can't lift me," Howard said, and then his tone changed to inquisitor. "What are you doing here anyway?"

His father's anger and suspicion, so familiar, settled him into the scene, and with that he could feel his own anger kindle. "What do you think?" Frederick challenged.

"She got a hold of you, didn't she?" Howard interrogated his son. "She told you to come home, didn't she?"

Frederick stood over his father, looking down at him. "I'm your only son and you greet me like the tax collector."

"Ain't you *smaht*?" Father interrupted son, and before he could go on, son interrupted father.

"You fall out of a tree stand, half drunk, no doubt," Frederick said, full of power from his self-righteousness, "and now you're grouchy, housebound, shut-in. I'm back to save your ass."

From his spot on the floor, leg aching, crick in his neck, Howard Elman looked up at his boy as if he were someone else's son, one of these young fellows with his balls where his brains were supposed to be, and he was rather impressed with this young stranger's outburst. "Ah, pipe down and help me get off this goddamn floor and we'll have a beer," he said.

Frederick hoisted his old man into the wheelchair, grabbed a couple bottles of Schaefer from the fridge, handed one to Howard, and sat himself at the kitchen table. It was the same table his parents had always had, heavy wood painted a dirty cream color, the top full of burn marks from Howard's Camel cigarettes. The table was among a few possessions saved when the Elman house had gone up in flames, the same year Frederick had quit college and hit the road.

"I wish the house hadn't burned down. I don't feel like this tin box is really home," Frederick said.

"When I set fire to a place, I have my reasons."

"Sure, Pop. How did you get out of the woods with a broken leg?"

"Crawled a mile to the nearest house."

Frederick laughed at his old man. "So where is this tree stand you couldn't stay in?"

21

"That's for me to know and you to find out." Howard was not merely defending psychic territory; he was issuing a challenge, and his son knew it.

"Okay, and I will, too."

"I doubt it," Howard said. After a moment of uneasy silence, Howard's voice softened. "Bring your stuff in. You can have Heather's room. Mrs. Cutter's paying for her schooling in France, and she don't come home no more."

"Who can blame her? If it's all the same to you, I'll sleep in my camper."

"Whatever you want," Howard said.

"Whatever I want?" Frederick posed the question to himself, and then he faced his father. "I go someplace and I'm temporary help. I don't see why it should be any different here."

Howard was wounded by his son's words, but damned if he'd show it. Rather, he turned his thoughts to business, which allowed him to let some affection creep into his tone. And it was this affection in his father's voice, as opposed to the words, coming out of nowhere as far as Frederick was concerned, that wounded Frederick.

"I'm a full week behind in my pickups," Howard said. "If you could make a run tomorrow morning, Honeywagon Incorporated would be deeply appreciative? Go get Cooty Patterson. He ain't worth nothing for work, but he knows the route and he's good company."

Frederick raised his bottle of beer in a toast. "To the Honeywagon," he said.

When Frederick Elman awakened on the morning after his arrival in Center Darby, he found freshly laundered work clothes on a hanger hooked over the driver's-side door handle of his camper, left there earlier by his mother. He brought the clothes inside, and, standing in his underwear, hunched over in the cramped quarters of the Live Free or Die, he held the clothes at arm's length and studied them, the heavy cotton forest-green trousers and a shirt to match, over the left breast pocket of which was sewn a label with the name of his father's company. His father owned racks of these outfits. They hung in the shed-porch entry of the mobile home, they hung in the bedroom, they hung in the barn. He wore them seven days a week for work and play, in hot weather and cold, and for every occasion save weddings and funerals, when he exchanged the uniform for a more formal one, an out-of-date blue suit and tie, a red-striped one for weddings, a gray-striped one for funerals. The shirttail might hang out of the back of his pants, but the tie would always be squared up to his throat in a perfect Windsor knot. While his personal appearance meant nothing to Howard, the quality of the tie knot was a matter of pride and identity. He would want people to say of him, "Now, there's a fella who knows how to tie a knot," rather than, "My, what a snappy dresser!"

Frederick pulled the shirt and trousers off the hanger and tried them on. Before Frederick had left New Hampshire, he'd never been able to wear his father's clothes, because they were too big, but today the trousers were only a little loose around the waist and the shirt fit perfectly. He looked at his own clothes, the blue jeans and flannel shirt, the T-shirt, and something told him that while he was on the job he must wear his father's uniform, so that on his own time his own uniform might have some meaning.

He'd eat breakfast at his parents' place, then he'd pick up old Cooty Patterson, and they'd collect the trash. The thought of the Honeywagon made Frederick wince, but he was looking forward to seeing Cooty. Besides renewing the friendship, he had another motive for seeing the old man. Last night Howard had been cagey about the location of the tree stand he'd fallen

23

out of. Frederick was determined to find it, and then to make sure Howard knew he had found it. Cooty might have some information.

He left the camper and went into the house for breakfast. His mother was waiting for him at the door.

"Been a while," he said. Though he avoided contact with Howard, he had talked to his mother on the telephone with some frequency.

They paused to look at each other before awkwardly embracing, then parting. Her dusty-gray hair and the lines around her eyes and mouth provoked Frederick to silent anger. He wished he could believe in her God enough to shake his fist at Him and ask, "Why?" In the background, he could hear his father muttering from the bathroom. Frederick was about to reach for the kettle of boiling water when Elenore snatched it from his hand.

"I can get my own coffee," Frederick said softly.

"Yes, you can, but I want to," she said.

Elenore Elman's great discovery in life was that out of the chaos of existence there was a power, a guiding light. She called this illuminated force God. She understood that you could not make people believe in Him. You could only suggest His way through example, good works, and prayer, and to this end she was committed.

An uncomfortable moment between son and mother, while she spooned instant coffee into a mug and poured the hot water into it, was aggravated by occasional oaths and moans from Howard offstage.

"What's his problem?" Frederick was annoyed.

"He won't let me help him on the potty," Elenore said.

"Well, jeez. Can't he do it himself?"

"Just barely."

"What'll happen if he ever gets more incapacitated than he is now?"

24

"I'll shoot him."

Mother and son stood suspended in the moment. Then they burst into laughter, and the unease between them vanished.

"He's not a wicked man, you know—just himself: unbearable," Elenore said.

"I know," Frederick said. "He could hire one of the Jordans to do his route for the three or four weeks he's going to be off his feet. He doesn't really need me."

"I know," Elenore said.

"You knew all along."

"That's right."

"You tricked me into coming home."

"That's right."

Mug in hand, Frederick made to leave and then, as an afterthought, he gave his mother a shy kiss on the cheek. The Elmans were not a family that displayed much physical affection, so this was a rare moment.

"Gotta get Cooty." Frederick headed out.

"Freddy?" Elenore called.

"Yah."

"I know you feel trapped here."

"Yah."

"But you do look natural in his work duds."

Frederick strode quickly to the Honeywagon, swung into the driver's seat, started the engine, fumbled a bit with the gear shift, backed down the dirt drive, and shifted into first. With a jerk and a growl, the Honeywagon rolled forward.

Frederick was driving about thirty-five miles an hour on the twisted roads of Darby when he came upon a bicyclist. The rider heard the farting engine of the Honeywagon, and glanced back over his shoulder. Frederick recognized him as a Prell, one of the families of the Upper Darby elite. The bicyclist began to bear down; he'd decided to race. The road dipped into a gentle curve, and the bicyclist actually gained some ground on the Honeywagon. Frederick estimated the bicycle was going fifty miles an hour. The operator of the machine wore a helmet and a tight-fitting uniform; his machine had probably cost more than the current market value of the Live Free or Die. The bicyclist was fastidious, athletic, attractive, and determined. He had everything for success that Frederick himself did not have, and Frederick knew it. He'd enjoy running the guy over. Frederick gunned the engine and roared by the bicycle. He glanced in the rearview mirror. The bicyclist got a whiff of the Honeywagon as it blasted past him, and he pinched his nose. Frederick, who'd thought he'd won this contest, now realized he'd lost.

When he arrived at Cooty Patterson's cabin, Frederick found the door open, a fire going in the cookstove, but the old man not at home. It was a one-room cabin of rough pine boards, built by a forgotten Frenchman, in a time gone by, for reasons that would make no sense today. The door had no lock, nothing to keep out an intruder but the smell of Cooty Patterson himself, like the fragrance of a flower that had survived a war by absorbing its stink. Frederick knew Cooty wouldn't mind his entering the cabin, but he backed off anyway out of the odd mix of superstition and common sense that the Elmans displayed: You didn't go into the wizard's lair unless the wizard was on the premises to extend the invitation. Never mind that the wizard was not a wizard.

Frederick wandered down a path in the woods, hoping to find Cooty bringing in firewood or tending his traps. It had been a long time since Frederick had been in New Hampshire, and he found himself thinking about these tree-infested, rock-strewn hills and the kind of people who hunkered down among them. A breed—the Jordans, his own family, Cooty—was dying out, replaced by people with money, education, culture, people "wise in the ways of the world," a phrase that suggested to Frederick that the "world" did not include the physical planet, but only the people on it. These "worldly" people commuted to jobs in Tuckerman, and perhaps in their free time they hunted or fished or hiked or cross-country skied; they lived in the woods, used the woods to some degree, but they were not really part of the "out there" that was the real home of the old breed, for to be of that forest you had to depend on it for sustenance, spiritual and physical. No more. The Jordans, his family, he himself had changed, becoming like those new people who were replacing them; only Cooty remained true to the old breed, and only because he was crazy. Frederick figured, if he ever went off the deep end, he could lose himself in the haze of failure, extend the effort necessary for renewal, or choose the course Cooty had taken.

He walked through the woods, thinking about the old man.

3

Cooty

Cooty Patterson's shack was near the road, but screened from it by brush and forest. The cabin had no electricity, no inside toilet, no paint, no wallpaper, no amenities of modern life.

By the standards of society, Upper and Center Darby both and even Darby Depot, Cooty was a mental case, a man who conjured rather than lived his life, proceeded from point A to point B not like a man—that is, in as straight a line as possible—but like an animal, sniffing and meandering, in which every point was point A, point B, and every point between. There was no room in such a life for growth or improvement, or even for the human way of love. Who would have him? It was a life made of pure animal inquisitiveness.

If he had had a bent for literary expression, which of course he could not have and still be Cooty Patterson, Cooty would have said, "I am not a man as such, I am a poem."

Cooty was a poem. He lived his life as an expression of the things that had meaning to him, and those things were integrated with the natural world in a natural way; he behaved as if he himself were a metaphor, as if all things were metaphors at play. When he heard the spoken word, when he himself spoke, he listened for the music in the words and showed no interest in making sense of those words, and yet sense came his way. In his interior life, in his travels through space and

28

time, in the mysterious zone of self normal people called the soul, Cooty Patterson found . . . something. Who can say what it was? Not Cooty.

There were times when Cooty's world clashed, and there would be times when Cooty's world would clash, with the day-to-day world of things and clockwork, and during those times he had been/would be mentally incompetent. There was no doubt that Cooty was crazy, loony, out to lunch, spaced, nutty as a fruitcake, totally bonkers; yet any fair-minded person would have to admit that Cooty was not mentally ill. Not in contact with what normal people think of as reality perhaps, but not mentally ill if the phrase meant dis-hyphen-ease with self. Cooty was at perfect ease with himself, and he would remain so as long as society did not disturb that ease.

Cooty made a life of noticing little things, collecting them, touching them, looking at them, dreaming himself into and out of them like a lover. Some of these things could be properly called collectibles, because they were useful or pretty. They included a beaver-chewed tree branch, a ceramic pot by Sam Azzaro, nails, monofilament fisherman's line, Popsicle sticks, a 35mm SRT-101 Minolta camera (which he had never used), a slingshot (which he had never used), an alarm clock (which he wound faithfully every day but never set and never looked at to tell time, for in Cooty's mind time was not something that could be told, but he liked the feel of the clock in his hands during a certain moment of the day: that was time). However, most of Cooty's things, by any measure other than his own, were of no consequence as things to collect. Cooty did not actually collect "things"; he collected reminders of his moods. Although he might have forgotten a particular event, when he picked up one of his objects it evoked the mood of that event, and thus Cooty was in constant touch with himself and with time.

When Cooty was not looking for or thinking about "things,"

he was doing chores or searching for food. He preferred to find food, rather than to buy food. To Cooty, bought food was spoiled food, tainted by the money. Not that Cooty held any economic theories. He didn't know capitalism from communism, Catholicism from atheism. It was just that to Cooty some things, such as food, had poetry; some things, such as money, did not. What did not have poetry did to what did have poetry what fire did to wood, warmed the world prettily with destruction; what did have poetry grew out new from its own ashes. Not that Cooty understood the meaning of the word "poetry." And if you asked him what a phoenix bird was, he would have said he had never been to Arizona.

Cooty's main chore was gathering firewood to stoke the small stove in his cabin. (Cooty did not own the cabin and the ten acres of woodland it sat on. He was house-sitting for a criminally insane fellow he had been incarcerated with during a brief stay at the state mental hospital in Concord.) The wood stove warmed Cooty in cold weather, cooked his food, and provided him with company. In hot weather, he cooked outside over an open fire. So he needed wood and plenty of it. It was there for the taking. The trees grew faster than Cooty could use them up. That's New Hampshire. Place that loves to grow trees. The trouble was, the trees did not dismantle easily. A realistic man used a chain saw. Cooty was not realistic, and, besides, he was frightened of chain saws. He worked with tools given to him by his friend and protector, Howard Elman—buck saw, ax, wedges, sledgehammer.

Dismantling trees with these tools is hard work for a strong, young person. Cooty was old and frail, yet for him the wood-gathering job was not hard, because he did not work hard, did not drive himself; the work was merely time-consuming. But it was time well consumed, for Cooty loved the woods, the sunlight tinkling through the trees, the zzzzz of his saw, the krch-echo, krch-echo of his ax, the sweet aroma of the freshly exposed juices of a living tree.

Howard taught him the basics of logging firewood, for these country crafts did not come naturally to Cooty. He was brought up in a tenement house in Lowell, Massachusetts. He lived most of his life in a furnished room in Tuckerman, where he came to work in the old Lodge textile mills. It wasn't until the shop closed and after his stay in the mental hospital that Cooty moved into the woods. With Howard's teachings as a base, Cooty worked out his system for getting in the wood. He began by picking the tree he wished to dismantle. He chose the tree much the same way as a cat picks a place to nap, by fretting, walking around and around, and sniffing. Finally, trembling, he'd say to himself, "This is it."

Say it was a red oak, ten inches in diameter. The immediate issue was how to bring down the tree. Cooty would take a few whacks with his ax, stop, walk away, return, take a few more, and so forth. Sometimes he'd walk all the way to Tuckerman, fifteen miles, and would not return until the next day or the next week. The difference between a day and a week was not meaningful to Cooty. What was meaningful was that felling the tree was the most unpleasant part of the job, and so he frequently postponed what he thrillingly referred to as "the tim-berrrrr!" At any one time on his property there might be half a dozen trees half felled, poised, as it were, in the philosophical limbo between making a sound and not making a sound. Not that Cooty had any formal knowledge of philosophy or limbo.

The immense power of a tree crashing to earth frightened him. And well it should, for Cooty Patterson had no understanding of how to arrange the felling of a tree, no more than the beaver who chewed the branch that was now part of Cooty's collection and who one day was killed by the very last tree it chewed through. Howard showed Cooty how to saw or chop a notch, and he explained the principle of the hinge in the felling of a tree, but none of this information came round in Cooty's mind. Cooty would chop and chop until he heard a crunching sound from inside the tree, and then he'd stand in awe and watch. Occasionally, he had to duck out of the way. Cooty did not understand how the law of averages worked, but he did understand there was a chance that some day a tree was going to fall on him, so sometimes he worshipped the spirit of the tree. He did not concern himself with the problem of whether the man upon whom the tree falls and whom it kills has heard the sound of the tree falling—and therefore it made a sound—or not. He thought: As I kills it, it kills me. We lie together, until the tree's remains take hold in my remains, and we grow into a new living being. By Cooty's logic, man becomes tree, tree becomes man; together they become God. It was no wonder, though, that, when people heard Cooty saying, "God is rot," they did not understand what he meant.

Once the tree was down, Cooty bucked it into six- to eight-foot lengths. Rarely could he cut all the way through with his saw, because it bound on him—it bound on him because Cooty could not saw straight. So he stopped frequently to chop free his saw with a hatchet. This was a pleasant tool to use, and Cooty was not sure what to think: The saw went fast but made him unhappy; the hatchet was slow and pleased him—what did this mean? The tree would fall on his head and kill him and the question would be answered, or the tree would not fall on his head and the question would be answered. Made no difference. But these—zzzzz, krch-echo—his apprehension of these sounds made a difference.

After the trunk of the tree was cut into billets, Cooty split them with wedges and sledgehammer into pieces three inches or less in thickness. Splitting was pleasant work. The sound of ripping wood rippled through his hands, right to his groin.

Naturally, his thoughts turned to romance—he thought not of a woman, or even of any real creature; he thought about fur, warm wetness, and rich stink.

The slender, gnarled lengths of wood were now easily cut with the buck saw. The tree had become firewood. Cooty lugged it back to the cabin in a carrier Howard made from the canvas of his old GI duffel bag. Cooty never let the wood sit too long in the forest. He was afraid for it out there. He had this idea somebody would steal it, or it would merely vanish. Things like that happened in the woods. He knew, he'd seen the evidence: every time he went into the forest, it was different. Somebody kept rearranging the furniture. He weighed down his wood carrier with only a few sticks, so he had to make many trips to bring the dismantled tree to the cabin. It was hard work but no hardship, for Cooty enjoyed walking. There was something about slow locomotion that calmed the whirl of his constant sense of amazement at the wonders— moss on a rock that had not been there yesterday, new sticks on the forest floor, new shards of light through the trees, new aspects to familiar boulders, new shadows to make him jump inside and hear his own voice say Ooo!, new footprints of the creatures who were there before him, before everything that was himself, and would be there afterward. Footprints . . . footprints . . . footprints.

He piled his wood in rows between trees outside the cabin, and covered the stacks with plastic that he rescued from dumpsters. Cooty loved dumpsters almost as much as he loved trees. He approached a dumpster with the awe and greed of an ancient thief cracking the treasure room of a pharaoh's tomb deep in a pyramid.

Cooty fussed with his wood piles. He wanted them to look just right. He watched them for line, form, and color, and he frequently realigned them. They delighted and frustrated him. Something always seemed to be out of place. He hadn't figured

out yet, and likely never would, that what was out of place—
or in place—was a convergence of the light of the moment on
a thing with his mood within that same moment. When, finally,
the wood pile was just right, he would sit by it for a long time,
dreaming. Whatever Cooty thought about or felt for his wood
piles will never be known, for he could not tell, and if he could
he wouldn't, but at any rate the wood piles were special. A
chain-saw cut left a ragged face on the log, but the cut from
Cooty's bow saw left a smooth, buffed face. The objective difference to the eye of the beholder was the intensity of shine.
The ends of Cooty's wood piles were bright. An observer might
not know exactly what he was seeing, but he would feel the
convergence of the light on the moment with his mood.

Cooty aged the wood a year or two before burning it, just
as Howard Elman advised him. Howard explained that the
wood must season. By "season" Howard meant that the sticks
must go through the cycles of the four seasons of the year in
order that the moisture in the wood cells dry out. But Cooty
misunderstood. He thought "to season" meant "to spice up."
He imagined that wood contained some mysterious element,
oregano or something, and it took a year before the flavor of
this element spread through the fibers of the wood. He had
burned unseasoned wood and knew how it smoked and refused
to release its heat, so he knew that Howard was right: the
wood must season a year. Accordingly, he told people that, the
spicier the wood, the better the burn.

Cooty picked up sticks in his travels. In the carrying, many
took on the quality of "things"; these he never burned. He
would lay them against a rock on the property, or put them in
the crooks of trees. Often he forgot where he had left them.
It didn't matter. They were invested with his spirit to become
part of the forest, and anyway Cooty had plenty of firewood.

———

At a turn in the path, Frederick spotted Cooty coming toward him, a sack over his shoulder. He smiled when he saw Frederick, smiled easily with eyes as well as mouth. Cooty was happy to see him, Frederick could tell, but the old man would want nothing from him, would ask nothing, would expect nothing. For the first time since he was back in his hometown, Frederick was comfortable and relaxed with a loved one.

"Cooty! How long has it been? Five years?" Frederick hailed Cooty.

"Five minutes. I seen you drive past in the Honeywagon." Cooty giggled, sounding like a cooing pigeon.

"I'm parked at your place. Howard says you know his trash route."

"Uh-huh. I'll show yuh."

Cooty wore baggy pants, suspenders, several layers of shirts, and a soiled out-of-date suit jacket, too big for him. In this outfit, picked from a Salvation Army clothes bin, Cooty resembled Professor Irwin Corey. He gave the impression he had worn these clothes since the beginning of time and would wear them till doomsday.

Frederick pointed at the sack. "What did you get?"

"Road meat."

"For your stew pot."

"Yes, for the pot. I beat the crows to him." Cooty reached into the sack and took out an animal, holding it by the hind legs. It must have been hit by a car only hours ago, for it had not yet stiffened.

"Nice rabbit," Frederick said.

"Not easy to come by, you know. You walk the roads for a meal and you find dog and cat and raccoon and bird and porcupine and skunk, plenty of skunk, but rabbit, which is common in the pucker brush, is rare in the road."

"Rarer even than deer?"

"Actually, a lot of deer get hit, but the police get 'em off the highway real quick. People will drive by a dead cat all day and not say anything, but if they see a deer, they call the cops."

They walked in silence for a minute. The morning light slanted in through the trees. "I've been all over the country but I never tasted anything like Cooty Patterson's stew," Frederick said.

"Road meat's special. The taste has got a little hurry-hurry in it, but no fear. The animal don't know it got run over and killed. Its spirit crossed that road and kept on going."

"You pick your spots?"

"I can get meat as long as cars go sixty on a road that cuts across an animal trail, because, you see, game been crossing the road there since before there was a road there."

Frederick thought about the animals. Every crossing was an emergency; every day, for a few seconds, the world of forest, earth, and sky gave way to a world of pavement, blurred behemoths, roars, and whines with changing pitches. "You'd think they'd learn," he said.

"The animals make it across clean or get killed, so they don't learn nothing. And the drivers keep on going, and you can't learn nothing about what's dead if it's back there. You gotta stop and look at it and smell it and touch it and, if you're hungry, eat it. It's only the man, laying in wait along the road for the demise of another creature, who knows that feeling alive is no more, no less than his own hunger."

"So what's death, Cooty, a full belly?"

"Oh, I don't know. I ain't dead yet. But I imagine death's a big relief, like a good fart."

The pine-board walls of Cooty's shack were decorated from floor to ceiling with little pieces of trash, Cooty's "things," collected from the roadside, trash cans, and dumpsters. Frederick looked around for a place to sit.

"You got a chair?" Frederick asked.

"What do I need a chair for?"

Frederick picked a Mounds wrapper on the wall. "I see you've added to your collection," he said.

"Dumpsters make life too easy; I feel spoiled sometimes." Cooty meant it; like every other sentient creature, animal or human, he was nostalgic for days that had never been.

Frederick sat on the edge of Cooty's bunk. He could smell the old man's sweet, musty sleep. Cooty stood by a crude cutting board in a homemade wooden sink over which presided an old-fashioned hand water-pump. Slowly and with pleasure, he began to skin the rabbit with a homemade knife a little too big for the job.

"Haven't I seen that knife before?" Frederick said.

Cooty looked Freddy in the eye and giggled.

"I remember now," Frederick said. "My father made it from a car spring when I was a kid. Took him a month of Sundays." Those were the days when his father worked at the old Lodge textile mills. Howard had been a foreman and a loom fixer; Cooty had worked for him as a cleanup man.

"He gave it to me. If Howie makes something, he gives it away."

"Maybe to you. Not to me," Frederick said, then, after a pause, added, "Cooty, I've been wondering."

Cooty heard something in Frederick's tone, and he smiled. "You been wondering."

"Where's this tree stand that Howard fell out of?"

"I don't know exactly, but somewhere up there on the Trust lands."

"The what?"

"Remember that Upper Darby land where you and Howie used to hunt? Well, Squire Salmon, before he died, closed hunting, closed everything. Can't hunt, fish, trap, or pee-pee on the trees. The idea is to give the plants and animals a break. But you know Howie. If somebody in Upper Darby says go this-a-way, he'll go that-a-way."

"Town's changed." Frederick frowned. He didn't really care what they did to Darby; what he resented was alterations to his memories.

"Yes." Cooty glowed. "Lots of changes. New school going up, new apartments."

"School?"

"They're going to dig up the bodies in the old cemetery, move 'em on out to the new cemetery, and build a school."

Frederick pointed at the pot on the wood-burning stove. "You just keep adding to it, do you?"

"Yep." Cooty finished skinning the rabbit, and pulled out the entrails.

"When'd you start it?"

"Can't remember the date, but it was some time before you were born."

"What would make you leave this place, abandon your stew pot? Freedom? Money? What?"

The old man stopped and thought for a moment. "It would have to be something carnal. . . ."

"Carnal?" Frederick was surprised. This was something new from his friend.

"I never had no carnal," Cooty said with a faint blush and added, "They say it's overrated."

"I don't know about that." Frederick knocked on the walls of the cabin as if testing the soundness of the wood. In fact, he was trying to change the subject. He, too, could use some carnal.

"You're going up there, ain't you, Freddy? Up there on the Trust."

Frederick smiled but did not speak.

"Your old man won't tell you where his tree stand is, and

you want to get a piece of him by finding out." Now Cooty smiled.

"Cooty, you eat too much meat; you ought to eat more vegetables," Frederick said.

Cooty's sunken chest shook with silent laughter; he dropped the animal carcass whole into the big pot boiling on the stove and wiped his hands on his pants.

4

Rash Acts

Lilith Salmon opened her eyes, glanced at the digital clock on the dresser. Eight-thirty. Plenty of time before her class with MacKavitt. She drifted off for another fifteen or so minutes and, halfway between here and there, fell into a dream.

She was in an enormous man-made cavern. A family of dark-skinned people wearing shabby but colorful clothes passed by. She watched them through a wedding-veil fog: a man, a woman, a boy about thirteen, a girl about eight, an infant carried by the mother. They spoke in a language she could not identify.

A voice, familiar and female (Was it her long-dead grand-mother Salmon?), spoke over a public-address system: "See how they cling to one another. Contained within themselves. Now watch them come apart. Note the intruder."

A black fellow with a boom box on his shoulder blaring heavy-metal rock music materialized out of the fog.

"See how his music attacks the family," the dream voice said. The mother drew in the infant to her bosom, the father doubled his fists as if protecting his loved ones against an invisible enemy, the boy searched outward.

"Lilith, do not look at the girl," the voice warned.

Against the advice of the dream voice, Lilith turned her attention to the girl, fat, ugly, holding in: herself.

The voice said, "See how she stands on a ledge between the abyss of the music on one side and the abyss of her family on the other. Now look around. See how this place is in a state of construction or deconstruction, hard to tell which, things, having been torn down and rebuilt and torn down and rebuilt, failing to provide comfort, appeal, illumination, convenience, or even shelter, or even . . . Never mind that, don't get close to *that*. . . . You, dear child, exist somewhere between this, that, and them . . . them . . . who you . . . are . . . them. . . ."

"Wake up! Wake up!"

Lilith opened her eyes again. Her roommate, Harriet Snow, stood with her hand on Lilith's shoulder.

"What? What's the matter?" Lilith sat up in bed.

"You were moaning," Harriet said.

"I was having a dream," Lilith said.

"Good, tell me. I can use it in my psych class." Harriet leaped from the edge of Lilith's bed to her own, grabbed her pocket tape recorder, and clicked it on.

"It was about, I think, immigrants," Lilith said.

"Borrrrring!" Harriet, catlike, waited a moment after delivering her judgment, then pounced. "Where?"

"I'm not sure, maybe Penn Station. I always go through there on the train home."

Harriet interrupted. "Oh, I love New York. The cars behave like people, and the people are like terrible little machines." Harriet aimed the tape recorder at Lilith. "Let's get down to the details of this dream. Sex, power, repression, guilt—tell Dr. Snow all your Witch Island secrets and you will be free." Harriet was pretending to be joking, but in fact, as Lilith was aware, Harriet meant every word she said. Harriet exhibited the sprightly sadism of a young person destined for a career in psychotherapy.

41

"I can't remember; it's gone," Lilith said. It was a half-truth. The images in the dream were fading, but she did remember enough to titillate Harriet and was determined not to.

"Um. Let's discuss your fears." Harriet was practicing her therapist delivery.

"My fears! My fears are my own." Lilith defended her territory.

"Don't be shy. I won't tell anybody. I'll tell you my greatest fear if you'll tell me yours."

"You, Harriet—you scare me with your noodle-head inquiries."

Harriet giggled.

Lilith rose from her bed, put on her robe, and began to gather her toiletry. Lilith showered at least once and sometimes two or more times a day, not because she had a fetish for cleanliness, but because she liked the feel and sound of water and the privacy afforded by the shower.

Harriet made one last try. "My greatest fear is that, after a long and successful career, in which I have sacrificed the joys of marriage and family to devote myself to humanity, I publish my magnum opus—*What Makes Us Tick*—and it hits the newsstands and nobody cares. I'm like shouting into a void."

Lilith stopped for a moment to think. She felt wistful; she could almost smell the fields behind her house in Darby. "I have this fear—I have it right now, and I don't know why— that everything around me is coming apart and it's all my fault."

"Sounds like you used to overhear your parents arguing," Harriet analyzed.

Lilith looked away. Her mother had told her: Never let them get too close.

Harriet realized that she had hurt her friend, and she apologized. "I'm experimenting—and it's all so serious with you. I'm sorry, Lilith," Harriet said.

"Sure—no problem," Lilith said.

Harriet reached out a hand in friendship, and Lilith brushed it with her own. She opened the door into the corridor, and stood there for a second, half in, half out. The dream, this oddly intimate conversation with her roommate sent a message to Lilith: She was ready for experience again. It had been so long since she'd felt like this—senses keen, emotions hot-wired to life.

"You know what I'm going to do today, Harriet?" Before Harriet could respond, Lilith answered her own question. "I'm going to change."

"It's about time. You've been morose ever since . . . last year." Harriet avoided specifics. She wouldn't mention the death of Lilith's father. While Harriet might be fearless in probing her own living, psychological demons (although she preferred the demons of others), she was squeamish about human mortality. As a result, the roommates had skirted the subject of Reggie Salmon's death and the yearlong torpor Lilith appeared now to be coming out of.

Harriet grabbed a nail clipper and, sitting on the edge of her bed, began to trim her toenails. Harriet's feet were short and wide but not unattractive as feet go, with toes of even length and undistinguished, as toes should be.

Headed for the shower, Lilith glided down the long, dreary corridor of the dormitory, carrying herself in the manner of a Salmon woman, head held high, body stately and squared away and moving with just a little John Wayne wiggle, proud, distinctive, and, but for her beauty, a little ridiculous. She imagined she was walking in a pathway of purple lilacs, caressed by their aroma.

In the shower, in the artificial rain and the artificial fog, Lilith thought back to a time, on a warm sunny day in June when she was about twelve, when her father took her in the woods to help him survey a piece of land. He lugged a transit over his right shoulder and a board-foot measure in his left hand. He had her carry a stake with an orange flag on the end.

"Use it as a walking stick," he had said.

They didn't talk much, but once in a while he commented on the trees. It was as if, instead of being a Yale-trained forester concerned with fauna, he was an anthropologist, and the trees were offspring of the human family.

"That's a white pine, soft, pliable wood, fit for a king or a pauper." He had pointed with the ruler. "These are red maples. Weed trees, like the people you find in Darby Depot. You wouldn't want to see them become extinct, but you do strive to keep their numbers down. Now look at this tree, the scaly bark, the shimmy in the trunk. Wild cherry, lovely reddish heart, good for spoon carving."

Some ways later, he had cut a black birch with his pocket knife so she could smell the sweet sap.

When they reached the work area, a ragged logged-over land he was thinking of buying, he planted the transit on a flat spot as if he were setting out a rare and precious sapling. He made her stand far away from him, holding the stake with the bright-orange flag at the tip. He sighted down the transit, motioning her with an impersonal wave of his right hand to move the stake this way or that. She knew that, looking into the transit, he could see her face clearly, but she could not see his. She had stood holding the stake, posing for her father's hidden eye.

At breakfast in the college dining commons, Harriet launched into an analysis. "Lilith, you've got the small-town rich-girl troubles: nobody treats you like everybody else. I've seen it in operation. The boys don't know how to flirt with you, and the man at the corner grocery is a tad politer, and the girls are jealous, and sometimes people are hostile and not sure why.

It's no wonder you don't know how to invite attention—you push people away."

"I guess so, but it doesn't seem important." Lilith understood that Harriet's observation was probably true, but she didn't feel the full brunt of that truth. She knew her place: at the distance that people had always kept her from themselves. It was the Darby way with the Salmons, the Salmon way with Darby. She knew that most people judged her as aloof while she was merely preoccupied, but what could she do about that? And, too, she liked the fact that, in their presumptions, they also judged her as cautious. Because cautious she was not, and she liked the idea she'd put one over on the general populace. If she stopped and thought about her actions, she froze. Rashness was her entry into strong feeling, new experience, and personal freedom. She was coming into that mood today, that mood that led to rash acts.

A snappy male voice behind her said, "So when are you coming over to Pi House with me?"

Lilith turned. The speaker was Sherman Adams, fraternity brother of Harriet's fiancé, Joel. Ever since Lilith had broken up with her boyfriend, Peter, Sherman had been asking her out. It was a joke between them. She'd never taken him seriously, in part because she found it hard to imagine herself as an object of desire. No matter what the mirror told her, she still felt the way she had when she was fourteen—overweight and shy, compensating with an erect carriage and a suggestion of haughtiness. Sherman was about her own height of five feet ten, and he was slender but wiry, a tennis player's body. He combed his short dark hair to the side. A wisp of a cowlick gave him a boyish appearance. He was confident and earnest, and she did not dislike him. Her standard reply to his question was "When you get your car, Sherman." (Sherman's father had promised him a new car for graduation—if only he'd graduate.) But this day she said, "All right—tonight or never." She wasn't sure she really wanted a date with Sherman, but she was certain she wanted to test her rash mood. She couldn't wait to see what would happen next.

"I don't believe this." Harriet feigned extreme wonder.

"We'll go to the house for beers, then down by the millstream with some of the brothers." Sherman looked at Lilith, not sure just what she'd say; he was still a little wobbly from Lilith's change of tack after all these months.

"Sure," she said.

Sherman sat down at their table. His fraternity, Delta Pi Delta, was known as the frat from the burbs, a middle-grade fraternity, respectable if undistinguished.

Sherman and Harriet talked, and Lilith fell into the role of sounding board. Harriet claimed that she had intellectualized her way toward a state of permanent bliss.

"Concentrated thoughts can cure illness, concentrated thoughts can fold a skirt or make a ball-point pen write in blood. Or Kool-Aid. I can do it. Well, almost," Harriet said.

"You're not thinking, you're fooling yourself," Sherman countered.

"I most certainly do think," Harriet said, and this rhetorical shift from hyperbole to simplicity staggered Sherman, but only for a moment.

"Thinking goes against happiness," Sherman said. "Thinking is an effort, a strain; I would go so far as to say that thinking, real thinking, is unhealthy. My philosophy is: let be be." He turned to Lilith for some kind of acknowledgment of his idea. She twitched a smile. She had little interest in the discussion, but she did enjoy the musical counterpoint of the banter between Sherman and Harriet.

It was during a lapse in her attention to the lecture during her ten o'clock class that Lilith decided it was time to do something about an academic matter that had long troubled her. She would change her major.

After class, Lilith followed Professor MacKavitt back to her office. Dr. Merryjay MacKavitt, a musicologist and booster of the artistic life, was Lilith's adviser and favorite teacher. The professor always wore a dress or skirt to class and high-heeled shoes. Like so many of the second wave of professional women, she went out of her way not to resemble the feminists of the first wave. Her office was crammed from floor to ceiling with books, sheet music, and a gargoyle or two. In this academic cocoon, Lilith could almost hear music. In her science courses, she learned that certain instruments could detect a sort of electronic hush from the sound of creation fifteen or so billion years ago. That was the music that Lilith heard now, and she resisted a desire to weep, a child grieving for the loss of a universe.

But Lilith did not cry. She spoke in a businesslike tone. "I don't want to be a music major anymore."

"I thought when you quit the cello, you might have some trouble," the professor said in a soft voice. Lilith liked Dr. MacKavitt because the professor believed her own lectures and because (apparently, and erroneously, to Lilith) she did not trade in irony (a professorial penchant that Lilith found despairing and offensive) and because she was so unlike Professor Hadly Blue, who was the latest of her mother's lovers.

"I'll never be good enough to play in a symphony orchestra," Lilith said.

"Self-knowledge is education enough. You started too late in life to master the instrument," the professor said.

"I want to change my major to premed—I want to be a doctor," Lilith said. In fact, Lilith had no idea what she wanted in life. She knew only that, without a career or plans for a career, a woman did not get much respect. Medicine was a noble profession and she liked biology, especially botany, and she knew she could survive chemistry, so why not premed?

At the end of the meeting, Dr. MacKavitt asked Lilith a question without looking her in the eye: "Any news from home?"

"No," Lilith said. Something was wrong, something about the way MacKavitt posed her question, from a distance. Lilith withdrew, from the professor's office, from her own suspicions.

For the rest of the day, Lilith talked to a dean, a guidance counselor, her adviser again, and several administrative assistants; she invented ambitions; she related her desires to heal; she filled out paperwork. She canoed adroitly through the college bureaucracy, and by the end of the day she felt herself carried along by the current of the system. It seemed inevitable that she would become a doctor. Never mind that she'd failed to meet her own standards in trying to learn the cello. She remembered now that she did not like the smell in hospitals.

She got through her usual late-day down time (anxiety that passed with the evening meal) by swimming some laps in the college pool. After showering and dressing, she read in the library. Exercise and escape into books took the edge off the familiar, daily feeling of near-panic. She was in touch and calm when Sherman arrived at nightfall to walk her to the frat basement. Harriet and Joel would meet them later at the river.

"The way to be happy is to keep track of your life," Sherman said to Lilith as they walked, talking as if she were not there, as if in fact he were still arguing with Harriet. "Put your life in boxes, time boxes."

"Time boxes?" Lilith played the stooge.

"Every human being has certain things he has to do. For me, it's eat, drink, be merry, and study for exams. In that order. You follow me? Boxes." Sherman tapped his temple with a forefinger. "Boxes in your head. Inside, you put in the time notes. Now it's time to study. Now it's time to eat. And so forth."

"You put your feelings in boxes, too?" Lilith wasn't probing; she was curious.

"I don't get hung up on that. I keep busy, I keep my foot to the floor."

"So, what's in your time box now?" Lilith asked.

"Drink. After that, be merry." Sherman added a sly laugh that Lilith liked.

The moment they arrived at the Delta Pi Delta House, Sherman changed in his behavior. His innocent eagerness to put his ideas on display vanished, and his attention to Lilith wandered. She knew the routine. The frat boys ignored their dates, concentrating instead on their brothers and a game called "beer pong." They liked having girls to show off for, and eventually, during the course of the evening, they would get around to the male-female stuff. Until then, you couldn't really have a conversation with a frat guy. That was all right. Lilith needed some between-time herself. After her father had died, she had found herself indifferent to love and sex and relationships. Now she sensed, if not yet felt, a renewed interest in the offing. Here, the frat house: was this an environment where a person might come back from the dead? What a strange thought! Perhaps she had been dead, dead inside for a year. Now it was time to come alive. She'd begin tonight by having fun. What she wasn't sure of was Sherman. She liked his clean-cut looks and unconceited confidence, but she didn't know if she liked him. So she watched him carefully, waiting—hoping—for that good feeling of likelove to spread through her.

Beer pong was played on a Ping-Pong table. Empty paper beer cups were placed on each side. The idea was to plop the ball in the cup on your opponent's side or knock the cup over. Every time your opponent scored, you had to drink a beer. Some players were slammers, attempting to knock the cup over. Some were cuties, attempting to drop the ball in the cup. Sherman challenged the table holder, a beefy guy named Chug, a visiting Delta Pi Delta brother from another college. A permanent, insincere smile seemed stitched on Chug's face. He sneaked glances at Lilith, who was dressed for the weather in shorts and a cotton shirt. Sherman started with delicate shots, but when he wasn't successful, he reverted to a power game. He did a little better then, but in the end he lost. When no one else challenged Chug, Sherman came back for more.

The competition between the two young men, covertly nasty—for they exchanged no words of hostility—disturbed Lilith. She couldn't get over the feeling that the animosity between them was her doing.

She turned her thoughts away from the players and toward her own future. Instead of spending her summer in Darby, where there was nothing to do but lifeguard at Darby Lake, perhaps she'd stay on campus, take a course, get something part-time at the medical center—the phrase "administrative assistant" popped to mind. Something told her that a return to Darby would mean a return to that old frame of mind—dead inside. And, too, there was nobody in Darby she wanted to see. Because she'd spent most of her life in private schools, she had made few friends in her hometown; and her cousins, whom she'd been fairly close to, had moved on when her uncle Billy Butterworth took a job in Houston. No reason to go home.

She lost herself so completely in these thoughts that she missed a few moments in time. Then she heard Chug calling, "Earth to Lilith, Earth to Lilith." The next thing she knew, Sherman took her hand and they were headed for the river. It was warm, sultry, about as warm as it ever got at night in her hometown of Darby, but an ordinary late-spring evening here in the South. The students, half a dozen college men and four women, started walking. Sherman seemed wary, and it took a moment for Lilith to reason why. His rival, Chug, was among the two guys with no dates who tagged along.

Down by the Millstream was a game the students played with the campus police. They'd malinger in the vicinity of the college dock, where the sculls were parked. Some walked along a narrow beach below the docks, some made bonfires. Couples carrying blankets and beer found privacy in the forest behind the beach. Once or twice a night, the campus police would cruise by the area and shoo away the people they could find.

When the group from Pi House arrived at the dock, Lilith looked around for her roommate, but Harriet and Joel hadn't arrived yet. The air was even warmer and thicker than it had been higher up on the campus. Reflected light from the stars and a few private homes cast shadows on the glassy surface of the water. There was no moon. The river was impounded, and by the dock it was still, more a long, snaking lake than a moving stream.

Sitting on the broad, spacious wooden dock, Lilith spotted the dark shape of Witch Island. The story went that a woman hermit had lived on the island before drowning herself under a full moon. With tall trees against the distant bluffs, the island looked mysterious and foreboding. Lilith wanted to go there. She walked to the edge of the dock and kicked off her shoes.

"It's scummy water and it's full of snakes," Sherman said.

"I don't care." Lilith sat on the dock's edge and dangled her feet in the water.

"Blood suckers, too. I'd be careful." Sherman was not kidding; he was truly concerned for Lilith's welfare.

Chug overheard and said, "That Yankee girl is braver than you are, Sherman. Watch out for those suckers."

Sherman joined in with the few titters of laughter from the group, but Lilith could tell from the stiffness of his body that he was not amused. Chug, beer in hand, left the dock, and

51

Sherman's mood improved. The river browsing around Lilith's legs was warm as the touch of a hand. Sherman—brave Sherman—actually put three fingers in the water. "Feels like stale beer," he said. The others drifted to the opposite end of the dock; Sherman and Lilith could now talk in private.

"I absolutely have to convince my father that I need a car." Sherman sounded fierce and determined. After a pause, he added, "Your family . . . You could have your own car."

It was common knowledge on campus that Lilith's family was well fixed, but nonetheless she was put off by Sherman's oblique reference to the Salmon fortune.

"I always wanted my own car," Lilith said. "A red car, violently red, but my father was against it. I think he believed that denying me a car would be good for my character or something."

"You have to respect that, but, frankly, I'd rather have wheels than character," Sherman said. "You can't get anywhere with character. Now that your father is gone, it's time to go to work on your mother, isn't it? Just come right out and tell her you need a car." Sherman's voice, though thick with drink, was under control.

"I don't know," Lilith said. "Maybe a car wouldn't make me a better person. Maybe I'll learn more by wanting it than having it."

"Oh, sure." Sherman was amused.

Lilith was looking at the island. It wasn't that far away, perhaps a half-mile, but something about it, its isolation, the lack of lights and buildings on it, its jagged irregularity, made it seem apart from this civilized place. Lilith thought she knew why the hermit lady had gone out there: the island offered beauty, strangeness, and privacy.

A moment later, Lilith heard her named called. She recognized Harriet's voice.

"On the dock!" Lilith shouted into the night, her words

faintly echoing. The water made a sucking sound as she pulled out her feet and stood.

Harriet and Joel appeared from out of the shadows. "You have some express mail from your mother." Harriet handed Lilith a letter.

"Express?" Lilith was alarmed. The last time her mother had sent her a message smelling of emergency, it had been by telephone, getting her out of a class, to inform her of her father's sudden death. He had cancer, but the doctors had expected him to live on for some time. He had died of heart failure up on the ledges of the Trust lands.

Harriet sensed Lilith's uneasiness. "If it was real bad news, I'm sure she would have called," Harriet said.

"So what's this about?" Lilith said, more to herself than her friend.

"Hey—mail," said Sherman, comprehending but not feeling the tenseness of the moment. He was already like an experienced middle-aged drunk, like Lilith's uncle Billy Butterworth, capable of thought but slow and mushy with his emotions.

Barefoot, Lilith walked alone from the dock to the road and stood under the street lamp to read the letter. She winced a little when she saw it had been typed. (In fact, Persephone Salmon had typed the letter because her arthritis had come on and she didn't want her daughter to read her shaky handwriting.)

My dear, darling Lilith,

This is coming to you a little later than it should. I delayed in sending it. Not sure why. Many things to talk over with you, but they can wait until you arrive. This much you must know now. Please come home a week earlier than scheduled for summer vacation. You won't have any trouble with the dean. I've explained the situation to him.

So this was why MacKavitt had twisted in her chair when she'd asked if Lilith had heard from home. MacKavitt had been informed! That was the way her mother operated. Never really up front but always ahead of her daughter and always with a plan. Lilith read on.

The bodies of your father and brother are going to be exhumed. The town of Darby is taking the property of the old cemetery to build a new school. Reggie and your brother are the only ones in the old cemetery from this century! After the bodies have been removed, the town is going to hold a memorial service. You should of course be there for this event.

When her father had died, he had been buried very quickly, according to his wishes. (Everything had been done according to his wishes.) Lilith had never had time to take it all in. Now—now was an opportunity for her to bear witness, to understand and absorb the meaning of that death. And, too, she was being presented with an occasion that might lead her to deal with the brother she had never seen, gone before her birth. She read the rest of the letter.

There's another reason you must come home early. You're coming of age. Your father requested that you be informed of his intentions upon your twenty-first birthday. One more thing. If you so choose, you can take your father's seat on the Trust board (the seat I now hold) at an official meeting of the board at the town hall. Garvin Prell, who helped Reggie write the will, and the town officials will also be on hand. More about these matters when I pick you up at the railroad station in Springfield.

The letter was signed "Your loving and (I'm afraid) fatigued mother, Persephone Salmon."

Lilith needed to talk, not about the letter in particular but about a strange excitement she felt at the prospect of putting her father to rest again. She looked for Sherman or Harriet.

But while Lilith was reading her letter, another drama had been unfolding. Sherman and Chug were arguing. Lilith heard her name used by both. She strained to listen, but their words were loud and garbled, as if she wasn't hearing right. She imagined herself in a cage; alien creatures giving her passing stares, others studying her, others shouting among themselves. She shook away the images and was left with a clarity of vision. Her sometime dreams were foolish and fanciful, her goals (what goals?) discordant with her destiny, and her understanding of her circumstances out-and-out wrong. This entire, uplifting day had been a fraud, a dirty trick she'd played on herself. Medical school! Crazy. She didn't want to go to medical school. She didn't want to go to school at all. She didn't want anything or anybody. She only wanted to be.

Neither Sherman nor Chug had thrown a blow, but they were pushing and shoving so that they resembled awkward dancers. Neither the combatants nor the bystanders took anything more than a passing notice when Lilith joined them for a moment, then slipped away. She was the object of the argument, but not the objective. When she leaped off the dock, however, the sound of her hitting the water stopped the disagreement. The students froze, recovered, and ran to the edge of the dock.

"What happened?" somebody shouted.

"It's Lilith," said Harriet. "Lilith! Are you out there?"

No answer but the sound of Lilith's body slicing through the water.

"Did she fall or jump or what?" Sherman ran to the edge and halted; he was beginning to feel as if he wanted to boot.

"She swims like a mermaid," Harriet said, then called through her cupped hands, "Lilith! Lilith!"

There was another splash. Chug had plunged in. Sherman followed along with another fellow and one of the women. In the water, the swimmers realized they could hardly see one another, let alone Lilith. They paddled and splashed around a bit, then returned to the dock.

Lilith swam with powerful strokes, heading for the dark shadow over the rim of the water that was the island.

Through the sounds of her own body knifing through the still water, through the sounds of her own hard breaths, Lilith heard Harriet's voice from the shore, and in Harriet's desperate anxiety to locate her she heard the voice of her own mother calling from fifteen years ago. She was six then, hiding in the woods, not so much listening to her name as trying to locate the voice in place and time, for it seemed to come from everywhere. At that moment, she'd known she was lost, and she'd huddled in the rocks.

Her father had found her. He had held her at arm's length and, speaking in the unique idiom of Upper Darby, the up-country prep-school accent slowed to a drawl, he had put to her a question he had asked many times before: "Are you a *Saamin?*" She had answered, "No, I am not a *Saamin.*" As always, they both laughed. "Well, what are you?" he had asked. "I am a *Sahl-mohn,*" she had said. "Yes, my love, you are a *Sahl-mohn.*" As always, he brought her close, holding her by the shoulders, directing her into his being.

Her father dressed like an English gentleman from another century, with a jacket that had patches on the elbows and a tweed cap and pleated trousers. People in Darby called him the Squire. Sometimes in her dormitory room, frightened or joyful, she'd catch her own reflection in the dresser mirror, and she would see a face beyond fright and joy—beyond all emotion—the face of the Squire's daughter.

She never stopped until she reached the island. It was heavily wooded, but she found a place where suddenly the depth of the water gave way, as she bumped hard into a rock. Still a good fifty feet from the shore of the island, Lilith stood on the just barely submerged rock and gazed out at the world left behind.

5

Money

The rail platform in Springfield was open to the weather, but under a gable roof held up by pillars. Lilith stepped down from the train, and scanned the area. She heard her mother calling her name, as if from long ago, before she actually saw her coming forward, bursting into the light from under the roof of the rail platform. Persephone was a Butterworth, petite and pretty, not at all like herself, who, people had been telling her for years, was a Salmon to the bone.

The Salmon women embraced. Persephone smelled of honey, flowers, earth from her greenhouse, and cigarettes.

"You're smoking again—you always do something weird when you start smoking," Lilith said.

"How observant of you." Persephone smiled mirthlessly. She hadn't meant to be sarcastic, although she noticed her daughter took her remark that way. She couldn't quite find a way to set it right, so she let it go. She was too preoccupied with other matters to repair minor damage to feelings. She had so many important things to say to Lilith, things that should have been said long ago.

Lilith felt her mother pull away from her.

The Salmon women headed for the parking lot several blocks away. The sidewalk was ripped up and they walked on gravel. Slabs of concrete the size of truck tires were stacked here and there. The downtown district in Springfield appeared ripped open for surgery that would accomplish nothing, since the patient was too far gone to begin with. They passed under a stone-arch railway bridge, where layers of the drab red dust of natural forces had collected between layers of the greasy black grime of human industry. It was as if the accretion of the inevitable had lain, in the Biblical sense, with the malevolence of the accidental.

Lilith heard church bells ringing.

"It's Sunday," she said.

"Yes," said her mother distractedly.

"I sat with some religious people, Catholics, I think." Lilith stopped. She didn't know what to say next, because she was unsure of the relevance of her thought.

"That's nice," her mother said in a tone that, as Lilith translated it, clarified the question of relevance—not relevant at all.

"Daddy's Bronco!" Lilith said, with a thrill she hadn't expected, as she caught sight of the used and abused four-wheel-drive vehicle Reggie took into the woods with him.

"The Saab is being serviced, so I took your father's car," Persephone said.

"Can I drive it home?" Lilith asked.

"Why not."

Her mother's easy acquiescence put Lilith on guard. Persephone was not one to surrender territory, even if it was only the driver's seat, unless she planned to wage a battle on another front.

Lilith was right and Lilith was wrong. Persephone was preparing a campaign, but she had no wish for war, and the reason she was happy to have Lilith behind the wheel was that her hands still ached from the arthritis flare-up. She concealed her disease from Lilith partly because she hadn't faced up to it herself and partly out of the habit of concealment.

Lilith slipped into what had been her father's place in the

Bronco. She could still detect, or perhaps imagined she could detect, his smell, the essence of trees picked up from his clothes. She started the car and a minute later was on I-91, headed north. Beside the highway ran the Connecticut River. Between herself and her mother were two bouquets of flowers wrapped in green tissue.

"Are we going to stop at the cemetery?" Lilith stared hard at the flowers.

"Yes, do you mind?" Persephone said.

"No, I want to," Lilith said.

"It will be the last time you'll see the old cemetery undisturbed," Persephone said. "The bodies will be moved to the new cemetery so the town can build its school."

Lilith tried to picture the caskets, the bodies resting in them—her father, after a year a mummy in a business suit; her brother, bones. She should be horrified at conjuring such grisly images, but she wasn't. They filled her with reverence for her own life, her own power, which was the power to endow events and things with meaning through the medium of her feelings.

"You drive too fast," Persephone said.

"Is that why you wouldn't let me have my own car?"

"Not exactly." There was an indefiniteness in Persephone's tone that Lilith perceived as smugness.

An hour after leaving Springfield, Lilith turned off the interstate highway and crossed the Connecticut River into New Hampshire. Soon they were in Darby. Lilith left Route 21 for Center Darby Road. It was on that twisting blacktop, driving sixty miles an hour, that she had to swerve to avoid hitting a big dog.

"Critter Jordan's hound. Still hasn't figured out roads are dangerous to animal life," Persephone said with a trace of affection. "Damn the Jordans, and damn the dog, and damn Darby. And welcome home, Lilith."

A few minutes later, Lilith pulled the Bronco to a stop on the side of the road beside the cemetery, which was bordered by a rock wall upon which grew green moss. Beyond the wall was the forest and a steep hill that ended in the ledges where Lilith's father had died. When she shut the ignition off, she felt the quiet of the surrounding woods, and the realization made her feel quiet inside herself.

Only people who nosed around town records, such as Selectman Arthur Crabb and Town Clerk and gossip Dorothy McCurtin, knew that the proper name of the old cemetery was Darby Cemetery and the proper name of the new cemetery was Center Darby Cemetery. Most people got by nicely with common, unwritten knowledge. The old cemetery had been called "the cemetery" until the new cemetery had been built, and then the names had been set—the "new cemetery" and the "old cemetery." That was two centuries ago. Upon the death of his son, Reggie Salmon had bought the last of the lots in the old cemetery. The act prompted local people to conclude (correctly) that Reggie believed that the Salmons were too good for eternal rest with the folks of his own time in the new cemetery. It was only later, when he could see his own death coming on, that Reggie had the idea to be buried on the Trust itself.

Lilith stared at the tips of the oak trees. The fresh new leaves were not yet green, but orange-brown. The color was similar to the autumn red she'd seen in junkyards and decaying buildings from the train, and yet it was very different. It was fresher, shinier; the difference was like the difference between sunrise and sunset.

Without a word between them, the Salmon women walked toward the graves, the rank smell of last year's fallen leaves in their nostrils. The ground under their feet was spongy, the grass matted, drab, sickly wet, and cold. It awaited warm days, warm rain, warm sun.

Some of the history of the early settlers was on the gravestones. As children, they died in droves from infectious diseases—"Beloved Joshua, Called home, Age 2"—and the women often did not survive childbirth—"Beloved Martha, blood lost, blood gained, in Labor, Age 28." Less often, men in their prime perished in accidents—"Beloved Abner, at Work, age 40." But those who made it into their middle years stood an excellent chance of living to eighty and beyond.

Persephone stopped at a stone partly covered with dark-green moss. "My favorite inscription," she said. Cut into the granite were the words "Remember me as you pass by. As you are now, so once was I. As I am now, so will you be. Prepare for death and follow me."

Most of the gravestones were low with rounded shoulders, the colors blotchy and irregular, the texture rough, as much part of the earth as the granite boulders that littered the countryside. By contrast, the gravestones of Lilith's father and brother were tall, straight, smooth, and shiny, thrusting up to the sky. Like the trees of Reggie's Trust, the Salmon stones identified with the heavens.

When Lilith and Persephone reached the grave sites, they stood between the two monuments of the Salmon males— "Raphael Salmon II, Beloved Son, Age 4"; "Raphael Salmon, Beloved Father of the Trust Lands, Age 57."

Persephone placed one bouquet in front of Reggie's grave, the other in front of her son's. She stood staring at the grave of the dead boy. With her head bowed, her wrists crossed before her, she looked like a hostage.

Right from the start, Lilith had understood she would always be in second place in the hearts of her parents. She ought to be angry at this situation over which she had no control, and perhaps in a deep, dark, secret part of herself she was, but at the surface she felt only an immense sadness.

Her parents had stopped communicating as man and wife

long before Reggie became sick, perhaps even before she herself was born. Those last few months when her father was ill, her mother was having an affair.

"Daddy would take long walks up on the Trust," Lilith seemed to be talking to the white daytime moon in the blue sky over Darby. "It was as if he was hiding. He had a place, you had somebody, I was alone."

Persephone put her arm around Lilith, who now, finally, could feel tears coming up. "Reggie wasn't good with people," Persephone said. "He showed his love with this—land."

"Love? That's what Daddy's Trust is about?"

Persephone answered with a single, ironic laugh. "Your father measured love by the acre." She led her daughter away from the gravestones, along the grassy cemetery lane to a patch of sunlight on the stone wall that bordered the cemetery. Behind them, the tops of the trees, shimmering in a wind unfelt below, seemed to flicker in the sunlight like the tongues of a green, heatless fire.

"The school's going to be there." Persephone pointed to the woods beyond the cemetery. "The trees are going to be cleared to the boundary of the Trust. The town wants to put in a park, connect it to the Trust with hiking trails. Just up the hill is a new development. The Prells are building condominiums."

Persephone stopped talking, lit a True, and continued. "Lilith, your uncle Monet is against this town plan, and Garvin is for it because it's going to help his development. I've had to stand between them."

The board that governed the Trust consisted of Persephone, Monet Salmon, and Garvin Prell, who had been Reggie's lawyer.

"I hate to see fighting—I can't deal with it," Lilith said.

"At the bottom of all this is money, Lilith."

"Money? Money is a problem?" Lilith did not understand.

"Money has always been the problem. Some families can't

face questions about sex or death; the Salmons can't face questions about money. It's been slipping away for generations. Now it's all gone. Reggie used his inheritance to consolidate land for his Trust."

"People said we were rich—the Salmons are supposed to be rich."

"You wanted to believe it, so you did, but you must have suspected something was wrong."

Lilith thought: There comes a time when everything is about money—she knew that—*but it's too early for me.* "I thought Daddy wouldn't buy me a car for my own good. Why didn't you tell me this before?"

"Your father," Persephone said.

Lilith felt tricked. "So, who do I blame?" she said. "You, conveniently alive? Or Daddy, conveniently dead?"

"Lilith, I made mistakes; your father made mistakes. But we both loved you. And he did provide. There's money to finish your college education, some for graduate school—if you so choose. And as soon as you're of age, you'll have the house to sell, or to keep, if you can find a way to maintain it."

"The house, for me? What about you?"

After a pause, Persephone, looking off toward some faraway point, said, "Your father did not include me in his will."

"It's not your house—it's mine?"

"That's correct." Persephone's inner rage at her former husband showed itself now as coldness to her daughter, a coldness that she did not intend but could not prevent, any more than New Englanders can prevent winter from lingering into spring.

"Please stay, Mother. You can have the house. I don't want it."

"It's yours. You are your father's daughter, and you've inherited his world—his house, a place on his Trust board."

Lilith understood now. "You're leaving, aren't you?" she said.

"You know I've been seeing Hadly."

"Professor Blue."

"He's asked me to marry him."

"Oh." Her mother deserved love, deserved a new life. Lilith hated her own resentment.

"He's signed a contract for six years at the University in Sydney," Persephone said. "He's there now. After the bodies are legally deposited in the new cemetery, I'm going to join him. Lilith, you're coming of age. According to the terms of Reggie's will, you'll take my place on your father's Trust board, if you're crazy enough to want the job. Also, you'll come into your inheritance—the house."

Lilith hadn't known her father had squandered what was left of the family fortune on land, but she did know he had squandered his love in the quest for land, and she knew he had used deceit in acquiring the land. Now, in her confusion, in her surprise, in a sudden painful giddiness, Lilith thought she saw a way toward reparation, toward nobility. "I want to give it back," she said.

"Give it back—what?"

"The house, the land, the Trust—all of it. If we could give it back, everything would be all right."

"Give it back? To whom?" Persephone was annoyed, puzzled, and just a mite amused.

"The Indians. If we could give it back, Garvin and Monet wouldn't fight. There'd be peace. And . . ." Lilith could feel the sweetness of discovery going bad with her attempt to bring logic to the idea.

"Lilith, the Trust is tied up in confusing and shaky legal language. It's not yours or ours to give, only to maintain or, perhaps, to lose. The house is, well, an albatross."

Now Persephone embraced her daughter. How could she explain to this child that she had no more strength to give her? She and Reggie had endured an impossible marriage through the stimulation afforded by domestic warfare. The war was over—Reggie was dead. Although she realized she should stay and help her daughter, Persephone had first to heal her own wounds, by necessity away from Upper Darby. Then perhaps she could come back and be of some use to her daughter.

"Come on. Let's go to Ancharsky's store and put gas in the Bronco." Persephone lit a new cigarette off the stub of the old.

6

Darby

Center Darby Village was several miles away from the Route 21 highway turnoff. In contrast to the old cemetery, the grass on the common was well tended and already beginning to green up; the fine eighteenth- and nineteenth-century houses surrounding the common had never looked better. The reason, in the language of the times, was gentrification. Educated, prosperous people from downcountry had moved into the neighborhood. The new people (which was the local term for anyone whose family had not been in Darby for at least two generations) liked to fix things up, and they had the money to get the job done. Unlike the natives, the new people believed in the idea of New England, even if the idea wasn't exactly true to the place, whereas the natives believed in the place and lacked any true idea of that place.

Lilith pulled the Bronco beside the pumps in front of the general store.

"Everything looks so spruced up, except for the store. It's run-down."

"He's lost a lot of business to the convenience market Critter Jordan built in his father's auction barn."

"Up on the highway."

"That's the way it is today. The guts are gone from the center of town." Persephone gave Lilith some money from her purse.

67

"I'll pump the gas and check the oil. You can go in and pay."

The store had once been a big rambling house, and now it was a big, rambling grocery store. The proprietor, Joe Ancharsky, had made sure it retained that classic look when he bought it several years back from the estate of Harold Flagg, a local farmer turned merchant. Joe had been a Hazelton, Pennsylvania, coal-mine foreman. "Nothing like the dark to make a man dream of light," he'd say.

As Lilith went into the store, the crackle of Joe's CB raked her spine—"Town Hall's going to be a mortuary while they move the bodies from the old cemetery to the new. . . ." Lilith recognized the voice of Dorothy McCurtin, the town gossip. Lilith experienced a vague, unspecified fear, like one far away from shelter sensing bad weather coming on. The remainder of Mrs. McCurtin's words were lost in static. Then there was silence.

"Welcome home, old-timer," Joe said to Lilith, and she returned his greeting.

Joe called anybody who came into his store "old-timer." Joe propped chairs against the wall and around his Mamma Bear wood stove, encouraging the "old-timers" to use his store as a social center. Lilith liked the storekeeper, with his sad hound-dog eyes and his unsmiling but kindly face. She looked at his hands, big hands attached to ordinary arms on an ordinary man's body. The way his palms spread out on the smooth-rough oak-plank countertop seemed to testify to pride, both in those hands and in the countertop itself, built by a forgotten carpenter for a forgotten proprietor in another century.

Lilith recognized most of the patrons in the store, but because she had spent most of her time in schools far from Darby, her knowledge of the people behind the faces was broken, unshaped by continued presence in a place.

The "old-timers" included:

—An elderly senile woman sitting stiffly in a chair against

the wall, a resident of the Village Common Nursing Home (which was actually not on the common but just off it). The woman had wandered away from the nursing home today, and Joe had sat her down and given her a bag of potato chips.

—A husky out-of-work farm hand, a big man who wore denim overalls all the time. His name was Leonard Parkinson, but everybody called him Pitchfork. He was the brother of Bud Parkinson, Darby's road agent. Pitchfork had dreamed of being a farmer. But the Parkinsons had no land to speak of, and the price of farmland in the area had gone beyond the reach of ordinary working people. Pitchfork would sit in the straight-back chair with his arms folded, saying little, usually taking everything in, but sometimes lost in himself.

—A small, wiry man with long, stringy hair, and a youth who was a Southeast Asian refugee. The older man wore mottled military fatigues; a hunting bow he carried everywhere leaned against the wall. The youth was dressed in black cottons. The older man was Abnaki Jordan, a member of the infamous Jordan clan. Abnaki had no trade (although he was good with his hands and he found work when he needed it), no immediate family (although he was related to hundreds of Jordans in Tuckerman County), no property (although he squatted on land owned by his cousin Critter Jordan), no education (although he knew everything he had to know to survive among his own kind), no philosophy of existence (although he was a pretty fair judge of character and situation, and he liked to hold forth), and no home as such. He was a wanderer of Tuckerman County, familiar to the town of Darby but not strictly a native of Darby. Local people called the youth Whack Two because that's what Abnaki had dubbed him, because he could not pronounce the boy's given name. Whack Two was the son of E. H. Prell's gardener, Lok Toh, but he was estranged from his family and he lived in a shack with Abnaki.

—A woman about thirty wearing too much makeup, attractive in a hard way. Her name was Noreen Cook, and she was the only person in the store besides Lilith who was actually shopping. Local people had started referring to Noreen as the Pocket Witch, just as they had started referring to Monet Salmon as the Pocket Squire.

Before paying for the gas, Lilith poked around the store, eavesdropping on the chatter between the old-timers and Joe.

"My cousin Critter's kinda *put'nit* to you since he opened his store on the highway," Abnaki said to Joe.

"What gets me down is that his store is not the real item," Joe said. "It's a franchise operation. Some accountant in Chicago orders the stock. Cheap beer, expensive everything else. No individuality. One like it in every burg in the U.S. of A."

"Joe, your problem is your heart's soft," Abnaki said. "Now, Critter's like me—a Jordan, crazy but hard. 'Course he's not as crazy as Whack Two here."

The Asian burst into a short laugh that might have been a cry.

"These highway corner marts moving in on country stores— they're like fast-food joints, like McDonald's," Joe said, his voice rising with discovery as he stumbled into the simile.

Abnaki grabbed his bow from the wall and began fiddling with it. "Pretty soon, everything McDonald's. McDonald's schools—kid goes to classes until he's old enough to work a cash register. McDonald's weddings—instead of white, the bride wears yellow. McDonald's funerals—won't have to get out of the car while the loved one is planted in a foam coffin. So the body stays warm." Abnaki bopped Whack Two on the head with the string end of the bow, and the two of them laughed. Joe clapped his big hands once and laughed; Pitchfork Parkinson shook with silent laughter. The old woman did not laugh, and Noreen Cook did not laugh. Lilith smiled with mild discomfort. She wondered if you could make music with Abnaki's bow by rubbing the arrow across the taut string.

Lilith gave Joe some bills for the gas. Joe took her money and rang up the sale.

"You going to lifeguard again this summer?" Joe asked.

"Well, I'm a little old for that," Lilith said.

Lilith's use of the word "old" elicited snickers of superiority. Even the senile woman understood Lilith's ingenuousness and reacted to it with a drop of her jaw.

Lilith blushed. "I don't know what I'm going to do," she said. How alone she felt in her hometown. "Darby's changing," she added in an attempt change the subject.

"In the school year you've been gone"—Joe halted in mid-sentence, turned toward the smoky window, and gestured—"there was Mrs. Bell—"

"Died," said Abnaki. Lilith heard in his pronunciation the heavy rural New England–accented English of a past generation—*doy'd*.

"Connally—" Joe went on.

"*Doy'd*," Abnaki said.

"Miss Price—"

"*Doy'd*."

"The Souters—"

"What happened to the Souters?" Abnaki asked.

Whack Two giggled like a girl.

"Retired to Florida," Joe said. "All of 'em: gone. Houses sold for big bucks. The McAdam heirs made a bundle selling to the Inn people."

"Who can blame them?" Abnaki said.

"I don't know why it gets me down, but it does," Joe said almost to himself, paused, and turned to Lilith. "The memorial service is a fine thing, the idea is fine, too: move an old cemetery, build a park and a school."

71

"Schools take you right out of your game—ain't worth *nothn'*," Abnaki said.

Noreen Cook arrived at the checkout counter. Lilith made way for her. Joe rang up Cheerios, potato chips, doughnuts, packaged pies, and a six-pack of expensive Mexican beer. "And gimme some Sweepstakes tickets," Noreen said.

Joe produced a string of tickets. "How many?" he asked.

"All of 'em," she said.

As Noreen left the store, Abnaki spoke just loud enough for Lilith and Joe to hear. "Pocket Witch for ailments of the heart and whatever." He and Joe knew the Mexican beer meant Noreen would be entertaining a certain customer tonight.

Outside, Persephone was finishing pumping gas when she saw Garvin Prell pedaling toward her on his English racing bicycle. "Per-seh-phoneee," Garvin called. "Garrrvinnn," Persephone answered. The two greeted each other in the Upper Darby idiom, and to an outsider they would have appeared to be old friends.

Garvin pulled to a stop, swung down from his machine, and removed his helmet. Persephone studied him. He stood as if posing, headgear in hand, at thirty-three, prime age, dressed in a European racing outfit, looking like some new breed of jet pilot. He was handsome in the way of the Prell men, not too tall and tending toward stockiness, but fit, with solid legs, sharp, even features, his manner confident, predatory, but not mean-spirited. Not yet, anyway. For meanness of spirit, there was Garvin's father. With that thought, Persephone chose her amenity. "How's E.H. doing?" she asked.

"Dad—the same."

Lilith stepped from the store into the sunshine, and Garvin noticed the change in her. "Time and a Southern climate have done wonders," he whispered to Persephone.

The sight in Joe's store of the Pocket Witch and the old woman, of the backcountry bum and the dazed Asian boy, of

Joe Ancharsky himself, and now, as her eyes smarted in the outdoor light, of a Prell in recreational garb troubled Lilith. Something was wrong—terribly wrong with this Darby world. It was . . . She had no word for her thought. She didn't even have a grasp of the idea but, rather, a feeling of misalignment. Her good manners swamped any notion of revealing her thoughts. She said, "Garvin, I haven't seen you since last summer at the lake. Are you going to sail this year?"

"I might test the Lightning in a race or two, but bicycling keeps me fit. You're looking well." He attacked her with the compliment.

Lilith felt awkward. She wanted to move on, but a sense of obligation prodded her to continue with the prattle. "So, what have you been doing?" she asked.

"Practicing law, a little business. Plodding on as a board member for your father's Trust." He folded his arms and looked long and hard at her.

Persephone guffawed. "He does more plotting than plodding."

"A Prell takes the world as he finds it." Although Garvin spoke his words to Lilith, it was obvious they were meant for Persephone.

Abnaki and Whack Two left the store, making their way toward benches on the town common.

"So many strangers in town. And I don't know what to think about Mrs. McAdam's house," Lilith said.

"Lilith, it's not the town it was," Garvin said.

"Your development—Mother told me about it," Lilith said.

"That's right. I'll show it to you sometime." He paused. "After I take you to the Inn for dinner."

Lilith didn't know what to say. She glanced at her mother.

"Oh, go ahead," Persephone said. "A Salmon and a Prell on a date. It thrills me to think what Mrs. McCurtin will say about that."

73

Lilith lied—"I'm going with someone right now"—then hedged, "but maybe later in the summer."

"I don't give up. I'll try you down the road," Garvin said.

Joe Ancharsky watched the old-timers leave, Garvin Prell on his bicycle, the Salmon women in the Squire's Bronco, Noreen Cook in a Plymouth Valiant, Abnaki and Whack Two on the park bench on the common, sitting motionless as statues. An attendant came to fetch the senile woman. Joe stood alone at his cash register, staring out the smoky window.

The Bronco turned onto Upper Darby Road. A feeling of being uneasily lifted, as in an elevator, came over Lilith, as it always did when she sensed the presence of Upper Darby, for there were no legal boundaries designating where Center Darby ended and Upper Darby began; these were places of mind and geography, not law.

"You see what's happening to this town?" Persephone said. "For centuries, the town common is the town common. Then a restaurant comes in and suddenly it's the town green. But the food is good, and—" Persephone abruptly stopped short.

"What?" Lilith sensed she was stepping into a trap.

"Nothing."

"What?" She was already in the trap.

"I saw the way Garvin looked at you," Persephone said. "If you could handle him, well, who knows what could happen between the Salmons and the Prells?"

"Nothing should happen between a Salmon and a Prell."

Persephone smiled. "Garvin represents everything I've been taught to despise—greed, deception, single-mindedness, insensitivity to the natural world. But he's not a bad man, you know. He's just a man—he wants to win. You could do worse than Garvin."

"Oh, Mother, please don't do this to me."

"Lilith, you're young—you're a dreamer. I know what's on

74

Garvin's mind. By marrying you, he'd have the Salmon prestige that the Prells have always yearned for."

"Is that why you married Daddy—prestige?"

"I married him because I was head over heels in love."

Lilith remembered herself as a young girl suddenly coming upon her reflection: made wrong. "I'm sorry, Mother."

"No reason to be sorry. I'm a scheming middle-aged woman. There's a name for it. Soon I'll be a scheming old woman, and then it will be all right. There's so much at stake—the future of Upper Darby. Your father wanted the land preserved in the name of our son. Garvin wants to turn the Trust into a city. Monet can't stop him; Monet has the brain of a hare. You could have at it with Garvin's money."

"I don't know what to think," Lilith said.

"Poor, half-equipped little knight. Forget what I said. Sell your house, get your money, and get out of Upper Darby."

The Bronco labored up the twisting road. They passed the original Butterworth house, now owned by Monet Salmon, Reggie's younger brother. Like the Salmon house and the Prell house, the Butterworth house of Upper Darby belonged to that Shingle architecture stage of the early twentieth century, great sprawling places put together with generous amounts of local wood by skilled carpenters who would have been happier as farmers. Designed by Byronic architects for baronial clients in the episode between the Victorian and Modern eras so that Gothic gewgaws coexisted with Japanese roof lines, these were houses with enormous porches and not enough bathrooms, houses with separate and unequal quarters for relatives, friends, servants, and pets. The Salmons, the Butterworths, and the Prells had built their dwellings to rival one another, each one bigger than the last. That was why the Butterworth house was the least—because it had gone up first. It had been the first because the Butterworths had been the most daring of the Upper Darby families, if not the most successful. It was the Butterworth daring which accounted for the fact that, of the three great houses of Upper Darby, the Butterworth house was the most unconventional. Never mind that the last two generations of Butterworths were reserved, cautious—anything but unconventional (not counting alcoholism); never mind that the present owner fit the spirit of the house much better than any Butterworth for half a century; never mind that he was not a Butterworth but a Salmon.

Persephone always winced a little when she passed by the place. Monet's occupancy of the house was another Upper Darby aphid taking little bites out of her soul, for Monet's house had belonged to Trellis Butterworth, Persephone's mother. Trellis' house had hidden behind its screen of trees in neglect for almost a year after she died. Then Monet returned to Darby after years of wanderings and bought the place (with drug money, Persephone guessed). Persephone had the consolation of knowing it would be called "the Butterworth house" for as long as Monet lived in it. That was how it went in Darby. You had not only to reside in a place for many years before the town recognized you as the true owner, but you had to die in it. The house made her yearn vaguely for her childhood.

"What's going on with Uncle Monet?" Lilith asked, the sight of the house kindling her curiosity.

"Has a girlfriend, quite exotic. I'll say this much for him: he's taken an interest in the Trust, made himself the unofficial caretaker of the forest."

The Bronco soon reached the end of the town road. Here was an open area used by the road agent to turn the snowplow around. Beyond were the Trust lands. The entry to the rough dirt road was barred by a chain hooked between two trees and a sign, "Salmon Trust—No Trespassing." Just before the turnaround was the driveway to the Salmon house. The drive twisted slightly upward through the trees, coming out in a clearing on a knoll upon which sat an impressive house, the finest in Darby by reputation if not in reality. The building rose from a mortared stone foundation to three stories. The downstairs rooms were so enormous that sometimes Lilith could hear her voice echo in them; the second-floor bedrooms were large, but smaller than the rooms downstairs. The third floor, chopped up into small rooms for servants, was closed off. The lawn undulated pleasantly; here and there shade trees grew. A wide porch wrapped around half the house in a sweeping curve. The cedar shingles that covered the house had darkened until they were almost black. To the rear was Persephone's greenhouse, then a shingled barn (meant to house not animals but machines), a field, a stone wall, then the forested hills of the Trust lands. Lilith brought the Bronco to a stop at the front door.

"I'm going to the greenhouse for a minute. I'll see you inside," Persephone said. Lilith was puzzled and a little frightened as Persephone for the briefest moment doubled her right fist; then she opened the car door and walked quickly away.

Lilith paused at the Bronco a moment and looked at the house, half in morning sunlight, half in deep shadow. The lighted half was so bright it hurt her eyes; the darker half seemed to forbid her entry. She approached the house cautiously, as if it belonged to someone else. The porch screens were rusted, and the screen door stuck when she opened it. She retrieved the key from a crack in a floorboard and opened the door. Inside, the house smelled cold, musty, unlived-in.

She headed for the Hearth Room, the place she always automatically gravitated to. It was so big it easily accepted a large cherrywood meeting table and a piano in addition to parlor-type furniture. Among the wealthy New York families who had built country homes in Upper Darby at the turn of this century, the Butterworths called their main room the Ball Room, the Prells the Hall, and the Salmons the Hearth after the centerpiece of the room, a fieldstone fireplace large enough for a child to walk into, wide enough for an adult to lie down in. The Hearth was home. Here her father burned alligator-sized logs and brooded by the flames for hours, but he never told anyone what was on his mind.

After the fieldstone fireplace, the main feature of the Hearth Room was the long cherrywood dining table, the site of the meetings of the Trust board and huge family gatherings from the bygone era. Wood for the table came from the property, as did the wood for the entire house, from the hand-split cedar shingles to the oak- and maple-paneled walls, to the spruce and birch flooring. The present-day Salmons had not used the table for dining, except for special occasions. Like most things in the house and like the house itself, it was a relic of a previous age. Originally, the native oak panels had been varnished and the wood played off against papered, plastered walls. Later, Lilith's grandmother had had the varnish stripped and the wood painted. Finally, Lilith's father had stripped the paint down to bare wood and paneled over the plaster walls with more wood. He refused to finish the wood, so that it had dried and cracked, and the finish was dull. "Unlike people," he would say, "wood and stone grow more beautiful with age."

The shelf space in this room was considerable, since it had been designed in part as a library, but even so the shelves were almost filled with books, knickknacks, things of her family, her father's surveyor's transit on the same shelf as her mother's fine ceramic pots, a logger's pulpwood hook sitting on a stack of *Smithsonian* magazines, a box of crossword puzzles (a family winter pastime) beside a box of wood matches for the fireplace. The juxtaposition of such objects gave the room an air of refined clutter.

Her cello leaned against the wall. She stood before it for a moment, then picked up the bow and ran it across the strings. Her dream had been to play in a symphony orchestra, but as MacKavitt had said—indeed, warned her early on—she'd started too late. She'd been possessed by a child's dream carried too far, for her original interest in the instrument began when she was an eighth-grader in private school. She'd been lonely and self-conscious. At a concert, she'd seen a beautiful young woman with tanned skin and a black dress play the cello. Lilith had envied not her beauty but her serenity. In a child's search for that serenity, she'd demanded her parents buy her a cello. She pawed at the stuff on the shelves—old cross-country skis, a sailcloth sewing kit for her father's old Lightning sailboat, a fur coat stuffed in a cardboard box, little carved chunks of wood in a tin cylinder (who knows what they were about), a cabinet with her father's shotgun left over from the days when he hunted, a pair of reading glasses.

Perhaps she should go into business, open the Salmon Flea Market. People would come for miles around to gawk at the Squire's daughter. They'd say, "She's broke, poor dear."

Persephone appeared from the hallway. "Can you give me a hand in the greenhouse?" she asked.

Lilith was surprised and a little thrilled. From the day Persephone had commissioned its construction, the greenhouse had been her sanctuary, off limits to husband and daughter. During the awful time of his illness, her father had found solace at the ledges in the Trust lands, while her mother sequestered herself in the greenhouse. Lilith could not reach her father—he was too far away—but her mother was in plain view behind wavy glass. Yet it was as if she were not there, as if the image of Persephone moving gracefully and purposefully behind the glass were insubstantial as an image on television. Lilith wanted to hate the plants because they had sucked up her mother's love and there was none left for her. But she loved the plants—they were her mother. Sometimes in the summer, at night, she would sneak into the greenhouse, nervous and alert as a burglar, and sit among the plants, breathe in their essence—her mother's perfume.

She had never taken an active interest in Persephone's plants, for the very reason that growing things was her mother hobby. There was another reason. All creatures come and go under the sun, Lilith knew, but she could not bear to see living things fail to thrive under her care. She'd had a cat once; it died because of her actions and poor judgment. In the screech of the desire to mate, the cat had asked for out, and Lilith, in violation of a family rule that Salmon cats were strictly house cats, had complied with the screech. She'd opened her upstairs window and watched as the cat softly bounded onto the abutting porch roof, then onto a lower shed, then into the night. The cat never returned. It was likely that a wild animal, a fisher or a coyote, had dined on it. One of the few traits her parents had had in common was an inclination to keep their feelings to themselves. They were like that animal on the Trust land that had killed her cat, full of knowledge about how to survive, the number-one rule of that knowledge being to keep to oneself that selfsame knowledge.

Now, after all these years, it seemed that Persephone had finally decided to share her private world with her daughter. Mother and daughter walked through the gloomy back hall to the greenhouse. Persephone opened the door that led into the greenhouse, and Lilith anticipated the pleasant shock of warm, moist air, smelling dankly of greenery and earth. A trace of the smell remained, but the greenhouse was dry and empty except for a single hibiscus plant, severely trimmed back, squatting in a giant red clay pot. Lilith felt a wave of vertigo. "What happened?" she asked.

"I gave my *plahnts* to the garden club," Persephone said. "The only one left is this lovely monster. It's my favorite, and I couldn't bear to part with it as long as I was in Upper Darby. I even thought about taking it with me to Australia before deciding to give it to Natalie Acheson."

"Maybe I could care for it," Lilith said.

Persephone laughed. "You silly child. Where in a college dormitory room is there space for a plant buried in a hundred-pound dirt ball?"

Lilith touched the leaves. They were thick, soft and smooth as flesh.

"It's a Chinese hibiscus," Persephone said. "Strictly tropical. Needs the greenhouse. The magic of this particular specimen is that it only blooms for one day in a year. I'd wait for that day. This year, on the very morning it bloomed, Hadly telephoned to ask me to marry him. I took it as an omen to say yes."

"All those years, all that magic. Why didn't you tell me?"

"I didn't think you cared. And maybe, just maybe, it was a personal thing with me."

Lilith understood, but her understanding didn't make her feel any less left out of her mother's life. "What color are the flowers?" Lilith asked.

"They're yellow, with a trace of pink radiating out from the centers."

Mother and daughter skidded the hibiscus and its pot on a blanket to the door. Then they pushed it up a plank into the rear of the Bronco. The work seemed to smooth over the rough moments between them. Lilith was impressed by, even proud of, the way her mother plotted out the task, with no wasted motions and with a confidence that the job would get done.

They drove the hibiscus to the Acheson place and dropped it in the driveway with Natalie Acheson looking on. Her husband would move it when he returned from golf, she said. Since his retirement, he liked to play golf before breakfast. It helped his appetite, which otherwise was not good. Natalie and Brooks Acheson, like many residents of Upper Darby these days, were not natives and were not young. They were people who'd bought into the abstraction of upcountry. They were good for the town, Persephone said, because they had money and taste, and because they didn't load up the school system with children. But Lilith didn't know what to think about the Achesons and their ilk. Mrs. Acheson had a grown son a few years older than herself, but she rarely talked about him, and Lilith had never seen him. It was the same with the rest of Upper Darby. People moving out, selling out, new people coming in who were older, done with pushing a new generation onto the scene, done with careers—done. Where were the young people?

When the Salmon women returned to their own home, Lilith watched her mother stare at the greenhouse through the French doors of the dining room, turn, and hurry upstairs. Lilith wondered if Persephone would cry. If she did, Lilith would never find out.

Lilith returned to the greenhouse. Without the hibiscus, the emptiness of the place seemed like a desert, and yet it still smelled vaguely of moist earth. She thought about the cemetery, the monuments of her father and brother, deep in the earth, grass growing, flowers growing, strange tangles of things growing. The thought of the sound of rain beating against the ground made her feel euphoric and strange. She decided then that she would be at the old cemetery when the town moved the bodies.

7

The ChaMadonnan

Garvin Prell snapped on his helmet, pedaled his bicycle to the edge of the driveway—and paused. Usually he bicycled down to the village, then back to Upper Darby, before leaving in the BMW for his law office in Tuckerman. On occasion, he'd bike all the way to the city. He'd shower and change at the office, and return home in the evening with Horace DeBussey Jones or stay with whomever he was dating. (At the moment, there was no woman in his life.) In that pause at the driveway, Garvin decided to head up the road instead of down.

He'd left on his bicycle ride even earlier than usual because the doctor was going to examine his father this morning. Doc Butterworth was an Upper Darby resident and a family friend (also a cousin of Persephone Salmon) who once a week looked in on E. H. Prell on his way to the county clinic. Garvin didn't want to be there when the doctor was around. Garvin was more or less fearless in dealing with most people, but where the issue of his father and/or health arose he was a coward. Like father, like son—type A; blood pressure on the high road; cholesterol count the age of Darby. So he exercised and watched his diet and stayed away from health professions. He liked life.

He pedaled up the steep grade to the top of the hill and the Trust lands. Garvin believed, perhaps rightly, that because his legs alone took him up the road, he could appreciate better than most the steepness of the grade between the Prell and Salmon properties. He understood this truth both as a metaphor of Darby and as a fact of physics.

Once he got to the Salmon house, he was winded but still full of energy. He pulled the bike into the driveway of the Salmon place because he wanted to get a good look at the house. He didn't expect to see Lilith outside this early, and he had no intention of stopping at the door; he merely wanted to feel proximity to the building and to Lilith. He imagined her sleeping, on her back, legs raised slightly, eyes shut, dreaming perhaps of him. He was surprised to find her outside, taking out the trash. He was so surprised that he stopped short. He stood there, astride his bicycle, watching her, wondering whether she'd see him. She wore blue jeans and a man's shirt tied around her waist. Her long blond hair was in a braid. He thought she looked beautiful. He didn't feel shy so much as unprepared to deal with her at the moment, and he was sweaty from his exertions, so he retreated.

The ride down the hill to home was exhilarating. There were stretches when he must have hit fifty miles an hour. In this mood, his thoughts, too, raced. He didn't so much think about his ideas for Darby as enjoy them as scenery. Then, unsummoned, the image of Lilith entered those thoughts. The world of Upper Darby was changing, and Lilith wasn't sure what was going on. She was vulnerable; she needed somebody to take care of her. With Persephone leaving Upper Darby, the Salmon house was going to be Lilith's, and so was Persephone's seat on the Trust board. Garvin wondered what Lilith planned to do with property and power. Probably she had no plans at all. The moment he'd seen her at Ancharsky's Store, he'd changed inside. He was more alive, more aware. Garvin had never felt about anyone like this before, something beyond mere love and affection, beyond even desire. It had to do with injury, revenge, and finally unification, peace, and property; it had to do with the old Salmon-Prell rivalry. Garvin understood, in the lingo of his father, that his heart was getting in the way of his head. E.H. would say, "Son, don't mix business with romance."

It was clear early on to his father that there was not going to be much room in Darby for advancement, so he had eased Garvin's brothers and sister out into the world. But when Garvin's mother died and E.H. was impaired by a stroke, Garvin found himself with an unspoken directive to carry on the Prell name in Upper Darby. At first he had rebelled. It was rebellion that had influenced him to accept Reggie Salmon's offer to be his lawyer. That act had chagrined his family while it satisfied his own need to chagrin them. But as time passed, his rebellion wore away, replaced by a sense of obligation and a desire to replace E.H. as leader of the family. But there was something else. In working with Reggie Salmon—the great man of Upper Darby, the head of a family that traditionally had competed against his own family—Garvin found himself with a distinctly un-Prell and un-Salmon dream, his own dream, and that was to unite the Upper Darby families, and furthermore to unite the town.

The new school and park being built by the town would support his bid to draw buyers for his condominiums; sure to make money for the Prells, he was thus assured of proving himself to the family. But Garvin was like any man who has achieved a goal. He dreamed bigger dreams, while at the same time he defended his gains. His future plans depended on what he and Selectman Arthur Crabb, his ally in the town government, referred to as "the links"—town and school/park, the Prell development, and the Trust. The weak link was the Trust. The problem was that the very thing that made the Trust valuable to the plan, a guarantee to incoming residents that a large area of the town would remain forever pristine and undeveloped, also made it difficult to tie it into the other links. People could hike on the Trust (in violation of the Trust charter), or pick berries there (violation), even fish in its waters (violation). The Trust must be made legally accessible for limited use, and it must be promoted as a lure. Garvin envisioned an entry point on the Trust for his ideas to pour through. He believed he had found that entry point in Reggie Salmon himself.

The Squire of Upper Darby was a local legend, and he'd cemented his place in the town's memory by founding the Trust. He had also stipulated in his will that his remains be interred on the Trust. As Reggie's lawyer, Garvin was well aware of the details. But Reggie had not been buried on the Trust, because his widow had other ideas. She wanted Reggie beside the grave of their son. Garvin had not thought to challenge a widow's authority, despite the command in the will. But today everything was different. The bodies were coming out of the ground. Time had passed. Persephone was headed for Australia to marry again.

A monument memorializing the Squire and his Trust built right on the Trust: that was Garvin's plan. The Prells would donate the money, and the town government would front the enterprise. The monument would serve as a gateway to open the Trust to the public for limited use, and yet the spirit of Reggie's wish to keep the landscape undisturbed would be preserved.

Garvin should have approached Persephone with his plan immediately after the town meeting in March when the voters approved the bond for the new school, but he didn't have the plan fully worked out then. It wasn't until he'd seen Lilith that he knew exactly what he wanted to do. It was time to get started. He had to talk with E.H. again, before approaching Persephone. Nor was it lost on Garvin that Lilith was sure to approve of his idea for a monument honoring her father.

Garvin pumped his racing bicycle up the long, paved way to his own house. He spotted the gardener, Lok Toh, bent over a hoe in the garden, like some Old World peasant.

"You don't look too perky today, Lok Toh," Garvin said.

"It's my boy."

"Yes, I see him everywhere with Abnaki Jordan. I'm sorry."

As Reggie Salmon had been fond of pointing out, Tuckerman County tracked its citizens by social and economic class. No matter who the new immigrants were—Irish, French, Hispanic, or Southeast Asian—the Jordans remained below them, laughed at, feared, but also admired in particular ways, as apes are admired by unsophisticated people for their strength and by sophisticated ones for their social structures.

The Prell house was built about the same time as the Salmon house and in the same Shingle Style so popular with the New England rich of pre-Depression years. As E. H. Prell was fond of saying, the Prell house actually contained more square footage than the Salmon house, thanks to a wing E.H. had built, a "modern" addition of the late 1950s, big glass windows, and a flat roof butting up against the main structure. Where the Salmon house was spent and neglected, the Prell house was spruced up and attended to, the inside completely renovated by an interior decorator from New York after Sylvia Prell had died, the lawns and gardens looked after by the full-time grounds keeper, Lok Toh, a refugee who had received his landscaping training from a Catholic archbishop in a lovely tropical garden in Southeast Asia. Yet, despite all the money E.H. had put into the house, and despite his preoccupation with its status, the house lacked the appeal of the Salmon place. Perhaps it was the wood paneling on the inside, which E.H. had finished and which Reggie had left raw, that made the difference, or perhaps it was the contrast of an imposed to an organic order, like the contrast of a park to a forest, or perhaps it was only the habit of the collective mind, but the people of Darby still regarded the Salmon house as *the* house of Upper Darby and the Prell house as the other house. It was a situation that troubled E. H. Prell, ate away at his innards.

Garvin parked his bicycle in the garage in a special stall beside his BMW. He removed his helmet and hung it on a peg. He slipped up the rear staircase to his room, cleaned up, changed, and walked back down the main stairs. E.H.'s private nurse, Gee, a Filipino, was waiting for him at the bottom. From the anxious look in her eyes, Garvin knew she had something to tell him regarding his father's medical condition.

"What did Doc Butterworth say?" he asked.

"He is going to call you on the telephone."

"I know that, Gee, but what did he say?"

"He say *Mistah* E.H. could have stroke today, tomorrow, any tomorrow."

"How is he at the moment?"

At this question, Gee dropped her look of concern and smiled thinly. "*Rathah lyyyvely,*" she said in perfect Upper Darby English that she'd picked up around the Prell household.

Garvin brushed past Gee, opened the door to his father's room, and shut it behind him. As he knew it would, the presence of his father, sitting up in bed talking to himself, drained away his confidence, leaving him feeling like a boy.

E. H. Prell was seventy but he looked ninety. His latest stroke had left him with a twisted mouth and distorted speech. He sounded not quite like a man but, rather, like a prototype model of a man, an early experiment by the Creator. E.H. stared at Garvin, but he did not see his son. He saw an old enemy. He held up a frail fist and said, "I am the ChaMadonnan."

"Father," Garvin whispered.

E.H. looked deeply into his son's eyes, and spoke to those eyes as if they belonged to his archenemy, Reggie Salmon.

"You used our friendship to swindle me out of half a mountain. You could never make money—you were a fool about money. What's that? What?" Suddenly his mind circled back to the real world and, without breaking the rhythm or construction of his speech, shifted his address from enemy to relation. "To give the devil his due, Reggie was able over the years to acquire property to feed his appetite for land. You understand what I'm saying? You see the iron in the irony? The poor man who in the end owns the soil we walk on—you see it?"

"Yes, Father."

"Somebody has to balance the ledger."

"Yes, Father."

"Somebody has to balance the ledger."

"Yes, Father."

"Somebody has to balance the ledger."

Garvin hated these stroke-caused stall jobs in time, but he repeated dutifully, "Yes, Father."

"I lie here in the dream of that mad dog." E.H. spoke to the sky in his room. "No new blood. No new money. Properties going to ruin. Shacks and trailers taking their place. People whose only talent is for breeding and bleeding. The distinction between Upper Darby and Center Darby fading into history . . . into history. You know what history is, my boy? It's nothing—a fabrication, a dream, a fear. An invention to satisfy our craving for order. Myself, I've settled for acquisition, but that, too, is nothing. In the woods, Reggie's triumphant, raven-black spirit looms over Darby. I can't stop it—I'm going to die." E.H. huffed and puffed, and then his voice softened, full of pained love. "Your brothers, your sister left Upper Darby."

"Yes, Father."

E.H. seemed to notice something in the room. He looked around, as if for a misplaced hat. "Where is your mother?"

"She passed away, Father."

"Sylvia?" E.H. called, then listened. No answer. He turned to Garvin. "So, then, we are alone."

"Yes, Father."

A moment passed, and then E.H. came to his senses again. Garvin could tell by his eyes, shrewd and focused. Garvin bent closer to him, and raised his voice slightly. "We have to talk about the condo project—okay?"

"You've made some progress on that one." E.H. brightened, and his words were spoken kindly.

Garvin was suspicious.

"It's time to put the monument proposal on the table," Garvin said.

"He's on that one again." E.H. stared off into space, as if his son were not in the room but far away. Then he turned to Garvin. "It was a frivolous idea to begin with. And Persephone will never relent. So, what's the point?"

"We could threaten a court suit since Reggie said clearly and in writing that he wished to be buried on the Trust." Garvin spoke in his courtroom voice.

"Don't you understand? I don't want a monument glorifying the Squire of Upper Darby," E.H. said.

"I'll drop it—for now," Garvin said.

E.H. had zeroed in on Garvin's hidden agenda, hidden even from himself, a drive to install a monument to his father's enemy, in the name of Prell profit, and while his father was still alive and sentient to witness the action. This was not so much revenge that Garvin was after as it was justice and notice.

"What about the girl?" E.H. asked.

"She's home for the memorial service."

E.H. chuckled.

The visit ended with E.H.'s losing his ability to form words. "I am the ChaMadonnan," he said.

Garvin understood now. His father had been the chairman of many boards. "Yes, father, you are the ChaMadonnan," Garvin said.

8

Grave Labor

The morning was gray and chilly. Rain was forecast. The work and Lilith would go ahead anyway. Disagreeable weather was always impending in Darby. Local people hoped for the best, knowing the odds were against them. If it rained, it rained; if it snowed, it snowed. Lilith put on a bulky sweater, wool jacket, blue jeans, and hiking boots—an Upper Darby outfit for all seasons but summer.

"Going somewhere?" her mother snooped, as Lilith was about to leave.

"A drive," Lilith said, and hurried out the door. She wasn't about to tell her mother she was headed for the old cemetery. She wished to avoid the draining discomfort of elaborate explanation, for Persephone would not have been satisfied with the only clear and honest answer she could give—*I just want to see for myself.* Of course, it would have been worse had Persephone tagged along with her to watch the bodies being exhumed. The presence of her mother would freeze her just as surely as if Persephone had accompanied her to a raunchy concert. And for the same reasons, having to do with privacy, pleasure, parental presence, and release.

As Lilith was about to get into the car, she heard her mother call her from the doorway.

"What is it, Mother?" Lilith tried to sound nonchalant.

91

Almost a hundred feet separated the parking space of the Bronco, the space that Reggie had taken for himself, from the house. Neither woman made an effort to close the space. "I know where you're going," Persephone said with a shout. "You're in for a shock."

"All right, then."

"Yes, maybe it's better that you see what's to see," Persephone said, and went back into the house.

Lilith drove off. The Bronco made Lilith feel small, innocently childlike. Her imagination infused the car with personality and spirit. The Bronco was strong, steady, reliable. She had covered a couple of miles when she came to a sign: "Welcome to Sugar Bush Village, a Prell Project for Progress." Impulsively, she wheeled onto the freshly paved road. It wound upward through the woods for about half a mile, dead-ending into a parking lot. The development sat on a small plateau. Half-built condominiums loomed in front of her. The structures, with their bare plywood sheeting, seemed to intimidate the somber, dignified forest, like women of the night staring down respectable people. Above were the ledges of the Trust lands. Below was the old cemetery. It was not visible through the trees, but she could hear the groan of heavy equipment transforming it. She turned the Bronco around and headed down.

She was surprised to find that a good-sized crowd of local people had gathered at the old cemetery. Apparently, she wasn't the only one curious and excited. She parallel-parked half on, half off the narrow road, behind a row of pickup trucks and late-model cars, vehicles of spectators and workmen. Someone had cranked up a radio in a pickup truck and left the door open; the familiar yet instantly forgotten words of Barry Manilow pierced the base roar of the chain saw. A station wagon pulled up behind her, and a tall, attractive man about forty stepped out. She thought he was looking at her, before she realized that he'd caught sight of the fist-sized rust holes along the fenders of the Bronco. In his eyes, she read amusement and pity. He seemed, she thought, to guess the truth about her—no money. An unfamiliar feeling washed over her—shame. A Salmon without means did not fit into Darby; she was an embarrassment to her own people. Lilith forced a smile. The man returned the smile in the direct but cautious way of married men, then turned away.

The cemetery was roped off so that only workmen were allowed inside. Town Constable Godfrey Perkins and a couple of teenage boys paced inside the rope to keep people from spilling onto the grounds. The boys wore brown uniforms that made them look one part boy scout, one part storm trooper. She recognized among the crowd Selectman Arthur Crabb and Dorothy McCurtin, the gossip. Lilith knew then that soon everyone in Darby would know that the Squire's daughter had been on hand for the removal of the bodies.

Most of the trees and shrubs had already been cleared, giving the land a rough, abused look. Huge boulders, parked by a passing glacier millennia ago, were now revealed, still in place but nicked by the blade of a bulldozer. Perhaps some future archaeologist—a professor, like the man her mother planned to marry—would translate these marks into meaningful language. The bulldozer waited without an operator beside a couple of brush piles, from where the smell of the pine slash made Lilith ache for something long ago, she knew not what, the event forgotten, only a hint of the feeling remaining.

The casket of Lilith's father had already been exhumed. It lay on the ground beside the opened grave, dirt piled to one side. Someone had toweled clean the casket so that it looked as new as the day it had been put in the ground. It was as if her father had died only days ago. Most of the gravestones in the cemetery, including her brother's, had been loaded on a flatbed truck. Her father's was in the process of being moved.

Wrapped in chains, the monument dangled from a tripod of cut tree trunks. It swung in the air like a hanged man.

The soil at the grave of her brother was undisturbed, but workmen were getting ready to dig. She recognized the men from the store, Abnaki Jordan and Whack Two.

Her eye caught a motion from the crowd, and Lilith turned to look. Selectman Arthur Crabb waved as he started toward her. Crabb was a retired dairy farmer, whose suit coat and tie went back to days when farmers were the political kingpins of all the towns in Tuckerman County. He still wielded considerable power, as the chairman of Darby's three-person board of selectmen and as the town's nonvoting representative on the Trust board.

Showing teeth with gold fillings, the old selectman grinned at Lilith as he came near. "Miss Salmon," the selectman exaggerated the pronunciation of *Sahlmohn,* and bowed as if to a princess. "Sorry we have to move your loved ones, but it's for a noble cause."

Lilith was put off by Crabb's courtly manner. It made her feel fifteen. She didn't know what to think about him and, she could see, he didn't know what to think about her. They were from the same town, but the differences in age, breeding, experience, and life-style made them aliens to one another.

The sound of the chain saws died down, and Crabb filled the space with rambling talk about this civic project and the Prell development; the new school, the town park, the condominiums were going to make Darby the best place to live in Tuckerman County. Crabb suggested the Salmon Trust board ought to approve hiking trails, which, as Crabb read the Trust charter, were not specifically barred. Lilith conceded the logic of Crabb's argument. But she was suspicious about her father's Trust being used by the public. He himself had not been public-spirited. He had loved nature, disliked human beings. On the other hand, he had valued renown, not for

LIVE FREE OR DIE

himself but for the Salmon name. So, if this work at the door of the Trust honored his name, perhaps he'd approve. She should think about this matter more. After all, she was going to have vote on the Trust board. Monet and Garvin, the other members, would be after her to support their pet ideas. But what about her ideas? What were her ideas? She did not know. Lilith wished she was older. She wished she had wisdom. She wished she had force of character. It seemed to her that the gains she'd started making in school were now completely lost. She was back in Darby, back at the beginning.

A hearse pulled onto the grounds, and two men Lilith did not recognize stepped out. They wore suits, and looked to her like hit men she'd seen in countless TV shows and movies. One of them supervised while the other and some workmen loaded her father's casket into the hearse.

When the hearse had sped away, Lilith interrupted the old selectman and asked, "Where are they taking my father's body?"

"Town Hall, temporary mortuary," Crabb said. "A two-day job, a dozen bodies a day," Crabb said. "Saved some money by doing it ourselves, instead of jobbing it out. That's why so many of these small towns are in financial trouble: they don't do for themselves. When we're done, the only evidence there'd been a cemetery here will be in the town records."

A minute later, her uncle Monet arrived with his new woman friend. A scientist with a Ph.D. in zoology, her mother had said. Monet was the black sheep of the Salmon family. While Reggie had committed himself to preserving the land and the Salmon name in Darby, Monet had been off on an odyssey of self-knowledge. Or so he put it. In fact, as a youth he'd been perhaps Darby's first—and certainly most notorious—hippie.

Monet and Crabb shook hands like boxers before a match. Monet introduced his woman. "Lilith, this is Dr. Marcia Pascal." Dr. Pascal seemed to probe with a metallic hand as

95

she took Lilith's hand. She wore a full skirt, a heavy sweater with a deep V-neck that showed a generous bosom. From her dark, chiseled features, Lilith guessed that blood from all the races in the world ran through her veins. Dr. Pascal (as Lilith thought of her) was perhaps only a decade older than herself, and yet she seemed more mature, more certain, more knowledgeable by a century.

"What will happen to the old wooden caskets?" Lilith asked Crabb.

"Throw them in the brush piles and burn them up," Crabb said.

"The brush fires will contribute nicely to the greenhouse effect," Monet grumbled, as he edged into the conversation.

"Greenhouse effect," Crabb repeated softly and sarcastically.

Monet went on: "Smoke will be one of the minor errors of this ill-conceived idea: sneak condos into the town by putting up a school for a front." Like his brother, Monet was a big, handsome man, but he lacked the Squire's poise and mystery.

"Mr. Salmon, why don't you let up?" Crabb said. "The old ways of farmers in the valley, shack people in the Depot, and rich folk up here on the hill are gone. We're a bedroom town today for the city of Tuckerman."

"You down there in Center Darby pretend we're all the same breed, but nothing's changed," Monet said.

"Created equal, with equal opportunity: that's the idea we're working with," Crabb said.

The two men argued softly; except for their words, one would have thought from their demeanor that they were old friends.

"It's only the old rich of Upper Darby and the old poor of Darby Depot who understand we're as different as bird dogs and basset hounds in this town," Monet said. "It's the Center Darby commuters that fool themselves, they and the farmers who have made deals with developers."

"Cow patties to that," said the old farmer.

Monet pressed on. "You track the kids with your school curriculum, fence in their parents with zoning laws."

Crabb interrupted: "I used to be against zoning, but without it the town goes to hell. In the modern world there's too much difference between the good, the bad, and the riffraff."

"And you folks down there in Center Darby call us up here on the hill snobs," Monet said.

"I'm not a snob," Crabb said. "I'm just a farmer bred for common sense who can see what's to see."

Monet laughed. "Okay, Crabb—you have the last word this morning, but I'll find a way to stop you. There'll be no school here, no Prell condos up on the hill, and the Trust lands will be protected."

Lilith was troubled by the hushed jocularity in the men's tones. Were they really friends, kidding one another? Or bitter enemies pretending an atmosphere of friendliness? It was not so much the uncertainty as the false air their conversation created that disturbed her, made her feel some essence deep inside her was being polluted by exposure to that air.

The backhoe operator gave a signal with his hand, and the workmen and crowd came to attention, like soldiers responding to an order barked by a tough sergeant. It was time to open the grave of Raphael Salmon II. Lilith watched with an intentness that seemed to brighten the gray day.

Behind the controls of the backhoe was Darby's road agent, Bud Parkinson, a bald-headed man about fifty with smooth reddish-gray skin who was almost never without a soggy Parodi cigar in his mouth. He was a big-bellied man who wore his pants so low on his hips they always seemed in danger of falling off. Bud had discovered that, although the girth of his stomach varied with the seasons, his hips always remained the same size, so by wearing his pants low he never had to buy new ones before they wore out. Bud, unlike his brother Pitchfork, was a jack of all trades and a leader of men. Even such strong personalities as Howard Elman, who contracted to plow a couple of roads for the town in the winter, did not mind bending their wills to Bud Parkinson.

The steel mouth of the backhoe took a bite of ground over the grave. Standing beside the backhoe were Abnaki Jordan and Whack Two, temporary laborers for this job. Lilith watched them. They held long-handled shovels at parade rest. Tan soil marks showed on the young Asian's black clothes. Abnaki's camouflaged fatigue uniform looked the same as it had in the country store.

Lilith remembered now who Abnaki reminded her of—her former boyfriend, Peter. He, too, owned a camouflage outfit, from his father, who was a veteran of the Vietnam War, and he liked wearing it. Peter had graduated—where was he now? She was vaguely curious but she did not really care. Last year, after her father had died and she had returned to school, it had been as if the students in her college had grown younger and more foolish, but she herself felt no older or wiser. She was merely alienated from them and damaged inside. She had not perceived the damage until a late-night hour when she realized she did not want Peter or anyone else to touch her.

The backhoe dug into the earth easily and quickly. Within minutes, the shovel reached the casket. Bud Parkinson operated the backhoe with such skill and precision that it seemed to Lilith that man and machine were one, a great unthinking creature of flesh and metal. When the backhoe came up with a rotted board in its maw, Bud Parkinson swung the arm of the machine out of the way and shifted into neutral. "Hey!" he yelled to Crabb.

The selectman ducked under one of the ropes, brushed past a kid guard, and walked bowlegged to the grave. He looked down in the hole, then up at Bud Parkinson, still in the saddle of the backhoe. They exchanged a few words that Lilith could not hear. Crabb returned.

"I have to warn you, Miss Salmon," he said. "Apparently, your father had his son buried in a wooden casket. Violation of New Hampshire law. Steel liner required. The backhoe cracked it open. I don't know what we're going to find when we dig some more."

Lilith understood now what her mother had meant—You're in for a shock. "Wood was sacred to my father," Lilith said with defensive fierceness.

"Yes, ma'am," the selectman said, then shouted to Bud Parkinson: "Get on with it."

One of the workmen brought Abnaki a gas mask. Abnaki slipped it on and eased himself into the hole. Whack Two stood like a soldier. Lilith watched dirt fly off the shovel until Abnaki shouted, "Bag!" Whack Two tossed a plastic body bag into the grave. Abnaki continued to work until he disappeared from view. The crowd was quiet. Trees and the clouds above seemed to still.

Lilith watched Bud Parkinson for signs of what was going on in the grave. She didn't care so much what Abnaki saw, as he stripped away the rotting boards of the casket, as what he felt, and she thought she might see an intimation of those emotions reflected in the face of Bud Parkinson—revulsion or fear, or perhaps wonder, verification that this brother she had never known had been real and that now, after decades of rest and natural corruption, his remains could still move a human being to demonstrate his human feelings. Bud Parkinson's face registered nothing human except human industry. Abnaki tossed some rotting wood out of the hole, and handed up the body bag to Whack Two. It lay on the ground, a bulging, distorted shiny "S," the color of overcooked spinach, yet with a suggestion of translucence, like the surface of a pond with a sunset lying upon it. Abnaki climbed out of the grave and removed his gas mask. His face betrayed nothing; he simply looked pooped.

The workmen stood by while Mrs. McCurtin, in her role as Darby's town clerk, tagged the body bag. The hearse returned. One of the men in suits set up a dolly behind the hearse. He opened the back of the hearse and a steel-lined casket slid out electrically onto the dolly. The other man opened the casket, where soft, silky fabric contrasted with the hard, shiny metal outside; then he placed the body bag inside. The casket closed without a sound and magically, it seemed to Lilith, receded into the womb of the hearse. The men drove off.

Bud Parkinson went back to work, cleaning from the grave the decayed boards from the old wooden casket. Abnaki and Whack Two picked the wood from the pile of earth and tossed it in the back of a town pickup truck that had pulled up. From there, the refuse was deposited in the brush pile.

The man she'd seen earlier at the Bronco walked past. He never looked at Lilith, but lingered a moment until he established eye contact with Selectman Crabb.

"Looks like rain," the man said.

"Good for burning brush. No chance of a forest fire," Crabb returned the amenity, and the man walked on.

"Who's that?" Monet asked.

"Name's Dracut. Lawyer. One of the new people," Crabb said.

Lilith hurried away from the cemetery just as the sun broke through the clouds. She was almost running when she reached the Bronco. She touched the fender. It was cool, smooth; the sensation of coolness made her aware of the sudden flash of warmth of the sun on her shoulders. She could hear birds singing, a suggestion of the wind in the trees, an echo of past springs, and the creak of heating metal. She could swear she was smelling the burn of leaves bursting from the buds of trees, the green fire that created as it consumed.

When Lilith returned home, the sight of Persephone's Saab, back from the service station and parked in the Bronco's space, sent a jolt of defiance through her. Persephone was her mother; a mother should prepare a daughter for the world. *You haven't prepared me, Mother.* Knowing that her reasons were not entirely defensible, knowing that in this mood she might provoke a confrontation with Persephone that she did not in truth want and that in the end Persephone would win anyway, Lilith stayed outside.

She parked the Bronco beside the Saab and walked around to the rear of the house in ankle-high field grass, moist, cool, smelling of the sun now shining brightly through a hole in rolling clouds. Soon Persephone would be gone. This house and land would be her own. For the first time since Persephone had told her the news about her father's will, Lilith experienced a moment of possession, of pleasure at thinking about what was to be hers. As her father had done, she ought to rent the fields to a farmer who would cut the grass, bale it up for hay, and feed it to his livestock. Which farmer? And how much should she charge? She'd have to find the answer to this and a hundred other questions.

Maybe she could make her property pay for itself. She wouldn't limit herself, as her mother had done, to a greenhouse and a garden of flowers and ornamentals—she'd work the land. She pictured herself driving a tractor, mowing the fields, plowing them up, scattering seeds; she pictured acres and acres of corn; she pictured a roadside vegetable stand, people giving her money and speeding away with bushel baskets full of corn and . . . what else? Perhaps beets and green beans and scallions. And tomatoes—of course, tomatoes, those red, pulpy jewels of late summer. From the scattering of seeds to the gathering of the harvest, from the distress of want to the comfort of means, from the absent father to the abandoning mother, from the dead son to the living daughter, the ancient cycle of seasons and soil might heal the hurt heart.

A yen to explore the Salmon lands now took hold within Lilith. Like almost all the fields of Upper Darby, this one was edged by a stone wall, and then the forest began. Lilith followed a path up through tall hardwood trees, until the land grew steeper, the trees fewer, the granite outcrops more numerous. It was at this point that she decided on a destination. She walked on the narrow path, at once dark and dazzling with green-yellow light; she fought her way through new growth of young hemlocks; she broke through to hard light, blue sky, and the ledges, where the bare bones of the earth shoved up through the soil. Here she stopped, thrilled by a sense that she'd entered a higher world. Her sensations seemed so much more acute than what she'd felt at the house and at the cemetery. She heard not only the birds but the hum of insects, and the wind, which, though not strong, seemed to carry the authority of an entity come with messages from a great distance; the deep-sweet, flower-berry fragrance of the forest washed her like a breaking ocean wave.

And then, for a moment, all was quiet. The suddenness of the silence alarmed her. She wheeled around, and stood looking at the face of a heavyset young man with a furious dark beard.

9

The Trust

Frederick, like his father, used a trail to do some thinking. Howard, deep into his middle age, had gone through the trouble of building a platform high up in a tree. Why? Frederick knew his father as a restless hunter, a tracker, a beater of bushes, not the kind to sit patiently for hours on end waiting for his quarry to come to him. Frederick figured that Howard was not hunting at all. He'd built the tree stand as a private place to brood and drink. The evidence for this idea was strong. Howard admitted he had fallen out of the tree stand. Must have been drunk. Believing in the soundness of his hypothesis, Frederick reasoned from it. Howard, being Howard, would want to know that he had a chance, even a small chance, for a kill, even if killing wasn't his primary purpose for building the tree stand. Therefore, he would have located the platform near an animal trail, but not necessarily on it. Howard would want a view. He'd say, "I like to see two, three states at once." Accordingly, Howard probably built the tree stand overlooking Grace Pond or up high. It was this line of thought that brought Frederick to the ledges, the very same place where—unknown to Frederick—Reggie Salmon had gone to die.

Frederick climbed a tree to get a better look around. He liked places where no one would reach him. He preferred looking down at the world, rather than up. So there he was, literally out on a limb, when he saw Lilith Salmon hurrying along the trail below. He dropped out of the tree just before she turned a corner. He wanted to surprise her, startle her. There was no cunning in him, for he hadn't calculated that this approach would gain him anything. Instead, he was merely exercising a minor cruel streak in his nature. He'd enjoy seeing just a twist of fear in her eyes.

The fear was there, that and something else, a sadness that had nothing to do with him, and he was immediately sorry that he had set out to frighten her. He stepped back, and hunched his body somewhat as animals will to demonstrate their submissiveness, and said softly, "I don't mean any harm."

She seemed about to run away, and then, as if making up her mind to face him, she said, without any real curiosity, "I've seen you before."

"I'm your trash man—Frederick *Elm'n*," he said, sliding over the "man." Shame vied with pride as Frederick identified himself. Lilith did not have to announce herself. Everyone in Darby knew the likeness of the Squire's daughter, if not the person.

"You're looking for something, aren't you," Frederick said.

"How did you know?" She was frightened again.

"The way you came up the trail. Walking pretty fast. Looking around. Stopping. Walking again."

His matter-of-fact tone relaxed her. "I was looking for my father's campfire," she said. "It's where he'd go when he wanted to get away from my mother and me . . . the world."

"The Indian camp—my father took me there when I was a kid," Frederick said.

"You know where it is?" She was animated now. He'd taken on some importance in her eyes with his knowledge.

"Let's go." He started moving and she followed.

He liked leading the way, sensing her behind him. They walked up some rocks, around some rocks, onto more ledge, through some trees. And there it was, the scar of an ancient campfire on the ledges. Before it was a log, obviously put there in more recent times as a seat. She sat on the log and stared into the blackened embers. Frederick didn't know what to make of her. She seemed more lost now that she'd found what she was looking for.

"People been coming here for thousands of years," he said. "This is a side street of an old Indian trail. Natural place to camp. Protected by the wind. Easy to defend. Firewood handy. A view."

Lilith stood, and they gazed out at the Vermont hills, the sky, the Connecticut River visible below. She found herself content for the first time since she'd returned home. This place, so much a part of her own family past though its essence went back through the ages, made her feel as if the burdens of her own life and time were not so important, not to be taken so seriously. Lilith thought about the Indians of long ago. She could see them, dancing around the fire, playing music—drums or something. This young man seemed not so much a man as another feature of the landscape.

"You know how to build campfires?" she asked.

"My father taught me. I'll make you one," he said, and set to work. She watched him peel bark from white birch trees and lay the strips on the granite; he broke dead branches off the hemlock trees. Nothing to it, thought Lilith, and she pitched in and helped.

The work and this situation, having come upon both of them out of the blue, combined to relax the young people so that very soon they felt like old friends instead of recent acquaintances.

"I wish . . . I wish it was ten thousand years ago, and I was an Indian," Lilith said, breaking off a branch and cradling it in her arms with other sticks.

"Be hard for you," Frederick said, and from a playful little smile on his face, she could tell he was going to tease her. "No panty hose, no pizza, no bridges to ford the waters, no combs for your golden hair."

Lilith did not smile, but she ran a hand through her hair. In the summer, it grew lighter from the sun. "I think, if life was hard, instead of only being complicated, we'd all be happier, even if we didn't live so long," she said.

Frederick was interested but skeptical. "Well, yah, but . . ."

"See, if life is hard, you're a success or you die." Lilith was excited now. "If you die, that's that. If you don't die, you can be happy, because there's no reason to be unhappy." Now that she'd voiced the idea, she didn't quite believe it.

"Maybe," he said, half convinced.

They worked on. Lilith liked the way he moved, not with grace but with economy. They put their sticks and kindling in a pile, all the butt ends facing the same way. Lilith sat on the log and watched Frederick kneel beside the campfire scar and lay in the strips of white birch. "That going to work?" she asked.

"Well, I don't know." He spoke these words with the easy self-effacement of a man cocksure of his enterprise. "Fact is, the best way to start a fire is with kerosene."

"That's not very romantic," she said.

"Survival takes charge over romance any day." He concentrated on his work as he talked, never looking at her. She watched his hands—tools, good tools.

"We can always go home and push the thermostat button to get heat," she said. "I think, if a fire like this, outdoors in the woods, isn't romantic, then it isn't worth anything at all."

"I'll buy that." Frederick struck a match. "Birch bark burns nice. It's saturated with an oil, nature's starter fluid." He touched off the bark and added twigs and a couple of sticks perhaps half an inch thick. "You don't want to put on any big stuff too early. The fire will just smoke and go out." The flame was yellow, the smoke black and stringy in raw, still air.

He sat on the log, leaving a space of about a foot between them. She wasn't sure how close she wanted him to her, and he seemed to sense her uncertainty and respect it. Accordingly, she felt comfortable with him.

"Do you still build outdoor fires with your father?" Lilith asked.

"I came home a few years back, and we went hunting—I shot a deer. Otherwise I haven't been in the woods with him since I hit the road. It's too bad. The only place we got along was hunting or fishing." He paused for a moment, then added with a note of frustration, "See, Howard is like a big, slobbery dog who scares everybody. I rebelled against him. I tried to be a . . . I don't know . . . a poet, anything he wouldn't understand. Because, if he didn't understand, I had him, I had him right by the"—he showed her an open claw of a hand—"and then I was free from him. I was me."

"My father was distant," Lilith said. "He made sure nobody understood him. He was a statue, and I worshipped him. He never responded—he had his own secret craziness. It's here. That craziness is here in the Trust, hidden in the rocks."

"Let you down, I bet. They all let you down."

With sudden clarity, Lilith understood now something of what had come between herself and her father, and she poured out her thoughts. "Let me down by dying on me before I had a chance to know him. I always had the idea that he'd love me if only I loved him enough. That was the whole problem: I didn't love him enough."

"But you must have."

"I guess I did, but I never thought I did. When he died, I had this strange feeling that I had killed him. Something in me said, If only I had loved him more, if only I had loved him the way you're supposed to—whatever that is—he would have loved me, he would have loved my mother. All of us—him, my mother, me—we would have been all right. But at the time I didn't think about any of this. And then it was over."

Frederick looked a little puzzled. Lilith wondered whether to tell him the rest. Her father had died up here on the ledges, near the campfire, under circumstances Persephone had never made clear. When Lilith had struck out for the ledges, she'd only had a vague notion, a feeling that she wanted to find the campfire. Now she understood that what she really wanted was to learn more about her father's death. She felt a need to tell Frederick everything, if for no other reason but that he was here, someone about her own age, someone not from Upper Darby. And then something important struck her, which reversed her thinking: the real reason people lie. The fact that he was puzzled, the fact that he didn't know the whole truth about her, the fact that she had the ability to withhold that truth from him gave her power over him. It wasn't as if she wanted power so much as she wanted to keep him (and other people) from having power over her, and one way to achieve that end was to seize power over him (them) by keeping him (them) in a state of bewilderment. She watched him as he considered a follow-up question and she was satisfied, because she was not going to tell him anything more. He seemed to think better of pressing the matter, and gave up. Lilith felt a surge of victory, not over this young man but over the world.

The fire was burning brightly now, and they watched the flames in silence for a while. Lilith stirred the fire with a stick, and then something dawned on her. Frederick was on the Trust illegally.

"What are you doing out here anyway?" she asked.

Frederick thought for a moment, and then he lied: "Sometimes I just have to get away, that's all."

Frederick's deception revolved around his reason for being

on the Trust lands in the first place. He was looking for his father's illegal hunter's tree stand. He felt it necessary to conceal this information from Lilith, since of course it was her own father who had established the Trust lands that his father had violated. Despite this situation, Frederick might have confessed his errand anyway and avoided deception, except that, as it turned out, it was their talk about their respective fathers that had brought them together, and he wished to preserve this bond between them, this bond of fathers.

The two, their private worlds at least partly intact, headed down the mountain. They had almost reached the rough, unimproved dirt road that meandered through the lower parts of the Trust, where Frederick had parked his truck, when he saw animal tracks in the soft mud.

"What is it?" Lilith asked.

Frederick knelt on one knee, and touched the dirt. "A bear," he pointed. "Look, another track."

"Smaller—a cub?" Lilith said.

"Yah, a black-bear sow and her cub."

They both apprehended the fearful thrill of the forest.

They walked down from the ledges until they reached the truck. He drove very slowly, two or three miles an hour; she guessed he was drawing out the time they had together. She noted that he had a scholarly look behind the wheel. Lilith felt good; she must be in love. Not with this young man necessarily—with herself, with her living being, in these woods.

When they reached the main road, Frederick accelerated. He drove fast, too fast. Lilith loved the contrast, slow and easy on the Trust, fast and hard on the road; and she liked the feeling of danger, the feeling she was falling off the edge of the flat earth.

"Did you ever see a body?" she asked.

"A body?"

"A dead person."

"Lying there, not breathing?" He wasn't sure whether or not she was kidding him.

"Yes—gone," Lilith said.

Something in her voice told Frederick that she was serious. He didn't want to tell her about the girl on the bridge. "I've seen dead animals, and people in funeral homes," he said.

"They don't look really dead in funeral homes. They just look strange. Powdered skin. Closed eyes. I want to die with my eyes open," Lilith said. "Drive me to the town hall."

"They're laying over the bodies there until the memorial service," Frederick said. "You want to take a look?"

"Yes."

The clouds thickened overhead; everything felt different. They drove to the town hall in silence, both victims of a sudden uneasy mood that neither understood or wished to articulate, or knew that the other shared. It was the difference between being together up there and separate down here.

Constable Godfrey Perkins stood by the main door of the town hall, hands behind his back, eyeing Frederick and Lilith curiously as they stepped out of the pickup and approached him. "This is not the town hall today. It's a mortuary," he said.

"I want to go in," Lilith said.

"I don't know." Perkins blocked the way. He wasn't hostile, merely undecided on the correct course of action.

Frederick hung back, uncertain of his own role. On the Trust lands, he'd been confident, in charge. Now nothing was clear to him. Lilith sensed his insecurity, and she felt alone. In the woods, they had an affinity to one another; in the town, they were strangers. It wasn't until both of them felt this strangeness that they understood just how close they had been at the ledges.

Mrs. McCurtin, the town clerk, appeared at the door. "Miss Salmon," she said, pronouncing the name the Center Darby way, looking over the two young people as one might look at a radically new clothes style, interested, appalled, not quite ready to judge it yet.

"She wants to go in," Perkins said to Mrs. McCurtin.

Mrs. McCurtin gave Lilith a mouth-only smile, then turned gun eyes onto Frederick. "You have kin in the old cemetery, do you?"

He didn't like the way she framed the question, but he couldn't find a way to challenge her, so he gave her the whisper of a no with a bare shake of the head.

"Then you have to stay outside." Mrs. McCurtin gave no reason for this pronouncement, but her tone of voice made it irrevocable.

Frederick assumed the pose of the offended workman—stooped, sullen, no eye contact.

Lilith, like Frederick, assumed the pose of her own class, body carriage erect, head and shoulders straight to the front, commanding with her eyes as well as her voice. "Go ahead, Frederick. Constable Perkins can drive me home."

"Yes, ma'am—sure will." Perkins grabbed at his gun belt as if to hoist his potbelly up to his chest.

"See you later." Frederick barely acknowledged Lilith's goodbye, turned away, and started toward his truck. He determined he'd been dismissed by Mrs. McCurtin purely because of who he was; he experienced just a mosquito prick of resentment for Lilith purely because of who she was.

Mrs. McCurtin led Lilith to her office. They walked past the main hall, where Lilith saw rows of caskets. Mrs. McCurtin hurried by, but Lilith slowed. The caskets, all shiny and new, replacing the rotted wooden coffins of the old cemetery, and marked with chalk, reminded Lilith of rows of identical cars on the lot of an automobile dealership.

The town clerk's chambers were cramped with file cabinets, straight-back chairs around a folding table set up for conferences, a big black metal desk upon which set an IBM-clone computer. Only a calendar decorated the puke-yellow walls. The place was as faded as the green acrylic sweater and loose brown slacks that were Mrs. McCurtin's uniform. The room smelled faintly of busy mold spores perusing the town records.

"I want to see my father's casket," Lilith said.

"Not here." The words shot from Mrs. McCurtin's mouth.

Lilith blinked, her smile twitchy with confusion.

"Your mother didn't want the Squire and the boy with these others. So she made her own arrangements."

"Where are they?" Lilith asked. As usual, her mother was several steps ahead of her.

"Town crypt."

"Shouldn't all the bodies be in the town crypt?" Lilith said.

"Not enough room—there's only so many seats in the first-class lounge; but you understand that." Mrs. McCurtin's tone was intimate and friendly, with just an edge of sarcasm, as if she were sharing very important information with a very special person.

Lilith didn't know what to say. Mrs. McCurtin walked to the window of her office, put her hands behind her back, and stared out at the town green. An uncomfortably quiet moment passed. Then, with her back still to Lilith, Mrs. McCurtin said, "What's your interest in these bodies, Lilith?"

The sound of her name uttered by the town gossip sent a shiver through Lilith. She understood now that Mrs. McCurtin had invited her in to size her up, perhaps extract information from her. Lilith mumbled an awkward goodbye and slowly retreated. If she knew anything, it was that to reveal any part of her true self to this woman was to stand naked before all of Darby.

Outside, Frederick headed for Donaldson. He'd visit with Cooty, spend the night sleeping in his truck in Cooty's yard. If he appeared in public again with Lilith, he would be forced to eat more of the same shit that Mrs. McCurtin had served him up; he did not like the taste, but he had to see Lilith Salmon again.

When Lilith returned home, her mother asked her where she'd been. Lilith told her about taking a walk in the woods and meeting Frederick. Something in her wanted to flaunt him. She left out the fact that she'd gone to the ledges. Persephone said softly and almost to herself and with a private little smile, "Oh, that's great, some thug from Center Darby."

That night Lilith went through her father's books on New Hampshire history. She tried to find information about Indians, how they lived, what they ate, their family arrangements, their small pleasures and pet peeves. All the stories were about warfare and politics, but she did find a note that puzzled her. Reggie had scribbled it on a piece of paper, which later he had used as a bookmark. The note said, "My old girl has an albino cub. Heredity? Freak of nature? Who can tell?"

It was almost as if Reggie Salmon, who had dreamed and connived his land Trust into being, had anticipated the coming of the dreaming, conniving bear, for the bear defined the boundaries of her sanctuary—and, indeed, even dreamed the notion of sanctuary—as the boundaries of the Trust. And for the same philosophical reasons Reggie had: she was fond of the place; she was not fond of people. In her sanctuary, she could nurse her cub in comfort and security. When the sow bear had a need to leave her sanctuary to search for food for herself, she did so with great caution and uneasiness, but also with a certain pleasure, a heightened awareness, a concentration of energies, and with the daring that spring brought on, for the bear was hungry and restless. Her cub was demanding. The sow's teats were sore, and she was going to have to wean him this year. The sow had no notion that there was something strange about her cub. She knew only that she must eat, and she'd felt herself called by the smells from the lower world.

She rose up on her hind legs, threw up her big head, and sniffed the air. Her cub stared at her, then attempted to imitate her by standing on his own hind legs. He balanced uncertainly, and then enjoyed the familiar sensation of the world suddenly topsy-turvy as he fell backward and tumbled down slope a few feet. The sow ignored him. Her brain was wired to her nose, and she was thinking. Dry, harshly windy weather produced the worst conditions for the transmission of smells, and on such days she holed up, for she couldn't trust her eyes to tell her much. Her vision, always poor, had deteriorated the last few years and she was nearly blind. But this particular morning was a good one for smells. It was cool and damp, with an occasional, shifty breeze that brought her information from all directions, if not all at once. Because she knew she could not be caught unawares under such conditions, and because she was hungry, she chose this morning to move down from the ridge in search of a meal. Down into the lower world. Two smells interested her. One was the beckoning smell of food a fair distance downslope, and the other was the menacing smell of coyote coming faintly from everywhere. She paused at a hemlock tree and rubbed her great back against it, and headed down, her cub following.

Reggie Salmon often talked about coyotes. "When white people came here," he'd say at social gatherings, in the somber lecturing tone that never failed to hold an audience, even while it made them edgy, "there were few if any coyotes, because the resident wolves would not tolerate their presence. But as time passed, the farmers drove off or killed the wolves, along with the cougar and most other natural predators, and had seriously reduced the bear population, which are not predators at all, but merely opportunists—in their own way, good Americans. Later, when the farmers themselves had been driven off by the wolves of economic circumstance, and the forest grew back in the neglected fields, the environment invited predators. But the wolves were long gone, so the coyotes filled the niche. If coyotes were people, they would be on Wall Street, or in law or politics; they'd rule us, and they'd probably do a pretty fair job, too. They're not violent creatures, like fisher cats; they are merely acquisitive, cruel when something is at stake, otherwise quite tolerant and shy."

The sow was not frightened of the coyotes for herself, but she was concerned in behalf of her cub. Coyotes competed with the sow for carrion, and they had a knack for picking off the young of careless parents. The sow continued to move down toward the lower world and the food smell, which in fact was the smell of Cooty Patterson's "honey," the nauseating (to humans) swill he used to bait his leg-hold traps. Like the bear, the coyote, and the crow, Cooty was a carrion eater. He did not trap like a man, for he was not particular about what he caught. He did not run a trap line for furs but for food and to satisfy his curiosity, and in this sense he was like the animals he sought; but, unlike the bear, the coyote, and the crow, Cooty lived not by wile but by whim, and in this sense he was like a man.

The cub was frisky and as inquisitive as Cooty Patterson about what was out here in these woods. When the cub wandered into clearings or along trails where the sow did not trust the smells, she cuffed him with a huge paw. And all the time, she steered him toward the food smell. Because the cub was still nursing, his interest in the food smell was more or less academic, but his mother was hungry. As they moved down, she stopped from time to time to turn over a log and feed on the slugs and other insects she was sure to find there. She enjoyed these tidbits, but they did not make a meal. She'd eat roots, tubers, bugs, just about anything, but she favored meat. Meat—now, there was food! She had no qualms about horning in on the kills of other creatures. She'd often happen on the carcasses of dog- or coyote-killed deer, and once she'd actually surprised a deer fawn herself and killed it, but she was no hunter.

She found this food smell on her nostrils full of promise, and somewhat mysterious. It was of course the smell of garbage, and for the sow it was an intoxicating smell indeed. It came from the lower world, where there were two other smells she could not abide, the smell of human beings, which was frightening to her, and the smell of dogs, which she reckoned as dangerous. But as the sow and her cub continued on down the ridge, the smell of people and canines seemed distant, and her hunger was stronger than her fear of the lower world.

The sow was drooling with the anticipation of a meal, and she was loping easily through the woods, well ahead of her cub, when she reached the smell. Right away she halted suspiciously. She sniffed the "honey," which was squeezed between two leg-hold traps, designed to immobilize animals the size of raccoons. The bear sniffed the traps; there was something about them she didn't like. Very carefully, she dislodged the lump of honey from between the traps with her paw and then popped it into her mouth. It satisfied in quality, but disappointed in quantity. She sniffed the traps some more, and backed off. Now that she'd eaten the food, the smell no longer captured her attention, and she realized she had come down too low, and that she should start moving higher up with her cub.

It was at that point that the cub came on the scene, going for the area where the sow's nose told her there was danger. When the cub stepped into the trap, springing it on his right forepaw, he let out a shriek that provoked his mother to roar and charge into the brush for the enemy she sensed. She found no enemy.

———

116

A fine, cold, seemingly endless rain was falling. If the weather had been better, Lilith would have hiked to the ledges. She knew—just knew—that Frederick would be there. Maybe he'd call. In another place, Lilith might have taken the initiative and telephoned him herself. Not in Darby. Here she might be impulsive, but not forward. She waited for the telephone to ring and pretended she was not waiting. The telephone did ring. It was the new recreation director at Darby Lake, wanting to know if Lilith would be working at the lifeguard station this summer. Lilith said maybe. In the afternoon, she drove to Ancharsky's store to buy a Boston *Globe* and a Tuckerman *Crier*. She heard Mrs. McCurtin's voice crackling over the CB: "Bonfire tonight at the old cemetery. Burning up the pine slash and what-have-you from the coffins." It wasn't until dark that the telephone rang. Lilith fought against the involuntary urge to run to the sound. Persephone picked up in the hall.

"Lilith—it's for you." Persephone's voice drifted into the Hearth Room, where Lilith sat. She strolled to the hall. Persephone's hand muffled the receiver with her palm. "It's Garvin." She stared hard at her daughter, as if to say, This is your big chance. Lilith refused to look at her mother and took the phone. Persephone slunk off. After Garvin hung up, Persephone said, "Well?"

"He was nice, kind of stately," Lilith said, not exactly sure what she thought about Garvin, except that over the telephone he sounded like an older man.

"Ah, he was in his lawyer's mode—I know it well," Persephone said.

"I think you should let Garvin build the monument for Daddy," Lilith said.

"So, that's what he wanted." Persephone chuckled.

"You don't have to laugh."

"Lilith, it's just a cheap stunt to make money for the Prells. If you take that seat on the Trust board, you'll spend your waking hours trying to decide between Monet's crazy schemes and Garvin's."

"Why do they have to fight? Why?"

"Cannibalism. They devour each other because nobody else suits their taste."

Lilith heard an echo of despair in Persephone's thin, ironic laughter. Her mother voiced truths, but they were almost always negative truths.

Thoughts of school flitted through Lilith's mind: friends, ideas, music, med school, the future. Her college seemed unreal, far away, the rewards unattainable. Was she going to miss out? "What if I don't want to be on Daddy's board?"

"Monet, Garvin, and myself will elect a member to replace me."

"Easy as that."

"Easy as that."

"I'm not really needed."

"The world goes on, Lilith; no one is really needed."

Lilith thought: Those Indians from long ago, they must have needed one another. "I don't know what to do," Lilith said.

"The position on the board carries responsibilities and some powers, but only over the Trust," Persephone argued. "It won't clear a path for you in the world, Lilith, and it definitely will tie you down to Darby."

Something about Persephone's tone, a little too offhand and cordial, didn't feel right to Lilith. She looked at her mother, but said nothing. What was Persephone really thinking?

Persephone lit a cigarette, took a deep drag, and said, "There's no advantage to serving."

"Who would be the new member?" Lilith put the question in her mother's curt manner.

"We'd work it out." Persephone averted her eyes from her daughter's.

It was dark and dreary outdoors, but Lilith was seeing dawn

over the horizon. "Since Monet and Garvin will never agree, they'd turn to you. Somebody you pick—right?"

"A compromise candidate—probably," Persephone said.

Now that she thought about the matter, Lilith realized that her mother had done nothing to encourage her to serve on the board.

"You should have told me about all this board stuff a long time ago."

"I thought it best to shelter you."

"You've already decided you don't want me on that board," Lilith said.

"It's a very stressful," Persephone said.

"You have someone in mind," Lilith said, desperate to know, knowing the answer was going to hurt her. "Who, Mother—who?"

"Roland LaChance." Persephone spoke the name as casually as she could.

"LaChance! Your lover!" Lilith stormed out of the hall and headed for the Hearth Room. Persephone followed on her heels.

"He is not my lover." Persephone was angry now, bitter and hard—found out.

The two women were about six feet apart, standing in front of the fireplace. "LaChance was your lover when Daddy was sick."

"It's over, Lilith. He's married and has a child. Lilith, he's levelheaded, and he has the best interest of the Trust at heart. He'll be able to stand up to Garvin and Monet. You have to understand that he thinks like your father. He'll do for the Trust what Reggie would have done."

"No, he won't, because I'm taking the seat." Lilith felt a surge of triumph, sudden relief.

"Of course you will, darling, and you'll do a wonderful job."

Persephone's easy submission drained the anger out of

Lilith. She felt empty and ugly. "I'm going," she said, and started out.

"Where?"

"I don't know."

As Lilith was leaving, she heard her mother shout, "It's raining. You should put your raincoat on."

Lilith ignored her mother's counsel. The Bronco's wipers were old, leaving a scummy film across the window. Lilith, head forward, eyes intent, peered into the fuzzy glow of the Bronco's headlights like some scholar of old reading by candlelight.

She didn't head for the bonfire on purpose, but found her way there, directed by some inner compass. The old cemetery was completely transformed. The bulldozer had filled in the graves and smoothed the terrain, leaving nothing but bare ground. Lilith thought for a moment she would burst into tears. How could a person compare her memories with the landscape of her childhood if that landscape had been completely obliterated?

Lilith plunged into the crowd, raucous and raw as the night. Something kindled the people's enthusiasm; a cheer swallowed the sound of the fire; tinny taped music played. In the sticky feel of shoulders brushing against one another in the rain, Lilith allowed herself to be engulfed by the mood of the gathered. Someone shoved a bottle of tequila in her hand and she took a long pull. It went down smooth, warming her immediately. The bottle was swept from her hand, and she walked deeper into the crowd. These were the outcasts of Darby Depot and Center Darby, mainly young people, men with beer bellies and beards, women with bad teeth and long hair, everybody in blue jeans.

The smell of fresh and burning pine slash commingled; but there was another, subtler smell, dank, wet, deep. Lilith picked up a piece of rotting wood from the ground. This, the wreckage of the graves, was the source of that second smell. Its corrupt nectar made her want to dance. She threw the board into the fire.

The rain came down steadily. Lilith hugged herself for warmth. This, she thought, this feeling, raw and desperate and cold, is the feeling of home. Upper Darby: high up in the hills, forested, with outbreaks of fields and outcrops of granite, inconstant and foggy in the transitional seasons of spring and fall, summer unsatisfyingly brief, a taunt, only in the winter a measure of security for the consistency of unpleasantness. She should remain in this weather; it was warmth, the warmth of the more temperate climate of her college, that weakened her with hope.

She'd come to associate the idea of home with chill, and the idea of chill with distance, so that when she was cold it seemed to her that everybody was far away. She—she herself created warmth in the closeness of her own being. Here, in that make-believe warmth, she found in the intensity of her awareness of her loneliness a freedom from the boredom of common sense and the ugly dictates of survival. So now, in this most dismal of weather so typical of Darby in the springtime—cold, raw, unnerving—she felt oddly relaxed, as if after a long journey she had finally arrived home.

Flames from the brush fire seemed to struggle upward. Lilith remembered the fiery glow of a sunset over Grace Pond, deep in her father's Trust lands, the orange of the flames like the orange of the dying sun rising up from below the horizon to the clouds, rising up, rising. The flames seemed to form the shape of a face. For a split second, Lilith thought she knew him.

Her father had been a tall, handsome man, but disease had bent his body and disfigured his face, and her understanding of him was itself disfigured, so she wasn't quite sure of the accuracy of her memories of him. He'd always been far away, and there were times when she was perfectly happy to contemplate him from that immeasurable distance. Perhaps she had contributed to the distance between them by her own aloofness (which of course was her mother's aloofness). Her father had died as he had lived, in a kind of dream, deep within his secrets. What was worth loving about him was in what she did not—could never—know: those secrets. Everything else was disfigured.

It was at this point that the miracle occurred. The fire was so hot that the falling rain was dispelled before it reached the ground. Dry warmth bathed the revelers. Everyone seemed to notice at once what was happening, and the dancing stopped. People joined hands. Someone turned the music off. Lilith listened to the fire, like a voice full of meaning but speaking a foreign language.

Images flashed—black sky, car headlights, these burning ruins of trees and coffins. The smell of the caskets had been transformed by the fire. What was in the smoky, rainy air was the emotions of the people who had been buried in the old cemetery. The wood of the caskets had soaked up every joy and agony. And now that the wood had been rent and burned, it was surrendering its essence.

The rain started coming down harder at about the time the fire died back. The canopy of warm, dry air vanished in a deluge of cold rain. The music returned, and the sound of the fire was extinguished. The crowd thinned out rapidly. Lilith grabbed for the tequila, danced, tried to lose herself. Soon only a few people remained in the pouring rain. She began to shiver, but she told herself she wasn't cold. In a few minutes, Lilith slipped into the early stages of hypothermia.

She spotted Abnaki Jordan and Whack Two at the base of the bonfire, rocking in place to the music. She approached them. The Asian circled around her menacingly. She halted, feeling his presence like some weird radiation. Then a sound in the crowd, a sort of half-screech from a dancer, startled him, and he slunk away. Lilith approached Abnaki, his camouflage outfit now blending into the night, now highlighted against it.

"Sir?" she called.

Abnaki turned and looked at her. "I'm going to puke," he said, and plopped to the ground in a sitting position.

"I have to talk to you." She knelt by him.

He leaned to one side and vomited. Then he wiped his mouth and said, "Get me on my feet."

She took him under the arms. He was wet there. He smelled like some terrible stain in a terrible bathroom in a terrible house, and he was surprisingly heavy. He reminded her of so many boys she'd known—bulky, unyielding, and profoundly insensitive to her.

She looked into his eyes, and she saw nothing. The eyes were bottomless pools of stagnant water. He pulled away from her, and stumbled off into the darkness.

Lilith, half out of her head, began to retreat, moving not toward the Bronco and shelter but toward the woods, the hills, the ledges.

Frederick Elman intercepted her near the stone wall. She was shivering, hugging herself for warmth.

"That was dumb—real dumb," he shouted at her like a frantic parent given a scare by a wild child. He put his arm around her waist and led her to his truck.

"Cold—cold—cold," she said.

"If you didn't feel the cold, then I'd be worried. You'll be all right." He half supported her with one arm, opened the door in the rear of the camper, and boosted her up. It was cramped inside and no warmer, but at least it was dry.

"Cold—cold—cold." Lilith stood hunched over, trying to make herself smaller.

"You're soaked through. Jeez, don't you own a coat?" He turned on a gas heater, then unzipped the sleeping bag from his bunk. "Get out of those clothes, get into the sleeping bag. Can you handle it alone?"

Lilith nodded a yes. She didn't make out his next words, muttered under his breath, a half-assed prayer in behalf of her well-being. Frederick eased his bulk through the tiny rear door of the camper, went around front, started the truck, and drove off. Lilith undressed and, still shivering, slid into the sleeping bag.

For a few minutes, she felt nothing but the cold, and then, when she started to warm, she felt the motion of the truck— a soothing drone. A short time passed in which she wasn't asleep exactly, but her perceptions of time and space were blurred. The truck turned off the pavement and started jouncing around. By the time it stopped she was warmer, more centered mentally.

She listened to the thunk of the front door, Frederick's footfalls as he walked around to the rear, and then to the camper door opening.

He snapped on a dim, car-battery-operated light. "You look better. How do you feel?" His voice was kindly.

"I'm fine. Where are we?"

"Take a look." He pulled open the curtain of a tiny window. He managed to appear dramatic and forceful without being show-offy.

Lilith sat up in the bunk, holding the sleeping bag tight to her throat. She peered out at the tops of trees against the sky. "The Trust lands," she said.

"At the end of the road, a hundred yards from Grace Pond." He fired up a gas stove and put some hot water on. Lilith stared out the window. She couldn't see the moon, but she could distinguish some of its light reflected off husky, hurrying clouds. She guessed the weather would clear.

"Want some coffee?" He knelt by the bunk, holding a ceramic mug in his hand.

She tested the hot brew. "It's delicious, best coffee I ever had in my whole life." She meant it.

"Instant," he said.

Frederick sat on a stool in the cramped camper, watching Lilith. She sipped the coffee as if it were tea from a cup.

"I saw you out there with Abnaki," he said. "Was he bothering you?"

"I was bothering him. I wanted him to tell me what he saw when he opened the grave of my brother," she said.

"What he saw? What did he see?"

"He couldn't say. He was drunk, and I don't think he could tell me even if he was sober," Lilith said. "I think he just forgot everything, or maybe he blocked it and never knew. Do you think that's how people get by who have to do unpleasant things—block?"

"Maybe." She'd hit close to the truth; he wondered how much he had blocked during years on the road, taking jobs up high and out of the way of the human world.

An awkward moment passed when neither said anything and they didn't look at one another. Finally, Lilith said, "Frederick, thank you for helping me."

"You scared me."

"I'm dumb sometimes—real dumb. You like it up here on the Trust lands, don't you?" She lay back down.

"Beats my folks' trailer. I don't have a home—I don't want a home," Frederick said. "So I stay in my truck. All over. But I like it up here, up and out."

He crouched in the tight confines of the camper to be nearer the bunk. "I've been thinking about you. All last night. All day today." His voice was low, almost a whisper.

"I was going to go to the ledges, but it rained," Lilith said.

Frederick unzipped the sleeping bag a few inches to reveal Lilith's bare shoulder.

"It rained," she repeated. She was looking at his eyes—hungry for her and something else she could not fathom.

"Are you warm now? Are you sure you're all right?" he whispered.

"I'm all right." She held out her arms to him.

He buried his face in the crook between her shoulder and her throat. And then he kissed her. His beard was long, thick, beastlike. She found herself lost in him. The bunk was narrow, squeezed between the wall, the aisle, and a cabinet overhead, and they had to make love without any gymnastics. They struggled between a search for comfort and a release of passion. Finally, he lay on his back and she settled in on him. He was very hairy all over. It was like riding a big teddy bear.

Afterward, they lay together side by side. She rested her face on his beard. She looked out beyond him through the tiny window of the truck. The rain had stopped; the moon was coming out.

After the cub had stepped in Cooty Patterson's trap and the sow's confusion and rage had subsided, she'd chewed free the paw of the cub and urged him to follow her. They didn't get far. The cub was in shock, stunned, eyes distant, chest heaving. She had curled up in some leaves with him, and he'd nursed. He drifted off in the uneasy sleep of wounded creatures, and she licked him. When the rain came, she dug out a shelter in the side of the hill. She stayed all day and into the night with the cub. Late the next day, her hunger returned, strong and urgent.

That night, the sow left the cub and moved down into the lower world. At a stone wall that to people acted as a legal boundary between the land known as the Trust and a privately owned house lot, the sow paused and sniffed the air. Smells drifted up to her nostrils: the complex, sweets-feces smell of a human child; the heavy meal smell of the 4-H pig the child was fattening; the wonderful aroma of the garbage cans sitting in the shed; the life smells of the house itself—pungent, interesting, exotic even in their extreme repulsiveness.

The sow roared with hunger and to feel the shake and roll of her own being. Later, when the moon was dying in the hills and all the humans of Darby were asleep, the bear began to descend. She had picked this place to raid because the smell of dog was faint. In the house, the child slept on, perhaps dreaming about her pig, but the adults in the house awakened. They jerked to sitting positions in bed, and the woman snapped on the light.

"I *hoid* something," the woman said, in a heavy downcountry accent.

"The *gohbidge* cans. Probably raccoons," the man said.

Another sound, deep and strange, as if the earth itself had groaned, filled their ears—then the squeal of the pig. In the silence of the "out there" that followed, they themselves were silent. And afraid.

10

Coming of Age

"He's an obstinate man," Persephone said, as she and Lilith prepared the Hearth Room for the special meeting of the Trust board, called to swear in Lilith as an official member.

"I don't think he's so bad," Lilith said. She felt no desire to defend Selectman Crabb; he meant nothing to her. But she did feel compelled to speak out against her mother's unfairness. Crabb might or might not be obstinate, but for sure Persephone was obstinate. Persephone's way of dealing with her failings was to criticize others for those very same defects. Her mother chose her target shrewdly. In physical appearance, Crabb was unattractive, in aspect cloying, in speech portentous, in thought ponderous as his cows, although even Persephone would admit he was not stupid. She must have sensed that Lilith could launch no effective defense of Crabb and that Crabb would not defend himself.

In fact, Arthur Crabb was more than capable of defending himself. The selectman was a man beyond pride, beyond dignity, and even beyond self-worth. He sustained himself on habit and a vaguely felt inclination toward the idea of public service. Ultimately, he was a New England farmer/politician of the old school, which is to say he was practical. As long as he stood a chance to achieve his ends this way, it cost him nothing to suck up to the Upper Darby folk, but if things changed and the occasion arose, he could just as easily machine-gun them into the ditches. The issue all came to this: if Upper Darby can help Darby, why, okay; if not, not okay.

Lilith enjoyed tidying up the room. Housework contained no surprises, no promises, no betrayals; the goal of order was achievable. And, too, she liked housework because her mother despised it. The meeting of the Trust board was scheduled to be brief and to the point. Persephone would resign the Salmon position on the board, Lilith would express her desire to take Persephone's place. Papers would be signed, Selectman Crabb and Town Clerk McCurtin would witness the proceedings. End of meeting. Lilith found herself in high spirits. She was twenty-one, coming of age; for a change she would be the center of attention.

Selectman Crabb and Mrs. McCurtin arrived in Crabb's pickup, then Garvin in his BMW. Lilith escorted them to the Hearth Room, where they circled about Persephone, who held forth with witty remarks and droll stories. Meanwhile, Lilith performed her familiar duty of getting the drinks. Without quite realizing it, the Salmons, Reggie and Persephone both, had broken in their daughter as a servant early on, perhaps because the two of them had both been raised with servants and it seemed natural to them that someone else should do the menial labor. For Lilith, the chore was an extension of the housework. She had only a flicker of conscious recognition that her parents had used her in a way different from the way they themselves had been used by their parents.

Monet arrived a few minutes later, accompanied by Marcia Pascal and his attorney, Charles Barnum.

Garvin was put on the alert from the moment Barnum came into the room. Like Garvin, Barnum was a Tuckerman attorney. He'd represented the Magnus Corporation, which several years back had attempted to persuade Darby to accept a regional shopping mall on agricultural land in the town. Garvin

129

and Reggie Salmon had led the fight against the mall—and won. Now Barnum was representing Monet Salmon, current leader of Darby's antidevelopment forces. The irony did not trouble Garvin. After all, he, too, was a lawyer. What did trouble him was that he had not a clue as to what Monet and Barnum were after.

"Let's sit down," Persephone said, and she took her place at the head of the meeting table. To her immediate right sat Mrs. McCurtin. She pored over the minutes of the last meeting. Beside her were Garvin and Selectman Crabb. Monet sat to Persephone's left, then Barnum, Dr. Marcia Pascal, and Lilith.

Persephone opened the meeting by slapping her hand on the table. She began with a formal declaration, designed perhaps for Lilith's sake. "The governing board of the land Trust that memorializes the memory of Raphael Salmon II does not have an official chairman," she said. "With three voting members and a nonvoting representative from the town government, we're too small a body. Nor do we conduct our meetings according to *Robert's Rules of Order*. Or any other order." Persephone paused while the others tittered with barely audible laughter. "Because of the principles involved, discussion is on occasion—how shall I say?—spirited. We are, however, civil, and we all understand how important this Trust is to the town of Darby."

"Hear, hear," Crabb said.

Persephone went on as if Crabb had not spoken. "Only one item on our agenda today—installation of a new member. As you are all aware, I am leaving Darby for Australia to marry Professor Hadly Blue. When my husband died, I took his place on the Trust board. It is only fitting that our daughter, Lilith, who this year has come of age, should take my place."

Only fitting—what did her mother mean? Hadn't she'd tried to steer her away from the board and set up her former lover in the position? And yet her mother sounded sincere. Had she changed her mind? What did her mother truly think? Was deception—constant, unrelenting deception—a kind of truth in itself for Persephone and anyone in the Salmon house?

Lilith now remembered a long-forgotten incident with her father. It was September. They were in the far end of the field near the stone wall. Lilith found a wounded butterfly. It lay in some grass, feebly attempting to fly with a ripped wing.

"Can you tell me what this creature is?" her father had asked.

"It's a monarch butterfly," she said.

"Listen closely to me." Her father held the orange-and-black butterfly in his cupped hands. "The monarch butterfly is a lovely animal, and it is conspicuous by that loveliness, by its bright coloring and habit of flying in full sunshine. This would seem to go against natural law, for by being conspicuous it invites birds who prey on insects to attack it. But, you see, the monarch feeds on the milkweed plant, which is poisonous to birds. Down through time, the birds have learned to leave the monarch be. By advertising its presence, the monarch guarantees its survival. It depends, however, on the good judgment of birds. Do you understand?"

Lilith had nodded her head yes.

"No, you don't understand," he said. "This is not a monarch butterfly at all. This is a viceroy butterfly. It is not poisonous. It is a perfectly acceptable meal for a bird. The viceroy is a mimic; it deceives the birds into believing it is a monarch. It, too, relies on the good judgment of birds. But in this case good judgment is poor judgment. Then again, note that this particular specimen has been attacked and surely will die." He placed the wounded butterfly gently in tall grass.

She had only been a child then, and she hadn't thought about the story as a fable with a hidden meaning. But of course it was clear to her now that Reggie had meant for her to search for just such a meaning. He was not talking about butterflies, but about Upper Darby. What was the point? Was it that Upper Darby was populated by monarchs, like the Prells, and viceroys, like her uncle Monet? Was her father telling her to live a life of deception for her own survival? Because he hadn't explained exactly what he meant for her to take from the fable, she could take what she wanted or nothing at all. She would never know his own meaning, but in telling her the tale in the manner in which he did, he seemed to be suggesting that the story itself was a deception.

When Persephone finished speaking, she yielded the floor with a casual glance at Garvin. The Trust might not have an official chairperson, as Persephone had said, but in fact Garvin had taken charge of taking charge. He had that turn of mind, and in addition to being a board member he was the Trust's attorney. He dug out papers and put them in front of Persephone.

Garvin talked about legal matters, and Lilith studied him for a moment. There was a crease where the slant of the underside of his lower lip met his chin, which then jutted out brazenly—typical Prell. But, unlike that of most of the Prells, his upper lip protruded a tad over his lower lip, giving him a pouting look, and where his lips met on the sides, instead of curving downward into a scowl, they swooped up like the handles of Saracen blades. As a speaker he was compelling, because he managed to seem both in command and out of control, as if the things on his mind might explode from the volatility of their import. As if to emphasize this dynamic, somewhat endearing quality, he often ended his sentences with the word "okay" and a hazy inflection that suggested the question mark as a universal sign-off for the publicly uttered sentence. "According to the terms of the will, Persephone as spouse has first choice regarding the Salmon seat on the board—okay? Persephone has indicated her desire to surrender the seat. Should Lilith decide to step down from her position on the board, the seat reverts to Persephone—okay? If Persephone declines, the remaining members, myself and Monet, will name a third member—okay?"

Persephone and Lilith signed the papers, and Lilith accepted congratulations from the gathered. The group was ready to disband when Monet rose to his feet. "I'd like to introduce another item for our consideration, which affects both the town and the Trust board. Since this is a legal matter, I've asked attorney Barnum to explain. Attorney Barnum?"

Barnum was a plain-faced, plain-brained, plainspoken, over-weight, middle-aged man who nonetheless commanded enough attention to be heard, because he knew when to speak, when not to speak, and what to wear. Had this been a meeting of a town board—say, the conservation commission—he would have worn a casual tweed sports jacket and one of his old ties, the idea being to appear like the town itself, dignified if a little out of date. But for this occasion, he deliberately wore a business suit. He knew his message had the element of surprise behind it, and he wished to appear as having come down from the height of a great metropolitan area (say, Manchester) to deliver it.

Barnum told his tale leisurely. There was no rush. He had a bombshell to explode. Might as well gather the crowd good and tight before detonating it.

Lilith listened with fascination. She felt as if she were at the movies.

Since his return to Darby, Monet had been doing nothing but studying the Trust lands, Barnum said. Monet had un-covered Indian ruins by the ledges, campfires and perhaps burial grounds dating back to pre-Columbian times. There was also the possibility that ancient mariners, perhaps Phoene-cians, had made their way from the Atlantic Ocean up the Connecticut River. For evidence, Barnum showed photo-graphs Monet had taken of scratches on rocks on the Trust lands. The point of all this, Barnum said, was to show that the Trust was not only a land preserve but a valuable archaeological resource for the community, the state, the nation, and, indeed, the world.

Barnum paused, smiled, and said, "Now I must address, first, Selectman Crabb, as a representative of the town of Darby and as nonvoting member of the Trust board, and, second, Mr. Garvin Prell, as a principal in Sugar Bush Village Development Corporation."

Monet folded his arms; Garvin seemed about to interrupt Barnum, but then thought better of it; Crabb frowned deeply, an old man taking refuge in the folds on his skin.

"Monet and his associate, Dr. Marcia Pascal, have discovered evidence of a rare animal, a possible endangered species of bruin on the Trust land, a breed of white-colored bears," Barnum said. "This evidence has been submitted to Judge Michael Barnicle. Based on the United States Endangered Species Act and upon applicable RSAs, we've asked the judge to bar any further development in the likely range of these animals, which includes—and Monet has the map—the town's land for a new school and park and also the so-called Sugar Bush Village development."

"Whoa!" A trace of color showed in Crabb's pale cheeks.

"Selectman Crabb?" Barnum smiled like a man who had just had sex after years of abstinence.

"Counselor, we're building a school on that land." Crabb was angry.

"Yes, it's unfortunate," Barnum said. "Work on the Cemetery School project will cease immediately." Barnum turned to Monet. "Mister Salmon?"

Monet slid a paper across the table.

Barnum held the paper up and gestured with it. "Judge Barnicle has issued an injunction barring any further disturbance of the property in question until a court hearing, which has been set for July ninth. At that time, the judge will rule on our petition to ban all development until the rare animal can be studied and a determination made regarding its viability and status as an endangered species."

"July ninth! That's six weeks from now. That'll set us way back, even if we win this crazy suit," Crabb said.

Monet's tempered flared. "It may be crazy to you, Mr. Selectman, but for some of us it's a step toward saving Upper Darby from development, toward preserving my brother's vision for the Trust."

"What is this evidence you have of white bears?" Garvin's voice was cold.

Monet was about to speak, but Barnum cut him off. "Our evidence is filed with the court. As an interested party, you'll have access to the evidence, and you can present your own evidence and a response at the hearing."

The meeting quickly broke up after that. Garvin and Crabb huddled briefly before departing. Mrs. McCurtin appeared antsy to spread the news of the events. Monet, Marcia Pascal, and Barnum slunk off. Persephone telephoned her lover across the seas. Lilith sat alone in the Hearth Room. She felt cheated. She hadn't really expected anything, but this was supposed to have been her moment, her coming of age.

Outside, Lawyer Barnum lectured his clients. He'd run the bluff, he told them, but in fact he had no case unless they could produce this hybrid bear or whatever it was. Monet and Dr. Pascal assured him the bear was real. Monet had seen it. But what was needed, Barnum said, was physical evidence. Monet said his cleaning lady, Mrs. Howard Elman, knew of such evidence. An old trapper named Cooty Patterson had found a white bear paw in one of his traps. "Well, let's go get it," Barnum said. The three of them drove to the trapper's cabin and offered to buy the paw. Monet was willing to go four figures for it. When Barnum made the offer, the trapper walked to the wood heating stove and lifted the lid on the cooking pot. It took a moment, but Monet, Marcia, and Barnum seemed to realize the meaning of the gesture at the same time. Monet spoke their thoughts: "Oh, Lordy, he ate it."

11

Memorial

It was Memorial Day, a special day for Darby, a special day for the Salmon women. After the memorial service, scheduled for the afternoon at the new cemetery, Persephone planned to start packing. She viewed leaving the town of her birth with the fear and hopefulness of one facing impending surgery, severing a grim connectedness, separation from a hated Siamese twin. To complete her mental preparations for this event, she had to bury, again and finally, her husband. She looked forward to the memorial service for another reason. In a secret part of her soul, she regarded it as a triumph. She had never wanted her son buried in the old cemetery; she'd never wanted him buried in a wooden casket. Now fate had stepped in. Husband and son were going where she'd wanted them in the first place, together, in the new cemetery, with the rest of her people.

Lilith, too, saw the day as a new start. But while her mother attempted to cut herself off from time and place, Lilith hoped to join with her past. The memorial service was going to connect her with her brother; the memorial service was giving her a second chance to put her father to rest, and therefore put her own feelings about him to rest. She was ready for ceremony; she needed ceremony. Also, the thought that her mother was going far away filled her with fear and secret pleasure. The presence of her mother was like a large rock rolled before the dark cave of self. Alone, she would know her house; alone, she would know the Trust; alone, she would come out into the light and open to the world like a flower in morning sun.

After the memorial service, she and Frederick were going to go for a drive. "For beers, grinders, and dreams," Frederick had said. It was a holiday—no Honeywagon. But it was also the traditional planting day in the Elman household. Frederick was going to help out in the morning. Meanwhile, Lilith decided to pass the time by painting the windowsills. Once she'd realized the house was going to be hers, she'd looked at it as if for the first time. It was so big—and run-down. A few more years and it would no longer be regarded as *the* house of Darby. The thought of fixing the house centered her, gave her a mission. The shingles had darkened with age, and they had given the house an increasingly brooding aspect, and she thought that was all right, but the green paint on the windowsills was peeling. She'd always hated that color. Now, with each brush swipe of brick-red paint, she was remaking the house into what she believed to be its own authentic image and likeness. She had started her repair project on the outside, because it was what other people saw. The main value of the house was not what it was, but what it meant.

Persephone watched her daughter on the ladder, in yellow shorts and a white top, legs already taking on a golden-brown color, blond hair sticking out of her painter's cap. She had a Salmon body all right—tall, straight, big-boned—but she was blessed with Butterworth skin, fair yet receptive to the sun, good tanning genes. With that thought, Persephone got an idea.

"I'm going to take your picture," she said.

"Do you want me to change?" Lilith said from her ladder.

"Stay put—you're standing hip deep in a burnt-sienna

shadow. Oh, I wish I'd followed my heart and become a painter." Persephone hustled into the house and returned with the ancient Leica Reggie's father had bought in the 1920s, before the crash. She stalked Lilith with the camera.

For a couple of minutes, the women were silent, Lilith painting the windowsill, Persephone snapping pictures, the shutter noise of the Leica so quiet that Lilith was not distracted by it. Persephone took perhaps a half-dozen pictures, and then a cloud crossed in front of the sun.

"The light just changed," Persephone said.

"Just for a minute or two," Lilith said.

"It never comes back the same."

"Don't you have a light meter?"

"It's broken. Everything we own is broken," Persephone said. Lilith didn't sense despair in Persephone's voice but, rather, a kind of determination to face up to what was real and get on with life. Her mother's courage made her feel reckless.

"I'll fix it—I'll fix everything," Lilith said, continuing to paint.

"Of course you will." Persephone fiddled with the f-stop setting on the camera, cigarette dangling between her lips, eyes filling with smoke. "Lilith, are you thinking of not returning to school?"

"You never finished your schooling."

Lilith's accusation didn't exactly put Persephone on the defensive, but it did send her back to a time when she, not Lilith, was the young darling of this house. The Salmons had a daughter. Her name was Justine, but she had escaped the family at eighteen, never to return. Persephone heard she'd married a Swiss cross-country ski racer and lived abroad. The Salmons had been injured by their daughter's flight, and they'd held out no hope at all for Monet, so when Reggie had brought home the young Butterworth girl from just down the road, they'd embraced her with open arms. Persephone had spent most of her teen years in the Salmon house as part of her rebellion against her own family.

"I was going to be an artist. I was going to show them." Persephone shook with self-mocking laughter.

"Oh, yah, I forgot that you took painting lessons."

Lilith's offhand comment stung her mother. Her own dreams made no impression on anyone in Darby, but she'd hoped glancingly that something of her own spirit would filter down to her daughter. Children didn't listen. They resented— or perhaps feared—the private lives of their elders. They were too busy trying to be themselves to pay any attention to adults trying to be themselves.

"I've wanted to be a painter since I can remember," Persephone went on, determined to sear her story in the memory of her daughter. "When I was eight, I had a tutor. His name was Ralph, but he called himself Rolf. Oh, he was a gifted one with a capital 'G.' I was painting a pumpkin, and Rolf messed over my strokes with his own. I went crying to Mother. 'Rolf is an abstract expressionist,' she said. 'All the young painters today are abstract expressionists.' I wept, wept for real pumpkins." Persephone flicked her lighted cigarette butt into the grass. She watched a wisp of yellow-gray smoke rise, catch the breeze, and disappear.

"My mother never thought I'd make it as a painter, and of course she was right. Your grandmother Salmon, on the other hand, was encouraging. Until it was time for Reggie and me to marry. And then it was clear that I was going to be a Sunday painter, because Reggie wanted to stay in Darby. No art school for Persephone. That was that. I couldn't bear the idea of painting like an amateur, so I didn't paint at all."

Her mother's reminiscence reminded Lilith that she, too, had had some ambitions in the world of art: a desire, pure and unselfish, to make music from the cello. To forget her anguish,

Lilith changed the subject. "Grandmother Salmon was so stat-uesque," Lilith said.

Persephone believed that Lilith just wasn't listening to her. It had always been this way, Persephone thought. People didn't believe that she could hurt. "She looked like you, Lilith—tall, strong, and very beautiful," Persephone said. "She was certainly more beautiful than I—I was merely cute—and Trellis was smarter, and both of them knew who they were and where they stood. Women in those days were more successful than today. I mean, they could do more successfully what was expected of them than we can. Because no one's quite sure what we're supposed to be. And, let's face it, it was hard for them to fail, because they had help."

The spoken word "help" pealed like a church bell for the Salmon women.

"Robert the butler," Lilith said. She yearned now for the glory days of the Salmons, yearned to belong to that time that was not her own.

"That's right. And the twins, Iris and Irene . . ."

"Maids." Lilith tried to imagine the house then. Everything would have looked shiny and kept up. The driveway would be loaded with fine old cars. The house full of life. The women wore gowns and the men dressed for dinner.

"Actually, Iris was a maid and Irene was—I think—the cook," Persephone said. "And there was dear, sweet Jen-Jen, who was a nurse to both Reggie and Monet and to all the children in Upper Darby in one way or another, even the Prells."

"What happened to her?"

"Went off with a man on an Indian motorcycle."

"And there was a gardener."

"Bunch of 'em. Your grandmother Salmon just chewed up gardeners."

141

Persephone started taking pictures again. A couple minutes later, Lilith asked, "What happened to Rolf?"

Persephone laughed with such deep satisfaction that the image in the camera viewer jiggled. "I had the little ditz fired." The laughter triggered sadness; Persephone said, "Even then the money was slipping away. It killed your grandfather Salmon."

"What did it do to Daddy?"

"Impossible to tell exactly."

"Because Daddy never told anyone what he felt."

"Even as a boy, Reggie was full of secrets. I loved him for those secrets, whatever they were. I think because he knew the money was going and because he knew he wasn't the type to make money, he decided instead to make a stand, as the Squire. He might have not had that name in mind, but he invented the Squire. I think he figured if he just acted the part it would come true. Well, it did come true—for him. But for the rest of us, you and me and Upper Darby, he held us back. Do you see what I'm saying?"

"Yes."

"So, you agree?"

"Yes, I agree." Although she wasn't sure why, Lilith was sure that, at this moment, she hated her mother.

Lilith painted, Persephone resumed taking pictures. Lilith had to reach out to do her work, and it was this effort and the lines it made—a dangerous, strained grace—that Persephone attempted to capture in her photographs, the very kind of work she would have done had she fulfilled her dream to become a fine-arts painter.

A couple minutes later, the Salmon women were distracted by the sound of Selectman Arthur Crabb's pickup truck pulling into the driveway. They watched the old farmer dismount from his vehicle and, sternly shy, stride toward them. Lilith came down off her ladder. "I don't like this," Persephone mumbled.

"Good day." Crabb bowed slightly.

Persephone looked Crabb in the eye. "What brings the town government this far up the hill, Mr. Selectman?" she asked.

Crabb looked Persephone in the eye. "Court papers," he said, and then it seemed to Lilith that the old farmer's dour face cast the shadow of a mischievous inner smile.

Persephone read the papers. She took her time. Most other people in the same situation might have scanned a few lines, missed most of the points until later, when they had time to sit down and think straight. But Persephone possessed the on-call ability to concentrate at will.

"The Prells put you up to this," Persephone said in a pained hiss that suggested to Lilith what her mother might sound like in ten years if she continued to smoke.

The old selectman did not respond to the accusation. "I'm sorry, Mrs. Salmon," he said, backed up a couple of steps, keeping his eyes on Persephone, as he might on a bull as he crossed a field, then turned and walked back to his pickup. It made a coughing sound upon starting. The puff of blue-black smoke from the exhaust reminded Lilith of the Bronco. She scurried down the ladder. "What's the matter, Mother?"

Persephone looked at her with that stony, mean-spirited expression for a long moment, as if Lilith had done something wrong. Then she explained. The town and the Prells had struck back at Monet through the Salmons and the Trust. The town had filed a countersuit against Monet, and they had also introduced another element in the court case, Garvin's pet project. The town asked the court to remand the body of Raphael Salmon to Darby for burial on the Raphael Salmon II Memorial Trust Lands. The basis for this suit was Reggie's will.

"What does it mean?" Lilith asked.

"It means war," Persephone said, and Lilith heard a thrill in her mother's voice. "They want Reggie. They won't get him, because I won't allow it."

"You're going to stay?"

"Until I see the remains of my loved ones disposed of in my own way. There'll be no reason to attend the memorial service. Both Reggies are going to stay in the town crypt until this is settled." Persephone stormed into the house. Lilith followed.

While she awaited Frederick, Lilith tried without success to ignore her mother's presence in the house. Persephone called a lawyer, called her lover down under, called Natalie Acheson. Between telephone calls, she paced about the house. Smoke from her cigarettes drifted in the light of the hall and hung there like a fog. Finally, Frederick arrived, and Lilith fled from the house.

As they drove down the hill, Lilith told Frederick about the selectman's visit. A certain overly formal expression of sympathy for her situation told Lilith that a part of Frederick was glad to see the Salmons getting theirs from the town. But she shook away her doubt. She needed somebody to be behind her all the way.

"You plant your garden?" she asked.

"Got the tomatoes in." Frederick was happy not to be talking about the problems of Upper Darby. "Howie bothered us for a while, sitting outside in his wheelchair, criticizing, and then my mother sent him in the house. He didn't care. He screws around with his new computer the way he used to screw around with cars. . . . You want to go anyplace in particular?"

"You think the memorial service is over with?"

"I imagine." Frederick hoped Lilith didn't want to go there. He didn't like cemeteries or ceremonies.

"Drive down. I want to see," Lilith said.

They arrived as the Reverend Spofford Hall, minister of the Unified Church of Christ, was saying words over the graves. The old soldiers had honored their dead and now, decent souls that they were, stood with bowed heads for this additional ceremony to bury for a second time the original settlers of Upper

Darby. Frederick slowed, and they peered through the trees. The caskets were lined up in rows with American flags slung over them. In the soft green spring light, they struck Lilith as pale and insubstantial as foam sculptures for an ad display of the containers of fast-food hamburgers, and the mourners were actors, and the service was a theatrical event, and the audience was History. Maybe they were all living for History; maybe History was the only thing worth living for, the only achievement of the human species. After all, a spider made better and more purposeful art, a cat displayed more grace, any number of creatures were stronger and swifter, and some lived longer. Feelings, those precious mental reactions all humans valued as their own, in fact were common to almost all mammals. As for intelligence, often it went bad, making useless inventions, or cruel gadgets, or just ugly stuff, or it turned me against you, or you against me, or me against myself. Science killed as easily as it saved. But History, that was something, that was unique to people and beautiful and strictly human.

Selectman Crabb, standing on the grass with hands crossed in front of him, recognized Frederick's pickup easing by. He bore Frederick and Lilith no ill will, but he didn't like the slow-look-see, drive-by. He wished they'd get about their business or stop and pay their respects. That was the trouble with the world today. No one paid respects. Everybody drove on by— and too fast. Too fast—everything. A man's life, his kids, his ideas about the world—they were like crazy teenagers in hot rods: going no place too fast.

It had been Crabb's idea to hold the service on Memorial Day. He was a veteran himself, and he'd seen a decline in the observance of the holiday, and he had thought this service might give people an added incentive to turn out for the regular Memorial Day march from the firehouse to the new cemetery. He believed in honoring the dead. He believed in the idea of honor. But pretty much the same crowd as usual showed up,

145

vets who knew what loss was all about, their loved ones, and widows. He was sorry more people hadn't come for the service, and he was especially sorry that the descendants of these long-dead town folks were so scattered across the country that most of them were unaware of the proceedings today.

Crabb knew the reason: Upper Darby was a hill town. Hill towns—goddamn 'em. They drove the children away from home; they forbade return. A hard climate, poor soil, and isolation from the rest of the country had worn down his own kind, river-valley farmers, but it had completely defeated the hill farmers. It had hurt his own father when the rich folks took over Upper Darby at the turn of this century, but Crabb figured better the rich than the poor, for a hill town was no place for a man without independent means. These upland towns didn't provide; these upland towns thrived with the first generations, which always seemed to be lucky, and then the inevitable bad year would come—not enough rain or too much, or early frost or late frost, or the national economy bad. The valley towns made it through these times, not the hill towns. God might live on a hill, but he didn't favor the common man for a neighbor.

Lilith looked beyond the burial sites to the town crypt. It was made of huge laid-up stones built into the side of the hill, so that the structure was exposed on one side only. Her father and brother were the current residents. They'd be there until Judge Barnicle heard the case. Lilith had few opinions on the legal matters involved in the situation. Monet and his white bear roaming the Trust lands, Garvin and his determination to inter her father's bones on the Trust lands, her mother's stubborn resolve that she get her way—these issues all seemed to be part of something else, something that belonged to Monet and Garvin and Persephone, but not to her.

PART II

PART II

1

Listen, Freddy

Elenore Elman, on her knees in the garden, watched her husband. Astride his shaving horse, putting the finishing touches on a crutch he'd made from a maple sapling, he looked like some kind of maniac cowboy. When the cast had been removed from his leg, and the medical people had issued him aluminum crutches, she had watched his face pucker up. "You look like Music turning up his nose at strange food," she said. "Damn cat, damn daughter—at the end, they all leave you. Damn 'em all," he had said. Howard hated the crutches, hated the way they looked, hated the way they felt, but mainly he hated the fact that someone else had made them. So he'd complained about the cost of renting them, even though insurance paid the bill. Following the law, two nurses, one male and one female, had rolled Howard out of the hospital in a wheelchair. He'd grumbled and fumed, and when they were outside, he'd faced the nurses and said, "Am I on my own now?" And when the male nurse had said yes and offered Howard the crutches, Howard had said, "Put 'em up your uncle Henry." Hanging on to her arm, pretending he wasn't—the nurses shaking their heads, thinking, What a fool—Howard had hobbled to the car. They weren't out of the parking lot before he'd criticized her driving; they hadn't gone a mile before he announced that he was going to make a crutch and it wouldn't cost a dime. So he had made Freddy cut some ash saplings. He'd cut them, put them in the bathtub, and poured boiling water on them so he could bend the wood to shape. Today, with her help, he'd hauled the shaving horse out of the barn so he could finish up the job. She'd was proud of him in a way she couldn't define, or wouldn't, or didn't want to if she could, or maybe she wasn't proud at all. Maybe, like him, she was only a fool.

"I wish they'd get here." Howard frowned at his watch and went back to his labors, pulling a draw knife over the wood, stripping off slivers, sanding the rough spots inch by inch. He was doing the finish work, the "fussy stuff," he'd say, as if he wanted to get it over with. But she knew he liked the fussy stuff. He was a big gruff man, and the only tenderness in him was in his hands.

"I don't see why you have to work on Sunday," Elenore said. Nagging was her way of getting his attention. She weeded around the marigolds at the foot of the pedestal of the statue of the Virgin Mary.

"Because the landfill's open on Sunday. Dumping is not real work. Pickups, that's the real work." Howard stared at his crutch, talked more to it than to his wife. "Another five, ten, twenty, thirty, a hundred years and I won't be fit for real work." He paused, boosted his decibel level and continued. "It wounds me to the soul that he parks my Honeywagon at Cooty's instead of here. Why won't he sleep on these grounds? He gets in that camper and he parks it on lonely roads, and he sleeps there— my word, but he sleeps in the pucker brush, like some animal, but he won't sleep on these grounds. Now, I ask you?" He paused again, feeling the wood with his fingers, then went on with the same rising voice: "It wounds me to the soul. . . . I suppose it don't matter. . . . Today's only a test day. No real work to be done. I'm just going to find out if my leg's healed good enough to drive the Honeywagon. If I can I will, if I can't—"

"You will anyway," Elenore interrupted.

"That's correct—I will anyway. Might as well go to the landfill, too, while I'm at it. Do some work while I'm not working. You understand? No, you don't understand. Goddamn woman."

"Oh, pipe down. I know work when I see it, and dumping or picking up garbage is work—all the same—and Jesus knows that, too. I wish on the Lord's day you'd go to church with me instead of tending to your business."

"Why should I go to church? I'm doomed to perdition anyway."

"Oh, he doesn't believe in God or in heaven, or in the Virgin, but he does believe in hell."

"Only in a manner of speaking. I mean, there ain't no evidence of the place upstairs, but plenty for down," Howard said.

The telephone rang. Howard (who loved gimmicks) picked up the portable phone which lay in his toolbox, beside the shaving horse. After his usual shouted hello, he didn't say much, but mainly listened, the look on his face interested but noncommittal. Elenore wondered if somebody had died.

"Who was that?" she asked as soon as he'd hung up.

"Your boss, the Pocket Squire," Howard said.

"It's Sunday. I'm not about to leave my garden to clean his house—he'll have to wait."

"He don't care about that. He wants to see me and Cooty. Got some job for us."

Howard might profess contempt for the Upper Darby crowd, but now that one of them had come to him for some kind of deal, he was pleased by the attention. Elenore moved several feet on her knees to the tomato patch. She felt holy down here with damp, cool earth on her knees. God was watching over her, and she knew it. She prayed silently: Blessed are the poor in spirit, for theirs is the kingdom of heaven. . . . Blessed are the sorrowful. . . . Blessed are the meek . . . the hungry . . .

151

the thirsty . . . the persecuted. Elenore did not expect to inherit either heaven or earth; the blessings were enough for her. She pinched off yellow flower buds on the big-boy tomato plants to encourage the fruits to grow and ripen. She plucked one of the green tomatoes, no bigger than a crab apple and hard, and held it under her husband's nose and said, "Who do you think makes these plants grow?"

"The Scott fertilizer people."

"You are about the most ignorant man in Tuckerman County." She knelt again in the soil. "There's where you need to pay attention." She rose up on her knees, facing the statue of the Blessed Virgin Mary.

Howard Elman noted that the sun was on the Virgin's face. It was he who had set the lady in concrete. Elenore wanted her facing the garden instead of the mobile home, because, whereas a house needed a woman's touch, a garden needed a saint's blessing. With her outstretched hands the Virgin seemed both to engulf and to protect them, while at the same time she held them at bay.

"I put a high degree of value on my ignorance," he said. "It's all I have besides common doggedness."

"Do what you can for him—he don't know any better." Elenore addressed the Virgin.

This was how they talked. They argued more or less, but it was mostly kidding. If for some reason he was mad at her or she was mad at him, they'd ignore one another. Elenore called these times "the cutting quiets." It used to be they never talked at all. He'd grumble, or yell at her, or suddenly he'd be all mushy—and that was all right—but he never actually talked. As for herself, she had nothing to say. Too darn busy to think when you're raising five kids. It was only after the children had gone and he'd lost his job and she'd been sick and their house had burned that, miraculously, they'd changed. She couldn't explain how it had happened, but she'd woke up.

152

Jesus had said, "Open your eyes, Elenore, and look at the world without fear." Meanwhile, Howard had gotten over his bitterness and confusion over losing his job, and he had forged this trash-collecting business. He'd even taken up reading, and—miracle of miracles—one fine day he'd engaged her in conversation. They'd been talking ever since. Howard, this man who at one time could speak to no one without barking orders—or defying orders—liked just to talk. Talked with anyone except his son, of course. With Freddy he was the old Howard, mean, loud, unreasonable.

"There—that'll do it," Howard announced. He adjusted his hearing aid, stood, put the crutch under his arm, and ambulated down the driveway, then back again. The crutch was a success, as both of them knew it would be. That established, Howard, using the crutch as a lever, maliciously tipped over the wheelchair he'd been saddled to for more than a month.

"By gosh, you're ungrateful," she said.

"That's true, there's ain't a grain of gratitude in me," he said. The whinny sound in his hearing aid told him the Honeywagon was coming down the road.

As Frederick Elman pulled the Honeywagon into the Elman driveway, neither he nor Cooty Patterson was prepared for the sight of Howard Elman standing in the middle, between the dirt ruts, pointing at the truck with his crutch, like some backwoods Moses facing the Red Sea. Frederick hit the brakes, the Honeywagon jerked to a stop, Cooty lurched forward and banged his head on the dashboard. "Jeez, he's up and around," Frederick lamented.

Cooty touched the place on his head where he'd hit it and giggled.

"Hold on! You trying to kill me!" Howard snarled.

"It crossed my mind." Frederick stuck his head out the window. He enjoyed looking down at Howard from the elevation of the Honeywagon's driver's seat.

153

Howard grinned. That was the kind of humor he liked to see in a young buck. Laugh at your fellow man, spit in his face; laugh at God, spit in His face—'k' em all, the long, the short, and the tall. Howard struggled up to the driver's side and opened the door. "Move over, goddamn it!"

Frederick did as he was told, sliding to the center. Cooty hugged the passenger door, as if he wanted out. Howard shoved his head through the window, and hollered to Elenore, "Going to the landfill—see you in heaven."

He backed the truck out of the drive, alternately whooping with heartfelt enthusiasm and cursing with leg-felt lameness.

Once they were on the road, Howard spoke. "Cooty, how was the Honeywagon without old Howie? Pretty awful, eh?"

"Peaceful, Howie—real peaceful," Cooty said.

"And civilized, real civilized," Frederick said.

Howard roared with laughter. "Oh, come on, boys—you know you missed me. The Honeywagon missed me. Didn't you, old girl?" He patted the dash with the stiff, exaggerated affection of people who despise people who shower their love on dogs.

Frederick, in the unfamiliar and inferior center seat, brooded. He had actually begun to get used to the trash route. He didn't like the work but, rather, he had grown to respect himself doing it. He had come to know the route well and, as the driver, ran the operation according to his own lights. Now Howard was taking over, and Frederick found himself feeling like an abused boy again. The labor of collecting trash was tiring, unpleasant, demeaning, and dreary. With Howard along, it would be tiring, unpleasant, demeaning, frustrating, and, eventually, intolerable. Usually when Frederick was upset he calmed down by imagining himself in the Live Free or Die, the road ahead vanishing into distant Western mountains. But when he tried to conjure that image, all that came to mind were thoughts of Lilith. He was going to see her later. She worked at the lifeguard station on Sundays until 2:00 P.M. At this moment, while he was on his way to the Tuckerman landfill, she'd be sitting high up in the guard chair, scanning the waters. He had asked whether she daydreamed up there to pass the time, and she had said, "No, I watch and I count heads. One, two, three, four, five . . . Where's sixteen? I haven't seen sixteen. Okay, there's sixteen. Seven is horsing around. Where's twelve? There's twelve. One, two, three . . ."

He had to tell her that he couldn't stay here any longer. It was time to hit the road. He had half an idea to ask her to come with him. She'd never go. He had nothing to offer her but a spree. That was the trouble with his kind—no future.

"I ain't seen your camper; where you been?" Howard demanded.

Frederick said nothing.

A moment passed. Howard turned to Frederick, but looked right past him to Cooty. "I know where he's been. Girling around," Howard said.

Cooty's face turned red, and he smiled in shy confirmation. The mere mention of an encounter between the sexes confused and titillated the old man. Frederick said nothing, but he squirmed inside. His father's method of inquiry unsettled him. Howard forced the issue. "It ain't Noreen Cook, is it? He ain't going out with no whore, is he? You ain't going out with no whore, are you?"

The sudden change in tactic, from addressing Frederick through Cooty to a direct question, startled Frederick into shouting the truth. "No—not a whore. Lilith *Sahl-mohn!*" Frederick pronounced the name the way the Upper Darby folk did, as a direct insult to his and Howard's own people in Center Darby.

"Well, that's what I heard," Howard said. "Dot McCurtin

155

has spread the news all over town. Howie Elman's son sucking up to the Upper Darby snobs. But I said to myself, Self, this can't be true."

"It's none of your business, Howie," Frederick said.

"None of my business," Howard mocked, but he knew Frederick was right. If there was anything Howard Elman believed in, it was another man's right to his own business. So he paused for a moment to try to fit the passion of the moment into his timeless philosophy. Thinking only messed up his mind further. He wanted to tell his son that he had big ideas. He'd bought the computer, and during the five weeks he'd been in the wheelchair, he'd done nothing but study up. That's what he wanted to tell his son: "I studied up." But that didn't make any sense. What did make sense was what the computer told him. There was room for expansion in the trash-collection business. He'd go to the bank, borrow some money, get another truck. That would be Freddy's truck. The trash business was good, and it was going to get better. If there was one thing that people nowadays had a lot of, it was trash. Yet he knew how Freddy felt about the business. He struggled for a way to invite his son into his life, into his business, into the business of his life, into the life of his business. That didn't make any sense either. Elenore had counseled him on fairness, decency. Be kind, even-handed, treat the boy at least the way you would a dog. That was the last thought in his mind when Howard heard himself blurt out these words: "She's going to make a fool of you!"

"So what? It runs in the family," Frederick said.

"My son shacked up with the Squire's daughter. I feel like going back to the house, getting down on my knees in front of your mother's shrine. Holy Virgin, what have I done to deserve this? Did you know the Salmons"—he pronounced it Saaminnzzz—"were part owners in the Lodge Manufacturing Works?"

"Big deal. Lodge went out of business."

"Closed up. Cooty and I lost our jobs. They had to lock Cooty in the nuthouse."

"Howie, Lilith had nothing to do with that. And, listen, she's only a friend."

"You mean, you're not getting anything off her? It figures."

"Enough, Pop—enough!"

Howard could see now that things had gone too far, but he was still mad, and when he was angry he just had to act angry, or else he'd explode later. So he turned to an old, familiar pet peeve upon which to vent his emotion.

"I'm not complaining," he complained, "but it's a crime against common sense that we have to drive fifteen miles just to dump our trash. We had a perfectly good dump right here in Darby. A feller would go there with his car, trunk full of trash, and they'd just set everything on fire. And what's more"—*what's mo-wah*—"the dump was public as the town common. Remember Ollie Jordan? Now, there was as fine a dump rat as this fine country has produced. Today— no dump rats allowed. Is this a free country? Not anymore, I say.

"Now, a poor bachelor like Cooty can get by raiding dumpsters," Howard continued, heading off the counterargument that he'd anticipated, but which neither Freddy nor Cooty was about to mount. "Think about it: a dumpster is only good for one dump rat, but a dump—a fine old burning dump—serves the public good. From a dumpster, you can't get, say, a dining-room set for a family. For one thing, you gotta pretty much be sneaky about taking the stuff out, because a dumpster is private property. No respectable businessman wants some idiot like Cooty Patterson sniffing around his property, sticking his nose in his dumpster. But, see, at a dump—I'm talking about a town dump, now, a burning dump, a fine old burning dump, a dump with heart—it's to everybody's benefit to have some

157

local dump rats to come and haul off the stuff that some fool in Upper Darby don't want. You ask why?"

"I didn't ask why," muttered Frederick, but Howard ignored him.

"I'll tell you why. For the obvious reasons that the public dollar don't have to pay to bury, burn, or bamboozle some other town to take your garbage. The town dump used to be like a supply depot for poor folk. You needed something, you didn't go to the welfare department. You went to the dump. You understand what I'm getting at: a good dump saves those who got it from dishing out to those that don't. And then . . ."

"Pop, what in hell are you talking about?"

"I'm talking about . . . I'm talking about"—as Howard struggled for words, Cooty began to laugh—"you shut up, old man, you talk too much. I'm talking about society, the world, the universe . . . the goddamn universe that the Creator, that guy your mother knows, kneels to, created, that went, like, ah, back in time to, ah . . ."

Frederick broke in. "Howie, if it wasn't for the landfill, you couldn't make a living. . . ."

"I could so."

"Not in the trash-collection business. You said yourself, people would take their own stuff to the dump."

"Because a local dump is convenient, and pleasant on a Saturday, and entertaining—fire always makes for a good show."

"So, what are you complaining about?"

"Was I complaining? Was I?" Howard turned to Cooty for support.

Cooty was now weeping and open-mouthed like a desperate actor hired for a laugh track tape.

"Like I say, I'm not complaining," Howard said, having long ago lost what it was he meant to say.

"Come on, Pop, you just don't like driving fifteen miles twice a week to dump the Honeywagon."

Now Howard understood everything. Frederick was right. "Well, it is an aggravation," Howard said.

That ended the conversation for the moment. The trash men drove on in silence.

Pretty soon the landfill was going to be closed. Frederick had heard talk about a housing project on the dump site. It was the kind of idea Howard would approve of, because it was so practical. But it vaguely troubled Frederick, and he didn't know why. The reason had something to do with the present impinging on the past. And yet who was he to judge, he who hadn't done anything, who did not even harbor ambitions? While people were out there trying to make a profit on this old landfill, local officials were discussing about what to do for a replacement. It was one of the touchier issues in Tuckerman County. What to do with waste? Burn it? Recycle it? Bury it? Ship it someplace? Some combination of these possibilities? No one had the answer, or so Frederick read in the newspaper. All this made him wonder: why are the important things of life so boring, and why are the things that matter to a person— say, what somebody else thinks of him—so trivial?

Howard was right, Frederick thought. The drive to the Tuckerman landfill was an unpleasant chore. It lengthened a workday, or it had to be done on Sunday morning. When Frederick was in charge of the Honeywagon, he had dealt with unpleasantness in the age-old manner of laborers, imposing upon himself a kind of stupor, so that he saw nothing, felt nothing, but today, because Howard had taken over the Honeywagon and because they'd been arguing, Frederick was alert to his surroundings. When they arrived at the landfill, he saw it as if for the first time since Howard had taken him there as a boy.

In those days, Howard was not Darby's trash man. He was

a foreman in the Lodge textile mills, and he took the family trash every Saturday to the landfill like any common citizen. Even then he complained about the drive. Local people in those days wouldn't think of paying someone to haul away their trash. It was a time when a week's worth of family trash could fit, if just barely, in the trunk of a big car. Never mind that one had to spend an hour on the road to get to the landfill and back. People still had the habit of going to the dump once a week. The Tuckerman landfill had just opened, in a deep valley, shrouded by steep-sided hills and dark forest. They had to descend down a long, windy road to reach the site. From here, Frederick could just barely see the tip of Mount Monadnock to the southeast. Howard would say in his kidder's voice, "What do you see?"

"The mountain," Frederick would say.

"Keep looking. As you grow, it'll grow," Howard had said with a chuckle and Frederick had believed him. For a couple of months, every Saturday, when they went to the dump, Frederick would look at the mountain. It never seemed to get bigger.

"Have I grown?" he would say to his father.

"Not that I've noticed," Howard teased him.

"Will I ever grow?"

"Look at the mountain," Howard would say.

"I can only see a little bit of it, and it's so far away."

"Keep looking."

Frederick looked at the mountain another month or so, but nothing changed, so soon he lost interest. Eventually, he forgot the whole thing. Now it came back, and he understood. Over the last twenty years, the steep valley had been filled with layer after layer of the county's trash. Today the level of the dump had actually risen above the surrounding hills. Indeed, there were no hills. The landscape was rearranged to form a mesa. The view of Mount Monadnock was magnificent. Beyond the

tan earth and blowing newspapers and other trash, the mountain rose up like a figure with outstretched hands. It reminded
him of his mother's statue of the Virgin. The mountain was
immense; it was God. It was what his father had meant. Look
at the mountain. Just as he had actually never noticed himself
grow, he had never noticed the mountain. All those years,
when he could have been seeing something, he had missed
out. He ached now to thank his father, to apologize, to reach
out to him in some way, in gratitude, in love.

"Hey, Pop?" he said lightly, winding up, choking back a tear
of love.

"What do you want?" Howard's droll sarcasm tripped up
Frederick. Something snapped.

"Fuck you, Pop," Frederick said.

And so the argument resumed, going on and on until Howard backed the Honeywagon to dump its contents, and the
Elman men got out of the truck, Howard easing himself down
with orgasmic groans, Frederick following him out with a leap
and a whoop.

"You're out of your mind, crazy as Cooty. That girl's going
to hang you by your privates. You watch," Howard perseverated.

"It's my life," Frederick perseverated.

"It's his life."

"Can't you talk to me straight on?"

Howard did not understand his son's question, but anyway
he decided to try reason in reaching this stubborn boy. "Listen,
Freddy. . . ." And then he stopped. As far as Howard was
concerned, "Listen, Freddy," delivered in a mild voice, was a
form of reasoning, even an apology, and Freddy ought to be
able to figure that out.

"Listen—what? You don't have anything to say to me," Frederick shouted, and inside the truck Cooty Patterson marveled
at how much Frederick was becoming like his father.

161

"Listen, Freddy"—Howard kept at it, different tone now, more teacherly—"it's guys like the Squire, all those guys up on the hill, that use guys like me and you and Cooty to make themselves rich. Ream jobs—these guys go to college to learn how to give 'em."

Frederick rolled his eyes. "What the hell! That has nothing to do with anything."

Howard struggled for words to frame his argument. "A leopard don't change his spots, even if he's a girl, and the Squire's daughter to boot."

"Oh, Pop!"

"There'll come a day when she'll double-cross you. You'll think you're putting it to her, but all along she'll be putting it to you. It's in her blood."

"You listen to me for a change—" But Frederick's train of thought went off the tracks when Howard shouted, "Hit it!" and Cooty pulled the dump lever. The argument stopped abruptly, and the Elman men, with the intensity of children at an air show, watched the Honeywagon dump its contents—food, paper, glass, metal, wood, plastic, the leavings of a world sculpturally in motion.

When everything was still, and the soft putrid smell wafted up into their nostrils, Howard said, "Listen, Freddy . . .?"

"Listen, Freddy," said Frederick, mimicking his father, talking to the trash.

"Listen, Freddy." Howard revved up again. "If you want a girl, go down to get her, bring her on up to where you're at. You won't have no troubles then."

"I'm at the bottom now, for cry-sakes," Frederick said.

"Listen, Freddy."

"Listen, Freddy." Frederick huffed and puffed like Howard, but Howard remained calm.

"Go up after your woman," he said, "and she's going to knock you on your ass."

Frederick turned his shoulder away from his father. Howard grabbed the shoulder. Frederick pulled off the hand, plucked Howard's crutch right from under his arm, and bounded up the Honeywagon into the driver's seat.

Howard stood on one foot, a hand on the Honeywagon for support. Damned if he was going to beg for his cane. He'd crawl out of here, the way he'd crawled out of the Trust when he broke his leg, before he'd ask his son for anything.

"Upper Darby uses Center Darby and Darby Depot as whores." Howard spat out the words. He could feel his ability to articulate come round. "Listen, Freddy! Ever since the quarries. Killed men with the dust. Ever since the mills. Put men and women to work in sweatshops. Brought in scabs to knock their blocks off. Turned Frenchman against Irishman. Killed Indians with disease. Clear-cut whole mountains for a few dollars in timber. You don't know your history, boy. Where's my cane? Goddamn it, gimme my cane!"

The crutch came sailing out of the cab of the truck, landed at his feet. Howard picked it up. It was a little scuffed. It could use some linseed oil to bring out the grain of the wood.

2

Driving Around

Darby Lake was two miles long, a mile wide; in the middle was an island thick with pines, spruces, and birches. The lake's rim was crowded with houses, but the area did not seem crowded, because the houses were hidden by the forest. In Northern New England, the idea behind owning a house on a lake is to have a place to get away from it all, "it" being the drone of day-to-day life. Upper Darby people called their lake houses "cottages," Center Darby people "camps." Never mind that these structures, both cottages and camps, often ran bigger than the average three-bedroom house, and never mind that Darby Depot residents rarely owned property at all and never lake property. Although Tuckerman County was being transformed by newcomers, most Darby Lake property continued to be owned by the same families that had always owned them. People moving out of the area might sell the family home, but not the camp. They kept the summer place on the lake, or passed it down to their children, or sold it to someone else in the family. The reason for this is that a place on a lake begins as a dream and endures as a dream, and dreams are the last thing to go.

The Darby hills unreeled from the heights right down to the shore; along most of the lake's edge, gray boulders protruded out of the water like the bums of basking hippos. But at the west end of the lake, where a brook had spread out over weeds and, having lost its identity as a stream, entered the lake, the land was flat and the water shallow. It was here that, many years ago, a young entrepreneur, one E. H. Prell, had bought land cheap, finagled a dredge-and-fill permit from the authorities, channeled the brook, filled in the swamp, created a beach, and sold at a profit. Today the beach was divided into two sections, the Lake Club and the Town Beach. At the Lake Club, members docked Lightning sailboats for races on Sunday, while their families and friends watched from a huge screened-in porch in the clubhouse. The Salmons once had a Lightning boat, but winning brought Reggie little pleasure, and he hated, just hated, to lose, so he sold the boat. The Salmons were still nominally members of the Lake Club, having been grandfathered in, as the term went. It was a club joke that Reggie's ghost wouldn't rest until he came and got his sail, which was still stored in a locker in the boathouse. Although the club, owned in common by the members, had no written rules keeping certain people in and excluding others, in practice the membership of the club managed to remain composed of the same kinds.

A small fee was charged for entry into the Town Beach, and a concessions stand produced a modest profit, year in and year out. Although the Town Beach was called the Town Beach, it was not publicly owned. The principal owner, a newcomer to the Darby area, attorney Lawrence Dracut, had just been accepted as a member of the Lake Club.

Lilith had been a lifeguard at the Town Beach since she was sixteen. When she entered college, she had planned to get another summer job, perhaps working in San Francisco for her uncle Thaddeus, who was a landscape architect, or (and this she'd only dreamed) doing something, she couldn't imagine what, for a symphony orchestra. Then her father sickened and died. After that, everything seemed to take tremendous effort. A kind of lethargy settled in over her. Out of habit, she returned to her post in the lifeguard's chair, sitting above it all, watching the waters, counting heads. Now, a year later, she was back. Her fellow workers had moved on, replaced by sixteen- and seventeen-year-olds. Most were new to the region, and they did not like Lilith. There was something about her that put them off, a reserve that they mistook for aloofness or snobbery. Lilith found herself alone, out of place and time. Her only friend for the last month had been Frederick Elman.

He picked her up after work nearly every day, but he never came to the beach. He parked on the shoulder of the narrow lake road and waited for her. When they were seen together in public, they were uncomfortable and alienated from one another as well as from their respective worlds. It was as if each knew some loathsome secret about the other. This strange feeling vanished the moment they were alone.

Lilith had showered and dressed, and she had just stepped outside of the bathhouse, when she was surprised to find Garvin Prell standing in the sand in deck shoes and white trousers.

"Did you see us out there?" he said, sounding not like a lawyer or even like a man of thirty-three but like a small boy, so that she found herself feeling tender toward him.

"The boats are so graceful in the wind—I love to watch them," she said.

"We won today," he said, as if that fact had led him from boat, to clubhouse, to beach, to her.

"That's nice," she said.

"I've been real busy with Sugar Bush Village, but I haven't forgotten my promise to take you to the Inn for dinner," he said.

In fact, Lilith herself had forgotten, but Garvin made it sound as if she'd been waiting all this time for him.

"Are you free Friday night?" he asked.

On Friday nights, she usually drove to Brattleboro with Frederick for pizza. But things had changed. Frederick had announced that he was leaving Darby. His father no longer needed him; he couldn't bear the confinement of Darby any longer. "I don't know," she said.

"You're seeing someone else, and I'm not going to concern myself with that," Garvin said. "But you and I have things in common, things to talk about. We're on your father's board together. We both care about Darby. Right now I'm in a three-way battle with Monet and your mother—okay? But, believe me, I want peace and fairness for all. Have dinner with me; we should talk." Garvin spoke easily and persuasively, so unlike Frederick, who was at turns hesitant and overbearing, but who redeemed himself with his sense of humor and warmth. Lilith was swayed, not so much by Garvin the man as by his arguments. Garvin sensed she was wavering, and at a crucial moment he said in a commanding voice, "Thursday."

"All right—Thursday," she said.

When she reached the Live Free or Die, she was thinking about Garvin. He was a Prell, and yet he did not seem so dangerous. He was aggressive, but she sensed something in him that was, well, not warm, but shy and needy. She wished Harriet were here to give her advice. Harriet might be wrong ninety percent of the time, but Lilith could use some of her brassiness. Lilith had talked to her on the telephone and told her about Frederick and Garvin. Lilith remembered Harriet's analysis now. "Trash man? Bridge painter? Beard? Built like the dump truck he drives? At the first sign of trouble, he'll run. Forget him. Go out with the lawyer. A lawyer will cheat on you because it's exciting for him, but then you can cheat on him. Doesn't matter. In the end, he'll take care of you, because that's what lawyers do: take care of people."

The engine was running in the pickup, and Frederick gunned it the moment she shut the door. He didn't look at her, but at the road.

"Bad day?" she asked.

"Good thing I'm leaving. My old man's driving me nuts."

"I thought so."

"How could you tell?" Frederick drove too fast; Lilith liked that.

"I read your mind," she said.

"Did you, now?"

"Actually, I smelled the beer. You don't usually drink so early."

"That's how Upper Darby judges Center Darby: by the smell, right?"

"You don't have to be mad at me, I didn't do anything," she said.

"Yah, I know. Want one?" He reached into the brown paper bag on the seat beside him and handed her a beer. They drank from bottles (they'd agreed that when you drove you wanted beer in a bottle) and they put the empties back in the bag. They had at least two things in common: a weakness for drinking and driving, and a reverence for unspoiled countryside.

The truck pulled off the lake road onto the town road.

"Anybody drown today in Darby Lake?" Frederick asked in his father's gruffly affectionate voice.

"It's always the same on Sunday—families," she said. "On weekdays, you get the teenagers—God, they're only a few years younger than I am, and yet they're so far away from me."

"They work on better cars than we did, and they never seem to get dirty."

"Teenagers—and mothers with their kids," Lilith went on. "They're involved and bored at the same time. They depress me. But on Sundays it's families. And they really depress me. I look at them—the mothers and the fathers and kids, and somebody's aunt and uncle—and they all look tricked."

"You're jealous. Deep down you want kids and a guy around

168

the house to nag." Frederick was joking, but Lilith brooded over the matter. Maybe some day she'd be ready for a family. But not now. She had to know herself before she could bring someone else into the world. "I don't think so," she said. "I think they depress me because I don't know who they are. People from Darby don't come to the beach anymore."

"They never did—you're just noticing."

"What I'm saying is, I look around and hope to see somebody. And maybe I see a familiar face, but it's nobody I know."

"The people you know all have summer places. They don't need the Town Beach," Frederick accused.

"No—they're gone. Don't you understand that?"

"Rich people are never gone—you keep in touch. You hang out with each other. You got no complaints, you're rich." He spoke the way a child speaks to an adult, full of insult because he believes this superior being cannot be hurt.

"So, we're rich, what's it to you?" she said, knowing that she was not rich, knowing that Upper Darby was dying because of lack of money. Like everyone else in Center Darby and Darby Depot, Frederick assumed she had a large independent income. What puzzled and frightened Lilith was that she felt obligated to help maintain his illusion, an obligation not to Frederick and his kind but to herself and her own kind and, even, to the town as a whole, for reasons she could not grasp.

"You can be rich. I don't have any right to criticize," he said.

Lilith thought: I should tell him about the money.

Frederick said, "At least on the beach you see somebody every day. I swear that when people hear the Honeywagon coming they hide—because, listen, I never see anybody. Or they don't see me. Nobody looks at me."

"You and your father scare people. You make them feel guilty. They don't want to see you."

"That's the answer," he said.

She was sorry she'd been so frank, for she realized that her words saddened him.

"Where to? The road? Up on the Trust?" he asked.

"Let's drive," she said, not because that's what she wanted but because that's what she knew he wanted. She was falling into the same pattern with Frederick that she'd fallen into with Peter, suppressing her own wants and feelings to accommodate his.

They drove lazily along Route 21, crossed the river into Vermont, and headed north on the interstate. Both Frederick and Lilith liked Vermont. It was different from New Hampshire. The hills were rounder, softer. Fields on the lower flanks of the hills opened a view, whereas in New Hampshire the forest usually came right to the road, obscuring the countryside. New Hampshire hid in itself like a lie. The trees in Vermont seemed healthier, too, less twisted than the ones in New Hampshire. Even the rocks were different. In Vermont, they varied in color from white to almost black, with streams of red and yellow and blue flowing through them. To Lilith, the rocks of Vermont seemed about to melt, like the exotic ice-cream flavors of Ben & Jerry's. In New Hampshire, the rocks were gray and still, solid as the ideas of religious people, the colors in them shimmering like the surface of a pond, reflecting the surrounding light rather than revealing the inner constitution.

"Would you live in Vermont?" Lilith asked.

"It's not far enough away from Darby," Frederick said. "Besides, it's too full of out-of-staters."

He immediately realized the accidental illogic of his words. He glanced at Lilith. Her face showed nothing. A moment of silence passed in which neither spoke. He pointed at her with his index finger, as one saying, "Okay, that's your cue." And they both laughed.

It was, Lilith thought, not the sex, but this upon which their relationship was built: drink, a few foolish words, silences in which they were thinking the same thing, then spontaneous laughter as if in celebration of the shared moment. It was probably better that he was leaving. If he stayed around, they'd get to know each other only too well. Everything would come apart between them, because, after all, they had been born and raised on different worlds, if only a few miles apart. Now it didn't matter. He was leaving. Like everybody else. 'Bye, Frederick. She thought about Garvin. This much she was sure of: Garvin was her own kind, and he was staying.

Frederick stopped in the river town of Bellows Falls to buy some beer. They walked to the store, and she happened to notice their reflections in the display window. She was an inch taller than he, and her body carriage was straight, her shoulders squared away. She carried her head up. His body was much thicker, and his shoulders were broad but they drooped. He walked with his head bowed slightly, his eyes furrowed, and his trunk hunched over. His attraction for her was the contrast between his beastlike body and his all-too-human human mind. And, too, his presence in her life sent a signal of her rebellion to Upper Darby: Lilith Salmon seeks change in her world.

In White River Junction they turned off, and within the space of a half a mile crossed two rivers, the White and the Connecticut, and pulled into the Four Aces Diner in West Lebanon, New Hampshire. For dinner they ate breakfast— ham, eggs, toast, home fries, coffee. Frederick paid. He acted huffy if Lilith offered to buy anything on these short-hop trips. They sat tightly together in a booth. Over coffee, she asked, "Where will you go?"

"I don't know. I've got a little money saved. Maybe Jackson Hole or Laramie until the weather gets mean, then head south for a painting job."

"It sounds like a lonely life."

"It's the only life I've got. There's nothing here for me. And nobody. Except you." He left an opening for her to speak, but she had nothing to say.

"I'm not really in your plans for the future, am I?" he said.

"If I'm not in your plans, how can you ask me to include you in my plans?" she said.

"Good point," he said with punctuating self-mockery, then rose to go to the men's room. When he returned, she saw something hanging out of his hip pocket. She picked it, coming up with red-and-yellow cloth. "What's this?"

"My headband. I wear it on the road."

Lilith tied the headband around her forehead and looked at herself in the window of the diner, thinking that she liked what she saw. At that moment, Frederick took her in his arms.

"Not here, not in public," she whispered into his beard.

He did not answer her. He kissed her. When he released her, he asked her to spend the night with him.

"The night?"

"You and me, we steal some time together, we talk, we fool around, and I take you home. You sleep in your house and I sleep in my truck. I want a night with you before I go."

"Where's the right place for us? Your truck? Some awful motel room? Where?"

The answer came to them both, obvious as rain. They agreed to spend a night on the Trust later in the week.

"We'll sleep under the stars and pretend it's ten thousand years ago," Lilith said.

3

Smoke

It was the moonlight coming through the window that woke Lilith, stroking her, making her room seem strange and unreal, a replica of the place where she'd grown, run to, discovered herself. She sat up in bed, back straight, dignified—a Salmon woman. The oval mirror on the wall angled away from her line of vision, so that she could not see herself, and the mirror was blank black. She imagined herself rising from the bed, staring into the mirror, seeing beneath her own image her grandmother, who had given her the mirror for her thirteenth birthday. She snapped on her reading lamp. The clock on the bedstand said 1:50.

She crept out into the hall to Persephone's room. Before her parents had become estranged, they had both slept here. It had always been the master bedroom in the Salmon house, but in fact, with its mirrors and papered walls and flowered curtains on the windows, it was never a room for masters but for mistresses. She peered through the half-open door, almost expecting to find her mother and father together and she, a child again, between them, safe and comfortable. The bed contained only her mother, of course. She could still detect Persephone's scent, the hint-of-clover perfume she favored, the aroma of moist earth after a spring rain, and, riding over these good smells, the stink of cigarettes.

"Mother?" Lilith whispered. There was no answer. She could make out her mother's shape in the bed, but she could not hear her breathe. Lilith slunk away. This house was so fetid with memories, and she was like an embryo in its womb, turning and kicking, growing into a new being, both wanting in and wanting out. In the hall again, she was unaccountably taken by an urge to walk up to the next flight, the third floor, where before her time the servants had slept in cramped cells. Empty today. Years since she'd been in those rooms. Nothing there for her. She hadn't known the servants, only stories about them. She might be the legal owner of this house, but that third story did not belong to her.

She entered her father's room, with its massive oak bed, stripped wood walls, bookshelves, and fireplace. No smell of her father remained, only the heavy, musty odor of the house itself. Unlike her own and her mother's quarters, her father's room still felt the same in the moonlight as it did in the day-light—dead, pleasantly, securely dead. She snapped on the overhead light.

Lilith searched distractedly in the room, not looking for any-thing particular, but merely curious, engaged by all this male stuff. In the closet, she found her father's fly-fishing equip-ment. In a pocket of an equipment vest, she found a receipt for hatchery trout made out to the Salmon Trust. Reggie, de-spite his pronouncements about keeping things natural on the Trust, couldn't bear the idea of Grace Pond without trout, so he had had it stocked and charged the expenditure to the Trust. More wearied than disturbed by this information, Lilith re-turned the paper to the pocket.

She removed some of the artificial flies from a plastic tin in the vest and looked at them. With their subtle coloring, they resembled flowers more than insects. Her father had been a fisherman, Frederick was a fisherman; her father had been a woodsman, Frederick was a woodsman. What would Harriet

174

say about this connection? Lilith smiled inwardly. Fish, animals, trees—these belonged to the men. What about her? What belonged to her of the soul of this place? She thought about the house, the fields outside, the garden she did not have. She visualized pumpkins and squashes and corn, Indian crops—her plantings, her future.

It might have appeared that Lilith sensed her mother's presence behind her, for she whipped around a second before Persephone called her name, "Lilith!" the word spoken in that new raspy voice that made the daughter believe the mother had already gone and left behind a defective, inferior holograph of herself. But no ESP was involved. Lilith had smelled the pall of cigarette smoke that followed Persephone everywhere. Persephone's smoking, over an adult lifetime episodic and infrequent, had accelerated in a month to constant and chronic. The smell of cigarettes was on her breath, in her hair, and in the pores of her skin. Nicotine stained her fingers and her teeth. The inside of the house itself took on Persephone's weather, a thin blue-yellow haze.

Lilith was startled. "I thought you were asleep." Persephone wore a negligee, nightwear for a lover; at the sight, her daughter flushed with mild embarrassment.

"I don't sleep," Persephone said. "I lie between then and now. What are you doing in here at this time of night?"

With the spontaneity of any guilty creature that has been caught, Lilith invented an answer. "I'm staying overnight tomorrow in the Trust, and I'm looking for camping equipment."

Her mother absorbed this without knowing at first what to say. She circled her daughter like a predator circling a wounded but still-dangerous prey; then she noticed the headband Lilith was wearing.

"What is that?" Persephone said.

"Frederick gave it to me."

"Frederick!"

"I sleep with it—what do you think of that, Mother?" Lilith shouted a challenge.

Persephone snickered. Hostility from loved ones did not trouble her; hostility was food to her. "Lilith, that young man is going nowhere and taking you along for the ride. What is the point of a headband? Style? What?" Persephone interrogated.

Lilith's brief defiance fizzled. "I like Indians—Indians wear headbands." As Lilith spoke, the flaccidity of her defense became evident to her. She didn't know anything about Indians. She didn't know anything about anything.

"Indians? My word. What's become of you? What's become of me? Us?" Like many people on the verge of madness, Persephone paid homage to *sense*. Madness was the reason she had planned to leave Upper Darby in the first place. Her town was literally driving her crazy. Since she'd postponed her departure and contended for the right to dispose of her late husband's body, Persephone had felt as if parts of her mind were stranded, like seeds cast on stone under a blazing sun. In the past, she'd been held together by her labors in the greenhouse, where she could, as she felt it, regenerate herself through the contact of her hands with earth and growing things. Now, staying, the greenhouse shut down, her joints aching, she had no way to relax; it was the madness itself that sustained her, the excitement of scheming, the prospects of defeating her enemies, the drive to get her way, the desert heat of her rage. She would gather her departed loved ones, place them in a repository of her choice, and travel to that faraway place where the seasons were reversed. In her efforts in behalf of self and the dead, there was no room for a living daughter. And why should there be? The daughter was twenty-one; the daughter had acquired through inheritance Persephone's own house; the daughter was young, and the young get by.

"I don't care," Lilith said, but of course she did care. She looked closely at her mother—new lines around the eyes and mouth and neck, florid complexion, a habit of doubling fists. What was happening? Half the truth hit her then. A person does not grow old by increments but in episodes, and she was a witness to one of those episodes in the life of her mother.

"All right—forget the headband." Persephone pulled out a cigarette and a butane lighter from a pouch tucked into the cleavage of her negligee. The lighter threw a three-inch flame as Persephone lit the cigarette. She blew smoke in the air, and watched it. After the smoke had dissipated, she said, "Why does it have to be one of *them*? Why can't it be someone from Upper Darby, or even Tuckerman?"

Lilith stood mute before the rhetoric of the question.

"Why not Garvin? He likes you," Persephone pressed.

Lilith might have headed off further argument by saying she had a date with Garvin. But she was twenty-one, she didn't owe Persephone an explanation. So she designed an answer to put her mother on the defensive. "Mother, Garvin is a Prell. You're feuding with him yourself."

Persephone blew smoke, then laughed with a hiss. "I enjoy seeing Garvin squirm, but I don't hate him. E.H. in his prime was worth hating, but he's only a sick old man today. For hate, give me a husband."

"Mother, I can't stand this!" Lilith started moving away, but her mother cut her off, circling. Lilith stood frozen in place. She could see the moon outside the window seeming to hang over her mother's shoulder.

"You'll get over me—my anger is the least of your problems," Persephone said, her voicing softening a little.

"Mother, there's something terrible about what you're doing."

Persephone stopped pacing. "I'll soon be gone. After the hearing next week, everything will be settled. Then you can have your life back."

"What if the judge . . .?"

177

Persephone cut off Lilith. "It doesn't matter about the judge. I've made sure of that."

"I don't know what you're saying, Mother."

Persephone blew smoke and smiled. She had her own secrets, her own plans, and she was not about to divulge them to a daughter. Persephone gestured grandly, as if surrendering the room to Lilith, and then she left. Lilith was alone. A wispy cloud of smoke circled above her.

For the next hour, neither of the Salmon women could sleep. Lilith gathered things for her overnight hike on the Trust with Frederick. Persephone paced and smoked and, despite the hour, talked on the telephone. She called Bud Parkinson, the road agent, and talked to him in whispers. Then she called her lawyer, Lawrence Dracut. Lilith could hear her, calling from the phone in her bedroom. Persephone laughed, and Lilith thought she could hear desire, carnal desire, in the laugh. She's having an affair with Dracut, Lilith thought. She felt a wave of disgust in her stomach at the idea, for Dracut was a married man.

Lilith went downstairs to the Hearth Room, turned on the stereo, and played one of her rock albums, the music she had loved before her passion for the cello. She played the music low, the way her mother had always insisted, but it didn't satisfy her, so she went hunting for headphones. Then it struck her—this was her house. She cranked up the volume and shouted into the music, "What do you think of that, house?"

"Lilith!" her mother hollered down from the top of the stairs.

Lilith turned down the music.

Headphones over the headband, Lilith danced for a few minutes, staring hard into the eyes of the partner who was not there. She picked up a broom and, still dancing, started to sweep the floor. She swept the Hearth Room, she dusted, she danced, she sang, and then she arranged and rearranged the furniture until she was exhausted. She shut the music off, and the silence in the house was deep as the heart of the Trust. She returned to her room and lay on the bed. Outside, the moon was at the crest of the ridge. Another minute and it would be down. She looked about her room, and now she understood. This room had belonged to another person, a girl, gone today, swallowed up by time. As her parents had interred a son in the earth, so she, with this knowledge at this moment, buried a self in this room.

4

Dining on Perch

Frederick was already at the Indian camp when Lilith arrived late in the afternoon. His stuff was strewn about—a tent half set up, a hatchet on the ground beside a bag of potato chips, a plastic jug of generic cooking oil in the ashes of the old campfire, a roll of Bounty paper towels in some leaves, a bottle of champagne by the seat-log along with a six-pack of beer and mustard in one of those yellow squeeze-containers found in diners and family restaurants. Surely, he must have filched it for a joke. An iron frying pan hung from a broken-off branch on a pine tree, and a bow saw dangled from another, both implements slightly cockeyed. He'd gathered some sticks for a fire, but hadn't bothered to stack the wood, and it lay in a pile vaguely resembling the nest of some disreputable bird. Frederick had the same messy habits as the rest of his family. His truck, this campsite, his very person were disheveled. Why did some people have to be so piggy? The Salmon house might be a little shabby, because there was no money to keep it up, but it stood on its ground with the dignity of a tired sentry. As long as a Salmon—or, for that matter, anyone from Upper Darby—held sway over the house, it would remain dignified. Over time, the house would collapse within its own order. She thought about her father on the day of his death, and an accidental rhyme popped to mind: Putting on a jacket and tie, he walked into the woods to die. Her father had dignity, the likes of which Frederick Elman and his ilk would only scorn or back away from in envy.

As Lilith came forward, Frederick pointed upward. She was startled to see a stringer of fish hanging from a tree. The fish were green and yellow, from four to eight inches long, their mouths gaping open as if they were murder victims. "Perch—right?" she said.

"Yes, indeed—perch." He overpronounced the *p* and *ch* sounds, and accompanied his utterance with a fisherman's smile of self-congratulation.

Lilith unslung her gear from her shoulders. She knelt on the ground and began to unpack—sleeping bag, a half dozen candles, a salad in a bowl wrapped in plastic, cloth napkins, paper plates, wineglasses wrapped in tissue, and the best silverware from the Salmon house.

"You're early," she said.

"Went looking for Howie's tree stand."

"Last chance before you head out."

"Last failure. I'll never find it, unless by accident, and that won't count. He beat me—my old man whipped my ass. I'm not my father's son. I'm just me—nobody." Frederick grabbed the bottle of champagne, sat on the log beside the campfire, put the bottle between his legs, and pulled out the cork with the tool on his Swiss army knife. At his side, he carried yet another knife in a sheath. He drank from the bottle and handed it to Lilith.

Lilith poured a glass of champagne, toasted the Trust, and drank. "Well, at least you caught our dinner," she said.

"We call it supper," Frederick said.

"Actually, you call it *suppa*."

"*Dinna* and *suppa*, by gosh." Frederick exaggerated the accent of his own people. He laid the fish stringer on the ledges. "Not just perch, but yellow perch," he said.

181

"Any blue or magenta perch?" Lilith smiled.

"There's your yellow perch and your white perch and, I don't know—I guess that's it."

Lilith remembered asking her father how to tell the difference between a white birch tree and a gray birch. He had said, "By their behavior."

She watched Frederick clean the perch. Kneeling, he picked up a fish on the tip of the hunting knife and laid it on a paper plate. He slit it along the spinal cord and belly; then he put the knife down carefully beside him, cleaned the guts out with a thumbnail, and with strong fingers pulled out the gills and ripped off the skin. He managed to be both fastidious and sloppy at the same time.

"I guess I should make myself useful," Lilith said. She dug a hole with her hands to bury the fish entrails. The earth was cool, dark, and moist. When all the fish were clean, they washed their hands in canteen water. Frederick opened a beer.

"Your yellow perch is more green than yellow," Lilith said. Her use of the word "your" told Frederick she was inviting a playful joust.

"The background color of all your Darby fish is green, the color of the trees reflecting off the water," he said.

Lilith remembered finding the receipt for the hatchery fish. "What about trout? My father liked trout."

"Trout imitate the fall colors," Frederick said.

"And the white perch?"

"Noon sky? Pure light? I don't know; I never caught a white perch. But I caught a black bass."

"Black bass. Sounds big," she said.

"Yes, the black bass is big, but not black—green."

"We're all trying to get away from green, from the trees," Lilith said, then added, "Your yellow perch is a weeny fish."

"That's because your yellow perch is a true New Hampshire

native—small, aggressive, a school fish but ignorant and with an independent streak. Also, your yellow perch is greedy." Frederick took a pull on the champagne, wiped the bottle neck with his palm, and handed the bottle to Lilith.

"Greedy or only self-indulgent?"

"Let's get down to specifics," he said.

"The yellow perch is unattractive." Lilith touched one of the fish. The scales were hard.

"The yellow perch, your true native, pirates his neighbors' wealth, and breeds like a fiend; he's territorial but can't abide zoning ordinances. Knows they're scoped out to drive away the poor and ugly, his own species."

Lilith grabbed a fish, but released it with a shouted "ouch" as the sharp dorsal fin stuck her hand.

"He's mean!" she said.

"Doesn't like to be handled."

"Afraid of touch." Lilith revealed her insight with the arrogance of Upper Darby behind her.

"Scorned, despised, misunderstood, and unprotected by the state he swears his allegiance to," Frederick said, and now there was an edge to his voice.

Lilith could see that, behind the joking, he was serious. These fish meant something to him. The words brought home that meaning to him. His seriousness, perhaps because she suspected that he himself was unaware of it, sent a small fear through her. "I'm hungry," she said.

Frederick made a batter of beer and egg and flour. Lilith dipped the fish in the batter while Frederick heated up the frying pan over the hot coals of the fire. The fish were cool to her touch and flexible in her hands, so that they felt protestingly alive. She put them on a paper plate.

"Where's the cooking oil?" Frederick grumbled.

"I put it away."

"She put it away." He raised an eyebrow at her.

"Frederick!" she scolded him, but did retrieve the oil from his pack and handed it to him.

"All right, all right, I know I'm a slob." He poured oil in the frying pan, which was almost red hot. The oil immediately began to smoke.

She handed him the paper plate and he plopped the fish into the hot oil. They cooked very quickly. He watched them intently, and he knew just the moment to take them out. Lilith, too, sensed the moment, and because of this she felt fleetingly joined to him. They dined on perch, fistfuls of potato chips, and salad, washing down the food with champagne. The flesh of the fish was white, moist, and delicious.

Frederick ate with his fingers and wiped his hands on his pants; Lilith almost expected him to snort. She wanted to tell him that he needn't complain about the trash route as the source of the smell he claimed followed him around everywhere. He ought to look to his own table habits. She wasn't angry with him for his slovenliness or his occasional rudeness, but for his obtuseness. At the same time, she was drawn to him. He was like that grand old house of her father's, basically sound but in need of repairs, a project. In this respect, as in most others, he was completely unlike Garvin, who was, in his own mind and in the eyes of society, a successful and completed development, needing only minor upkeep. She watched Frederick strip the tender flesh from the bone between his teeth. His dark beard exaggerated the pinkness of his lips and tongue.

"Do you think you need saving?" she asked him.

The question took him off balance. "Religion? What do you mean?"

"Just saving."

He thought about the question between mouthfuls, and then he said, "Yah."

He was aware now that she was watching him. He didn't stop eating and drinking, but he did slow down. As she watched him, he watched her. She was now aware of herself eating. She should have been self-conscious, and in a way she was, but she was not shy or uneasy; she was enlivened; she felt like one called upon to perform. She used the silverware, eating carefully, consciously, with her head up and straight to the front, her elbows tucked into her sides, the way her grandmother had coached her as a child. She licked her lips with only the tip of her tongue and wiped them with a napkin. He imitated her, a student, doing exactly as she did, first in joking mockery and then with growing seriousness, so that by the end of the meal he was converted to her way. For that moment, she had made him over into someone else.

"Frederick—" she called for him.

"Oh, God, I love you," he said, coming toward her.

They kissed, rolling around in the dry leaves beside the campfire. It was, she thought, like kissing a bear with soft lips and tender hands. He even growled like an animal. For a few minutes, they were lost in one another. And then the sounds of the forest were too close, and the hardness of the ledges against her body began to hurt.

"Not now, I want to wait until it's dark." She pushed him away.

They decided to go for a walk. They hiked along the trail, Frederick in the lead, Lilith behind. Then they turned off on a side trail. The ground was rust-colored and soft under their feet from a mat of pine needles, for they had arrived at a stand of pines, huge and twisted, passed over by decades of loggers. Frederick looked up at the trees, stopped, grabbed a branch, and swung his body skyward. Lilith watched him scramble up the tree as if he'd been born in it.

Frederick looked out at the Trust, at the pond below, at the ledges rising above him, at the hills and mountains beyond.

185

Maybe . . . maybe he could stay in New Hampshire after all; maybe he belonged here; maybe he'd find a way to open up these hills—or open up himself to the hills; maybe he and Lilith . . . Then he saw something below that interested him. He shimmied down the tree.

"Strange place. Never noticed it before," he said.

"What kind of place?"

"I think it's an old quarry. Small one, though."

"My great-grandfather built those quarries."

"Let's take a look."

So off they went on an adventure, the heavyset young man with a big knife strapped to his hip and the tall young woman with the yellow-and-red cloth band around her head. The sun was going down over the ridge of the Trust when they arrived at the quarry, surprisingly near the town road but camouflaged from it by a dense cover of young hemlocks.

They explored, climbing down the rocks, which appeared unnatural because they were dynamite-split. It was the kind of quarry that had been a mistake. The vein of quartz had been thin and at the surface. The site was soon abandoned. At the bottom was a small, scummy pond. Below, it was hot, humid, and quiet.

When they reached the water, Lilith said, "You could hide in these rocks down here, and nobody would find you."

"Why would anybody want to hide in a place like this?"

"I don't know, but I think about it," Lilith said.

They meandered around a bit, then rested. Without realizing it, they parted, not by sight, but by self. Lilith sat wedged between some rocks, where she could feel the protection of the earth and the mystery of her secrets, and Frederick squatted by the pond, where he could feel the freedom of the sky and the mystery of the waters. For a few minutes, each was unaware of the physical presence of the other, and yet they were both thinking private thoughts about the other.

Whatever happened between herself and Frederick today, it would be tainted by her impending date with Garvin. If she had been sorry she had agreed to dine with Garvin, she might simply have decided to call off the date or told Frederick about it. It also would have been easy if she had decided she wanted Garvin, and not Frederick, but the issue was more confused than that. She wished to see Garvin out of duty and curiosity, reasons apart from the man himself. Perhaps her mother was right, perhaps Upper Darby was right. Her own people had no chance unless they stood together. It was odd but true, she thought, that the legal battles embroiling Monet and Garvin and Persephone and the town were family quarrels, desperate attempts not to divide further but to unite. So it was important that she see Garvin. Frederick, a wanderer with origins in Center Darby, was outside of this scheme; she had nothing to say to him about it.

Frederick, too, was withholding something from Lilith. He knew that Howard was hunting illegally on the Trust. He'd seen Howard and Cooty boiling the traps to get the man smell out of them. He'd seen the tranquilizer gun that Monet Salmon had given Howard after hiring him to track down and capture or kill this white bear that was supposed to be roaming the Trust lands. Howard might complain about his son dating the Squire's daughter, but he himself wasn't above taking money from the Squire's brother, especially if it meant a hunt. Even at this moment, his father might be on the Trust, hunting the white bear. It wasn't that Frederick wanted to protect Lilith or his father, and certainly not her uncle; he just didn't want any trouble.

Lilith joined him. "I want to go swimming," she said.

"Now?"

"Not now, not here, in Grace Pond," she said.

By the time they reached this new destination, it was dark and they were walking in a snake of light from above that

187

defined the path. The pond came upon them with a blast of moonlight out of the darkness of the forest. Several streams flowed through the Trust, but Grace Pond was the only water body of size. No road circled it, no cottages were built along its shores. Trees leaned over the waters, their branches tipped downward as if attempting to drink.

Frederick spread out his arms like some prophet of old and looked up at the stars. "I love this place—it's open. What I hate most about New Hampshire is that closed-in feeling, no sky, all of us hiding behind the trees."

"I like the rocks and the woods," Lilith said.

Lilith looked at the pond. The surface of the water was still, a distorted mirror of the sky above, so that she could see the stars as wavy yellow lines. When she was a girl, she had asked her father to bring her to the pond, but he had put her off. The waters on the Trust were part of his private world, and a daughter in tow would crowd that domain of self. But she had come here a couple times with her cousins. They had watched herons building nests in the highest trees.

Lilith and Frederick were at the water's edge when Lilith said, "Smells like dead fish."

"Probably hornpout fishermen. They clean the catch on shore."

"Nobody's supposed to use the Trust—it was my father's rule."

"Her father's law." Frederick chuckled. He couldn't see how upset she was, and he couldn't tell by her voice, because she was so practiced at excluding her emotion from her speech.

"Well, *he* didn't climb trees to get drunk!" Almost before her words were out, Lilith felt a need to apologize, although for what she wasn't exactly sure; after all, she was the injured party. She could never marry this young man. They would never be able to fight, because neither would know who the injured party was. Her ambivalent feeling—not exactly guilt, not exactly condescension—was the old familiar attitude of Upper Darby toward Center Darby. That attitude—unnamed, hidden beneath layers of amenities, manners, rituals, platitudes, and the gyroscopic directive to defend one's position, the discomfort of the feeling bound to it—was one reason Upper Darby had little to do with Center Darby. For Lilith the feeling was tied in with loathing and, strangely, desire, desire not only for Frederick, but for a way to make everything right.

Frederick translated Lilith's words as nothing more than another tease. He was going to one-up her. "Come here, I'll show you something," he said, leading Lilith along the shore until they came to a tiny hidden cove. In the weeds was a flat-bottom wooden rowboat.

"A boat? What is it doing here?" Lilith was offended.

"Your father put it there."

"My father? What do you know about my father?" She was shaking inside with rage, but she kept her voice under control. There was even a touch of jocularity in it.

"Maybe not your father. But somebody with the Trust. That boat has been here for years. Everybody knows about it."

"What are you telling me?"

"Grace Pond is a whore—everybody uses her," Frederick said.

"I hate that. I hate the way you say it." She pulled away from him, and finally he understood how hurt and upset she was.

"I'm sorry, I didn't know," he said. And his sensitivity and sincerity were all it took to soothe her. They walked to the boulder on the edge of the shore.

They sat side by side, looking out at the water. "I love you, Lilith. I'm just crazy, forever in love with you." He spoke these words with love's muddle of despair and hope. "I wish . . . I wish . . . I had something to give you."

"What difference does it make whether we love each other

or not? You're leaving." She loved him right now. But what about tomorrow or next year? She was not sure how she would feel then.

He put his hand on her knee and bent toward her. "Come with me, see the country with me," he said.

"In the truck?"

"You and me—live free or die."

She could smell his sweat from the exertions of walking; she could smell the maleness of him; and she could smell the fish they'd eaten together.

"I don't know," she said.

"Do you want to stay here, go back to your college, marry a lawyer or something? I can understand if you do. I just want to know what you really want. If I thought I had a chance for you, I'd stay."

"I want—I need—to find something here in Darby," Lilith said. "I don't even know what it is. There's nothing we can really do for each other," Lilith said.

"Maybe Howie's right—we don't belong together."

"Maybe," Lilith said. And again she heard the soft moan of the night on the Trust, the birds, the whisper of a rising breeze, the buzzing of insects. "When are you leaving?"

"Couple days."

Lilith removed the headband from her own head and tied it around Frederick's. She said, "When the legal stuff is over with, they'll bury my father and my brother. They'll have a service. Maybe then I can start over. I have this need, this craving for some kind of ceremony."

"You and me, we don't know what we're looking for," Frederick said. "But I know this: it's the same thing. But for you it's here, and for me it's out there. So let's say goodbye."

Lilith stood on top of the rock. Frederick watched her undress. Then he slipped off his T-shirt and blue jeans. The white of his jockey shorts was all wrong in this darkness, and Lilith grabbed them at his hips and pulled them down.

They moved from the rock into shin-deep water over some sand. The water was warmer than at Darby Lake, caressing their legs. Lilith stepped toward the depths. After two steps, the bottom fell away and she was up to her waist in the pond and she could feel muck pulling at her feet. She pushed off, going down. She swam underwater as far as she could before surfacing. Frederick was fifteen or twenty feet behind.

"Scared me—jeez." She heard his voice, some frantic splashing, and then a return echo. She could tell he was a sure swimmer but unpracticed and untutored. She swam a circle around him, her legs kicking hard, her hands cutting through the surface. Out here, she was his physical superior. She went under again. She could just make out his torso pushing up and vanishing into a silver radiance that was the moonlight on the surface of the pond. It passed through her mind to grab his feet and pull him under, right to the bottom, the bottom of everything. She surfaced beside him, and then they were swimming together, going out, toward the middle, the distant shore dark and menacing as the one they had left from. Out there, in the middle, they embraced, legs kicking, arms around one another, mouth to mouth, hip to hip. He was ready.

"Let's go in to shore," she said.

"No, here," he said.

They tried, failed, and swam back to shore. In the shallows, half in the pond and half out, they made love, like some new breed of amphibian, not sure in which medium they belonged.

5

Trying On for Size

After she said goodbye to her lover but before she saw the
white, vanishing wisps of the vanishing morning mist and
came down from the ledges, Lilith smelled the burn of the sun
on that mist, a sweet-dank smell of grass and thin layers of
dead leaves vanishing into soft humus over a granite shield
thousands of feet thick. It was going to be a hot day, busy at
Darby Lake this afternoon. She looked forward to her work,
her place in the lifeguard's chair, above it all, out of reach,
unnoticed and yet important and involved in the scheme of
things. She looked forward to playing her Counting Heads
game, tense because it was like trying to map moving clouds,
relaxing because the concentration shielded her mind from its
own weather.

After she crossed the stone wall between the woods and the
fields that surrounded her house, Lilith began to hurry. In the
distance, the dark shingles on the house seemed to hold on to
and hold off the summer sun. Lilith felt the call of duty: leave
the woods behind, leave love behind; come home and be the
daughter, come home and be the future; leave hope behind,
hold arms out to obligation. She was almost running when she
arrived.

Something didn't look right. It took her a moment to pin
down what it was. The Saab was not in its usual parking spot

beside the barn. It suddenly seemed important that she see her mother. She went into the house, calling out, "I'm home!" No answer. Persephone must be running an errand or visiting her friend Natalie.

Once in the house, her house, alone, Lilith calmed down. This is what it would be like after her mother had left for Australia. Nobody around to tell her what to do. Her house: she tested out the idea by shaping the words in her mind— *my house, Lilith's house, the Salmon house.* Her next thought was that it would take an act of will to make the house her own, or else it would disappear in the ether of memory as a place that belonged to others. She opened the windows to let out the odor of stale cigarette smoke. She marched around with a wastebasket, dumping True cigarette butts into it. Then she chucked the contents into the fireplace and burned them. She was almost finished cleaning when she ran across Persephone's typed note, right in front of her nose, tacked to the wooden mantel over the fireplace in the Hearth Room. "Gone— Legal business and then some! Preparing for departure. Monet to take Reggie's things, and to make offer. Hear him out! P." Monet? Reggie's things? Offer? Legal business? That last phrase shouted at her. What did all this mean? Scribbled in pencil under the typescript was a telephone number in Massachusetts. Lilith called the number.

"Archambault Funeral Home," said the voice at the other end of the line.

"This is Lilith Salmon. I'm looking for my mother, Persephone Salmon," Lilith said.

"Yes. Mrs. Salmon said you might call. She's not available at the moment. She asked us to tell you that she was busy on legal business. But you may leave a message." The voice grated with the Lowell accent.

"Message? I have no message," Lilith said and hung up.

Legal business? Persephone's phrase careened about in Lilith's head. She had suspected her mother was sleeping with Lawrence Dracut. Now she was sure of it. It would be like Persephone to seduce her lawyer. It would be like Persephone to couch the affair in the context of a legal battle. Or the other way around. It would be like Persephone to relieve her tension with illicit sex with a married man. Lilith had no basis for her suspicions. She was like those Biblical writers of old, finding God and the devil not through evidence in a search for truth but through need in a search for meaning.

Lilith showered, dressed, and discovered all at once that she was very hungry, for she had skipped breakfast. She whipped up an early lunch, a green salad with Cheddar cheese and English muffins. She was just finishing a cup of coffee, about ready to go off to Darby Lake, when she heard cars pulling into the driveway. She went to the front door to see who had come down her road. Her uncle Monet and Dr. Marcia Pascal stood beside a U-Haul truck. Behind the truck was Abnaki Jordan's ragged, jagged Jeep. At the sight of Lilith, the sly Jordan and the strange Asian dismounted from their vehicle.

"We're here for Reggie's things." Monet barged in, his momentum carrying Lilith and Marcia into the hallway.

Abnaki and Whack Two followed. Their presence in the house disturbed Lilith. Abnaki carried on his face the thin, wispy smile of a burglar; Whack Two's eyes searched about hungrily—he didn't covet the goods, but the way of life. It struck Lilith how oddly the four of them were dressed: Monet in blue jeans, Mexican print shirt and clogs; Dr. Marcia Pascal looking like a gypsy out of an old movie in her flowing skirt, white blouse, jangling earrings, and red, red lipstick; Abnaki in his camouflage outfit; the Asian sidekick in black cottons. By contrast, she thought about Frederick in his workman's jumper or on-the-road blue jeans and T-shirt, and Garvin in his standard suit and tie, uniforms for all time.

Monet said to Abnaki, "The room is upstairs, to the right—

with the red fireplace. Bring up some boxes and start loading."

"What's going on?" Lilith's voice was sharp. This was her house.

"I'm sorry, Lilith. I got carried away," Monet said, the softness in his voice so out of character that it revealed to Lilith a shadow of the resentment he was attempting to conceal.

"I'm sorry, too. Please come in." Lilith did not feel sorrow, but she did feel that her response should indicate some expression of vague remorse.

Lilith led Monet and Marcia to the Hearth Room. She should offer them something—snacks or drinks. But she fought against the directive to be gracious. "Please sit down," she said.

Marcia sat on the couch, crossing her legs, throwing her head back.

Monet remained standing and, in the tradition of the Salmon men who had come before him, displayed his nervousness and irritability by criticizing his help. "I should check on Abnaki. I trust him about as far as I can throw his pal." He went into the hallway.

"Monet is a little nervous, I'm afraid." Marcia smiled easily. Her beauty and sense of relaxed command took Lilith's breath away.

Lilith heard Monet shout something, and a moment later he had returned to the Hearth Room.

Marcia tossed Monet a knowing glance. Lilith caught the look and calculated that Monet would make some kind of speech. The offer her mother had mentioned? Monet answered Marcia with a smile of mouth but not eyes, an Upper Darby gesture signifying mild annoyance. He said to Lilith, "Persephone and I had a talk."

Lilith knew what that meant. Things discussed, things decided, her concurrence expected.

"Tell me." Lilith counseled herself to pay attention. After

all, he was her uncle, her elder, the only Salmon male remaining in Upper Darby.

"Persephone has agreed to support our case at the hearing," Monet said. "Dracut and Barnum are in discussions right now. Lilith, we have some new evidence."

"New evidence?" Lilith was growing uneasy.

"An Indian burial ground on the Trust. Can you believe it? Maybe even more than one. Tribe up in Maine laying claim to it. We're going to pool our resources with them. Barnum says it's much better stuff for stopping the Prell development than the white bear."

"Indian graves—where?" Lilith asked. The mention of Indians sent a little thrill through her. Maybe there was no reason for her to be uneasy. Maybe everything was going to work out.

"Near Grace Pond," Monet said. "We believe the Indians burned the bodies in pyres, then buried the bones of the deceased with their possessions."

Lilith was contemplating the wonders of pyres and ancient rites when she was distracted by banging sounds upstairs. "What are these men doing in my house? Are they in my father's room?" As she spoke, she felt as if she were pleading with someone to confirm that this really was her house.

Marcia caught Lilith's tone, read her as Monet could not. "We're intruders here; please forgive us," Marcia said, then turned to Monet. "You'd better explain."

"Lilith, after your father died, I asked Persephone for some of his things, clothes, desk, pipes, books—all his personal effects. At the time, Persephone couldn't see her way clear toward surrendering them."

"But now she says it's all right," Lilith said with just enough disbelief to rock Monet on his heels slightly.

"That's correct," he said.

Lilith wondered if her mother's sudden generosity meant she had decided to stay in Upper Darby. It didn't seem likely.

Persephone had battled Garvin on one front, to prevent Reggie from being interred on the Trust lands, and Monet on another front, to prevent Reggie from being returned to the old cemetery. So, what to make of this news? Perhaps Persephone had given up, had understood that this fight was draining away not only what was left of her money but what was left of her youth. Then it dawned on Lilith that some kind of deal had been made. Persephone had relented on Monet's request for Reggie's things, but it wasn't like Persephone to give something for nothing. Lilith was fatigued and confused; there was so much she didn't know.

"I camped overnight on the Trust," Lilith said. "I come back to find my mother gone, leaving me a strange note. Now you're here. What's going on?"

Lilith's forthrightness seemed to frighten Monet. "Marcia, talk to Lilith about our proposal for the house." He glanced in the direction of the hall. Then, with the grace and fear of a surprised stag, he bounded toward the stairs.

It seemed to Lilith that she was under bombardment from distant artillery. "The house? What about my house?" Lilith challenged Marcia.

"Your uncle and I are going to be married." Marcia deflected Lilith's question.

"Congratulations." Lilith did not feel particularly congratulatory.

"So many things to consider," Marcia said. "I can see that you are upset, and have an urgent need for information. It's such a problem with Upper Darby, this desire to understand everything. Where I come from, we narrow our anxiety to what we know. We worry that we are hungry; we worry that our children are sick. Here you worry about what you do not know. Listen to me for a while. Can you?"

Lilith nodded in resignation. Marcia began a long recitation about her life with Monet. Marcia had been born in Brazil.

197

She'd met Monet in Bogotá, where she was studying at the university for a doctoral degree in biology. Lilith surmised that Marcia considered Monet her intellectual inferior but her social superior; there was no doubt he was her financial superior. They wished to marry and have children. There was a problem. Marcia could conceive a child, but she could not carry a child. Science would save them, however. Tied in with these problems of parenthood was their longing to set down roots. They wished to start their own family and re-establish the Salmons as Upper Darby's first family.

"Monet wants to sell the Butterworth house. He wants to return to the Salmon house," Marcia said.

"My house?"

"We want to buy it, Lilith."

Lilith remembered the painful discussion she'd had with her mother in the old cemetery. "Money—you know about the money," she blurted out.

"Yes, we know about the money," Marcia said. "Your uncle was uncomfortable with the idea of approaching you. Because of the money."

"I don't know," Lilith said. "It's my house, and I think right now I want to keep it."

"Lilith, your father wanted a Salmon in his house. He wanted to carry on the Salmon name. Monet can do that. You cannot—"

"I can."

"A single college girl, with no resources but a house and a fund for her college education. Suppose you marry? What happens then to the Salmon name? If you have children, you'd have to go through the trouble of convincing a husband to allow his child to take your name. Who in Darby would accept that, even if it was legal? If you do not marry, there is the problem of money. This house demands so much in upkeep and taxes. Lilith, you can't afford to live in this house."

"Money," Lilith said, as if at issue was alchemy and the word "money" was an ingredient in a secret, only partly known formula.

"That's right. Lilith, your father meant for you to sell the house and collect your inheritance. Monet wants you to be financially secure—"

"And he wants my house! And how can you say what my father wanted? None of us knows."

"Be that as it may. Think about our offer. It's an option."

Maybe Marcia was right. Maybe what she should do is sell the house, finish her college education, and never come back to Darby. Start new someplace else.

"Give me some time," Lilith said.

"Of course," said Marcia.

Monet swept into the Hearth Room from the hallway. For a split second, Lilith felt thrown back in time. Monet was wearing her father's clothes, cotton-twill trousers, blue oxford shirt, yellow tie, madras jacket.

Monet was too caught up in the thrill of his own moment to notice that Lilith was stunned. "I'm devoting the rest of my life to keeping your father's dream for the Trust from being corrupted. Do you believe me, Lilith?" he said.

Lilith mumbled a yes.

The Asian came between them, carrying a box. He smelled of the sweet sweat of young men. Abnaki, behind him, said, "We got everything."

"Everything?" Lilith questioned, then added, "Please leave a few of my father's things. I just want . . . reminders."

"Not the clothes—I insist on keeping the clothes." Monet was still excited, a little crazy right now, as Marcia could see.

"Keepsakes—she wants keepsakes. Isn't that so?" Marcia glanced from Monet to Lilith.

Monet grabbed the box from Whack Two, and spilled out notebooks, a pipe rack, a compass, some audio tapes of classical music. "Do you want more?" Monet asked, loath to give up even this box. His face shone.

"This is fine." Lilith knelt on the floor and began refilling the box.

After Monet and his entourage had left, Lilith went outside, in the fields, where she'd had a dream to create a huge vegetable garden and a hedge of lilac bushes. Now it seemed that any thoughts she might have about this house and land were unrealistic. It had all been decided for her. She should sell the house, collect her money, and vanish forever from Darby.

She was just leaving for the lake when Garvin called to remind her of their date.

6

The Native

Frederick thought he'd drive to Tuckerman to buy some stuff for his trip, but when he reached the Route 21 turnoff, he impulsively veered off the road into the parking lot of the Jordan auction barn. A food mart along with a ramshackle store selling discounted retail goods were housed in a barn that had once belonged to a farmer named Flagg. The only outdoor evidence of the discount store was a crude plywood marker over the entry that said "Everything on Sale." The place had no name as such, so it had become known by its former name, "the auction barn." The parking lot was nearly always clogged with cars.

Around back was the convenience store that so offended Joe Ancharsky. Here also were self-service gas pumps, a coin-operated car wash, and a laundromat. The food mart, in contrast to Joe's store, was busy, alive, and, as Joe had pointed out, no different from any other convenience store in the United States. Nevertheless, the general-store atmosphere that Joe had consciously and lovingly cultivated in his store had in Jordan's Kwick Stop spontaneously generated of itself. People arrived, bought goods, chewed the fat, and went on their way. The owner, Carlton "Critter" Jordan, was making a mint.

Behind the cash register stood a tall, attractive woman in

her sixties, with long, almost white hair and a Mona Lisa smile. She was serene in her transactions with customers, never hurrying, but never wasting time either. She was one who had mastered living with herself and with the world. Frederick recognized her as Estelle, the Jordan Witch.

There was a lull in the business around the register when Frederick approached. At that point, the Witch said, "You're the Elman boy, *aincha?*"

Frederick looked deeply into the Witch's eyes. It was a fierce look he'd inherited from his father, and although he knew it for what it was, he did not know half its power for making people uncomfortable. He only knew that those under the gun of the look almost always turned away their eyes. Not the Witch.

"That's my name," Frederick said.

"You want to buy something." She looked at him curiously, as if she were a small boy inspecting a hellgrammite.

Frederick gave her his order.

"Going someplace?"

"Jeez, you're nosy." Frederick was enjoying the encounter.

" 'Course I am."

"Getting out of Darby."

"I don't blame you. You'll find your goods through the door." The Witch pointed. "In the auction barn."

"I figured."

"So, how's your old man? Healing up?"

"Nothing's going to heal his personality, but his leg's doing all right," Frederick said.

"It's a fine thing when a young man works in his father's business," the Witch said, and Frederick could feel the spit of her sarcasm. Then she gave him a just-fooling feint of a smile.

There were two entries into the convenience market, one from the lot outside, the other from the discount store next door. It was through that door to the discount store that Frederick meandered now. He had to step over a huge hound dozing in the entry. The dog glowered at him through one open eye. "What's your problem?" Frederick challenged the big mutt, who closed the open eye, as if to say, You're not worth bothering with. Natural light poured into the convenience store through display windows, but here in the discount store there was only the bluish-cream light of neon bulbs and the faint smell of a barn.

Just about everything could be bought here, from firearms to dolls, from furniture to Christmas-tree ornaments, from tools to paintings on black velvet, from pine-cone arrangements made by the Ladies of the Darby Grange to Korean-made computers gotten cheap by Critter in a deal through a broker in the Virgin Islands (Frederick's father had been among the customers). Things gave the impression not of having been laid out for display but, rather, of having been piled here and there. The haphazardness reminded Frederick of the forests of the Trust, a second- and third-growth forest; here grew second- and third-line merchandise; the goods, like the trees, were thickly displayed, tangled, varied, disorienting in the confusion of mind they could engender, sustaining in the protection of mind they could afford. Frederick figured that, if New Hampshire went to war against, say, Massachusetts, these—auctions barns and auction-barn-like forests—were what was worth fighting for.

He heard laughter, then the sound of a man's voice. A small crowd had gathered near the front of the store beside a table with a sign that said "Free Coffee." Critter Jordan was holding forth. Frederick did not know Critter personally, but he knew of him. Critter ran the auction barn, and he had speculated on real estate until he owned most of the run-down housing in Darby Depot. The Squire of Darby Depot (nobody used the term to Critter's face) was surprisingly young. But there was no boy left in him at all. In appearance he resembled a suc-

cessful stock-car race driver, rugged, almost handsome, but
going to fat. Jordan was kin to the Witch, and one of the few
financially successful Jordans.

"Oh, I fought it tooth and nail," he preached to the crowd.
"I used to say, 'When a woman's ready to calve, a man's place
is in the corridor.' I wouldn't admit it, but I was scared. Well,
my wife kept after me, kept after me, and so, to preserve the
peace, I says, 'Whatever you want, my sweet.'

"Come the big day, and her water broke and I brought her
to the hospital. They checked her in, weighed her and spread
her out to measure her you-know-what, and assigned her to
a room. 'When can I go to the birthing room?' she says. 'Not
until you go into hard labor,' the doctor says. 'You call me
when you're ready,' I says. 'You ain't going nowhere,' she says.
'This one's a trooper,' the doctor says. 'Yes, indeed,' I says.

"So I stayed.

"She lay there and she grunted and she groaned, and she
cursed me like it was all my fault, but do you think she'd go
into hard labor? *Nooo.* This went on all night, and I'm still
by her side, awake, holding her hand—when she'll let me.
Meanwhile, her attention—can you believe it?—is on the television set.

"She says, 'I wish we had the cable in Darby Depot.' I says,
'I'll work on it.' And that's how come today we have this satellite
dish in the yard. Gets every channel in the world, cost thousands of dollars—no lie—and do you think I ever look at it?
Never! No time."

At this point in his narration, Critter seemed to sense an
alien presence in his store. He stopped talking, looked around,
took in the scene. His eyes fell on Frederick. The audience
grew restless. One couple drifted off. Somebody asked Critter
for the exact number of channels the dish could draw in. Six
hundred and thirteen, Critter lied, then went on with his story.

"Finally, I says, 'I've had enough, I'm sacking out.'" Although Critter never looked at him again, Frederick had the impression he was being directly addressed. "So they rolled in a bed for me with a plastic cover on it. Lights glaring down, TV on, clank clank with the hospital trays, still wearing my paper clothes, I more or less slept. Next morning, five o'clock, I wake up, and there she is, watching the television. I says, 'You in labor?' She says, 'I think so.' I says, 'Sure—shut the tube off and go to sleep.'

"So we do the whole thing again. All day long and half the night, and the doctor says, 'This is not a go. We've got to induce labor.' And then he says maybe it'll be like the last one, where they had to cut. Delphina don't want to hear that. 'No way,' she says, and why can't we go into the birthing room, like that's going to do the trick. The doctor says they've got to induce labor and you can't go into the birthing room until you are actually in labor. Rule. Delphina says, 'I will not have this baby anywhere else but in the birthing room.' I look at the doctor, he looks at me, we shrug, we go into the birthing room.

"I says, 'Delphina, we're stuck; time we put it in four-wheel drive.' She laughed at that—and splook! I saw a head. I says, 'Hey, I can see the head.' The doctor and two-hundred-and-forty-odd nurses, they all gathered round. A minute later he flew out—whoosh! I mean, he was airborne. And the doctor caught him." Critter made a sound like a cork popping off a champagne bottle, then talked on. "As he arched over, I could see his two little—you know—that makes him a boy. I says to the doc, 'Hey, it's one of us.' I punched the nurse and I kissed the doctor. I was ninety-nine thousand feet off the ground, and I didn't come down for two days. Absolutely the most incredible experience of my life. Any man who doesn't sit in on the birth of his children is missing out on *the* big event in the history of everything."

Critter's story disturbed Frederick even while it sent a shiver of yearning through him. He felt as he did on a hunt, anticipating a deer about to leap from cover, loathing the idea of killing it, loving the motion of the gun swinging from his shoulder to a line, seeing the deer for one split second—perfect, still, immense in his field of vision—firing, making it his . . . his sorrow.

Frederick slunk out of the store without buying his provisions. Driving through Center Darby village, he spotted Lilith going into the new restaurant. She was on the arm of Garvin Prell, the Upper Darby guy he'd seen tooling around town on a bicycle. Well, he thought, she didn't waste much time. He stepped on the accelerator and headed for the Trust.

Usually, he'd sleep in the rear of his truck, but tonight he decided to stay under the stars, close to the place where he and Lilith had last made love. As he drifted off in his sleeping bag along the shore of Grace Pond, he could still smell dead fish.

Six- and seven-pound native brook trout used to populate Grace Pond, or so the stories go. No one knows for sure, because no one alive has seen a native trout that big. This we know. The brook trout, or the native, as it is referred to locally, is a beautiful fish to behold and a powerful fish to feel on the end of a line. This, too, we know. Grace Pond is not what it was. People busy themselves around ponds and try to improve them, as they try to improve anything that is perfectly agreeable. The local ponds were dammed early on by the white settlers looking for water power, so today the ponds are greater in area and depth than ever before. You would think the native trout, like the waters, would be bigger and lovelier. This is not the case. The native has lost out. The reasons for this situation lie in the nature of the people who settled the region and the nature of the fish.

As fly fishermen are wont to say, especially when holding forth before non–fly fishermen, the native trout is not a true trout, but a char, a northern-clime fish. It thrives in the cold; heat and the filth of heat—festering life—upset and disorient it. It's a primitive creature, narrow-minded, vulnerable to change. The only thing that saves it from being just another conservative is its beauty and fighting spirit. Unfortunately, it's not so smart. It responds to a worm like a liberal to a new idea. So there you have the native's problem: this fish is a mixed metaphor.

The most beautiful creature in its environment, the brook trout is touchy about environment. Warm water, dirty water, can kill it. When the white folk came to these hills and created Darby, they built factories and saw mills and tanneries along the streams and ponds. They polluted the water, and they killed the native. The government came along, serious and mannered, and its agents "managed" the trout ponds and many streams, poisoning the water (for the pond's own good), and introduced a government version of the native—a pretty-enough fish, just as stupid as the wild variety, but short-lived. That's why today's brook trout never gets big, but it's been here so long, and the true native is so far gone, that this newcomer is now being referred to as a native.

It is this "native," the state's put-and-take, foot-long-at-best brook trout, that is the local fly fisherman's sole pursuit—when, of course, he fishes locally. Trout fishing locally is generally unproductive. Success is measured in aesthetic moments. "Wonderful rise on Grace Pond," an Upper Darby fly fisherman will say to his wife. He likes this kind of fishing because it's solitary. The fly fisherman owns lots of land and a big house and he's proud to say his woman is his equal and he has a good job—he's a lawyer, for heaven's sake, or a doctor, or an insurance man, or a drug-rehab counselor, or a Realtor (don't you dare write him a note without capitalizing that "R"), or, simply, a businessman—but pity this poor fellow. He has a lot of everything, but he doesn't have as much as his father had in the way of free enterprise of the soul. Where the Darby Depot and Center Darby fishermen think of themselves as ones who are "getting ahead," the Upper Darby man knows full well he is falling behind. He can't get over the feeling he's living the American dream in reverse, and yet, despite all this, something in him believes his brand of human being is better than any other, and he also knows he mustn't be a snob—Grandfather was a snob—and so he cultivates some generalized guilt and that more or less takes care of that problem.

He dreams about a place and time that was, and he's scared of his kids, and periodically his wife goes crazy, and he suspects she's having an affair with her therapist, unless he's a therapist himself, in which case he finds his own feelings thinned by the dreary rain of his patients' tales, unless he's a patient himself, in which case he understands finally and completely that he's nowhere, what he wants never was—cannot be. He turns to his wife and blurts out those words from the front porch of his mind—"Cannot be!"

"Yes, dear?" His wife's question mark burns him like a brand.

"I'm restless," he says.

"It's your age," she says.

Several days later, she presents him with a book—*How to Turn Fifty and Like It*. He thanks her, he smiles; she can see the book will not do the job. She doesn't understand, but she says nothing. What's to say? He doesn't understand either. He's got a stoic streak, and he suffers himself in silence. Or he tells her everything, and now she does understand and tells him not to worry. That's how she phrases her advice: "Not to worry."

Either way—nothing. So he digs out the fly rod and goes fishing. Or perhaps he only thinks about fishing: if he's the type, that's enough. He dies happy.

He assumes that fly fishing is the only kind of fishing worth contemplating. He's right. Fly fishing is the cocaine of angling—instantly addictive for life. The euphoria of casting a fly is everything anybody can feel, and yet it is not enough.

"Not enough—it's not enough," he says to his wife.

"Yes, dear?"

"Bamboo," he says.

"Oriental brushwork?" She is curious now.

"Orvis," he says.

"Ohhh," she says. He's going to buy a fishing pole. He thinks of his rod and reel as instruments. He corrects her when she uses the term "fishing pole." She's smart enough to repeat her mistake from time to time, just to keep him on his toes; she's smart enough, too, to keep it a secret that she finds his intensity on this matter quite funny.

He becomes an equipment fanatic. He studies books about insects, so that he can "match the hatch," as the saying goes. But these stocked trout can't read. Soon he figures out he can catch them on imitations of hatchery liver pellets. Such a matched hatch is disappointing. So he goes to Vermont, to the Battenkill, where there are some real trout that eat real bugs on the water. Vermont lasts a year. Then it's on to Quebec. Canada is not enough. Montana is not enough.

His friends say he's quite the traveler.

"Mid-life crisis," his wife says, and his friends nod. Of course . . . of course.

The Upper Darby fly fisher will eat his catch, but since he releases most of the fish he catches—when, on occasion, he catches fish—he doesn't eat much fish. He will order fish in restaurants, because it's good for his health. Occasionally, he will express an opinion about the fish he eats in restaurants, but he'll almost always be talking about the sauce rather than the actual flesh.

Somewhere—say, on an overnight camp out in Idaho—it dawns on him: like the stocked brookies of Grace Pond, he

209

doesn't belong in Darby. Yet he was born there, he's a native. Home is nowhere. At that moment of realization, he understands why he fishes: to reach through a surface and come away with something alive. He says to his wife, "Something I have to tell you."

"Yes, dear?" She's on guard.

He can't speak the words; they are too painful. He buries his knowledge.

"I think I'll go to Argentina," he says. "I hear they have brookies there, ten-pounders. Brought in. You understand?"

"No," she says.

"Okay," he says, and that's that.

In the muck of New Hampshire water bodies lives a tough, ugly little fish we call the hornpout. Other places, he's a bullhead, a lowly member of the lowly catfish family, feeds at night, easily caught on a worm, but hard to kill, and prickly spines near his head (the horns) can stick you when you are removing the hook. The hornpout is black and slippery in the hand. Very tasty fried in butter.

Around dark on Darby Lake, when the trout fishers are sliding into shore in their canoes and the bass men are backing their motorized fiberglass platforms onto boat trailers, the harvesters of hornpout are launching their flat-bottom johnboats. They prefer aluminum for no better reason than that it's cheap. Sometimes they scrounge leaky wooden rowboats. Wooden oarlocks crick and creak in delicate night air over water; aluminum oarlocks clunk and clank. These are Darby Depot folk. The Darby Depot fisher pursues the hornpout for the purpose of eating it. The taste of his own fish brings him tremendous pleasure, because he's predisposed toward cannibalism.

Hornpout fishing is productive. Success is measured in numbers. "Caught fifty," a Darby Depot fellow will brag to his wife. Actually he caught twenty-two. Darby Depot people like the activity of fishing because it's sociable. You might find two men (drinking), or a man and a boy (the man bossing the boy around), or two men and two boys (the men drinking, the boys heehawing), or a guy and his girl (likely fishing from shore, he bragging about his *cah*, which might not *staht* when they leave, she complaining about the bugs), or a man and his wife (abstaining from quarreling during these hours), or an old codger and his old woman (silent), or an entire family (loud). The men bring six-packs of beer (beer is their salvation) and, standing half drunk in johnboats, they pee off the side.

Equipment for hornpout fishing is modest, consisting of a hook, a worm, a sinker, pliers to pull the hook out of the fish's throat, a flashlight to see by, a can to hold the worms, a bucket to hold the fish. It's desirable but not necessary to have a rod and reel. Such equipment is usually available from the shed of, say, a stepfather on the lam, or it can be bought used at a yard sale or new at the Woolworth store in Tuckerman.

For cleaning, a hornpout is staked through the head on a nail on a board. The skin is cut above the gills and pulled off with pliers. That's all there is to it. The guts that don't spill out are whisked away with a thumbnail. Some men can perform the cleaning task with their bare hands alone. They break the head off, ripping downward; this decapitates, skins, and cleans the fish. The men don't tell you how this task is done, and you can't tell from watching their hands, because it is all done faster than the eye can follow. A man about to clean a hornpout bare-handed gets the same look of concentration as a karate expert about to chop at a concrete block. A Center Darby or an Upper Darby man might dip into his reservoir of spiritual energy to help him catch a fish, but only a Darby Depot man will make the same investment in the interest of cleaning a fish.

The people of Darby Depot know the hornpout intimately and speak of him in the third person singular, as if he were a

flawed but important relative, a drunken uncle who has out-
lived his soberer brothers. It is whispered among those who
know better that the horns are poisonous, and so the hornpout
is also feared, feared out of all proportion to the danger he
poses. It's as if a quarry is not worthy of pursuit or consumption
unless it can hurt you. So the hornpout is at once revered and
despised. The people of Upper Darby understand in a felt, if
not a figured, way that they have found a creature even lower
in the order of things than themselves, and they rejoice in the
knowledge.

The hornpout is of little or no concern to the general public.
The state does not regulate the fishing of hornpout. The hornpout is not an endangered species, and even if it were, only
the Darby Depot folk would notice, and they wouldn't do anything about the situation. There is neither a need nor a desire
among the populace to concern itself with this little black fish,
because, unlike game fish, the hornpout invites no self-
congratulating symbolism. The hornpout is not "wary" or
"moody" or "discriminating," nor is it a great "fighter"—words
ascribed to fish such as trout and bass, fish commanding respect. Why should a trout or a bass command respect from
the general public, and not a hornpout? This is my answer: If
I were a foreign agent, I would write in my report, "The American male thinks of himself as wary, moody, discriminating—
a fighter."

The Center Darby man is what happens when the Darby Depot
man gets out from under clan and habit and strikes out for
the middle class. Often the origin of Center Darby folk is another place, far from Tuckerman County, perhaps even a foreign country. The Center Darby man has, so to speak, put the
Darby Depot of his past behind him. He schools himself a bit,
lands a decent job, and marries an ambitious woman. Or he
is transformed by war or religion or Dame Fortune—shit luck,

in the local idiom. Although he couldn't bear to think of himself as ordinary, as common, he likes to refer to himself as the common man, a typical American—"What do you want from me?" he says to his wife. "I'm a guy, just a guy."

A common man, to achieve a feeling of distinction, searches for a distinguished fish to pursue. Any distinguished fish will suffice, but a distinguished fish that the man can identify with is preferred. Thus the common man seeks a common fish that itself has achieved distinction. It's not surprising, then, that the preferred game fish of Center Darby is the bass, a distinguished member of the undistinguished sunfish family. Following the twisted streets of human reasoning, it makes sense, too, that the Center Darby man holds in contempt the common sunfish, because it reminds him who, underneath, he is.

The black bass is a school fish but with an independent streak. It can be daring, impulsive, on occasion brave, but not contemplative or philosophical, even as fish go. If a bass were a man, it would be a bar patron in a television beer commercial. The bass will chase a plug, sweep live bait off the bottom, even rise to a fly. It can be taken on just about anything, especially when it's breeding. But it's fickle. Sometimes it likes red, sometimes blue. Sometimes it sulks and cannot be roused for its dinner. During these moments, it sits on the bottom still as stone, from all appearances a deep thinker. Actually, the bass is like a guy who hates his job, who on Saturday night in the living room, after the wife and kids have gone to bed, sits drunk and inert in front of the TV, watching his perfected self in the beer commercials.

The bass likes structure; it camps in the shadows of rocks, in the camouflage of weeds, in the tangles of roots. It's not hiding, but lying in ambush. Without an enemy, it's unhappy. Yet it's not enmity that excites it, but the thought of an enemy. It may or may not attack. It's not battle that stirs it, but the film reel of battle in the mind.

The first boat the Center Darby man buys is, more than likely, a Sears aluminum runabout with an outboard engine of five to nine horsepower. Or it's a secondhand boat, slightly bigger than the new boat he can afford, and bearing the wear of another man's effort, probably with a fiberglass hull, advertised in the classifieds of the Tuckerman *Crier*. The seller bought a bigger boat, or had a heart attack and died, or got cancer and plans to die, or woke old, or his wife browbeat him into selling it. Whatever the reason, there are always fishing boats for sale, and there are always sad stories to go with them. But the anguish of the seller doesn't matter to a guy buying his first boat. What matters is the boat. He'll no longer have to depend on a friend with a craft to put himself on the water; alone (and sometimes a man has to be alone, if only to allow emotion to surface on his face), he'll no longer have to cast his lures from shore.

That first boat is usually the best boat for Darby waters. The helmsman can troll, anchor in deep water, row into weeds, paddle into stream inlets, float, and drift. It's a small craft but safe and dry, unlike a canoe (sometimes a Center Darby man dreams of canoes, but he rarely acquires one), and easy to trailer or toss in the bed of a pickup truck (and, yes, in a sense he regards the back of his truck as a bed). The upkeep is modest. And yet, from the moment he launches his new boat, the Center Darby man is dissatisfied. He's like a boy stepping into a shower stall of men: too small.

He frets. The sight of bigger, grander boats angers him. He has no words to explain his frustration.

"Everything's screwy," he tells his wife.

"So?" She doesn't look at him.

Why can't she understand? Why is she so stupid? Why are women so stupid? He turns his anger upon her. He spits words at her.

"I didn't do anything. Who do you think you are?" she says.

He doubles his fist and holds it before her. "Gaw-damn, gaw-damn you," he shouts at the fist.

At first she is cowed by the inscrutability of his anger, and then something tells her he's not Rambo, he's Ralph Kramden, and he won't hit her—not this time.

They collapse into the ritual of domestic argument. Before they are even aware it has started, it's over. He's miserable, she's miserable. Finally, it dawns on him: it's not her fault; it's his damn boat. It's a sniggling little thing that ridicules him.

"Aw, shit," he says, and because of the tone of his voice, she understands he is apologizing. She forgives him, but silently, so that he does not understand he has been forgiven.

That night, alone—he's singing half audibly, "All aloooohne"—outdoors under the stars, taking a leak (because it's his land, gaw-damn it), he realizes what he must do. Next day, he gets a loan and buys a bigger boat. The boat is beautiful. It makes him feel tender. He tells his wife she's the best thing that ever happened to him. They make love. Everything is all right.

The wife of the Center Darby man is jealous of the pleasure her husband takes from his moments on the water. She's discontented, and she scores his contentment as an insult to her. She understands in a felt, if not a figured, way that it is his very happiness—brief and private, in his boat, with a buddy—that prevents him from understanding her desperation and, further, that camouflages his own desperation from her, perhaps even from himself. The Center Darby woman knows there's no place for her in her husband's life. Sometimes that's okay. Other times, she'll say, "It's raining again. Why does it have to rain?" He'll answer, "How should I know?"

She's acutely female, this wife—beautiful and fashionable and desirable and passionate—but she has interred her femininity. She despises femininity; she regards femininity as the

215

turn of mind that shackled her mother. And of course she is right, and of course she is wrong. In our society, it is only drag queens for whom femininity is appropriate.

The women of Center Darby do not fish for real fish. Society has rigged it so they fish in the brine of men for status, prestige, money, and they are burdened by men's work and men's worry in addition to women's work and women's worry. If these women fished for real fish, they would fish with spears. They would don masks and snorkels and rubber webbed feet and they would weigh themselves down with lead bars and they would dive into the deepest lakes, where the waters are dark and cold, and they would stand immobile as statues (beautiful and oddly out of proportion, yet perfect, classically Grecian), and when a fish came by they would spear it. Breaking through water and into air and white light, they would hold the fish before their men and shout furiously, "There . . . see . . . understand?"

For the Center Darby man, the drama of boat buying repeats itself year by year. With every fishing season, his boat is bigger, faster, more elaborate. Eventually, he finds himself with a boat that has a horsepower rating equal to his car's, an electric trolling motor, a steering wheel, a winch for the anchor, an electronic fish-finder, a cooler to hold the ever-increasing amounts of booze he consumes, water wells to store the catch he will not eat, and rod holders so that he will not have to fish while he fishes. The boat builders struggle to keep up with his demands. Some day perhaps they will build a bass boat that will not require a fisherman, and then . . . and then the Center Darby fisherman will be content.

A Center Darby man will consume the fish he catches when he's camping out. But he won't eat fish at home—not his fish, anyway. He gives his fish away or throws them out, or releases them live if they're not worth bragging about, and, really, he doesn't brag, just thinks about it. He will eat somebody else's

216

fish, and he can be tempted at the table by ocean fish, but his preferred protein is on the hoof. He despises "meat fishermen"—Darby Depot folk, whom he despises anyway.

Eventually, the Center Darby man finds Darby waters too meager for his boat. He ventures out, seeking greater waters—Lake Sunapee, Lake Winnipesaukee, Lake Champlain, Great Bay, the Atlantic Ocean. Eventually (and this passes through his mind in dreams), he is lost at sea and ripped to pieces by sharks. With that image, it strikes him: he's getting old. Fear rolls over him like sea fog.

"What's this? What's going on?" He speaks to his folded hands at the dinner table.

His wife looks over. "What's with you?" she asks.

The fog clears and he can see. Beyond, there is nothing, just more of what was back there: years.

"Listen," he says, not aware of what he will say next but confident his words will shake a world, "I'm going to sell the boat. I don't care anymore. We'll take a vacation. We'll go to Florida. Or Atlantic City."

His wife looks at him, really looks at him. He can tell she is reading his age on his skin; he can tell because he is reading hers.

"When it's over, it's over," he says.

She bursts into tears. She does not know why she weeps, nor does he.

We have plenty of water in Darby, water of every kind but ocean water. We have a deep, clear, glacial lake, shallow tea-colored ponds, fetid swamps, beaver-dam impoundments, fast-running brooks, and a wide, slow-flowing river, the Connecticut. If you listen carefully, you can hear our waters whisper into the wind, "I hold a great bounty; cast your lines." But the waters exaggerate. The fishing here is not bad, but it's not great either. These are not rich limestone waters. This is the

Granite State, and these are granite waters, too poor for abundance, too pure for fecundity. Our waters please the eye, stimulate the mind, and disappoint the stomach. Our most prestigious game fish, the stocked trouts of the state Fish and Game Department, like our Upper Darby aristocrats, don't behave like the natives, even though they've been here through a number of generations; the common smallmouth bass, like our Center Darby commoners, battles spectacularly but only out of fear. The hornpout lives in the muck, like the Darby Depot folk who are nourished by him. There might be dignity and independence in such a life, but, still, muck is muck.

The native Darby brook trout survives in, of all places, Upper Darby, right under the noses of aristocratic fly fishermen. It resides in tiny, rocky streams shrouded by forest and pucker brush. It is deep-bodied and colorful as concentrated sunsets, but small—very small. If you can catch one six inches long, you have a lunker. It remains in proportion to the water bodies that hold it, a case where, finally, aesthetics and fitness become one.

These upland waters are too brush-strewn and tree-darkened, the fish of too little consequence, not to mention reclusive, to tempt most fishermen. But there is a breed of man who is interested. He's the stream worm fisherman, an outcast even by Darby Depot standards. He fishes alone, and he doesn't say much. He's not shy exactly, not reticent in the New England Yankee sense. He is misanthropic; his only virtue is patience. He likes the darkness and discomfort of the woods, because nobody bothers him there. He seeks these little trout merely because they are available.

Frederick Elman popped awake. He thought he'd heard a noise. He opened his eyes, and the sight of the stars overhead made him feel humble and noble at the same time. He shut his eyes and, between the worlds of wakefulness and sleep, finished the dream.

I come from the bottom of Center Darby, the bottom of Center Darby being not quite the top of Darby Depot. I have no wish to ascend to the village of Center Darby. It's Upper Darby that intrigues me. I fish for perch. It's a small, aggressive fish in the water but passive on the line. It's the best-tasting fish in Darby. It's been here forever. Nobody fishes it but me. I bring the fish to the daughter of Upper Darby. I cut off the heads of the fish and open up the insides and show them to her. She remarks on the awful smell. She watches as I roll the fish in a batter of beer and egg and flour, and cook them in hot oil. The white flesh steams as I lift it off the bone. It is tender and sweet. We make love; we re-create the world.

7

Dining on Sole

Garvin was in a good mood when he picked up Lilith, and perhaps that was why he teased her about driving around in her father's Bronco. "You're such a sight," he said. "Big, beautiful blonde in a grunty four-wheel-drive from another time zone." He laughed, reached over from his position in the driver's seat of his own BMW, and casually touched her shoulder.

"I'll have my own car soon." Lilith didn't want Garvin to think she was satisfied with the Bronco.

"Sure you will," he said with faint skepticism in his tone. "You'd be the convertible type," he said. "Beach girl. Showing off her tan." Garvin slowed as they came into Center Darby Village. The usual hangers-on malingered on the common.

"Maybe," Lilith said. She wasn't going to tell him she wanted a red car—violently red. For one thing, he'd want to know what kind of car. He'd want to know the style, the make, the dream. But only that color, violently red, came to mind when she thought about her dream car. It occurred to her that a woman had to know who she was before she knew what kind of car suited her. Or maybe you could do it the other way. Buy a car and suit yourself to it.

Garvin parked. Abnaki Jordan began to shuffle over in their direction from the green. When Garvin saw him, he said to

Lilith, "Wait here—I'll be right back," and he hurried across the street to intercept Abnaki.

Lilith did not hear the brief conversation between the Upper Darby lawyer and the Darby Depot bum. "Any luck?" Garvin said to Abnaki.

"We seen it. White bear cub. Real as sticks and stones."

Garvin did not believe any Jordans, let alone Abnaki. "Bring it to me, dead or alive—preferably dead—else there's no payment. Understand?"

"Yes, sir—you're the boss," Abnaki said.

Garvin returned to Lilith.

"What was that all about?" she asked.

"Nothing. He does odd jobs for us at the development."

The tone in Garvin's voice displayed his annoyance with Lilith for prying into his affairs, but he did take her arm as they were about to enter the restaurant. He said something she didn't catch, and she turned toward him. (It was at that moment that the Live Free or Die had barreled into the village, and Frederick saw Lilith with Garvin.)

"Getting chilly," Garvin repeated. "You didn't bring a sweater."

"I'll be all right," Lilith said.

Inside the restaurant, with the aroma of spicy food and the clinking of glasses and the aspect of the patrons—dressy, affluent, clean-cut, in such contrast to the people on the green—it was if Lilith had stepped into a different world. The decor was very New Englandy, perhaps self-mockingly so, but the atmosphere reminded her of a restaurant in a city. It was the kind of place Lilith had known since she was a child, and yet she'd never known it here in Darby, and perhaps, she thought, that was the reason the restaurant made her feel as if she were far from home.

As they were waiting to be seated by the hostess, Lilith

watched a waitress—dark, angular, looked like a boy—approach the bartender with a drink order.

"That's a very splashy shirt you have there," the waitress said to the bartender, a jovial lesbian wearing men's trousers and a short-sleeved Hawaiian shirt, who answered the compliment in a rich baritone laugh just this side of James Earl Jones.

"Well, you could always waitress for a living," Garvin said to Lilith as they were escorted to a table by the hostess.

It was an offhand comment, but Lilith considered the possibility. She could do it: take food orders, be civil to people. But could she make enough money to fix the roof, buy a new car, keep herself whole, fit, and fed? She didn't think so. Then, too, something told her the town would not want to see the Squire's daughter waitressing, at least not in Darby itself, and not in this place, owned by outside interests. But why should she care what the people of Darby thought? She did not know why she cared, only that she did.

The dark, angular waitress arrived at their table, lit candles, and took their drink order, Perrier and vodka on the rocks and half a lime for Garvin, Bass ale for Lilith.

"Enjoying your house?" Garvin looked up from the menu.

"It won't feel like it's mine until Persephone leaves."

"So you want her gone."

"I'm not sure."

They drank in silence for a minute or two, and then Garvin said, "Lilith, I want you to know that I've been in touch with your mother's lawyer."

"Dracut!" Lilith's fear of the man was in her voice.

"We offered to drop our case against Persephone. All we asked is some support for our case against Monet. It's his phony white bear that is costing us time and money. Dracut put us off."

Lilith knew that Monet already had made a deal with Persephone, so she didn't quite know what to say next. Everything was so false, and she was part of it.

"Why can't we just bury Daddy?" she said. "Why can't we have the service? With flowers and singing and the Reverend Hall saying words. And a walk to the grave site. Garvin, I even want the caskets opened. I want to see. I want to feel."

"That's . . . that's real psychological." Garvin was uncomfortable with this kind of talk.

"Why do you and Mother and Monet have to fight?" Lilith surprised herself with her own fury, but Garvin only read that fury as heatless female fire that could be extinguished with man's cold reason.

"Your father asked to be buried on the Trust lands," he said. "It will help my business and our town if his wishes are carried out. Your mother has a different opinion. Monet—well, he has an agenda all his own. There's no real animosity between us, only contentiousness."

"Something is wrong. . . ." Lilith had no words, no twist of logic, to explain herself.

"Lilith, what you have to get used to is, nobody cares about right or wrong. We proceed along lines that serve our interests. Don't take these court cases so seriously. Think of them as . . . as a . . . sport."

"Sport!" Lilith raised her voice.

"Listen, I'm sorry—okay?" Garvin was genuinely contrite. "I didn't ask you to dinner to resume the Salmon-Prell wars. Lilith, do you realize all that's left of our generation in Upper Darby is you and I?"

Even though she regarded herself and Garvin as belonging to different generations, his words moved her. She wanted to say, "Let's start over." Instead, she said timidly, "I hadn't thought about that."

She watched Garvin bask in a moment of triumph. He was exactly what her mother said he was: a man who only wanted to have his way. Is this what you did with a man, bargain your soul for his good humor? Hitch on to his train of thought and ride empty on tracks to his destination? She wished desperately to speak. She said nothing, but her good manners smiled cordially at him.

When their drinks were down, the waitress returned, and began a long speech. Lilith didn't actually take in her words until she was almost finished with an exhaustive description of the foods for the day. "With today's special of stir-fried shrimp served with an orchestra of vegetables, we have Québecois legumes slowly cooked in ceramic ware with ham hocks, white onions, white wine, and white pepper."

"What?" Lilith whipped her head from the waitress to Garvin.

"Pea soup." Garvin smiled at Lilith, then turned to the waiter. "Another round of drinks; then we'll order."

For the main course, they had the sole. They drank a bottle of wine through the meal, so the alcohol buzz lingered on. Lilith ordered dessert, coffee-toffee pie with blueberries. Afterward, Garvin called for a round of brandies. Like so many lawyers, he was a loose-lipped fellow after some drinks. When she began to enjoy listening to him, began to admire his confidence because it made her feel safe, she realized she was getting drunk. In the excitement of the alcohol, Lilith thought, I kind of admire him, kind of want him dead.

Garvin talked on. "You know the landfill in Tuckerman? Well, it's going to be closed next year. We have an option on that property—okay? It commands a view of Mount Monadnock. We are going to rebuild Tuckerman, we are going to rebuild this whole county. The state. The U.S. of A. The world. But I don't care about the world, I don't care about Tuckerman—what I care about is Upper Darby—okay?"

The waitress cleared the table. Garvin surprised Lilith by

breaking out a map from the inside pocket of his jacket. He spread it out on the table.

"This—" Lilith pointed.

"The solid lines."

"My house," Lilith said.

"And this broken line is my dream." Garvin stroked the map.

Lilith stared at the map.

"I know every room in the Salmon house," Garvin said. "I have copies of the original blueprints. I know what has to be done with it. It's all up here." He tapped his head. Then he took her hand again. "Lilith, come with me. I want to show you what I want to do." He released her hand. The matter was settled. She was going to go with him.

The waitress brought a drink, and Garvin knocked it down. In his drunken lawyer's mode—argumentative but not abrasive, bristling with eye contact, yet curiously impersonal—Garvin convinced Lilith totally and irrevocably that she could never love him. However, she was fascinated by his gift for command, the very character trait that repelled her. She admired Garvin as an older man who would take care of everything. Maybe she could work in Garvin's office. The phrase "administrative assistant" popped into her head. She smiled at him.

Garvin took the smile as a starving man takes bread. "Let's go," he said.

Outside, Garvin fetched the BMW while Lilith waited. The wind had picked up out of the north, and the temperature had dropped ten degrees since they'd gone in, but Lilith felt warmed by the drink. She stood illuminated by a spotlight from the top step of the Inn, and she took in the moonlit figures on the green, those troubled beings she'd seen around town, the mean little man in the camouflage suit, the Asian boy in black, the old woman in a cotton dress, the out-of-work farm hand in overalls. She had a mind to join them, sit among them, and await her fate. Wait with neither hope nor despair. Wasn't that what peace of mind was all about? And then—stupidly and drunkenly, she realized even as she spoke—she called out to the people on the green, "Hello, you out there." They turned to look at her. She stepped down off the top step, and for a moment they seemed frozen in time and space, like figures in a movie still. Then they parted, going off. She wished to call out—Stay! But by now it was too late, and she knew better than to say anything more. Her power was not in her words or even in her actions, but in who she was; she was a Salmon, she was the Squire's daughter.

Garvin pulled the BMW beside her and opened the door for her to get in. When they arrived at Sugar Bush Village, Lilith noticed the moon made everything yellow and blue. The wind moaned through the trees. Ahead, the condos were dark, angular shapes against the sky. She struggled to find an image in her mind that would define those shapes, but none appeared. The BMW came to a stop. Garvin traipsed in a disorderly crescent around to the passenger side in order to open Lilith's door.

"Well, what do you think?" Garvin gestured grandly at the half-made condos.

"Spooky." Lilith stepped into the night light.

"Spooky?" Garvin didn't like the word; he slammed shut the door of the BMW.

"I mean, at night," Lilith said.

"I suppose so, but let's not blame Prell Enterprises for the moon's mode of doing business," Garvin said. "Damn summer chill, I don't like it. Not fair."

She could see what was happening to him. Furnished with buoyancy by alcohol, the old Prell feelings of inferiority to the Salmons were rising to the surface. Her father had used this single weakness among the Prells to exploit them.

"Come on," Garvin said. "I want to show you the apartments."

But indoors it was pitch-black, so they stayed outside and walked around the structures under the moon.

Garvin held forth: "Tuckerman County is wedged between the New York megalopolis to the south and the Boston megalopolis to the east. When they converge, some of the towns in the county are going to explode with prosperity. The others will become slums. With our state taxing system—everything depending on the property tax—the quality of life is dependent on the value of the property—okay? You see how it is? Tuckerman County sociology is a machine that regenerates itself with use." After a pause he said, "Remember the map?"

"The what?"

"The map I showed you—okay?"

"Okay," Lilith said.

"Between the Salmon house and Sugar Bush Village is a strip of Trust land. Think about your house now, where it is—virtually at the end of the town-maintained road, isolated, run-down. I'm asking you to think about what it could be. The Salmon house as an integral part of Sugar Bush Village."

"I don't understand." Lilith did understand, but in her frame of mind, fuzzy with drink ("beer goggles" was the term at her college), the words seemed like play. Garvin was kidding her; she was kidding him; they were kidding each other; everybody kidded everybody, then died. The point of life was to confuse reality, so reality wouldn't sink in, because if it did you were sunk. Maybe she should tell Garvin. No, he was too earnest. His earnestness struck her a little bit funny—and sad, really sad. She laughed involuntarily.

"Something funny?" Garvin said.

"You are—you're funny; I think I'm going to cry," Lilith said.

"What's the matter with you?"

"I'm just a little weird from drinking." Lilith touched his arm in the night.

The touch, unexpected, sent a jolt to Garvin's loins. "Upper Darby with its own commercial center," he said seriously, in the manner of a modern young countryman courting his beloved. "Think of it—shops, restaurants, an Upper Darby Green. . . ."

"Not a green, a common—right?"

"Makes no difference. A meeting hall. Listen, Lilith." Garvin took her hand. "The Trust seals Upper Darby off from the world. It's a wall. But if we relaxed the rules a little bit, we'd attract the best of these new people. You see what I'm saying? We'd make a profit, we'd leave behind a positive legacy. What else could a Prell—or a Salmon—ask for?"

"Loot and legacy." Lilith giggled. She was afraid she was going to become hysterical.

"Yes, that's it—that's us." He slid his arm around her waist.

Lilith felt calmer then. She liked the night, the stars, the moon glow, the hard wind. Perhaps it was her enthusiasm for the natural world, that and her need for protection by an elder, that Garvin mistook for submission.

"It's only a short walk through the trees to the Salmon property," Garvin said. Still holding her around the waist, he led her up the hill. They walked along the rough ground of a recently seeded field. They followed a logging road through the woods. The trees obscured the moonlight, and Lilith, growing ever calmer, enjoyed the half-caress of the darkness. Garvin plunged on with his message.

"This old logging road? Here's your link between Sugar Bush Village and the Salmon house. . . ."

Lilith had ceased to listen. She was adrift from the reality of the moment. She looked up, keeping her eyes on a star, a tiny glitter of light—like a piece of mica a child finds and thinks is a jewel—and then her attention wandered for a moment and the star was lost among the other stars and the glare of the moon.

". . . The Trust was your father's vision," Garvin said. "He just ran out of time—and money. I can't dream his dream, Lilith—I can only dream my dream. But within that dream I can hold his dream. Lilith, we can do it together. I see Upper Darby with its own village, own economy. I see bicycle paths. . . ."

Quite suddenly they broke out of the forest in a field, her field. Lilith saw her house with the moon hanging over it. And then she heard Garvin utter the word that summed up his dream: "The financial base for this dream . . . is . . . SKIING!"

The word, at the moment of surprise at seeing her house, halted Lilith as if she'd been challenged by a border guard. "Skiing?" She was confused now, awakened from the doze of alcohol. Garvin wanted her, Garvin wanted her house, Garvin wanted everything. "Skiing," she repeated, attempting to orient herself by voicing the word.

"We've dialogued over names." Garvin was like a man placidly floating on his back in a quiet pool, who because his head is partially submerged does not hear what is going on around him, and who thinks he sees the shape of the world in a cloud. "Sugar Bush was the obvious one, but there's already an area in Vermont with the same name. Well, one day, as I was riding my bicycle, I happened to notice the ledges in the Trust, and I thought that's it: The Ledge."

"The Ledge."

"Yes—yes." Garvin's face glowed. "The Ledge. Nothing else. Not The Ledges or The Ledges Resort or The Ledges Ski Area. Just The Ledge. It has the right sound, on the wild side, mysterious. The skiers will love it." Garvin stopped abruptly, and stared at Lilith's face in the moonlight. A long moment passed when he said nothing, when Lilith thought, What happened? What happened to my life? Did I ever have a life? What makes

229

a life? And then Garvin said, as if to someone else, "My God, I'm falling in love with her. Think of it—a Prell and a Salmon. We can make the earth roll." He took her in his arms and kissed her.

After that she wasn't sure what happened. She stumbled, or he wrestled her to the ground. But there was a moment, only a moment, when she was lost in compliance to a rule she had not made, did not believe in, did not feel. The next thing she knew, her blouse was open and Garvin was kissing her breasts. She tried to push him away. "No—I don't want this."

Garvin ignored her.

She clawed him in the face, and that got his attention. He pulled back, wounded, hand against his cheek. Lilith struggled to her feet. Garvin rose and grabbed her wrists. "You led me on. . . . I was after something, you were after something. . . . What's the contention, Lilith?"

"The what?"

"The point, goddamn it! What do you want from me?" He shouted with the righteousness of a minister from his TV pulpit, and Lilith twisted free from him.

"I want . . . I want . . . I want nothing from you," she said.

"Lilith!"

A moment passed when she wondered just what she was doing out here with this man she had no feeling for. And then she knew what had kept her bottled up for a year. "I want to know what happened to my father," she shouted.

"He passed away, I can't help that." Garvin backed up a step, and for the first time his voice wavered.

Lilith pressed him. "I was in school when he died, you were here, his lawyer—you know, you have to know. I came home, and something was all wrong. He died, but . . . something . . . something."

"Lilith, your father took his own life," Garvin said softly.

"What?"

230

"He climbed up to the ledges and took an overdose of sleeping pills. Look, it wasn't like a tragedy or anything," Garvin tried to smooth it all over. "He was a sick man. You knew that. He just decided to get it over with."

"It's not true."

"Everybody in Upper Darby knows. Ask your mother." Garvin had regained his composure. He realized he'd drunk too much and let things go too far. Maybe it was better this way. Lilith wasn't ready for him—or for anybody. She had problems. He backed away.

"Come on, I'll drive you home." He ran his fingers through his hair, straightened his tie.

"I am home." Lilith pointed to the ground beneath her feet, then to her house in the moonlight.

"So I won't drive you home. You'll get there alone. Why do the Salmons always win? Why?" Garvin started down the path returning to the Sugar Bush development.

Lilith ran across the field, the tall grass like rasps against her legs. There were no lights on in the house, and Persephone's Saab was still missing. She couldn't bear the idea of going into an empty house. The moon glow on the Bronco made the vehicle seem new. She got into the car and started it up. The Bronco seemed to operate itself. It ripped up the driveway of the Salmon residence, and then, instead of turning right for town, cut left, into the chain stretched between the trees where the town road ended and the Trust road began. The steering wheel twisted in her hands for a second as the chain between the trees caught the front of the car, and then the chain snapped. The Bronco rocketed forward. No lights on, engine roaring, vehicle body whipped by tree branches, tires jouncing on the rough road, the Bronco plunged deep into the Trust lands. And then, without warning, it hit a pothole and was airborne. The steering wheel turned with incredible ease in Lilith's hands, as if she were piloting a spaceship. For that moment when she knew she was off the road and suspended in the air, she was at peace. And then she could feel herself banging around in the car. It was as if the hand of a giant child had picked up the car and shaken it like a toy.

The motor was still running. Lilith lay with her eyes closed for a few minutes listening to the engine race. When she opened her eyes and began to stir, she was surprised to discover she was on her knees and the Bronco was upside down.

Lilith stumbled home in a dream. It wasn't until she was in the house that she realized she was in shock. Her flesh felt numb and cold. She turned up the stereo system as if music could revive sensation. She tried to dance, but the effort only brought her attention to her weakness and nausea—and still she could not feel; she was all chaotic thoughts, no material being. If only a person didn't have to think. Blood flowing through your veins, eyes perceiving light and shape, ears registering sounds, but no thoughts. That would be bliss—heaven.

She ran into the bathroom and filled the tub with hot water. She stripped and stood for a moment looking in the mirror. The bruises made her face seem more dirty than injured. Her skin was pale, lifeless. But she smelled the hot, steamy water, and that suggested to her life and continuity. The water on the Salmon property came from a deep well. It tasted vaguely of minerals. She stepped into the tub and lay down. The water felt neither warm nor cold. She shut her eyes. The water closing around her was less a physical sensation than a physical understanding of the embodiment of an idea. She was going to be all right. She soaped her body until the water was soft and slippery on her skin.

When she returned to the Hearth, she turned off the music and started a fire so that she could listen to the hiss and crackle of the flames, and she lay on the floor wrapped in her robe before the fireplace. The moist heat of the bathroom had obscured her vision, but this dry heat shed light. She hadn't known where she was going, only that she must go on, but she had progressed in hesitation and fright, like a child. Now she was changed inside. *Suicide—you had to commit suicide!* At this moment, Lilith Salmon truly came of age. And she wept—she wept in mourning, not for those others in her life who had died or gone from her, she wept for the dead child in herself.

8

Howard's Dump

Joe Ancharsky was startled when Howard Elman came into his store. He knew Howard well enough, but he had never quite gotten used to the man. Elman had the eyes of a stick-up thug, and he had a kind of swagger about him, forgivable in young men, threatening and annoying in middle-aged men. Elman swung opened the door, halted, swept the store with those bullet eyes until they reached Joe's only customer at the moment, Pitchfork Parkinson, sitting in a straight-back chair. Elman, who was holding a homemade crutch in his hand, now pointed the crutch at Pitchfork. "There's the man I'm looking for," Howard said.

"What do you want with me, Howie?" Pitchfork was not one to be bullied.

"I hate farmers, you know I hate farmers—you know that, doncha?"

"It's well known." Pitchfork rocked back on his chair and folded his arms. He was wearing only a strappy white under-shirt under his denim overalls, and Joe experienced a mild jolt of revulsion at the sight, heretofore unapprehended, of streams of brown hair along Pitchfork's thick shoulders.

"You regard yourself as a farmer?" Elman leaned his crutch against the wall, but he remained standing in the doorway.

Joe wanted to tell Elman to get in or get out, he was blocking the access; but he held his tongue. He had the crazy idea Elman was going to pull a gun.

"I got the experience for farming, but I ain't got no land," Pitchfork said.

"The old farmers are all rich bastards," Howard said.

"Land-rich, not money-rich—God love 'em." Pitchfork put just a little STP in the tone of his voice.

"You correcting me?"

"Yes, I am, Howie."

"Well, that's good. See, I'm awful stubborn, and if you let me push you around, why, I'll be happy to do so."

"That's what they say," Pitchfork said.

Howard began anew before Pitchfork's words were out. "Now, this present-day batch of young farmers are a bunch of a different kind of bastards, because they all go to the aggie school in Durham—tell me I'm wrong."

"Except for the bastard part, you're not wrong, and maybe you're not wrong all the way around." Pitchfork's voice was even. He exhibited the resigned confidence of a defeated man who had stuck by his principles.

"You still holding out for a job on the farm?" Howard growled at Pitchfork.

"Farmers are poor. All the green stuff is in the field and not in the wallet. They hire these retarded fellows to shovel shit for low pay. They hire these darkies from the islands to pick apples for low pay. Then there's me, with experience. They're ashamed to offer me low pay. So I sit in Joe's store."

Joe was moved by these words, although he couldn't have said exactly why. "Pitchfork, that's the longest speech I ever heard you make," Joe said.

"But he didn't say *nothn'*," Howard said.

"What's on your mind?" Pitchfork's voice rose just a bit, as

Howard's purpose here was finally beginning to dawn on him.

"Let me ask you a question. Are you a proud man?" Howard said.

Pitchfork's face turned red with embarrassment, and he unfolded his arms.

"Now, Pitchfork, don't get unhinged," Howard said, sounding almost human. "I need a man. Cooty's disappeared again, maybe for good this time. My boy's leaving town, or maybe he ain't, but it don't matter. I got plans to expand my business. I need a man."

"Well, I don't know." Pitchfork plopped his chunky chin into his chunky palm. Joe knew this meant Pitchfork was retreating into what he sometimes referred to as "mental composting." Joe decided it was time for him to act.

"He wants a proud man, Pitchfork. A proud man." Joe spoke with great exclamation (at least for him), designed to keep Pitchfork from disappearing into his thoughts.

"I want a man so proud he ain't scared of swill," Howard said.

Pitchfork did not speak.

"It can't be any worse than cow shit," Joe said.

"Cow shit never bothered me." Pitchfork perked up.

Good, he's coming out of it, thought Joe.

"Pitchfork, make up your mind—I got things to do." Howard Elman grabbed his crutch.

"I could use some work," Pitchfork said in a low voice.

And that was how Howard Elman hired Pitchfork Parkinson. That day, he showed Pitchfork how to operate the trash masher on the Honeywagon. Pitchfork, who had been around machines all his life, caught on quickly. Then Howard presented Pitchfork with a computer printout of his customers and their addresses. "It's the route for the day. Just do the pickups in the order you see 'em, and you won't have no trouble. Go to it—time's a-wasting," Howard said, and Pitchfork drove off in the Honeywagon. Behind the wheel, he was thinking he'd better re-up his commercial-vehicle license.

Elenore came out of the house. "Where's Freddy?" she asked.

"I don't know and I don't care. I'm going hunting," Howard said.

"Men!" Elenore turned her back on Howard and went into the house.

She knew his problem. He was losing Freddy, and he couldn't handle the situation. He had no useful thoughts, no useful words, no useful actions to keep his son with him. He made do by dubbing around in the woods. Every day he went out with the strange gun Mr. Monet had given him, sometimes alone, sometimes with Cooty. They hunted; they set traps, baiting them with every manner of human food gathered from the trash route. He believed in the white bear, he said; he was going to get it for the scientists. He had no evidence to base his belief on, only the belief itself. Elenore scoffed at him. She knew that belief of Howard's variety was merely a form of human vanity. The only belief that mattered was faith, faith in God. Not vanity, but humility. You believed because God wanted you to believe. In Him. Howard's kind of belief—in his own ideas—could only get him in trouble.

While Elenore knew roughly what Howard was up to in his forays into the woods, she was ignorant of a number of details. She did not know, for example, that Howard had realized his methods—trapping and hunting alone—were lacking. Black bears were wary under ordinary circumstances. His quarry, this white-bear cub, had a mother, and she'd be especially cautious now that her cub had lost a paw in a trap. Bears had good noses for the smell of men, so it was unlikely he could come upon her. Howard had seen a few signs of bears, scat and scrapings, but nothing to indicate the bears, mother and

237

child, stayed in one place long enough for him to find them. The only practical way to locate these bears was with dogs, but Howard was not one to keep dogs, and most certainly wasn't about to advise the Pocket Squire that he wasn't the man for the job. And, too, he had a strange idea, which was that this cub with one paw and his mother didn't matter. He dreamed of a bear, a huge white-coated black bear that looked like a polar bear come to New Hampshire to take up residence, run the locals off, and he, Howard, was going to put a stop to it.

Howard drove his pickup truck into the Trust lands, parked, and set off on foot, hobbling along the paths with the help of his crutch. He carried the tranquilizer gun and a .44 magnum pistol. He didn't expect to happen on the bear, but you never knew. This was a terrible time of year to be in the woods. The trees were too dense with foliage to see anything, the humidity made a man sweat, and the bugs were everywhere. God, I love it, he thought.

He stopped by his tree stand, staring up at it. Something told him that this broken leg would set him back just enough that he'd never want to climb that high again. He made a guttural sound, and walked on. He checked the traps. No sign of bears.

His leg was beginning to ache, and he was some distance from his pickup, when he came on to an area that interested him. It reminded him a little of the old quarry where he had killed Mrs. Cutter's dog some years back, but this place was smaller, more hidden. And yet it was near the town road. What concealed the quarry from view was protruding ledges on three sides and a dense cover of young hemlock trees on the fourth. He hobbled about through the hemlocks, coming out on North-side Lane, a dead-end road that Howard plowed for the town in the winter. An idea began to take shape in his head. He could chain-saw out a little turnaround here for the plow, and at the same time cut a zigzag to the quarry. When his business was pushed up, he could dump the contents of the Honey-wagon in this old quarry. He smiled to himself.

Howard arrived home later that day, and Elenore asked him how it had gone.

"It pays to go in the woods; a man can think in the woods," he said.

"Did you see the bear?"

"I didn't see him, but he's out there—I know," Howard said.

9

A Course for Salvation

Frederick lingered on in the Trust lands for most of the morning. He fished (no bites) and puttered around, as if the Trust were his back yard. Sitting by the fire, he was content, distracted from the troubles of self and Darby by the sinuous movement of the flames, the smell of the trees in morning mist, the solitude of the Trust. Lilith, his family, his failed life no longer mattered. The whole problem with the world, he decided, was people and time. If, like Cooty Patterson, he could get used to the idea of self-worth without the confirmation of other selves, of action without the worry of time (which was no more than a man-made gizmo to measure mortality), why, he could be happy.

He decided to hit the road later today. Had no idea where he would go. He would surprise himself at the first traffic light he encountered by picking a direction, some variable of west. Traffic lights! That would be next in Darby; he didn't want to see that day. The only difficult part was going to be saying goodbye to his mother. In her hopes that he and Howard would reconcile their differences, she had conspired to bring him here. She had been right. A son should not remain estranged from his father. Such a condition was disturbing to the father, destructive to the son. But in the end, both of them, himself and his father, had failed her, failed themselves. So, Frederick thought, I'll OD on my drug—the road.

He was coming down off the ledges, was almost to the Live Free or Die, when he came upon the Bronco. Fascinated and detached—curious, chillingly unemotional—he crawled through the wreckage, searching for a body. When he found none, he crawled out, climbed atop a nearby boulder, and screamed at the top of his lungs, "Lih-lahhhhhhhhhh!" He started to shake, and then he broke into a run, headed for the Salmon house.

Fascinated and detached—curious, chillingly unemotional—Lilith watched Frederick Elman come through a window in the Hearth Room. When he had reached the house, he'd knocked on the door, but she hadn't heard him; she was in the greenhouse. He'd been too frantic to see the doorbell in plain view. At about the time Lilith left the greenhouse and entered the Hearth Room, Frederick had found an open window. He punched in the screen and dived in like a husky seal going through a hoop.

"Frederick?" Lilith said uncertainly, as if questioning her own mind rather than the figure before her.

He heard her while he was en route through the window before he saw her, and he started to speak before he actually hit the floor: "You're alive, Lilith, you're alive."

She stared down at him, ridiculous and anguished at her feet, and laughed. Her laughter provoked Frederick to laughter. He scrambled up, and the two young people stood grinning foolishly at one another for a long moment.

"My God, I missed you; it's like I haven't seen you for years," he said. And they embraced.

"I can smell the Bronco in your beard," Lilith said.

They both burst into tears.

For a few minutes, they were giddy with delight in each

241

other's presence, from a sense of release that they couldn't have explained, and then Frederick saw the bruises on Lilith's face.

"What happened?" he asked.

"I don't want to tell you everything—I never want to tell anybody everything," she said.

Frederick pulled away, not upset, just a little confused.

"I have to keep some things to myself, that's all," she said.

"Hey, whatever you want."

They sat side by side on the floor beside the black maw of the fireplace. Lilith told Frederick about her date with Garvin, the revelation of her father's suicide, and finally cracking up the Bronco, everything except her suspicion that her mother was having an affair with Lawrence Dracut. Events belonged to time and history, but the suspicion was hers, to protect and keep hidden, the way a child attempts to nurse a bird that the family cat has wounded. At the same moment, Frederick held his own suspicion: what Lilith didn't want to talk about was sex with Garvin Prell. Frederick did not wish to protect his suspicion, but to kill it and bury it. Neither Frederick nor Lilith would reveal these fears.

"Lilith, your father was sick," Frederick said. "He was going to die, so what difference does it make how he went out?"

"The difference is, nobody told me. He didn't, my mother didn't. They kept everything from me. They made me a stranger."

"Ask her, then. Just nail her to the wall with the question."

Lilith stood from her sitting position before the fireplace and kicked imaginary sticks into the cold hearth. She realized now that she'd been waiting all along for her mother to reveal the circumstances of Reggie's death, waiting without any real understanding that she had been waiting, waiting for her mother to realize her need and act upon it.

Frederick looked around, noticing the interior of the house now. "Quite a palace."

"I should have asked you in before, but . . ."

"Your mother didn't approve of me."

Lilith said nothing, and Frederick did not pursue the subject. But a barrier remained between them.

Frederick touched the oak paneling. "Raw wood, I love it. Somehow I expected this place to be more, I don't know, refined."

"Daddy had all the paint stripped off years ago; he liked the look of wood grain," Lilith said.

"Me, too." Frederick was sorry he had never known the Squire. It chimed in his mind that he and Lilith would have been better off if they could have swapped fathers.

Now that Frederick had changed the subject to her house, Lilith was happy to give him a tour. And yet her mother and, as Lilith saw it, her mother's misconduct with Dracut were still with her, so that unconsciously she led Frederick to Persephone's greenhouse.

Frederick grimaced at the sight of wooden shelves, unpainted, stained with water and dirt, full of the evidence of earth and plant life, but with no stem or leaf to be seen.

"What did your mother use this place for, a nursery business?" Frederick's sarcasm wounded Lilith, but she hid her feelings.

"She gave all the plants away," Lilith said. "I started a few pots. Coleus—I love coleus . . . the colors—but it's the wrong time of year for the greenhouse. Too hot."

"Too hot now, but it must a cost a fortune to heat this place in the winter." Frederick snapped the greenhouse glass with his finger.

Lilith said nothing, and Frederick, who had not heard his own arrogance, took her resigned silence as smugness.

243

What lay before the young people was a bog of misunderstanding and tangles of deception. Frederick could see that the Salmon house was run-down, the grounds barely kept up, the items of luxury belonging to the past, but his deep-seated belief that the Salmons were rich folk, a belief more in the guts than in the head, camouflaged the evidence of his eyes. He wondered: Are these Upper Darby people rich because they're cheap, or cheap because they're rich? For her part, Lilith was determined to maintain Frederick's illusions. She divined it important to pretend she was rich. If she denied herself the role of the Squire's daughter, as conceived by the town, she was lost.

Lilith brought Frederick through the house. He commented on the scale of the rooms, the intricacy of the woodwork. He offered admiring remarks for the veneration of those long-dead carpenters who had built the house (people Lilith had never actually thought about before), but said nothing about the vision of her great-grandfather, who had commissioned the house. At the third-floor staircase, he paused. "What's up there?"

"Servants' quarters."

He started up the stairs. She remained behind. He stopped and turned. "Coming up?"

She shook her head no.

When he returned, he grumbled about the "tightness," as he called it, of the servants' quarters. The narrowness of his observations provoked Lilith into mentioning some of the luminaries of the past era who had visited the house—movie stars, corporate heads, community leaders, and politicians. Frederick let her explanations go by.

"So, how come no servants today?" Frederick asked.

"You can't get good help—everybody knows that," Lilith lied to Frederick, pretending to be more snobbish than she was in order to preserve the illusion of the Squire's daughter.

"You can't get good help," Frederick criticized her with a smirk.

Lilith stood her ground. Frederick stood his. But neither wanted an argument. Both sensed that the contention between them was not strictly her snobbery and his resentment. It was something far greater, which neither understood or was prepared to confront. A signal from Frederick's stomach helped change the mood of the moment.

"You got anything to eat in this joint?" he asked.

"In the fridge. You can help yourself." Lilith started downstairs.

The Salmons did not have a kitchen table as such, because formal meals were served in the dining room. But there was a spacious countertop around which were bar stools. Lilith's father wouldn't sit at the bar stools—they were Persephone's idea. In the morning, he'd grab his coffee and his rolls and he'd eat in the Hearth Room or in the Bronco as he drove into the woods, but he insisted that the evening meal be served in the dining room with cloth napkins, silverware, fine china. Lilith determined that, if she ever had a family of her own, she would insist on the Salmon formality for the evening meal.

Frederick rummaged around the refrigerator, complained there was no meat, and settled for a bowl of wild raspberries in heavy cream. Lilith brewed coffee, and the two young people sat facing one another at the counter. Here, in the kitchen, was where they belonged.

"I knew he was sick," Lilith said. "But he never told me how sick, and my mother pretended he wasn't sick at all. I went along; I wanted to believe everything was going to be all right. Once I asked him, just blurted it out, 'Are you going to be all right, Daddy?' He said, 'You're the one who matters. You're the future.' That's as close as he ever came to telling me he was dying."

"What room was that in?" Frederick alternated between sips of coffee and spoonings of raspberries.

"What do you mean?"

"I mean, when he told you this, what room was he in?"

"Is that important?"

"I don't know why I think so, but I do. My father, when he has something hard to tell me, waits until he's in the pit working on a car. He can't talk unless he keeps his hands busy."

"It was on the phone," Lilith said softly. Frederick had inadvertently put his finger on the problem between herself and her family—indeed, the problem between Upper Darby and the rest of the world—distance. "I came home from school the day before the funeral. My mother told me he died on the ledges. Heart failure. She sort of implied that it was from his disease. As sick as he was, it seemed peculiar that he'd want to hike up that steep trail, but I never questioned her. I was afraid of being hurt. Before I had a chance to cry, to feel, it was over and I was back in school, numb and changed. I didn't know who I was before, and then I was somebody else. I've been trying ever since to catch up with myself. I was hoping I could get it over with at this memorial service the town had planned. I wanted a good cry, I wanted some memories—and I wanted to forget. So, it ends up like this: bodies in cold storage, lies in county court, and me nowhere."

"That's the only thing you and I have in common," Frederick said.

The young people stared hard at one another.

"We're in our hometown, and we're nowhere," Lilith said.

It was a moment of recognition between them. The past, of family and of place, now seemed unimportant compared with this shared despair.

"Lilith, come with me. We'll go away. We'll live on the road."

"I can't. If I go now, ghosts will follow me," Lilith said.

"Once the legal stuff is over with, your father will be buried—

you can put him to rest. You'll be free—we can get away."

"It won't happen. Persephone and Monet and Garvin won't stop fighting after one court hearing."

"Then you have to fight, too."

"I don't want to fight. I can't."

Frederick started to say something, then stopped.

For the moment, they sat drinking coffee and thinking their own private thoughts. Frederick had no more to say to Lilith now than he had had to say to that young black girl on the bridge. He always managed to maneuver himself into positions where his counsel had some value but he had no counsel to give. Still seeing the image of the black girl reaching out a hand to him, Frederick resolved that, whatever else he would do, he must remain close to Lilith, must hold her hand, even if that meant falling to the bottom of the world with her.

Lilith was thinking about those native peoples of a time gone by. She imagined a night, a fire, dancers, priests and priestesses, sacred words, chanting natives. She could almost smell the smoke, feel her own musk and sweat from the exertion; she imagined her dreams leaving her mind, taking shape in the real world, given dimension and plane by some secret incantation.

"What did the Indians do when someone died?" She posed the question aloud, not only to Frederick but to herself.

"I'm not sure."

"They must have buried their dead. That's what Monet says. An old Indian burial ground on the Trust, he said. They must have had a ceremony of some kind."

"They didn't have iron tools," Frederick mused. "They probably burned the bodies, then laid the remains in a shallow grave with, I don't know, a spear and some feathers. And, yah, I suppose they did it all up in some kind of ceremony."

"How would they burn the bodies?"

"Build a bier, stack some wood underneath. Up she goes."

247

Lilith rose from her stool. She looked away from Frederick, staring off to some faraway point. "I've seen a thousand fires," she said. "My father made fires—you make fires. It was the men who made the fires."

Frederick looked curiously at Lilith. He began to sense the strangeness in her. He knew she would ask something of him, knew she needed his help.

"Whatever you want, I'll do it," he said.

"What if it's something that's just crazy? What if I'm crazy?"

"It doesn't matter; I love you."

Frederick would help her. That was enough for Lilith. She didn't have a plan as such, the kind of thought-out scheme that her mother would come up with. She was full of feeling and bright colors. But it all came to this: If she could have her own ceremony, bury her father and brother her own way, she could be done with them, done with Darby. Then she would go away with Frederick. They would find a place where it didn't matter that she was the Squire's daughter and he the trash man's son. They could be somebody else; they could start the world anew.

10

Shrouds and Pyres

The caskets were too heavy and awkward to transport in the
Live Free or Die, and they would have to remove the bodies
anyway to place them on the bier, so they decided they would
open the caskets at the crypt and transfer the remains to
shrouds. They recognized that this, the few minutes in the
crypt when they would see and smell and touch the remains
of the Salmon males, would be the most difficult moment of
the ceremony. Frederick intended to protect himself by preparing to face the experience as a workman. He would turn
away from his own thoughts and feelings, and pay attention
to the task at hand. There was a job to be done; he had been
picked to do it. Lilith had no thoughts of protecting herself.
She had a vague faith that if she irradiated her senses with
the experience she would find salvation.

It was Lilith's idea to use sailcloth for shrouds. Her father
had had an old Lightning-boat sail stored at the Lake Club.
Although he had no apparent use for the sail, he had refused
to part with it. He'd told her once that a man's use for an object
with intrinsic merit lingers on after his death. Such pronouncements, delivered with not a trace of the irony they
apparently deserved, held Lilith in awe, unnerved her, and
finally disgusted her because she accounted them tricks to
keep her off guard. Now that she herself had found a use for

the sailcloth, she realized she had proved him right, herself wrong.

Frederick tied the sail to the roof rack on top of his truck. When they arrived at the Salmon house, he pulled off the sail and bear-hugged it into the house. The sail, stiff as cardboard, protested in his arms like a stolen bride.

By moving some furniture around in the Hearth Room, Frederick and Lilith were able to lay out the sail on the floor. Something about its whiteness and triangularity startled them pleasantly, as if they'd come upon a work of art in the middle of a wilderness. A touch of mildew gave the sail a sweet, corrupt smell. The fabric was Dacron, stubborn and crinkly, so that, when they knelt on the triangle, it sizzled like a campfire. Lilith measured the cloth, using the board-foot rule her father had carried everywhere in the woods. Frederick cut out the shapes for the shrouds with his hunting knife. Lilith found the hand-sewing kit her father had used to repair sails, and the young people sewed the cloth into shrouds. Kneeling, they worked trancelike and in silence.

After they had finished and, as it seemed, awakened into the real world of ambiguity and time, they stood and Frederick held Reggie Salmon's shroud up before his own body.

Lilith measured Frederick against the shroud. Her lover: medium height, wide body, solid, utilitarian; the shroud: tall, stately, ephemeral, mysterious.

"Is it all right?" Frederick asked.

"It's fine."

"Now the pyres," Frederick said.

They drove in Frederick's truck as far as Grace Pond. From here they hiked up to the ledges, just missing a search party that had completed its work only an hour or so earlier. Two people were missing, one of the female clients in the Village Common Nursing Home and a bum named Cooty Patterson.

At about this same time, Dot McCurtin was eavesdropping

on the police radio bands with her scanner. She soon discovered that the search party had located the lost woman from the nursing home, in shock, chewed up by bugs, but otherwise unharmed. The search party had found no sign of Cooty Patterson, but had stumbled upon something else of far more immediate concern to Mrs. McCurtin, a fresh car wreck on the Trust lands. Mrs. McCurtin contacted Town Constable Godfrey Perkins in his police cruiser. A few minutes later, she herself responded to an incoming call on the CB from one of her sources. It seemed as if Persephone Salmon had been seen in the company of a prominent Darby citizen. When Mrs. McCurtin heard the name, she was amazed.

At the ledges, Lilith carried a bow saw, Frederick an ax over his shoulder. He looked like Paul Bunyan, Lilith thought. Here in the woods, it was Frederick, not the memory of her father, who took on a stately bearing.

Frederick was thinking that it was going to be a dirty job lugging the bodies up the trail. (Frederick evaluated tasks according to a scale based roughly on relative cleanliness— clean jobs, decent jobs, messy jobs, dirty jobs, filthy jobs, rotten jobs, pissy jobs, and shitty jobs.) The kid would be nothing, just a bag of bones. But the old man—what would he consist of after a year in a sealed coffin? Surely, he'd be intact but dried out, and therefore not very heavy. Frederick hoped so. The idea of handling an oozy cadaver did not appeal to him.

When they arrived at the Indian camp, Frederick started piling up brush haphazardly, but Lilith made him create a neat, aesthetically pleasing pyre.

"What's the diff? It's all going up in flames!" Frederick exaggerated in tone his feeling of slight exasperation.

"You're just lazy, Frederick," Lilith said wryly.

"And you're bossy."

In their labors, Frederick and Lilith enjoyed the intimacy of

251

conspirators, and they reverted to the pleasant sparring sessions that had kept them close earlier in the month. Words meant nothing, tone and facial expressions meant everything.

"I'm beginning to believe your mother's right—there is a God," Lilith preached in mock seriousness. "But He's not the God she thinks He is. He's nothing like the gods that people worship. But He's out there, and He cares about how things look . . . nice . . . orderly . . . pretty. That's why He made them."

"How do you know that?" Frederick inoculated his question with incredulity.

"Because He's like me—and I like things neat."

"You're saying He's a Salmon."

"That's right."

"Maybe this God is an Elman—untidy," Frederick said. "Look at these woods. Things growing all twisted. Rotten logs on the ground. Pucker brush everywhere. Different kinds of trees growing every which way. It's untidy."

"Not to me. To me, everything here is in its place," Lilith said.

"That big room in your house . . ."

"The Hearth Room."

"It wasn't so neat."

"My mother let it go. When I have my own house . . . We'll have a house, won't we?" The playfulness suddenly left her voice; she was desperate and serious.

"Of course we'll have a house, with kids and chickens in the yard, and a new pickup truck and a garage and a lawn and a friggn' white picket fence." Frederick did not believe his own words.

"When I have my own house, it will be neat," Lilith said.

Frederick had no desire for a house—let alone a *neat* house; he wanted only Lilith and the road. Her ambitions for a home made him wince inside. He understood now that he'd have to give up something for this woman, maybe give up everything he had valued, which was only one thing: his freedom.

They constructed a platform to receive the bodies, a raised platform about six feet high, eight feet long, and four feet wide. They cut posts with crooked ends at the top, positioned cross-pieces in the crooks, then laid branches perpendicular to the crosspieces. Frederick had little trouble finding and cutting the posts with the crooked ends, but how to support them was a problem, because the soil on the ledges was so thin. You couldn't bury a wooden post in ledge. Lilith solved the problem.

"Cairns—we'll embed each pole in a cairn," she said.

Frederick approved. "Plenty of rocks up here—this is New Hampshire," he said.

Frederick cut and chopped wood for the pyres, mostly the dead lower branches of hemlocks. They were full of pitch, and they were dry; they would make a hot, crackling fire. Lilith gathered rocks. She enjoyed the rough feel of the stones in her hands as she laid them against the posts. The work went on almost the entire afternoon. When they had finished, they rested, sitting on the log beside the blackened embers of the old Indian campfire. Then they walked down to the pond and the Live Free or Die.

"Now what?" Frederick said.

"I don't know."

"I'll buy a six-pack."

"No, please. Don't drink. This is too important to drink."

Frederick folded his arms. He was about to complain, thought better of it, and said, "Let's go back to your house. We'll get something to eat. And wait until dark."

"Middle of the night," Lilith said. "After the teenagers are finished making out in their cars. After the drunks are home. And when the moon is down."

Side by side, taking up a tad less than two-thirds of the front seat of the truck, they started down the rough road that snaked through the Trust.

When they pulled into the Salmon drive, they were distressed to find the cruiser of the town constable parked in front of the house. The constable was standing on the grass, as if he'd tried the door, peeked into the windows, and now didn't know what to do next.

Godfrey Perkins was about fifty. He had a skinny neck, narrow shoulders, and long apelike arms. He might have resembled Ichabod Crane were it not for his spectacular potbelly. It protruded from his front without splaying out to his sides. And because he had no fat to speak of anywhere else on his body, he gave the impression of a rather masculine fellow who, much to his bewilderment, had awakened after a long sleep pregnant. He wore traditional policeman's blues, topped by a gray, cowboy-style hat.

"The sail—what's left of it is still in the house," Lilith whispered to Frederick. "Do you think he saw it? Does he know?"

Frederick touched Lilith's shoulder, stuck his head out the window of the truck, and said, "Something wrong, Godfrey?"

"I got some business with Miss *Saamin,*" the constable said.

Frederick and Lilith stepped out of the truck. Lilith stuffed her hands in the pockets of her blue jeans and with a stony face looked the constable in the eye. Frederick stood by the door so that he was not too close to Lilith. He was amazed at the transformation in her. In the pickup, when she had first seen the policeman, she was frightened, vulnerable. Now, on her own property, she was a *Sahl-mohn*—beautiful, cool, in charge.

"What business?" she challenged.

"It's about your father's vehicle. We found it smashed up in the woods."

Lilith said nothing, but she continued to look at Officer Perkins as if he were a collectible at a yard sale.

"Did you report it stolen to the state police?" he asked.

Lilith shook her head no.

"If you were in an accident, you have to report it, miss. Did you crack up that car?"

"Where did you find it?" Lilith asked.

"I told you. In the woods. On the Trust."

"The Trust is private property. Neither the town nor the state has a legal interest in the land or the roads."

Perkins puffed his cheeks, blew out some air, and grabbed the front of his gun belt. "What you say is true. Unless there was some pee-eye in that accident, there's no need to report it or remove the remains of the vehicle."

The constable now looked at Lilith, as if it was her turn to speak. But she said nothing.

"You can leave it there as a memento, if you want," the constable said, to fill the void.

"Right now I wish to rest, or else I'd invite you in for a cup of coffee," Lilith said, suddenly friendly, engaging. So that Perkins could excuse himself and make a graceful exit.

Frederick and Lilith watched the constable get into his cruiser and drive off.

"I wish I could handle cops like that," Frederick said.

"Did I handle him?" Lilith started toward the house.

"Lilith, you don't know your own power." Frederick followed her, lagging a step or two behind; then he caught up. They were side by side when they reached the door, and each of them stopped short, not knowing exactly who should go first.

11

Staying and Leaving

The bear and her cub, loping loosely if not gracefully on two hind legs and one forepaw, were headed for Grace Pond. Like most of the Trust critters, the sow regarded the place as a special eatery; the pond did for the Trust what the Inn at Darby Green did for the town: attract visitors from great distances and at the same time enhance the livelihood of the indigenous population.

Shorelines rivaled the lower world for their richness and variety of smells; the sow could always find something dead either to dine upon or to peruse. Sometimes the dead things had decayed beyond rot, beyond putrefaction, so that they could not be eaten. Such matter had come round until, to the nose of the sow, it possessed sweetness and charm, to be experienced rather than consumed, to be worn as a human might wear perfume, and she'd roll in the dead matter to take on its exotic scent.

The sow was in a good mood. The cub was better, moving around. She'd even gotten him to lick food morsels from her fur, blood and such. Soon he'd be weaned. She'd be free to mate again. However, the cub was slow, constantly lagging behind his mother. And she left him far behind. She could always locate him, for his scent was strong and true, and she had it fixed so securely in her bear mind that as far as she was concerned he did not actually exist as separate from her but, rather, as an extension of herself. When his scent was strong, she smelled him into being. All this was part of her instinct as a mother, and would vanish once the cub was weaned.

The sow kept in the shadows. She did not like the feel of direct sunlight, which she experienced as a threat from some unknowable predator that resided in the daytime sky. She preferred to move in tree shade, but there was a strong smell of dead fish down by Grace Pond, and it was imperative she reach the smell before some other scavenger did. Her competitors, crows and coyotes, also patrolled the shorelines of water bodies.

Often, when she left the den, the cub stayed behind, but this day he tagged along. It was the time of year for activity, for exploration, for exercise, for growth. He imitated his mother, poking his nose under logs he could not yet lift. On two hind legs and one forepaw, he moved with a distinctive shuffle, and there was no consciousness sufficiently subtle (save the Creator Himself) to appreciate it—that is, until now, when he arrived under a certain tall pine.

The sow had gone downslope from the pine tree, and even if the wind had been favorable she would not have smelled the men. They were too far above the zone of free-flowing forest air that carried smells. When Howard Elman had built the stand, he'd made sure he went above that zone, which he reckoned (arbitrarily) as thirty-five feet from the ground.

Whack Two had spotted the tree stand earlier that day, when he and Abnaki had been loitering about in the forest. While Abnaki had sat honing the points of his arrows, Whack Two had reclined in an essay of sunshine upon the leaf-mold-blemished earth. He'd looked up, not thinking exactly but experiencing the patterns in the trees, as another youth might experience a movie show, when he'd seen something strange—strange for this place, anyway—which was not strictly the four-by-eight sheet of plywood that Howard Elman had somehow managed to hoist up the tree but, rather, a suggestion of rectangularity. He pointed out the strangeness to Abnaki, who knew at a glance what was in the pine: a hunter's tree stand.

"This is worth a look-see," Abnaki had said.

They had climbed up, Whack Two first, Abnaki following, his bow over his shoulder. The view opened. Abnaki and Whack Two could see the pond and ledges of the Trust land at the end of the sweep of hills that rose up from the water. They could also see the Connecticut River Valley below and, in the distance, Mount Ascutney in Vermont. The deep green of summer made them feel peaceful and playful. Abnaki experienced a sense of command, Whack Two a sudden urge to plunge off the platform and fly away.

When the bear cub arrived under the tree, Whack Two stared down. He had never seen a bear before. In fact, he had seen few pictures of bears, and the idea of a bear cub had never quite taken hold in him, so that the creature below him seemed otherworldly. This feeling was reinforced by the fact that here obviously was the creature they had been seeking, for it was white. He had never thought it would be so young. It had occurred to him that television was a window between the United States of America and ancient Asian deities. Now, as he watched the animal, he couldn't get over the idea he was watching TV, a program on white bears.

The cub had smelled something interesting near the tree. He didn't quite know what it was, but he knew it was in the ground and that maybe he could eat it. The idea of eating was very exciting to the cub. He liked his mother well enough, her rough comfort, her wonderful smell, but she was cranky and she knocked him around, and though her milk made him dreamy, lately he'd discovered he could eat things the way she

258

did, sniff 'em, slurp 'em, and chew 'em. Fun that satisfied the belly—what else could an active cub ask for? He began to scrape at the pine needles with his good paw.

Up the tree, Whack Two noticed that the cub only had one forefoot, and he extended his hands and looked at them. Then he looked down, to study the cub, learn the secrets of its nature. He stared at his hands again. At that moment he heard the twang of Abnaki's bow, the extended thwip of the arrow in flight, then the short thwup as it hit its target.

"Got him!" Abnaki hollered.

Whack Two heard the cub whine below. The sound sent him back in time, to that other world, to his mother's wail, to mist in the morning, sun at midday, rain in the afternoon, darkness under the trees.

Several hundred yards away, the sow did not hear her cub's soft whine of surprise at his own pain, but she did hear Abnaki's cry of exuberance. However, because she didn't smell the man, she didn't quite know what to make of the sound. She could smell the cub. He was, she determined, upslope. She also caught the strong food odor of the dead fish, but it didn't come to her directly from the pond, for the wind had shifted. Rather, it was background smell, in the trees. The sow rose up on her hind legs and sniffed the air.

Abnaki possessed a clear understanding of the nature of his crime—killing for pay—but he felt neither guilt nor regret for having committed it. He would have killed the cub even if Garvin Prell had not promised him money for the act; Abnaki killed for the fun of it. In the next few hours, or perhaps for the entire remainder of the day, like a surfer riding a wave, he would coast on the remnant pleasure of the memory of killing the cub—the feeling in his fingertips of the arrow leaving the bow, the image of the arc of flight of the arrow, the sound of the arrow arriving home. He was so excited that he left his bow up the tree when he scrambled down. Whack Two was right behind. Abnaki's arrow had penetrated the cub at the shoulder, and the point had gone into the chest. It must have pierced the heart, because the cub was dead, sitting serenely in blood-stained pine needles.

Abnaki knelt to pull out the arrow. Whack Two knelt beside him.

"Whack Two, this is our lucky day," Abnaki said. He had trouble extricating his arrow from the flesh of the bear, and by the time he'd finished, his hands were covered with the cub's blood. Whack Two took Abnaki's bloodied hand in his own. Abnaki touched Whack Two's cheek.

"You've got blood on your face, boy." Abnaki laughed. Then he spread the cub's legs. Whack Two looked for the sex organs. They were small, hidden, male. "Come on, grab his feet," Abnaki said.

Whack Two took the bear by the legs; Abnaki put his bloody hands under the shoulders.

The cub was much heavier than Whack Two thought he would be. He sniffed the bear. The fur, long and shaggy and dirty, stank, but the blood was fresh and raw.

At that point Abnaki spotted the cub's mother downslope, roaring toward them like a freight train. They dropped the cub; Abnaki reached for his bow, which was not there. Then they ran for their lives.

After Constable Perkins left, Frederick and Lilith felt the barrier between them thicken. They could speak, they could touch, they could love, but a part of each was sealed off from the other. Frederick paced among the downstairs rooms like a restless burglar.

Lilith did not feel the strain of waiting directly in herself but through her apprehension of the sounds of her house. The wind against loose shutters, creaks and groans of beams, the conk-uh! of water pipes—subdued noises that normally she barely noted now seemed like the grunts of some pained and confined beast. It was her duty to care for that beast, feed it and make it comfortable and try to persuade it for its own good that it was not imprisoned but protected.

As they stood together in the Hearth Room, Frederick said, "I can't get over the feeling somebody's out there, watching us."

An image of those bare, third-story rooms appeared in Lilith's mind, at once bright and ill defined, like an Impressionist painting. A painting—now she could see her mother as a child struggling to bring forth her reality in oil paints. "Yes, I feel it, too," Lilith said. "But it's not a person. It's the land, it's ghosts."

"No such thing as a ghost," Frederick said.

"Ghosts in ourselves."

That stopped him. Memories, fears—maybe they had a life of their own. "I'm jumpy. I'm going outdoors and look around." Frederick charged outside with the hesitant aggression of a bull attacking a waved handkerchief.

Lilith stared out the window, looking now at Frederick skulking about, now at the fields where once she'd hoped to grow crops, now at the stone wall and the forest and the ledges beyond.

Outside, Frederick almost hoped Perkins would jump out at him from the "out there." At least then he'd know his enemy. He scanned the fields and the woods behind. It struck him how stupid it was for him to be standing in the open—a target. He started to walk. He stopped, turned, and stared at the huge shingled house—target! The dwelling protects the dwellers, and the dwellers protect the dwelling. He thought he saw a movement in the woods beyond. He imagined it was his father, striding toward him, carrying a can of gasoline, preparing to torch this place. Goddamn you, Howie! He visualized himself tackling Howard, gas spilling from the can, the gas igniting—everybody dead. He shook away the image, and soon, in the walking, he calmed down.

Just to keep busy, he measured the perimeter of the house in footsteps. Twenty-seven paces north-south. Sixty-seven and a half feet. Twenty-seven paces east-west. The place—immense, full of history and renown, commanding views of two states—was no more than a big square box with lots of protruding angles. He grabbed one of the porch pillars and swung himself up on the porch roof. From here he imagined the Squire walking away from the house, going up in the woods to die. His own father was out there now, with a mission to kill. I'm new, I'm new—and Howard Elman is old, used up. A voice from inside interrupted, *Wrong again, Freddy. You're old, older than these hills, while Howard is forever new. You think, he acts; you break, he fixes; you make up, he makes.* Then he remembered that morning when his mother had first laid out work clothes for him. She believed in God, she believed in ceremony; perhaps only she in Darby could understand how important this ritual of burning the bodies of Reggie Salmon and his son was to Lilith and, yes, to himself.

He took note of the clothes he wore—blue jeans, Monkey Hill T-shirt, track shoes, the on-the-road uniform; off-duty duds, his mother called these clothes. But it wasn't time to leave yet; he was not off duty. He shimmied down the pillar and walked to his truck where he changed into heavy forest-green cotton trousers and shirt to match, work clothes for a workingman to do his job in.

Inside the Salmon house, Lilith daydreamed about driving off with Frederick. They would put this world behind them. They would settle down in, say, San Francisco. They would work for her uncle Thaddeus. They would have an apartment with palm trees flanking a narrow brick entry. Did they have palm trees in San Francisco? The question took on some importance in her mind. She looked up San Francisco in the encyclopedia. Nothing about palm trees. The City—they called it "the City"—was cool and misty. So perhaps there were no palm trees. She tried to picture the Golden Gate Bridge in her mind, but the image didn't take on any life. She imagined docked apartment barges in Sausalito, homes for young people like herself—busy in their jobs and doing whatever they did. A moment later, her dream of flight vanished. As with Frederick, what took the place of the dream was duty—to her family, to herself, to her town: put to final rest the father and the father's only son, and it's over. Once she and Frederick burned the bodies, Garvin and Monet and her mother would have nothing to fight about. They would come to their senses. By then she and Frederick would be far away. So what did it mean, duty? Why was it there, as strong for people you didn't like as for loved ones? She had to leave because she had not the strength or the know-how to do her duty.

She showered, changed into fresh jeans, a plain blue shirt, boots, her hiking outfit. It seemed important to her that she be fresh and clean for the experience. She washed her hair and pulled it back into a pony tail. Her face in the mirror seemed drab and uninteresting. Those Indians of old probably marked themselves with paint. She slashed her face with lipstick. Her expression was too serious, too reserved to give the marks any meaning. Wild markings on the wrong face. She scrubbed clean, and put on a light layer of makeup, as if she were going out to dinner.

When Frederick came back into the house, Lilith saw that he was wearing his father's work clothes. The sight vaguely unsettled her. "Trash man's uniform," she said.

Frederick was startled by her words; then he grasped the "Honeywagon Inc." label over the breast pocket and ripped it off. "Not anymore," he said.

They left as soon as it was dark, Frederick behind the steering wheel, Lilith beside him, shrouds in the rear. The truck pulled out of the driveway, and Lilith glanced back at the house. "Maybe I'll never see it again," she said.

"My father says, Never say never; say instead, You never know."

"Where will we go? We haven't talked about that."

"I don't like to make plans," Frederick said. "Takes away the spontaneity."

"I want to talk about where we're going," Lilith said. She could feel that barrier between them, invisible but hard and impenetrable. She could tell it would always be like this. They would never quite agree on anything.

"West," Frederick said.

"West?" She put some schoolgirl sarcasm in her voice.

"Maybe New Mexico."

"Taos? Santa Fe?" Lilith pressed.

"I was thinking Alamogordo," Frederick said. "They've got Indians there and cowboys and Spanish Americans and scientists and travelers. There's a little bit of everybody in America in that town," Frederick said.

"I was thinking of Taos," Lilith countered.

The road melded invisibly into Center Darby, and soon they were in the village.

"When you're on the road, alone for hours on end, what do you think about?" Lilith asked.

"I think about the things I see. I think about stories."

"Stories?"

"It's like I'm in a waking dream. I'm telling a story to somebody I don't know, a long story, somebody else's story. I see this guy in my head who looks like me, except I think of him not as myself but as him, and this guy is telling a story about people I know. This goes on for miles."

"People you know? Your father?"

"Everybody."

"Frederick, it's your way of loving them."

Lilith's insight struck Frederick like a sharp, painful musical note. "Maybe," he said.

"What about your own story?" she asked.

"I have no story," he said. "Just other people's dreams. But once we're away from here together, we'll make our own dream, and we'll make it real."

"Dreams were ruined for me long ago."

"You were born a Salmon. How can you ask for better than that?"

"Don't you see, don't you?"

"No," Frederick said.

"The Salmons stopped dreaming. Because the dreams came true. Everything, house, land, money, prestige. And then—gone."

As Lilith thought about the situation now, she could see that her grandparents had some of the leftover dreams. She didn't think her parents ever had dreams. Her father had his Trust, but that wasn't a dream, it was a sickness. Her mother, now that she thought about it, had nothing. The house was a cruel mockery for her, because it was never her house. It was the Salmon house. In the beginning, Persephone had Reggie, and when the marriage went bad, she was left with nobody, nowhere.

Frederick didn't think he'd heard Lilith right. "What do you mean—gone?" he asked.

"Why do you automatically assume a Salmon is rich?"

"It's true, isn't it?"

"If it's true, I am who I am. If it's not, I'm nobody. Isn't that so?"

"Lilith, everybody with no money is nobody. So stop playing with the idea." He glanced over at her and caught the fury in her eyes, and he did not understand. "You're rich—tell me you're not rich," he goaded her.

Now was the time to reach out a hand to him, to say, "No, I am not rich. The Squire's daughter is not rich. Hold me, change me, as I change you." But Lilith could not speak. She said nothing for a moment, and then she announced, "I don't care about money."

Frederick took her ambivalence as criticism of him for launching an incursion upon her wealth.

"Lilith, I will never ask you for money. If I ask, we're doomed—we're dead."

She was sealed off from him. As long as they remained in Darby, she would remain sealed off from him. Only somewhere else did they have a chance. "Oh, Frederick, what's going to happen to us?"

Frederick again heard great emotion in her voice, and again misunderstood the meaning. "We can get jobs and we can share what we make, but if we use your family's money, it will be like we never left Darby," he said. "You'll still be the Upper Darby girl, and I'll still be the Center Darby boy. We have to start over—clean." Then he added with a laugh, "And penniless."

It was as if a wave broke over Lilith, and now she was listening to the retreating water. After tonight, she might never see Darby Lake again, never see Upper Darby. Once they were on the road, she would no longer be the Squire's daughter. When they were far away, she could tell him the whole truth about herself. Perhaps that was the reason she must go. Out there, in the desert, she would speak the truth.

Frederick was puzzled. He knew something between them had been left unsaid, but he was afraid to delve further to discover what was missing.

"I wonder where the old man went," he said, and his words, coming completely out of context, knocked her off center for a second.

"Your partner on the trash route—Cooty?"

"Yah."

"You said he takes off all the time. You weren't worried before."

"Something's different this time. I don't know what it is. Me and you, the bear, town troubles—Cooty's got a nose for these things. I'm afraid for him."

"Don't worry about him. He's an adult."

"I don't know what Cooty is, but 'adult' is not the word. I don't think he can survive out there."

"You mean without your help or your father's."

"That's right."

"That's not *right*—that's vanity, Center Darby style," Lilith said.

Frederick said nothing. He was thinking that so many local people went into the woods and disappeared, their remains revealed before the new spring growth, the bodies often half eaten by domesticated dogs on romps in the woods but rarely touched by wild animals. In contrast, few carcasses of wild animals were ever found. The beasts consumed one another, left no trace. They were part of the continuity of the forest. His own kind, human beings and the creatures brought under the umbrella of humanity, disturbed that continuity. It occurred to Frederick now that Reggie Salmon had been right, right to rob his rich brethren in Upper Darby of their ill-gotten land, right to establish a Trust where no man was allowed.

Frederick turned off Center Darby Road onto Owl's Hill Road, which led to the new cemetery.

"We're here," Lilith said.

"*Ayuh.*" Frederick mocked the accent of his own people.

When they reached the entrance to the cemetery, Frederick shut off the lights of the Live Free or Die and turned off the blacktop onto a dirt road. Under the rising half-moon and starlight, Lilith felt the peace of the place. Frederick drove to the rear of the cemetery. He backed the truck to about six feet from the crypt, and shut off the engine.

When Lilith stepped out of the truck, she felt unusually alert, frighteningly, thrillingly alive. Every sensation was heightened—the softness of the grassy ground on the soles of her boots, the smell of the damp air, the sound of peepers, the sight of fireflies dancing over the graves. The moon was just above the trees surrounding the cemetery. They'd planned to wait until the moon was down. It was more dangerous this way, she thought, but better—much better—because this was the alive part of the night. She couldn't have borne waiting for hours, watching the moon rise and fall, darkness diminishing, darkness growing, the night coming to its peak, then dying into her own sleepiness. She looked at Frederick. He was all business, mumbling to himself as he inspected the crypt. It showed a face of granite stones. The remainder was buried in the earth of the hillside. The door was made of heavy oak planks.

"How are we going to get it open?" The night air sweetened Lilith's whispered words.

"Chop through the son of a bitch," he said.

Lilith could hear the voice of Howard Elman from Frederick's throat. He rummaged around in the back of the Live Free or Die for his ax. Lilith fetched a flashlight from the utility box in the cab.

As Frederick swung the ax, Lilith heard first a loud kch!, then the returning echo, kch-eek!, a scream abbreviated by oblivion, and finally the -uh! grunt of Frederick's effort. A chip of wood flew clear. Again—kch! kch-eek! -uh!; again—kch! kch-eek! -uh!; again; again. There were no houses nearby, but someone out for an evening walk would hear them.

Lilith fetched the shrouds.

Frederick chopped a jagged hole a few inches wide and a foot long through the door. He shoved a chain through the hole and hooked the end onto the inside latch. He wrapped the other end of the chain around the rear bumper of the Live Free or Die. He started the truck, put it in gear, and stepped on the gas. The truck jerked forward, the door shuddered for a moment, then neatly pulled out, frame and all. What remained was the stone arch and a black, empty maw. It looked like the main fireplace in the Salmon house.

Lilith clicked on the flashlight. Yellow light slashed through the darkness, and yet it showed nothing. The shrouds over her shoulder, she walked into the crypt. The two caskets were side by side, the larger one her father's, the smaller one her brother's. The chamber itself was no bigger than her own bedroom. A smell suddenly on her nostrils surprised her by its softness, like spring earth waiting for planting. Lilith enjoyed a moment of peace, sweet because it was unexpected. The feeling passed when Frederick blundered into the room, stinking of anxiety and his labors.

"I thought I heard a car," he said. "Let's hurry up, and shut off that flashlight."

"You're afraid," Lilith said.

"Douse the goddamn flashlight," Frederick barked.

"I don't want to—I want to see—I have to see."

"Jeez!"

In her stubbornness, the strength of it, the certainty of her conviction—she had to see!—Lilith realized she was behaving like her mother. She'd always thought she was her father's child. Maybe, after all, she was destined to re-enact her mother's tragedy, and not her father's. Lilith shone the light on the large casket. Frederick pulled the shroud off her shoulder and threw it upon his own. He put his hands on the handles of the casket and pulled upward very hard. The exertion was

269

unnecessary. The casket top opened easily. At the very moment Frederick turned his head away, Lilith aimed the beam of the light inside the casket.

She recoiled, twisting backward as if struck. Frederick grabbed the flashlight from her hand, and the beam illuminated her face for a moment. She was as one stunned with pain and humiliation, as if somebody had spit in her face.

"What is it? What's in there?" Frederick said.

Lilith could not speak.

Frederick shone the beam into the casket.

"Empty! Nothing!" Frederick shouted at the granite stones of the crypt. He shone the light in Lilith's face.

And then a voice cried out, reverberating about the granite walls, *"Lih-lah! Lih-laaaaah!"*

Frederick whipped around, aiming the flashlight in the doorway. The beam fell on Persephone Salmon. It was she who had called out Lilith's name, but her voice was hardly recognizable. It was grating and harsh. Her face in the flashlight beam was bright red, creased with lines. She appeared to have aged ten years. Her back was hunched slightly, misshapen. Cradled in her arms were two urns.

"Mother," said Lilith, coming awake.

"How did you find us?" Frederick scanned the night for signs of police.

"Mrs. McCurtin," Persephone hissed.

"She knows we're here?" Frederick was alarmed.

"She knew about the sail. I put the rest together myself." Persephone addressed Frederick, then turned to her daughter. "You came for them, but you're too late."

Lilith stepped toward Persephone as if to embrace her, stopped short, and touched the urns close to her mother's bosom. "Ashes," Lilith said.

"Monet and Garvin are going to fight until doomsday—I knew that from the beginning." Persephone's words seemed to heat the air in the crypt, so that Frederick felt as if he were standing in front of a roaring furnace. "They'll fight until they're both exhausted, until there's nothing left of Upper Darby—no money, no prestige, no remainder of the old world. And still they'll fight. I played along with their infantile games. I even hired that fool Dracut to throw them off the track. But I knew from the start what I was going to do. Bud Parkinson and I fetched the bodies. . . ."

"What did you see?" Lilith cried out her question.

"We saw . . ."

"What did you see?" Lilith repeated.

"We saw nothing," Persephone said, and it was impossible to tell whether she told the truth or not. "It doesn't matter what they do at that court hearing; I had the remains cremated, and I'm going to take them with me down under."

"Don't go, please don't go, Mother," Lilith said.

"I must. I'm burning up inside. Another day here and I'll be incinerated," Persephone said. "You, you must stay."

"Mother! Persephone!"

"Listen, I know what you had planned tonight. You've got to destroy any evidence. If Mrs. McCurtin finds out, you'll both be spurned, shunned, outcasts forever. Not only from this town but from the world, from yourselves."

"Mother, help me!"

"There comes a time when a mother has nothing left to give. I have to save myself before I can save you."

"Help me!"

"Not now! Understand? Not now!"

Earlier that day, the sow bear had come into the sunlight and eaten hornpout heads and guts. She ambled around the entire pond, finding along the way tubers and a couple of dead fish washed up on shore; she raided a bird's nest for the young. Then she went looking for her cub. There was something strange about his scent. It seemed to stay in one place, it was not so distant, it contained no fright, and yet it was oddly weak. She followed the scent. She saw the men, but she did not chase them. She ran toward the smell of her cub. The smell was strong, but it was intermingled with the smell of food and the smell of the lower world. And before the sow was a carcass. She'd eat fresh meat but she preferred it aged. She sniffed the carcass—and pulled back. The smell of her cub was shot through the carcass.

The sow did not understand, and she did not know what to do. The smell of the lower world made her want to flee, the smell of food made her want to feed, the smell of her cub made her want to create him. She charged at a bush, roaring and slashing with her big paws, but there was no enemy present. She returned to the carcass and circled it, stopping every now and then to sniff the bloody spots and privates. It smelled so strongly of her cub that she licked it and nudged it, to enliven it. She knocked it over, but it did not move of its own. It was as if the smell of the lower world prevented her from smelling the cub into being. She reared up on her hind legs, stood over the carcass, and roared. The carcass did not move. She backed up, and stood on four feet looking at it.

The sow waited all night and into the next day for her cub to come to life. By then both the scent of the cub and the scent of the lower world had faded, and the smell of food from the cub was stronger. The sow was hungry, but she did not want to feed here. She made one more bluff charge, then left. This much she knew: something was over; it was time to leave this place.

Frederick and Lilith stood dazed outside the crypt, as Persephone sped off. A few minutes passed before the lovers returned to the world of measurement and judgment.

"I was wrong about Dracut," Lilith said. "I was wrong about my mother. I was wrong about everything. This—stealing bodies, burning them—it was so crazy. What was I thinking of?"

"Just shaking things up. It probably would have worked, too," Frederick said.

"It doesn't make any difference now. I'm back where I started from. Nothing is resolved. Frederick, I can't leave with you. I have to stay in Darby."

The thought of all those miles between himself and everywhere else, alone, no longer seemed inviting to Frederick. He was afraid of being alone. She had to come with him, or he could not go. His cherished idea of freedom had dissolved in his love for this woman. He tried to talk her into leaving, but even as he spoke he knew they'd both be staying, trapped here. He shook away his dispiritedness and reconstituted himself as a practical workman. "Your mother's right," he said. "We have to get rid of that pyre."

They drove back to Grace Pond. Lilith heard on the radio that the lost old woman had been found in the woods. Where did she think she was going—home? Where did Persephone think she was going? *Where are you going, Mother—home?*

They hiked from the pond up the trail in the darkness. Lilith carried the shrouds, and when they arrived at the ledges, she threw them on top of the pyre.

Frederick knelt between the cairns and struck a match to some dry pine needles. The young people knelt side by side until the fire was going well. Then, on the hard ground of the ledges, they made love.

Well after the moon was down, the coyotes came out from their lairs and fed on the carcass of the cub. One of the females took some of the meat back to her own cubs.

The next day, Frederick and Lilith scattered the stones and the ashes so that all evidence of the pyre was gone.

Downslope, crows picked what meat was left off the bones of the cub. At the same time, the bear sow was heading north. Cooty Patterson picked up her trail and followed.

PART III

PART III

1

Different

Once Dot McCurtin had passed judgment, decided what you were, who you were, that was it as far as the people of Darby were concerned. You were what she said you were. In the case of Frederick Elman and Lilith Salmon, Mrs. McCurtin's pronouncement came on Christmas Eve, between hymns at the annual Darby Common Christmas Caroling, sponsored by the Unified Church of Christ. The night was crisp and cold, but not frigid. It had snowed a couple weeks before, but most of the cover had melted, and patches of bare, drab ground showed through a smutty crust. Technically, it was going to be a white Christmas, but in fact Darby did not look very Christmassy.

Mrs. McCurtin, who practiced singing by staring in a mirror and shaping perfect "O"s with her mouth, gathered with the other choir members on the Darby Village Common. From here, the carolers could see Joe Ancharsky's manger brilliantly illuminated outside the store. Oh, it was spectacular all right, but Mrs. McCurtin reckoned it a little too showy, a little too Catholic.

The choir moved from house to house on the common, singing carols under the direction of the Reverend Spofford Hall. The roving concert was almost finished when the group reached the Village Common Nursing Home. It was at this point on the route that Mrs. Arthur Crabb, who had been on vacation in Florida, joined the singers; naturally she sought out her friend and confidante, Dot McCurtin. The two women chatted between "Hark! the Herald" and "Glory Be to the Newborn King."

"Arthur called the town attorney to find out the latest on the court hearings," Mrs. Crabb said, "but wouldn't you know it . . ."

Mrs. McCurtin cut in, "He's in Florida, too."

"Oh, Dot, you've got a line on everybody," Mrs. Crabb said.

Mrs. McCurtin understood Mrs. Crabb's need to know. The court cases regarding the town had dragged on for months. There were so many postponements and so much legal brouhaha, no one was quite sure just what the issues were anymore. But while the Crabbs were on vacation, Judge Barnicle had held a couple of important hearings, and Selectman Crabb wanted to know what was what. He'd sent his wife to get the info.

Mrs. McCurtin told Mrs. Crabb that Judge Barnicle had dismissed the white-bear case as fatuous, but found merit in the Indian-graveyard issue, and on that basis continued his injunction against any building construction at the old cemetery. As to where the Squire was going to be buried, the matter was still up in the air, what with the widow having absconded with the remains, or so the story went. What a riot! Another hearing was scheduled for January.

"Everybody in the town pretends to be up in arms, because the school won't get built this year, but a lot of 'em are secretly happy, because now their taxes won't go up. Tell me if I'm wrong," Mrs. McCurtin said.

"I don't know why they need a new school anyway. These kids are spoiled," Mrs. Crabb said, then veered off her original course and added, "I have some news of my own."

The Crabbs had decided that, starting next year, they'd

spend the whole winter in Florida, not just a couple of weeks. They had sold a piece of land to the Prells—"Oh, heck! You can't take it with you." Mrs. McCurtin did not have to press on to determine the meaning of this event to the town: if Arthur Crabb was going to winter in Florida, he wouldn't be running for re-election as selectman at the town meeting in March. Mrs. McCurtin took note.

The Reverend Hall cued the singers with a discreet, clenched-teeth order: "Glory Be . . ." The carolers began to sing: "Glory be to the newborn king. . . ."

Mr. Hall was a Southerner, overdressed in a parka and fur hat that made him look like a Russian. Mrs. McCurtin wondered if the church had erred in hiring him. When they had looked for a new rector after the Reverend Summerfield had passed away, old Mrs. Dorne had said that nowadays only Southerners could be said to practice true Christianity. The comment, uttered off the cuff, had the sting of truth in it, and the church elders had hired a Southerner. Mrs. McCurtin did not approve. She continued to attend church service, but she kept her distance from the new minister. In fact, she thought very little about God or religion, or any of the things religious people thought about. God and Christianity were just there, like a family history of nose moles. Not important as such. What was important was the necessity of a town-supported church. Without church and organized religion, people strangled in their own desperate questions. The church was in the same business as herself: it provided answers. But none of this had anything to do with Mrs. McCurtin's contempt for the Reverend Hall. Her animosity was based solely on his Southern accent.

The old folks stood in the yard under a spotlight or sat on the porch. Wrapped in blankets or wearing long coats, they resembled people waiting for a train to a concentration camp.

After "Glory Be to the Newborn King" and before "Silent Night," Mrs. McCurtin and Mrs. Crabb observed a pickup truck easing to a stop along the roadside.

"The trash man's son and the Squire's daughter, what a *pay-ah*," Mrs. Crabb said.

Mrs. McCurtin understood that Mrs. Crabb was seeking gossip regarding these young people. Everybody in town knew they were shacking up, but Mrs. Crabb, now that she was back from Florida, sought an update. Mrs. McCurtin timed her releases of gossip to coincide with what she believed to be the community's need to know. She understood that, to be effective, gossip cannot be squirted into the face of the world but, rather, must radiate naturally in all directions from a center, like the ripples made by a stone dropped onto the quiet surface of a pond, and must be beheld by the world from the respectful distance at which a lover of nature beholds those ripples.

"Miss Salmon was seen at the Tuckerman clinic," Mrs. McCurtin said.

Mrs. Crabb looked to Mrs. McCurtin for more.

In her role as town gossip, Mrs. McCurtin believed that truth was relative, but credibility was crucial. She checked up: that was her pride. Her gossip was not idle. "In the waiting room of a baby doctor."

"Oooo." Mrs. Crabb shivered with pleasure. "Well, Dot, what's your line on these two now?"

Mrs. McCurtin felt challenged to reply with just the right description. She sensed that it was time to pass judgment. She rose to the occasion. "Different," she said.

"Different!" Mrs. Crabb chuckled.

"Different," repeated Mrs. McCurtin.

"Different," said Mrs. Crabb, testing the word on her lips.

"Diff-frent," said Mrs. McCurtin yet again, almost as if the "diff" and the "frent" were two separate words, to be spoken with the care of a fastidious coffin maker driving in his nails,

280

drawing out the "f"s of the "diff," putting some nasal into the "frent"—"diff-frent."

Both women understood the local meaning of the word. Darby people believed in the free-enterprise system; believed in necessary laws only (though these should be strictly enforced); believed in fairness but not mercy, frugality but not conservation, independence but not liberation; believed in Live Free or Die. As Mrs. McCurtin put it, "No zoning ordinances or seat-belt regulations for me, thank you." Nonconformity was tolerated, but frowned upon. ("Frowned upon" was another local phrase. Persons who didn't put snow tires on their cars in the winter were frowned upon. Nonconformists were tied, so to speak, to the post and punished with the whiplash frowns of their neighbors.) Persons who displayed creativity were *different*. Persons who dressed expensively or fashionably were *different*. Persons with political leanings left or right of Dwight D. Eisenhower were *different*. Once the word got around that you were different, you were diminished in the eyes of the community. And so it was for Frederick Elman and Lilith Salmon. Beginning that Christmas Eve, Mrs. McCurtin and Mrs. Crabb spread the word. These young people, not necessarily as separate beings but as a unit, were different.

Coincidentally, it was on the same night that Frederick and Lilith came to the same conclusion about themselves. Frederick slowed the Live Free or Die as it approached the carolers on the lawn of the nursing home. He and Lilith sat in the manner of country folk of the American West, he upright, Celtics cap on head, sleeveless parka over a flannel shirt, hands high on the steering wheel; she close beside him, head leaning into his shoulder; space empty on the passenger side.

"Roll the window down, I want to listen," Lilith said.

Frederick pulled over and put his arm around Lilith.

The carolers were singing "Silent Night." Frederick and

Lilith sat listening through the entire hymn. They experienced the music as an emanation from the night sky rather than from the singers, who, in their winter coats under the yellow incandescent lights from the nursing home, seemed more like a whipped mob than a choral group. After the singing, when one of the carolers turned in their direction and appeared to notice their presence, Lilith said, "I want to go now," and Frederick, who not only understood her shyness but shared in it, stepped on the gas.

They were going to the city of Tuckerman to do some last-minute Christmas shopping and, in Frederick's words, "get drunk." Lilith had mailed out presents to her mother in Australia, to her cousins, and to Harriet, her former college roommate. But she hadn't bought anything for Frederick's mother, who had invited Lilith to join the Elman family for Christmas dinner.

"What am I going to buy her?" Lilith asked.

Frederick shrugged.

"You're no help."

"That's true."

"What are you buying her?"

"Same thing I got her last year—nothing."

"Nothing?"

"It's an Elman family tradition," Frederick said. "Once you're not a kid anymore, you don't ask for presents. You don't give to nobody, nobody gives to you. Saves a lot of hassle during years of prosperity, saves face in the down times."

"That's terrible!"

"I never bought her anything," Frederick chuckled.

"I don't believe you."

"It's true. She never wanted anything. It's a mistake to give her gifts, Lilith. She feeds on self-sacrifice. Offer her a present and you'll make her suspicious."

"I have to do something, a gesture—something."

"I know," Frederick said.

He spoke either too softly or too loudly. Either he kidded her or he was kind to her, but he was incapable of dealing with her squarely and seriously. He protected himself from people, including her, with quick anger, a sense of humor, and dreams of escape. Frederick was not equipped for the world—not yet, Lilith thought.

They drove on in silence for a while; then Lilith said, "Your family is so strange."

"All families are strange. The very idea of a family is strange. Ever see a parent that didn't have his life ruined by his kids? Ever see a kid who liked family life?"

"Having a family is natural and necessary. Just because it isn't fun doesn't make it strange."

Frederick pulled the truck into a parking space in downtown Tuckerman. Christmas lights gave Main Street a festive look. The stores were open another hour, and then the commercial sector of the city would shut down until after the holiday.

They strolled arm and arm, much too cozy for a couple in a New England city, as if they were from someplace else, far away, where people were more demonstrative.

Lilith and Frederick, living in her house on his salary as a trash collector, had agreed not to buy any presents for each other. That would come later, after they were on their feet. That was the phrase Frederick used—"on our feet"; it meant the future. They'd talked about this future, but the discussions had kept reaching a dead end until last September, when Lilith spoke the words that were on both their minds—"If you're going to support us the way we want, you have to get a college degree." That had led to a compromise of Frederick's position that he must not use any of Lilith's money. Lilith paid for night courses Frederick was taking at the state college in Tuckerman. Of course, she paid out of the money set aside for her own education, the only money she had.

283

Frederick was doing very well in his classes. He read during every spare moment. He entertained her with quirky theories, and infuriated her with opinions about subjects he knew little about. Sometimes he recited his poems to her. Once he blurted out, "I'm going to raise myself up to your level." She'd watched the shame envelop him for voicing the thought. She could say nothing, do nothing about this issue of class and privilege and culture and whatever else lay between them. She didn't have the right. When you were at the pinnacle, you didn't have the right. He was holding her up, his gun the poverty of his childhood, not the lack of money, but everything else—the injurious influences, the heritage of just-getting-by, the fear of language, the hatred of art and sagacity and elegance, and above all (and now she was remembering words spoken by her father) "the crummy, hypocritical public school system that selected some students for better things and sent the rest to tinker with machines or to master trivial facts and the latest lies about the American way of life." It hit her now why Monet was so hostile to the town's plan for a new school. He was imitating Reggie.

Lilith missed her own school life; mainly she missed friends of her own gender. Here in Upper Darby, she had her house and she had Frederick, and that was all. There were few women her own age in Darby. Meanwhile, Upper Darby had frozen her out of its social world because of her relationship with Frederick. Or perhaps there was more to it than that. Perhaps Upper Darby had harbored a deep resentment of the Salmons, and now—now that the father was dead, the mother gone—she, the daughter, was seen as an easier target. Or perhaps they steered away from her merely because they were uncomfortable with Frederick. Not that any of this mattered at the moment.

The lovers walked on until Frederick stopped abruptly.

"Here's the place to satisfy your dreams," he said. They were standing in front of Woolworth's.

"I've never been in there."

"Lived in Tuckerman County all her life, never been in Woolworth's," Frederick teased.

"All right, then. Let's go—you can pick the present."

"Hey, wait a minute. I was only kidding," Frederick said, but Lilith pulled him gently by the hand, and in they went.

The first things she saw were plastic imitation-porcelain animals—pigs, poodles, roosters.

"Buy one of those. Mom'll love it," Frederick said.

Lilith blanched.

"You can't do it, can you?" Frederick was enjoying himself. "I know you can't. You're too honest. Right?" He saw something in the women's clothes section. "Here's something she can use. She's got a closet full of them." He picked up a pair of XL women's slacks dangling over a hanger. "Your basic polyester pants. Pre-yard-sale goods. Size extra large." Frederick laughed at his own joke.

Lilith ignored him; indeed, she turned and walked away, so that Frederick found himself standing alone holding women's clothes. He blushed under his beard, returned the pants to the rack, and hustled to rejoin his woman.

Lilith eyed tea sets for children, in which the packages probably cost more than the cups and saucers. The sight made her sad. The manufacture of cheap goods seemed to her not only a deceitful and corruptible practice but a despairing one. Then she saw a package of tiny soaps. She held it up before Frederick and read from the label, " 'English bath cubes.' What do you think?"

Frederick took the box, and he, too, read from the label: "*Sels de bain*. The French will make her suspicious, and the soap will make her think you're telling her she needs a bath."

285

"I guess she is impossible to shop for," Lilith said, and headed for the exit.

"Lilith, play by the Elman rules; don't give her anything."

"Why should I play by your family's rules? You've been breaking them since you reached the age of reason." As she spoke, Lilith realized she was wrong. Frederick had rebelled to some degree against his father and his family, just as she had, but he had never actually broken the important rules of life set down in the canon of his class—until he had met her.

"I have yet to reach the age of reason, and do not intend to get there," Frederick said.

"You were right. It was a mistake to come here," Lilith said, pushing through the glass doors. And they were outside again, in the cold, on the sidewalk, under red, blue, and green Christmas lights dangling from utility poles.

"Cheap goods, Lilith. In the end, they'll bust your bankbook and break your heart," Frederick said.

The "goods"—give us the "goods"—the good, Lilith thought. Good equaled goods. Without enough money, you were left with cheap goods, a cheap good. Money. Good. Goods. But I have money for the goods, for the good of my child; we are well off, my child, we are wealthy, I am a Salmon; our goods are our good.

"Let's go to the mill," Frederick said.

They strolled along the old B&M railroad tracks for less than a mile to what had once been a series of textile mills and was now a shopping mall. The Mill by the Pond, it was called, although the pond had been filled in years ago.

"My father used to work in one of those buildings," Frederick said.

"Doing what?"

"They made girdles, briefs, stuff like that. Howie was a foreman. That's where he found Cooty Patterson. Cooty was a piece of lint under a machine loom. Then the mill shut down. Cooty,

Howie, my mother—they all went crazy for a while. I left college and hit the road. Howie became Darby's trash man. Wanted me to come back and work with him. Turned him down flat. Sometimes I kid you about being a snob, but I'm the biggest snob of all. My father earns an honest living, and I can't stand to be seen with him."

"You just want something else."

"I don't even know what it is, Lilith. But Howard's better off since he started his own business. He likes his life, because he's his own boss. He's successful—I can't believe it. Howie and I and Pitchfork keep the Honeywagon on the road a hundred and twenty hours a week. Howie's got the routes down scientifically. Pretty soon my mother won't have to work anymore. I don't think she has to work now."

"So why does she?"

"Habit—fear—I don't know."

The mill buildings, built by Yankees for the purpose of profit, had lain neglected for a generation before an enterprising and visionary local man, a Franco-American, had renovated them, created the mall, and resurrected the city of Tuckerman. It occurred to Lilith, whose own family had made its fortune in industry, that, in its brickwork, wooden beams, arched windows, and skyscraper chimneys, the mall was both a monument to and a mockery of those sweatshops of old.

The lovers were about to go inside when Lilith spotted an arts-and-crafts sidewalk booth. Here a red-cheeked clerk jogged in place to keep his feet warm.

"Anything made in Darby?" Lilith asked the street vendor.

"Only these." The man pointed to wire-wrapped bouquets of dried flowers and weeds. Lilith was touched by the beauty and delicacy of the plants; some of them apparently had been air-dried while others, from the look of them, had been pressed between books. Tags on each arrangement said a single word: "Estelle."

287

"Do you think your mother would like one of these for her holiday table?" Lilith asked Frederick.

"Maybe," Frederick said.

Lilith bought one of the bouquets. She was satisfied that she had completed her mission. She hadn't bought a gift as such, but she had committed herself to the gesture she believed so important. Gestures were the legacy of her own people.

"Time for me to get drunk," Frederick said.

Lilith didn't object to Frederick's drinking. He drank every day, usually in moderation, but every once in a while he liked to tie one on. He was a good-humored drinker, perhaps the way her uncle Billy had been before he went over the edge into alcoholism.

"Let's have dinner in the Boiler Room," Lilith said.

"We can't afford to eat there." Frederick's tone lacked the conviction of the words.

"I'll buy."

Frederick frowned—a charade.

"It's Christmas Eve," Lilith said.

Frederick's frown stood at the corners. "I'll earn my supper by reading you my latest poem," he said, and they went into the restaurant.

During odd moments, Lilith took great pleasure in imagining that the money in her bank account was being replenished by a secret benefactor. Because she couldn't bear to part with this fantasy, and because it pained her to watch the money trickle away, she'd stopped keeping track of the balance in her bankbook. She was squirting away the money set aside for her college education, yet she did not feel anxiety or resentment but, rather, a kind of pleasant, inner vagueness, as if on a bright day she'd suddenly found herself surrounded by a perfumed mist.

The best restaurant in the mall—and in Tuckerman—was

named after its location in the mills, the Boiler Room. All the boilers had been removed, of course; the brick walls and concrete floor had been meticulously cleaned, and the huge wooden beams that traversed the area had been sanded and oiled. With its interior view reaching to the roof rafters forty feet above the dining room, and its arched window frames refurbished with tinted glass, the place had the feel of a church.

"Let's eat at the bar. I love bars," Frederick said.

"I'm not going to drink—because of the baby."

"That's all right. I'll drink for two—I'll drink for three—or four. Maybe we'll have twins." Frederick blundered forward and Lilith, infected by his high spirits, followed. They sat at a slick black table in the raised bar overlooking the dining room. The restaurant was not quite half full.

Frederick got around the New Hampshire law prohibiting two drinks at one time for one person by ordering a shot of bourbon for himself and a beer for Lilith. He toasted the building. "Boilermakers for the Boiler Room." He raised the whiskey high, clinked it perfunctorily against the beer mug in Lilith's hand, downed the shot, then took command of Lilith's beer.

"Should we get married?" They'd already buried this subject after days of serious discussion, and now Frederick was resurrecting it for sport.

"Frederick, I know you don't want to get married—not now. So stop playing with me."

Frederick answered with such exaggerated seriousness— "You're absolutely right"—that she could tell he was deeply into his absurdist mode. "I can't get married now. I may have to take off for six months at the drop of a hat and hit the road. I'm not the husband type. I'm a playboy. Love 'em and leave 'em, that's my motto."

"Frederick? Freddy!"

"Oh, I hate it when you call me Freddy."

"Just trying to get your attention."

"All right, I know I'm not good husband material, but I swear on my father's garbage truck that I'll be a good father."

"You'd better." Lilith was serious.

A minute passed; then, reviving his silly mood, Frederick grinned mischievously and said, "So we don't get married. What is it going to be, then, a Salmon or an Elman?"

"We could hyphenate the last name," Lilith said.

"*Elm'n-Sahlmohn.*" Frederick pronounced the names correctly. "Doesn't sound right. Maybe *Saaminn-Elm'n.*" Frederick ran the words together.

"Or *Sahlmohn-Elmohn,*" Lilith said, her mood as playful as his now, even though she was not drinking.

"I've got it," Frederick said. "Say it's a boy—it is going to be a boy—we'll call him *Elmohn Sahlmohn Saaminn-Elm'n.* Pretty fancy, eh?"

"Or Howard Raphael Salmon Elman, and let him call himself what he wants, pronounce the names the way he wants," Lilith said.

"That's it; that's going to be your name, boy," Frederick said to Lilith's belly. "This is America. You can grow up to be a Reggie Salmon or a Howard Elman. Take your pick, kid."

"I think we ought to consider the possibility that it might be a girl," Lilith said.

"How is a girl going to support me in my old age?"

"Seriously."

"Desdemona—now, there was a woman," Frederick said.

"I was thinking . . . after my grandmother—Trellis."

"All right, I don't care."

"You won't love it if it's a girl."

"I'll love it if it's an orangutan," he said with forced conviction. "In fact, it may be an orangutan. Sometimes I think Howard is part wild animal."

When the next round of drinks came, Lilith asked, "Frederick, what are we going to tell your parents tomorrow?"

"Maybe we could take it one step at a time. Tomorrow we tell them about the baby. They won't get upset. In Center Darby, pregnancy is part of the courtship rite. They'll expect marriage, though."

"So what do we say, when we don't know ourselves what we really feel about that?" She couldn't bear to voice the word "marriage."

"I don't know. Let's have fun, let's not think about that now."

Frederick had finished the booze when the food came. He ordered wine to preserve the glow of the alcohol. They gabbed through the meal.

Lilith was finishing dessert, Frederick nursing the last of the wine, when he snapped out of his habitual slouch and sat upright, reached into his parka pocket, and took out a computer printout of his poem. "You ready for this?" he asked.

"What is it about?"

"Main Street in Tuckerman," Frederick said. "It's called 'Christmas Shopping for Dreams.' "

"That's a pretentious title."

Frederick ignored Lilith and began to read.

"Santa Clauses fill the city;
   they grow like tumors in the memories of kids.
   Near the liquor store,
   a woman in blue rings a bell for the Salvation Army.
   Despite high prices, shoppers mill about,
   make their choices, pay.
   Some are chic as tropical fish.
   Others, heads small upon dark winter coats,
   resemble their parents as immigrants.
   Hurrying in his Chevy, a sad priest

notices mannequins in a window.
They are perfect as the plaster shepherds
that stand in the manger of his church.
He carries the oil for extreme unction."

Frederick pushed back his chair and, Lothario-like, knelt on the floor before Lilith and continued.

"Cars in their quest for a space honk like geese,
  as if parking stalls were parts of a pond
  deemed by their blueness as safe for skating.
  (And so we are shocked when a child falls through.
  The cars do not honk, but escort the child to his grave,
  as if geese were mourners and as if
  stone forgave accident and injustice equally.)
  A policeman listens to the bell toll.
  The air sweet with sound makes him think of drink.
  Then he thinks of himself thinking of drink.
  'The drink will doom me.'
  The words form flesh on the bones of his thoughts.
  Insight into self has earned him drink tonight."

Frederick took Lilith's hand now. He was talking louder, beginning to attract the notice of the other patrons of the Boiler Room, not to mention the restaurant manager, who whispered to the bartender, "Don't give him any more booze."

The lovers were oblivious to everything but themselves. Frederick went on with his recitation.

"Like some shy Christ pretending to be Man,
  a young fellow, buried in a parka,
  molests the bell ringer with his pity.
  Does she pray for daintiness? he wonders.
  Something to remove the slick from her hair?

292

A new skin less white? Lotion for her hands?
Pretty blue stockings and shoes that shine?
If she were mine—if I dared approach her—
I would show her a way to love the cold.
I would . . . I would . . . He makes his statement:
a coin, a sly smile, and forever vanishes from the world.

If the bell ringer halted her ringing,
the shoppers might pause
and search the new snow as if consulting a fortune-
    teller,
before shuffling on with their busy lives,
or, heads curious as little cottages on Darby Lake,
they might turn to the bell ringer,
so blue against the blue snow,
and hear a gramophone play from her soul in a voice
. . . like the voice . . . of . . . W. . . . C. . . . Fields."

At this point Frederick rose from his kneeling position and
stood. "Get it?" he said. "The guy thinks she wants to be some
dainty thing, because that's what he wants, but in fact she's
thinking something altogether different." Frederick pinched
his nose and began to imitate the W. C. Fields twang.

"Summer is here. Why not summer all year?"

Frederick was now so loud everyone in the restaurant could
hear. But he was performing only for Lilith, who sat back in
her chair, shedding tears of laughter or perhaps only of joy in
the foolishness of this foolish love. Frederick went on, talking
in the voice of W. C. Fields.

"Open windows full of happy faces.
  Big, toothy city hailing a parade, a gold key, flags
    waving,
  sunshiny day, children with balloons,

men waiting with brooms,
intimations of a time before this,
a poster, Sunday, empty saloons,
and I, pitiful bell ringer of the small New England
    town.
Townsmen, throw your pity not at me,
for I am triumphant, loudest and finest,
am no bell but a tuba in a marching band."

Frederick ended by blowing through his thumbs, the sound like a tuba celebrating flatulence.

This moment between Frederick and Lilith ended with her laughter trailing off and their sudden apprehension of a critical silence in the restaurant. Frederick's display—and Lilith's raucous appreciation—had intruded upon the calm atmosphere of the place. It was at this moment that the young people recognized what Mrs. McCurtin earlier had perceived—they were different.

2

Christmas Prayers

The Elman kin packed Elenore's mobile home shoulder to shoulder for the Christmas festivities. The company included Pegeen, who had driven up from Massachusetts with her two boys and her new husband and one of his kids; Charlene, God bless her, and her three young ones (her husband, Parker, was working at the fire station; arranged it that way, Elenore knew). Heather, the youngest of the Elmans, telephoned from France to wish them well. Her tooth braces were being removed come New Year's. Lost that one, but she's doing okay, so thanks anyway, Jesus. Elenore kept waiting for a call from Sherry Ann, but it never came. Sherry Ann was their second eldest after Charlene and she had left home at age seventeen. They hadn't heard from her in fifteen years. She was living out west somewhere.

The late arrivals were the Elmans' only son, Freddy, and his fiancée (the word that leaped to Elenore's mind the second she learned Lilith was pregnant). She was beautiful, all right, and she had good manners. "Here—an arrangement of dried flowers. We picked them up in town," she had said, and handed Elenore a bouquet. Freddy, poor mixed-up Freddy, had taken up with this girl, had gone back to school. And why? To spite his family, that was why.

By eight o'clock, the only guest remaining was Pitchfork,

who these days was more like part of the household than company. Pitchfork and Howard sat at the kitchen table having a cup of coffee, while Elenore put the dishes away. Pegeen and Charlene had washed the dishes, but left them in the strainer piled to the rafters. Elenore was as glad to see her children go as she had been to see them come. She was tired. She'd gone to midnight mass, grabbed a few hours' sleep, then rose again to stuff the turkey and put it in the oven. But, despite her fatigue, Elenore was determined to end the day with a prayer of thankfulness at the foot of the Virgin. As usual, she insisted that Howard accompany her and, as usual, he grumbled about this duty, but he'd go along, she knew. When Pitchfork learned that he, too, was expected to kneel outside in the cold and pray, he was delighted.

"Pray—by gosh, what a wonderful idea," he said to Elenore, as if she had invented a new method of using the mind.

"Ain't you ever prayed before?" Howard asked Pitchfork.

"Why, no. Never knew anybody prayed outside a church, and I don't go to church, so I never figured that, well, like . . . ah, you know what I'm saying?"

"Pitchfork, if you don't know what you're saying, how am I going to know?" Howard whammed down his coffee cup on the table for emphasis. "But, to answer your question, I know what you're saying. Now, let me ask you this: you ever bump heads with any Catholics?"

"I imagine so," Pitchfork said. "Come to think of it, Joe Ancharsky's a Catholic. Said the Sisters used to crack a ruler across his knuckles."

"Elenore's Catholic, a convert," Howard said. "Meanest type of religious fanatic you'll find anywhere, and they'll pray at the drop of a hat."

"Shut up, Howie, and get your coat." Elenore put the last dish away. It was nice, this mobile home, but kind of cramped, and if you didn't keep it picked up, it got away from you.

"Praying—outdoors, at that. I can't get over it." Pitchfork patted his tummy, as if, by the way, thanking Elenore for the meal. The men got up from the table.

Elenore liked Pitchfork. He was big and gentle, docile yet manly, in the way of these middle-aged Northern New England bachelors. She liked him, too, because he was stupid. She hated smart men, whom she regarded as inherently cruel, full of themselves, and in the end not so smart. She gave Pitchfork far higher grades as a friend to and accomplice of her husband than Cooty Patterson. She had never actually despised or distrusted Cooty, but she felt threatened by him, because she could see that Howard liked Cooty as much as he liked her.

They put on their coats and went outside; Howard brought a blanket for them to kneel on. Starlight showed through patches of clouds; the air was cold but nearly still. Elenore lit three candles in tinted glasses and placed them on the pedestal of the Virgin's shrine. Last year the wind had blown out the candles. This night the candle flames trembled like the wings of the small birds that visited Elenore's winter feeder. At the foot of the Virgin was a Baby Jesus, about a foot long, carved in white pine, that Howard had made during those months his leg had been healing up.

Howard laid out the blanket before the Virgin and Child. "We don't need that," Elenore said.

"We don't but I do, being so much older and more decrepit," Howard said, exaggerating his distress at the oncoming of old age.

Elenore gave Howard a dirty look, but she thought, Well, all right. They knelt on the blanket, Elenore between the two men.

"What am I supposed to do?" Pitchfork said, the unfamiliarity of the position putting him into a panic.

"Shut up and pray," Howard said.

297

"You won't have to force it," Elenore said. "Pretty soon you'll find yourself talking to God."

Pitchfork nodded in the dead-certain, knowing manner of people who are neither certain nor knowing.

Howard grunted. His leg hurt.

Had Elenore been raised in the Catholic church, she might have led in the saying of the rosary, or at any rate she might have prayed aloud. But Elenore had come to her religion as an adult, after years of intercourse with saints, angels, and her God—that is, intercourse with intensity and emotion but without touch or noise. As far as she was concerned, what went on between a person and heaven was not to be spoken or sung, but thought and felt.

Pitchfork calmed down. The mild discomfort of kneeling seemed to focus his attention, make him aware of the passing of time, the stars above. By gosh, he thought, one of these days I'll pass on. He glanced over at Howard, who was glowering at the stars, then at Elenore. Her lips moved, but she made not a sound. Pitchfork, too, spoke his prayer soundlessly:

Well, hello, Allmighty, I don't know what prayer is, but I know what hope is. I used to have hope. I had hope for my own *fahm*. But I lost hope. For a while, I didn't have nothing. I was an idler. Then this fine specimen of humanity, Howie Elman, gives me a job. Maybe you had it figured this way all along. I don't know. I don't know nothing. But I know this: I gotta job. A job is as good as hope if you've given up hope to begin with. 'Course, if you got hope, a job gets in the way. Makes you cranky. But once you got no hope, why, you can just do the work and relax. So, that's it: I want to say thank you.

Howard liked to pray on occasion, because it gave him an opportunity to let off steam. Given the predicament of the planet, every creature eating another creature, Howard Elman figured that, if there was a God, that God would be like himself, a horse's ass, and he was perfectly at ease with the idea of giving such a God a piece of his mind.

Let's get one thing straight, Howard made *p-sss, p-sss* sounds. I don't believe you exist. I don't believe in nothing but myself and clockwork, but just in case you're out there, I want you to know I'm not afraid of you; I ain't afraid of nothing, least of all a God who won't show Himself except to nervous people. But if you're out there, why, let's just say I'm like You, not the humble type. But I get things done, and I expect You can understand that. Now, I know You can read my mind, so You figure You know what I'm going to pray for—a new Honeywagon. I got these trash routes going pretty good right now, and the problem is, I'm running the Honeywagon straight out. I need another truck, so I'm going to the bank for a loan. Don't laugh—I got the facts and figures from the computer to talk the bank into giving me the money. Well, maybe. I can keep the Honeywagon purring like a kitten until doomsday. I imagine You know something about doomsday, doncha? If the bank says okay, I'm giving the new truck to Freddy. His own Honeywagon—that'll smarten him up. I know what You're thinking: Howard Elman is going to pray for a new Honeywagon for his boy. I ain't going to do no such thing. Much as I want that truck, I plan on getting it myself: me and the bank. So what I'm praying for is not for me or for mine.

You remember a feller named Cooty Patterson? You probably created him and forgot. Cooty Patterson is the most forgot person I ever knew. Now, this is a little embarrassing, but I have to tell you that the last thing Cooty said to me before he disappeared was he had romantic notions for a she-bear. Last night I dreamed that this bear, of the *Saaminn* Trust, that I've been trying to catch, that's maybe white and maybe not, and I can't find no sign of, I dreamed she got Cooty. Ate him. He's there still, in the bear's belly. I dreamed it. Look, God, I don't care about saving Cooty or nothing like that. Let the rain fall where it may. I don't even know what I'm praying for. But I know this: something's wrong, so for cry-sakes fix it. One more thing, I hate Christmas—too much trash for the same pay. That's all I got to say. See You later.

When Elenore began her prayer she was, in effect, rehearsing the speech she would deliver later that night over the telephone to Mrs. McCurtin. Elenore was not herself a gossip. She had no wish to spread malicious rumors, and certainly not rumors concerning her own family. Elenore told tales about herself and her family because she hoped that, once in the public domain, the problems would come round, solve themselves. Asked to explain herself, Elenore might have said that, if you dump dirty water in a river, the filth goes away and becomes part of the beautiful stream. The stream she had in mind could not be polluted, because it came from the fountainhead of God: it was the stream of human consciousness. In another realm, the simple fact was that Elenore was lonely for a listener of her own sex. Howard was a good man, but he was a man. Mrs. McCurtin comprehended everything and she never criticized. It didn't really matter that sometimes she got the facts wrong. When gossip about her people was inaccurate, Elenore enjoyed a curious moment of triumph, as if she'd tricked the devil. (It had been Mrs. McCurtin's idea that Elenore invite Lilith over personally for Christmas dinner.) And so Elenore prayed:

Myself it don't matter—my dream was for my children—and that's over. I started out a dreamer, I made some dreamers—Sherry Ann, Heather, Freddy—I died a dreamer. I dreamed for myself, and then I dreamed for them, but that's over. I try to dream for the grandchildren, but there's nothing left in the tank. I try to dream for heaven, but the dream is foggy, because I don't know what I'm supposed to think about when I dream for heaven. So I don't dream for anything, I don't dream for nobody, I don't dream no more.

But I won't quit praying. Lord, I have this son, and he has this fiancée, rich girl lives up on the hill. She was here today. Going to have a child, she says. I probably shouldn't have, but I warned her. I says, God forgives the young for the sins of love. (Which I imagine to be true.) I says, God knows about love—God is love. (Which I know to be true.) When He decides to give you a baby, He's sending you a message: get married. The fun's over, the job of life replaces the job of love. (Which may not be exactly true, but it's close.) When you come right down to it, we're all just guessing most of the time, and calling it "fate" or "destiny," what-have-you. She didn't believe me. I don't believe she believes anybody; I don't believe she knows diddly-doo about anything. I believe she's got mysterious ideas that don't come from up on the hill, but from way below, below Center Darby, below the Depot—Ecuador—someplace like that. I know I should care about her, because my boy cares about her, but I can't. I care about my boy, I care about that baby You're giving them, so I'm praying that, whatever else may go wrong, save the baby and I promise I will raise it. I know You think I'm narrow-minded, and maybe I am, but what am I suppose to feel when my son's fiancée brings me dead flowers?

3

Dismantling the Manger

Deep in January, 6:00 A.M., the beginning of what would normally be Joe Ancharsky's fifteen-hour workday at the store, and he was writing on a piece of cardboard with a red crayon belonging to his daughter—CLOSED UNTIL NOON TODAY—when his scanner picked up Mrs. McCurtin broadcasting on her CB. Usually, he listened intently to the town gossip, because she was his main source of news in the town. But for the last week or so, it had seemed to him that the topics of discussions were getting too personal. At the moment, she was talking about the folks in Upper Darby. "You could see she was putting on weight. I thought she was just maturing. Naïve *moi*. Pregnancy—now, that'll give you a white hair or two. Whose? I suppose the Elman boy. He moved into the Squire's mansion, so he's the logical one. But they aren't saying anything, nobody's talking of marriage. And, 'course, back when all this was conceived, she was seen with young Mr. Garvin Prell dining at the Inn. So, who knows? Who really knows.

"You heard about Reggie Salmon's brother—Moann-ay? Married that scientist woman he's been living with. They didn't make it legal in this poor town, though. Went off and did it. And, well, imagine this: Noreen Cook has moved in with the two of them. Closed down her trailer, closed down her business. So you know who's supporting her. I talked to her. I says, 'Noreen, what's a nice Depot girl like you doing up on the hill?' Know what she says to me? She says, 'It's an experiment.' I'll bet. The Pocket Squire and the Pocket Witch and the darkie scientist femme—quite an experiment."

Joe shut off the inside lights of the market and stepped into the January cold. He hung the sign on the door, took a long critical look at it, and found himself dissatisfied. The sign didn't look right, incomplete somehow. Joe went back inside to get the crayon, and he added the words FOR THE HOLIDAY.

Satisfied, he walked down the four steps to the blacktop, where he could smell the gas from his pumps. Just beyond was the manger. He'd put it up close to the pumps so that everybody could get a good look at it. In the morning darkness of deep winter, the yellow light shining into the throat of the stable was warm and cheering; it promised a better world ahead. He decided to leave the light on inside the manger so he could see what he was doing, and because the sight gave him a sweet ache. A great man, maybe even a God, born in a barn—what a thrilling event! He felt humbled and ennobled by his appreciation of it, even if he had a hard time actually buying the facts as presented by the priests and ministers of the Christian world. He considered the basics: A baby! New, to save us! New! It was all so wonderful, too bad he had no words for his wonder, only a feeling whose expression was this manger.

Joe had been toying with the idea of displaying the manger 365 days a year. But the hints—from the wife, the kids, the customers, the bread man—poked at him: Take down the manger, Christmas is over. So he thought he'd kill two birds with one stone—celebrate the holiday by closing until noon and, during the time off, dismantle the manger. He'd put the pieces back in the barn, number them, and log them, so that next year the manger would go up fast. This year he had expanded the size of the barn. Next year he planned to add more statues.

He had plenty of shepherds, but he found himself short on angels. Angels were tough. You had to hang them with wires from a framework.

A couple of sullen fellows in a pickup truck with Vermont plates pulled to a stop. They did not look at the manger; it was as if the manger did not exist. "We're looking for this *Saaminn Truss*," the driver said.

Joe gave the directions and off they went. Joe knew what they were up to, illegally hunting the white bear that roamed the Trust lands. The legend had spread far and wide. Joe could almost visualize the creature, a giant white bear, some kind of mutant who had been seen (plenty of eyewitness reports) but who could not be killed or caught. Joe wasn't entirely sure he believed in the stories; still, he liked to hear them told. There was a kind of timelessness about them, like fairy tales, so that it seemed to Joe he had been hearing them all the years he'd been living in Darby, and his children would hear them, and their children, way into endless tomorrows. The bear had even been mentioned in the newspaper. The Tuckerman *Crier* had reported that, in testimony before the Superior Court, Charles Barnum, Monet Salmon's attorney, had given into evidence documents from Colonial times mentioning the existence of unusual bears. As far as Joe Ancharsky was concerned, there had always been a giant white bear in Tuckerman County, and men had always hunted it.

Dawn was breaking red over the hills when the road agent, Bud Parkinson, showed up to get his morning cup of coffee. He was so bleary-eyed he didn't notice Joe or his sign, but when he reached the entry he did notice that it was dark inside the store. Then he read the sign.

"What in holy hell is going on?" he grumbled.

"Door's unlocked, go in, coffee's on," Joe shouted from the manger.

304

Bud wheeled around, looked at Joe to make sure he was real, then turned his eyes back to the sign. "Jezum Crow," he said and went inside the store.

Joe chuckled to himself, and put a donkey and two sheep in a box. Seconds later, Selectman Crabb pulled in front of the gas pumps, driving his new Cadillac. He rolled down the window. "You open for gas?" he said.

"I'm not open, but the pumps are on, so help yourself and pay me later," Joe said.

"Uh-huh." Crabb got out of the Caddy.

Bud Parkinson, returned to bedrock by the coffee, was about to leave as he noticed Arthur Crabb pumping his gas.

"Crazy morning," Bud said, simultaneously addressing the storekeeper and the selectman—his boss. "First I see these weekend hunters sneaking up to the Trust—but it ain't a weekend. Then I come over to get my morning coffee, and the sign says HOLIDAY."

"It's kind of a holiday, *yaaas*," said Crabb, amused.

"Those hunters you saw?" Joe said to Bud. "They're from Vermont."

"I know that, I seen the plates," Bud said.

"Well, in Vermont a workingman has the day off," Joe said.

"The day off?" Bud was mystified.

"It's Martin Luther King's Birthday—national holiday," Crabb said.

"Why don't I have the day off, then?" Bud asked.

"Because it's not a holiday in the state of New Hampshire, and those are the rules the town goes by in setting policy for our employees," Crabb said.

"My word . . ." Bud said.

"Here in this country we have what you call states' rights," Crabb explained. "And this is one of the states that exercised the right not to have a holiday for the Reverend King."

"Well, I don't know about that." Bud didn't like being talked down to by the selectman. "King? King? *Mahtin Lutha King?* Colored feller, right?"

"A great man, a hero to the black people, a hero for us all," said Joe, who was a Democrat, Civil Rights Advocate, and, although he was loath to admit it in Darby, a union man. In his family's home back in Hazelton hung pictures of the Virgin Mary and John L. Lewis.

Joe's words, spoken with passion, stirred Bud. It hit him now that Selectman Crabb was going to be out of office come the second Tuesday in March, and Crabb would no longer be his superior. With that, Bud had a notion to bust the old geezer's chops. "How do you like that, Mr. Selectman?" he said. "A hero. The man was a hero. And us working people don't have the day off to honor his birth. Is that right? I ask you, is that right?"

"Take it up with the New Hampshire Legislature." Crabb could see Bud's game and wasn't about to kowtow to the likes of him. He knew the Parkinsons. Brought up in a barn, they were.

Joe Ancharsky changed the subject. He said to the selectman, "Now that you're not running for re-election, should be a real race at town meeting this year. Who you supporting?"

"I haven't made up my mind yet," said Crabb, who in fact had made up his mind. He did not consider his lie a lie, however, but merely a politic remark. He paid Joe, then said, "Nice manger," the lie slipping off his lips easily so that he never recognized the taint of it until the bad aftertaste. He couldn't wait to get back to Florida: retired, no politics, no easy lies.

"Think you'll miss it?" Joe asked.

"It?" The old man got in his car.

"The town. The selectman's position. Local notoriety."

"I won't miss the snow," Crabb said.

"Lots of sunshine in Florida," Joe said.

"I wasn't talking about the weather," Crabb said and drove off. Moments later, Bud Parkinson left, and Joe had a few minutes alone. He finished putting the animals in the carton, followed by the shepherds, wise men, Jesus, Mary, and Joseph.

He was cutting down the angels when Pitchfork Parkinson rolled by in Howard Elman's Honeywagon. They exchanged waves; then Joe heard the telephone ringing inside the store. He figured he better answer it, because this was about the time his wife was taking her shower, and it was his job to pick up the phone in the store when she was indisposed. He didn't run in, but took his time, hoping the party on the other end had hung up. No such luck. It was Mrs. McCurtin. "What's going on, Joe? I heard you're not open," she said. Joe was determined to keep his own counsel on this issue, but because he was who he was and because Mrs. McCurtin was who she was, in a few minutes he had told her about the manger and Martin Luther King—everything. Then he went back to the manger. The faint light of morning had penetrated the darkness. He had missed the lovely red dawn. He felt cheated. It was going to be a drab, cloudy January day. He wondered if it would snow.

What happened in the next few hours greatly surprised Joe. He was suddenly popular. People who had deserted his store over the last couple of years came by and gave him their opinions about the holiday. Others, new people who had moved in, dropped by to see this man, this freedom-loving Yankee (it didn't matter Joe was Pennsylvania coal town, born and bred) who would shut his business down for Martin Luther King. They went home thinking, What a kind, honest man. "Just wanted a morning off," he said. He was such a great listener. And so wise. "I may not agree with you, but if you believe it, there must be something to it," he said. And because Joe was such a great listener, and wise, they found themselves opening up to him, speaking their minds, earnestly and without shame. They felt like old-timers.

That day, Joe Ancharsky heard the voices of Darby: "We already have too many holidays this time of year. . . . I heard something bad about that man. . . . You won't find black people in New Hampshire because they can't stand our *wintahs*. . . . I don't see that he was such a great American, but he did a lot for his people. . . . Why can't they have a holiday for one of our own, maybe Daniel Webster or Mel Thomson? . . . It's about time we had a holiday for a woman. . . . Do you know how much holidays cost business annually? . . . In my book, he was a black jackass. . . . I have nothing against him personally, but . . . It's terrible that we don't celebrate the Reverend King's birthday here in New Hampshire; he was a great man. . . . You have this holiday for this guy, and pretty soon they'll all want one. . . . The government has got programs for the poor people, and tax breaks for the rich, but there's nothing for the middle class. Everybody who's a true American is middle-class." And so forth. The more the people of Darby spoke, the more Joe listened, the more credit they bestowed upon him for wisdom.

That morning something happened, an effect that even Mrs. McCurtin could not have anticipated, or encouraged, or prevented. A miracle occurred. The people of Darby realized all at once, but separately, that they appreciated Joe and his store. It was as if every citizen of the town had come outside that morning and seen the dawn Joe had missed, seen a message in the red glow of the east: Darby Village was defined by the general store; without it, Darby would not be Darby. Joe was not only the keeper of the store, he was the keeper of the town. By noon, a crowd milled about in front of the store to get in. When Joe opened the doors, they gave him a standing ovation. Meanwhile, Joe had been so busy explaining himself that he hadn't had time to do what he had set out to do. The figures from the manger were safely stowed, but the manger itself was only half dismantled. Joe didn't know what to make of his popularity. It confused him, even frightened him a little bit for its mysteriousness. But, as always, he did his job and he was polite and if, as was apparent even to him, he was going to be some kind of hero, why, that was okay, too.

Because Joe and his place had achieved instant celebrity status in the town, it was only natural that political candidates would come by. The first was Critter Jordan, the owner of Jordan's Kwick Stop, the auction barn, and half of Darby Depot. From the moment Selectman Crabb had announced his retirement, Critter knew he would run for Crabb's seat on the board of selectmen. But it took the events of this day, the phenomenon of Joe and his store, to get Critter off his duff, if for no other reason than that he wanted in on some of the publicity.

Critter arrived with a poster for Joe's public bulletin board and some handout sheets outlining his positions on the issues. Critter shook the hands of Joe's customers, most of whom were his own customers, and he sounded his themes, and, in the end, bought a six-pack of beer from Joe just to show there were no hard feelings. Critter needn't have worried. Hard feelings were not stocked on Joe's shelves of emotions. Although Critter was Joe's primary competitor, and although he did not approve of the Kwick Stop itself, Joe could not bring himself to dislike Critter the man. In fact, Joe couldn't bring himself to dislike anybody. Furthermore, Joe was a good citizen, and he scrutinized Critter as a candidate, a potential leader of the community, not as a competitor. Critter stuck pretty much to the script outlined in his posters. He promised to keep property taxes down and new people out, and to lobby against the power of the Darby Planning Board.

No sooner had Critter left than another candidate came in.

This one was a real shocker. The personage was no less than Monet Salmon, the younger brother of the departed Squire of Upper Darby. He, too, was running for selectman. Carrying a briefcase, he came into the store, shook Joe's hand, and said he was proud to live in the same town as he. A little embarrassed, Joe said, "Welcome to Center Darby Village, old-timer."

"Would you have a place for this on your bulletin board?" Monet asked, producing from his briefcase a poster of himself in a tweed jacket, gazing out from the heights of the ledges on the Trust land. Monet's motto, written in bold lettering on the poster, was "He knows Darby—you can Trust him."

Monet whipped around to face the townsfolk who had been lucky enough to grab the chairs Joe had set out for chewing the fat. Joe was left with the poster in his hands. It took a moment for him to realize that he was expected to tack it up. Joe was honored. His immediate impulse was to stick the poster above Critter Jordan's poster, but Joe was a fair man, and he put the posters side by side, making certain they got equal play.

Monet passed in review before the people, and after that he made a short speech. "As you know," he began, then repeated, "as you know . . . as you know . . ." His voice died down, and a quiet filled the store. Joe strained to listen. When the silence was almost unbearable, Monet started anew. "As you know, my fellow citizens of Darby, my brother, Raphael Salmon—called Reggie by those of us who knew him, called the Squire by those of you who respected him—established the Salmon Trust lands to memorialize his son and to preserve in a natural state a part of this town, so that in the next century, and the one following that, through the millennia, long after our day has passed, this part of the world can remain untouched by the dirty hands of industry, commercialism, the machine age. I stand for what he stood for. I stand for . . . for . . . for land."

Joe didn't exactly make practical political sense of these words, but he found himself moved by them.

"Hear! Hear!" said Ted Barkley, and a round of restrained but respectful applause followed. A moment later, having made his speech, Monet was gone.

Something about Monet was different, but Joe had not taken note of the change until today, when Joe was seeing Monet not just as another member of the Upper Darby elite but as a candidate for political office. At first Joe attributed the change to marriage. Monet seemed more reserved, grave; strain showed on his face. It hit Joe then that Monet was looking and behaving more and more like the Squire. The way he walked, back and shoulders straight, voice low and direct, made Monet resemble Reggie. In fact, Joe could have sworn he had seen the clothes that Monet wore on the Squire himself. It seemed to Joe that, in a manner of speaking, the Squire was back.

The last of the candidates was a tall, well-dressed man. One of the new people. His name was Lawrence Dracut, and he was a lawyer. He was accompanied by the Reverend Spofford Hall, who said, almost in a whisper, "This is the man we need to lead us." Dracut didn't really say anything. He introduced himself, announced he was running for office, shook a few hands, talked about the weather, the Celtics, the price of fuel oil, the Russians, acid rain, the greenhouse effect, ozone, profitability, and productivity, and walked out. Joe didn't know what to think about him. He looked good, had made a favorable impression, but what was inside of him? Joe was confused and a little uncomfortable in the gut. He felt like a man after a meal in a fast-food restaurant, staring at the paper and plastic, wondering what it all meant to his stomach.

Joe didn't think about politics for the remainder of his workday. He was too busy. If business stayed like this, he could hire somebody to work evenings. Maybe stay open until eleven, instead of nine. There were still people in the store at closing time, and it wasn't until nine-thirty that he was able to shut the doors. As he was doing the day's receipts, his wife came in through the divider between house and store. She had worked all day in Tuckerman at the Grange insurance building, and she, too, was tired. "Have a cup of coffee," she said.

"I have to finish taking down the manger," Joe said.

"Can't it wait?" she said.

"No, it's half apart. Looks disreputable like that," he said. His wife returned to the house behind the store, and Joe went outside.

As he worked, alone at last, he relaxed a bit. He wondered about these fellows running for selectman. None of them had touched the real issue in town—the school. Should Darby have it or not? The candidates weren't talking about the school because it cost money. Monet's court suit, by blocking construction of the school, satisfied a lot of people. Could Darby afford the school? Joe wasn't sure. Many people in town were working full-time jobs but just barely making ends meet. Himself included. Joe thought about the candidates—Critter, representing Darby Depot; Monet, Upper Darby; Dracut, the new people. Joe put himself down as undecided.

The manger was almost down when Godfrey Perkins, the town constable, drove up.

"Seen a couple guys, look like hunters, pickup truck, Vermont plates?" he asked.

"Saw 'em first thing this morning," Joe said.

"They got away from me," Godfrey said.

"You think anybody will ever get that bear?"

"I dunno," Godfrey said.

"You think there is a white bear?" Joe asked.

"Oh, sure, I seen it."

This was thrilling news indeed. "Tell me about it," Joe said.

"Well, it was back in early December, before the first snow. I was walking around in the woods, trying to find these poachers on the Trust, and he just stepped out of the woods. Maybe a hundred yards away. I looked again, he was gone."

"What did you see?"

Godfrey stopped to take a breath. He fondled his admirable belly. A faraway look came to his eye, like that of a man thinking about some momentous event in his childhood. "Gigantic. And white," he said.

4

On Ice

Before the phone rang and woke him, Frederick had been dreaming. Volumes of seated people watch from metal fold-down chairs. Voices cry out, "An Elman—pee-yew!" He glanced at the alarm clock. Half awake: Grandfather clock big as Reggie Salmon's coffin. Darn near asleep: Heirloom. Air loom. Air apparent. Hair apparent. Heir a parent. Waking: Neither-hear-nor-they're—here, there *they-ay*. Trouble telling the time. Roman numerals too complicated. Almost noon. Moon. Loon. Ghostly Howie voice from childhood: Get off your dead ass. And now he was more or less awake. Okay, I'll get up. And he fell asleep, and the dream started all over again. Volumes of seated people watch from metal fold-down chairs. Voices cry out, "An Elman—pee-yew!"

Seconds before the memory of the dream dived for oblivion in his skull, he realized the sense of it: today was town-meeting day. Those "volumes of seated people" were going to set the town on a course for the next year. Not that he planned on taking part. For one thing, the Elmans did not attend town meeting (as the dream earlier had reminded him); for another thing, the evening hour of the meeting interfered with his shift in the Honeywagon. Pitchfork Parkinson worked from 4:00 A.M. to noon, Howard took over from noon to 4:00 P.M., and

314

then his own shift began. Frederick finished up anywhere from 11:00 P.M. to 1:00 A.M. It was lonely without Cooty along.

He had to admire Howard. In his free time, he recruited customers, schemed for a bank loan for a new Honeywagon (unapproved as of yet), and on weekends did the mechanical work to keep the Honeywagon on the road. These men on the front porch of old age, all they thought about was business. What seemed to settle them down, civilize them, was brooding over ways to gyp your friends and kill your enemies and make a buck. Wiliness replaced wildness. Frederick was not ready for that. He had some wildness left; he had acquired no wiliness. Once the baby came, things would change. He was reminded of that every time he looked at Lilith. She was, in his father's words, "rounding out." He and Lilith had proved their capacity to make a human being—they had this potential, always, for creation. Frederick was surprised that he found her so sumptuous in a family way. No wonder humankind continued on. Men liked women pregnant; women liked themselves pregnant. They were accessible; they could deny access without hard feelings. They were grateful; they were objects of gratitude. They weren't likely to run away and, if you ran away, they wouldn't come after you.

The telephone continued to ring between dozes. *Lilith, get that, will ya?* She was probably in the greenhouse. Spent all her free time in that place. Kept the door locked. He got the message: Some of me you'll never see. Okay, he respected that. But damned if he was going to answer her telephone. Now, wait a minute, Freddy, who says it's her telephone call? Don't call me Freddy. It was probably Howard. Some kind of problem to be dealt with. Would you *frikn'ay* please run down to the Greenfield junkyard and pick up a *paht* for the Honeywagon? Not now, Pop, I limit my time to Honeywagon Inc. from four P.M. to midnight. Which was not true. If his father

315

asked him to go to Greenfield, Massachusetts, or Mars, he'd comply.

He heard Lilith answer the phone in the hallway downstairs. He couldn't make out her words, but an exclamation point in her voice told him the caller was not Howard. Maybe it was Persephone. Lilith—poor girl—had been trying to contact her mother for weeks, but Persephone was traveling. It was late summer in Australia—vacation time. Frederick pulled on blue jeans and a sweatshirt and, feet bare, mind burning oil, headed downstairs. Every night, when he arrived home from work, he'd shower; he wouldn't allow Lilith to touch him until he was clean. He didn't even want her close to him when he was soiled from his labors on the trash route. After he'd washed away the grit, he and Lilith would have a drink, make love on the rug in the Hearth Room, eat a leisurely dinner as they watched a VCR movie. Before bed, he'd wash her, and she'd wash him. They'd make love again, slower this time. Then, sleep—delicious sleep . . . dreams . . . dreams.

He had the sudden urge to tell her he loved her. He was about to speak the words when he saw her glancing up at him, turning away, romancing the phone receiver, smiling mysteriously, speaking in a lowered voice so he couldn't tell who she was talking to. In that split second, Frederick drew fully awake like any animal sensing danger.

He went into the kitchen, dubbed around for a while, stole a glance into the hall—Lilith was still on the phone—and went back into the kitchen. In a peeking frame of mind, he peeked out the window and gazed out at fields, rock wall fence, forest, hills, sky; no buildings except for the greenhouse obstructed the view. It was snowing lightly. He peeked at the fancy indoor-outdoor thermometer Reggie Salmon had installed. (From the evidence of Reggie's journals, Frederick determined that the Squire had gone on periodic binges of weather-record keeping. He'd kept detailed notes for a few weeks, then abandoned the game. All during his life, Reggie Salmon had returned to the weather theme, the enduring theme of Northern New England.) Today: eighteen degrees, a trifle nippy for a big storm. Still, you never knew about weather. Frederick didn't mind snow. The Honeywagon was heavy, the body so high above the roadbed that snow made little difference in how the truck handled. Ice—that was another beast altogether. He tried to peek through the heavy plastic sheeting over the glass of the greenhouse for a look-see inside, but failed; the only suggestion he had into that secret world of his woman was faint green-and-brown shapes. Attempting to see through the plastic was like trying to see the world of a lake through foot-thick ice. Hang up the goddamn phone! The thought was so strong, he almost voiced it.

A moment later, Lilith was off the phone, and Frederick was all over her. "Who the hell was that?" he shouted.

"Put your shoes on—you'll catch your death." She turned her back on him and walked from the hallway into the Hearth Room. Every time he was a fool, she'd treat him like a fool. Didn't she understand? Why didn't she understand?

Frederick followed her, watching. She swaggered; by gosh, she'd swiped his swagger. His feet were cold. "What's the big secret?" He framed the question as an accusation.

She ignored him, kept walking until she reached the fireplace in the Hearth Room, and there she stood like one making a stand.

"You love your secrets, don't you," he was shouting as, he bet, no Salmon man had ever shouted. "And you're awful good with them, good and awful."

"You're babbling." Lilith hit the nail on his head.

"You not only have your little secrets, you rub my nose in them."

"I don't have to tell you anything." Lilith turned and faced the fire. They had plenty of dry firewood—Lilith's father had

317

seen to that—and they kept the wood stove in the kitchen and the fireplace stoked to save on fuel oil. In another economy measure, they closed off most of the house. With all the shut doors, the Salmon mansion seemed not like a big house but like a small house with one big room, the Hearth Room.

"Oh, come on," he said.

"Oh, come on," she mocked him.

"You're messing with my mind." Frederick circled her. Lilith thought he resembled her mother. He added, "Tell me a lie, tell me something."

"It was Garvin."

"The Prell lawyer—I thought so." Frederick stopped circling and stood with his hands outstretched. "Next time I see him on his little bicycle, I think I'll run over him with the Honeywagon."

"I suppose you would, if you had the courage." Lilith smiled.

Frederick plunged on with his tirade. "I can see the headlines now: 'Distinguished Local Attorney Extinguished by Garbage Truck.' "

They stood eye to eye now. "He's driving me to the town meeting tonight," Lilith said.

"Oh, is he, now?"

"My father's Trust board hasn't met, because Garvin and Monet have been fighting, but next month they have to meet, because it's required. That's what Garvin wants to talk to me about." She turned, showing a profile, holding her protruding front in her hands. "How can you be jealous? He doesn't want me. Why would he want me?"

"The question is, do you want him?"

"You're so mean when you're jealous. And so stupid."

It wasn't the word "mean" that stopped him dead in the tracks of his anger—Elman men were expected to show some meanness—it was the other word. We Elmans aren't stupid, he wanted to say, we're bullheaded and ignorant. What he

318

actually said was "Too true, too true. I can't help it." He felt his anger sift through; he had a colander head for strong feeling. He sat down on the floor cross-legged and stared at the fire. "I'm sorry," he said. *She's right—the old man sicced me with a stupid streak.*

The argument was over, the animosity between them gone, and yet something lingered that stood between them. They knelt by the fire. It was an awkward moment, and then Lilith said, "Let's take the skis and go up to the pond."

"But you might fall."

"And if I do?"

"Lilith?"

"I want to go—it doesn't get steep until after the pond."

"Your impulsiveness scares me sometimes."

"My impulsiveness brought us together."

"There you go—big mistake."

They both laughed.

"I hate to see you risking the baby just to go skiing," Frederick said.

"Maybe you're right," Lilith said. "Do you want something to eat?"

"In a minute." He took her in his arms. They lay beside one another in front of the fireplace. Then Lilith said, "Feel—he's kicking," she said.

Frederick knelt by her. Her breasts were swollen. Her complexion was slightly flushed. He put his hand on her belly. He could feel a push against his fingertips.

"Wants out," Frederick said.

It snowed delicately all during the day. By the time Frederick started his route, the storm was letting up; about four inches of light, fluffy snow had fallen. Frederick noticed the sky clearing moments before he roared up on the tail of the snowplow. When, finally, he had a chance to pass, he was surprised to see his father driving the town truck. Frederick waved; Howard acknowledged neither son nor vehicle. Frederick visualized himself crashing the town meeting, kicking in the doors, facing the gathered. Then what? What would you do then, Frederick? Tell them you're not ready for fatherhood? Complain about your old man? You have nothing to say to them. You have nothing to say at all. You're still waiting for the mail. Frederick finished the route at 12:30 A.M. Why did the new day start in the middle of the night? The moon was out.

Usually when he arrived home, he'd give Lilith a bare greeting and run upstairs to shower. But tonight she'd been with Garvin Prell, and Frederick paused at the cool hello he received in response to his own cool hello. He told himself he didn't care what they had talked about, or even what they had done, but he had to know what the effect had been on Lilith. He stood half in the hallway, half in the Hearth Room, while Lilith sat on the couch pretending to read. She knew better than to approach him before he'd washed. He stood looking at her, trying to divine the secrets behind her eyes.

"How was the town meeting?" he asked.

"Sanborn House was elected moderator." She looked up from the book and stared back at him.

He couldn't tell from the way she was holding the book what she was reading, but he saw a flash of red and the name Boose. "Any laughs?" he said, standing still as stone.

"The road agent got them going," Lilith said.

"He hired Howard to do his job tonight." Frederick hardly heard his own words, he was so intent on Lilith.

"That was a big subject of debate," she said. "Richard Stole wanted to know what the road agent was doing in the town hall on the night of a storm. Bud said, 'I'd rather be out there, but I have to be in here, protecting my interests against you budget cutters.' That drew a laugh."

"And you?" Frederick did not smile.

"Me? I envied the women who brought knitting and cro-cheting projects."

"And in lieu of that?"

"I made do." She dragged out the "do," breaking into the Center Darby idiom, so distant from her own that Frederick could feel the Upper Darby aptitude for derision like hot frying-pan grease spattering into his face. She knew damn well why he was looking at her, and she was working hard to show him nothing. That's what you deserve, Freddy—nothing.

Frederick boomed, "Made do in the time-honored manner of a Salmon woman."

"How would you know anything about that?" she snapped at him, neither in anger nor in jest, but quickly, efficiently, impersonally as a lizard taking a fly on its tongue.

"I don't know. They were all jealous of you, Lilith," Frederick said, the coldness in his voice breaking into warmth. His body edged backward into the hallway, but his mind moved forward into the Hearth Room.

"I thought about my mother," Lilith said, "cool and reserved for so many years, and then, all at once, in flames."

Now that she had shown a trace of emotion, the deep-down hurt that he knew she harbored, he was suddenly ashamed of his jealous probing. "Oh, yah," he said, striving to be non-committal.

"You can take your shower now," she said.

"I'll be human when I finish, I promise." Frederick backed up, like a man trying to ease away from a bull in a field.

Lilith halted him for a moment. "It's bright as day outside," she said.

"Yes . . . the moon . . . the new snow." Frederick headed for warm, cleansing water.

When he came back down—clean, dressed, feet slippered,

revitalized—he was surprised to find Lilith putting on her parka. "I'm going skiing," she said.

Tiny stars seemed to burst from the new snow under the new moon. The only sound Frederick and Lilith heard was the slide-crunch of the skis on fresh snow over crusty snow. The skis moved them leisurely but swiftly, and neither felt the need to speak. When they reached the edge of the ice, they didn't hesitate but skied out onto it. Finally, they stopped in the middle of the pond to rest and to take in the night. Snow lay before them in ripples, as if the waves of summer had been stopped by time; in spots, the wind had whisked the snow away to bare ice, dense and full of design, like a cracked pane of glass a foot thick over another cracked pane of glass a foot thick and so forth, to the center of the earth.

After the moment passed, Frederick asked, "What were you thinking about?"

"The baby—I'm afraid for him . . . her," Lilith said.

"Oh." Frederick was afraid for himself. Not only did he rarely think about the baby, he didn't even know how to go about thinking about the baby.

"What was on your mind?" Lilith asked.

"Ice fishing."

"Frederick!" Lilith said, partly amused, partly exasperated. She started to move, sauntering on the cross-country skis.

Frederick lagged behind so he could watch her, enjoy her grace. Also, he was a little afraid she was going to fall and he'd have to catch her, although in fact she was much more stable on the skis than he was. She'd told him her father had put her on cross-country skis the day she could walk; Frederick remembered himself as a small boy, sitting on Howard's lap, barreling along in a skidoo at fifty miles an hour.

"A lot of married guys like ice fishing," Frederick said. "Out-doors, wind blowing, cold, miserable, winter weather of the wild world every man leaves behind when he takes up with a woman."

"And they get drunk."

"That's right."

They reached an icy spot and Frederick's fear was realized. Lilith slipped and lost her balance. Frederick grabbed for her, missed, and flopped ridiculously into the snow. Lilith caught herself, did not fall, then laughed at him. Frederick picked himself up without a word. It struck him that he was still angry from this morning, angry at Garvin Prell, at Lilith, at himself, at the universe; and for no good reason. He hated to feel like this. He wished he could be more giving, more generous. Giving and forgiving, thinking and forethinking—a generous heart—that's what being an adult was about. Nobody he knew was like that.

"What?" said Lilith.

"I didn't say anything," Frederick said.

"You were muttering to yourself."

"Guy in my head talking."

"Ever since you started that new work schedule and had to quit taking night classes, you've been restless," Lilith said.

He pointed at the moon with his ski pole. "I want to climb up there. I want to be something, be somebody. But . . . but." He could speak no more.

"But you can't, you have to work, you have to prepare for fatherhood, for the family life. You feel . . . What do you feel?"

His emotions rose up to the surface, strong, true, and awful. "Trapped." He started skiing again. "Everything's a trap— you're a trap, the baby's a trap. My father wants to buy a new Honeywagon—that's a trap. There, I said all those things I hate myself for thinking. Lilith, I don't know if I'm going to fly away or fly apart."

"Frederick, if you didn't have to do your father's trash route, if you could finish your education at the state college in Tuck-

323

erman—could you be happy here, with me, with the baby?"

"You want to bribe me. It won't work, Lilith. I can't just live on your money." Despite his words, Frederick was prepared to accept a bribe, and therefore, he realized, he was already lost; they had to get away. "Lilith, there's nothing for us in Darby. Why are we staying here?"

"I have a house, I have a past to catch up with. You do, too. We can make it work here." Lilith presented her case with passionate desperation, but without any real logic or depth. She thought, Now he'll defeat me in the argument, and he'll be happy, and we can forget about all this.

"Nobody stays, everybody leaves," he said. "Starting over is what it's about in America. Going is normal. Staying is strange. You and me—we're the strange ones. Because we're trying to get ahead in the place where we were born. You stay in your hometown, you end up more of a stranger than if you'd started new someplace else."

"It's not me or you who's a stranger here—it's us," Lilith said. "Upper Darby and Center Darby just have to get used to the idea of us. The baby will take care of that. Frederick, I know you can't stand working on the Honeywagon. I know you feel trapped, but I've got a way out for you that's better than just driving away. Frederick, you could be the caretaker on my father's Trust."

He wasn't sure whether he had heard her right. "Are you serious?" He whispered the words, but the night air carried them to Lilith. He felt uncomfortably giddy, as if he'd won the sweepstakes with somebody else's ticket.

"Garvin and I talked about it at the town meeting. The Trust is overrun with kids in four-wheelers and poachers trying to catch the white bear. There's some money in a fund for the Trust. If we log parts of the Trust, we can keep the fund up and pay your salary."

324

"This all comes from Garvin, right?" Frederick said.

"The Trust needs a caretaker. It would be the perfect job for you."

"Your vote and Garvin's vote against Monet's," Frederick said.

"Yes. It's the best thing. You, part of the Trust. I can see us, you in the woods at work, coming home across the field, and the baby and I on the grass, and the smell of lilacs. Oh, Frederick, I've always wanted lilacs. Everything is going to be all right, isn't it?"

Frederick knew he should turn Lilith down. He knew that this was Garvin's way of striking back at Monet, who fancied himself the unofficial caretaker of the Trust; Garvin was going to want something in return. Lilith was too young and inexperienced to be making deals with a Prell, but he said nothing about his worries. He was swept up in the idea: himself—caretaker, boss man of the Trust lands.

"Sure, everything's going to be fine," he said. Then, to escape from his guilt, he changed the subject. "How was the town meeting?"

"It dragged on."

"Who's the new selectman? Monet?"

"Who do you think?"

"My father doesn't vote, but he said if he did vote Critter Jordan would be his man. Pitchfork was going to vote for Critter. So, I figure Critter."

"Lawrence Dracut. He won in a landslide." Lilith was hurrying now, her long legs moving the skis effortlessly across the snow. Frederick had to struggle to keep up with her. They were almost at the shoreline when Lilith slowed, then stopped. "Listen!" she said.

"What? I don't hear anything."

"Can you feel it?"

325

A moment later, Frederick felt a great rumbling on the soles of his feet, and then a crackling sound echoed across the lake. It was like standing in the middle of a lightning strike.

"The pond's making ice," Frederick said.

They stood before the sound like patriots before the flag. "Isn't it beautiful, isn't it powerful?" Lilith said. She seemed transfixed, as if someone were calling her, and then she hurried for shore, heading for home. Frederick followed. In the woods, they surprised a deer which bounded across the path and disappeared into the night. They stopped for a moment, then went on. Frederick thought about the deer, struggling with winter weather, perhaps fleeing the domesticated dogs that formed packs and chased wild deer. And then he thought of Lilith. She was like that deer. Already he had an inkling of the tragedy that was coming, but not how and not how to stop it and not that he would be its instrument.

5

The Thaw

It had been a long winter, not severe, but consistently cold, with no relief. Now, finally, in early April, a warm spell. Spring fever! Everybody in the North Country had it, even Garvin Prell behind his desk at Prell Enterprises Inc. in Tuckerman. It was 10:00 A.M., the second day of the thaw. Yesterday the temperature had hit sixty-eight degrees. Snowmelt poured off the roofs; patches of bare ground materialized in back yards; Tuckerman State College students sunbathed on dormitory rooftops; shoppers crowded downtown, as if spring were on sale. Today promised to be even warmer.

It was Friday and Garvin decided right then and there to end his workweek immediately. He'd drive home, grab a bite to eat, and take a bicycle ride, his first in the new year. Maybe he'd pedal over to the Salmon house. He had the idea that if Lilith could see him and Frederick Elman together, measure him beside her bearded trash man, the comparison would raise an element of doubt in her mind. Lilith was prone to doubt, and such persons were subject to persuasion—here's how to get unstuck.

It was well before noon when Garvin pulled the BMW onto Prell grounds. He didn't bother opening the automatic garage doors, but parked outside and stepped into the sunshine. It was even balmier in Darby than it had been in Tuckerman.

Usually the extra thousand feet in altitude meant colder temperatures, not warmer. What a day!

He walked slowly from the car to the house, feeling the sun patting him on the back. The sun said, Here's to you and me, here's to the here and now, and forget yesterday ever happened. What he needed was some personal time, away from the business, away from the law practice, and, yes, away from his father. E.H. had been bedridden all winter, the victim of two more minor strokes since the summer. Some days he was coherent; other days he resided in a realm of his own. It was just a matter of time, Doc Butterworth had said. Garvin was weary of the death watch. It was so much like winter itself, a constant coldness, dark and white. Why couldn't people just die? Why did they have to wait around, putting the healthy on hold?

He was not the type to brood. He was a man of action. So he had immersed himself in his work. He couldn't seem to concentrate on a relationship with a member of the opposite sex. Once he had satisfied his physical needs, he felt empty, distracted, uninterested. Take a vacation, his friends said. He knew he should, but he didn't want to be away too long from E.H. He'd surrendered much of his life in favor of caring for his father, at first more or less unconsciously, but it was beginning to dawn on him that the reason he hadn't married, couldn't seem to find the right girl, had something to do with his father. He didn't want to think about this. It was dangerous stuff. He didn't want to wind up like half of his friends, paying some therapist big money to find out things you did not want to know about yourself. But forget that, he thought. Today belonged to the sun.

Garvin turned the doorknob (an exquisite thing from Brassworks), walked through the front hall to the Great Room, and here stopped abruptly. There before him stood Gee, a radiant smile on her face, and his father on his feet and fully dressed.

"Father?" Garvin said, as if addressing a ghost.

"Of course, I'm your father." E.H. spoke softly and oddly, for he did not sound like himself but like someone else. And yet the voice was familiar to Garvin. But whose?

"He dressed himself—it's a miracle," Gee said. She was one of those Oriental Catholics, full of belief and cunning.

"Yes, I even shaved myself," E.H. said.

"Actually, I shaved him," Gee said.

"I think I'm going to recover," E.H. said. "I arose this morning and the first thing I thought was, Something today is different."

"It's warm—that's what's different—okay?" Garvin said. Another man might have heard the resentment in his own voice, but not Garvin.

Perhaps the resentment did not matter, for E.H. did not hear it either, and Gee, who heard it, merely accepted it with respectful dread, as one accepts floods in monsoon rains.

"And then I knew what the difference was," E.H. said. "I feel like myself. No pain. No befuddlement. I've got a hold of myself. . . . I've got a hold of myself."

"I was going to go for a bicycle ride," Garvin said, and now he felt the resentment along with the accompanying guilt, like some malevolent oily wave, washing on board a sailboat.

E.H. turned to Gee and continued to speak in that smooth, alien, yet vaguely familiar voice. "The boy wants to ride his bicycle, isn't that lovely? You know the problem with your generation, Garvin? You spent too many of your early years outside the adult world. Too much time with peers."

"My Upper Darby peers left. . . ."

"Don't interrupt me." E.H. cut Garvin with a look, and then he turned back to Gee. "I expect it's partly our fault, sending children off to school, conducting our businesses in private. Young people have no choice but to grow up among themselves. It makes for delayed maturation. When is he going to marry, people this house with another generation?" He turned back to Garvin. "My boy, when? Never mind, your life can wait. Mine is getting short, and I . . . and I . . . and I wish to go to lunch."

"Lunch?" Garvin said.

"He hasn't had breakfast yet," Gee said.

"Cook him something," Garvin said.

"I want you to take me to lunch," E.H. said. "I want to be seen. Take me to the Inn. I want to show everybody that E.H. is still a functioning presence in Darby."

And so they left for the Inn at Darby Green, the young man and the old man. Garvin felt as if he were taking a stranger to lunch. It was as if he hadn't left work at all. This was not his father. This was a client, whom he had to entertain. Who, then, was his father? Where was the old bedridden man? Who was this fellow? What did he want?

It was barely noon when they reached the Inn.

"Mr. Prell," the hostess greeted Garvin, a familiar face to her.

E.H. took the stage away from Garvin. "I am Mr. Prell, thank you," he said gently and firmly.

The hostess blinked at this unfamiliar face. She was one of the new people in Darby, those who had swept Lawrence Dracut into office. She had heard of E. H. Prell, heard he had died last year. She'd gotten E.H. mixed up with the Squire, but, then, to the new people one old New Hampshire poop up on the hill was much like another.

"My father, E. H. Prell. Dad, this is Lesley, one of the owners of the Inn," Garvin said.

"They thought I was ill, but I've recovered—completely. Indeed, I was never ill. Let us say I was resting," E.H. said.

"Could we sit by a window?" Garvin said to the hostess.

"No, no—I can't bear too much light," E.H. said, easily,

disarmingly, so that it was natural for the hostess to listen to him and not to Garvin.

They sat in the middle of the restaurant. Here E.H. could watch people come and go. E.H. ordered a martini; Garvin, as if following the lead of a client, asked for the same.

"Olive or twist of lemon?" the waiter asked.

"Young man," E.H. said, "there is no such thing as a martini with a lemon. A martini is defined by the olive."

The waiter scampered off.

Garvin experienced a moment of despair. He wished he were somebody else, someplace far away, with someone he had never met before. Then something happened. E.H. spoke to him with the gentleness of God. "Garvin, I know this is difficult for you. You would rather be doing something else. But please humor me. I understand . . . everything. Nobody likes the richest man in town. He reminds them of their infirmities. For this next hour, be my son, and I will be your father."

With those kindly spoken words coming from a father so unlike his father, so unlike anybody he knew at all, Garvin found himself moved. In that instant, he no longer felt alienated from this man. Suddenly it was as if he were discovering his true father, the father under the skin of the skinflint, as it were.

From this moment on, Garvin's mood turned inside out. Instead of being resentful and distracted, he was respectful and attentive. He could feel the warmth of that light his father was frightened of, pouring in from the outside. The glow of the martini added more light, like the bright, intoxicating haze of a summer day. These two men, father and son, began to talk—easily and joyfully. They laughed together. They discussed. They schemed. E.H. spoke with a kind of formality, as if he were constructing prose for the ages rather than merely gabbing.

331

"Dad"—he'd never called E.H. "Dad" before—"you should have become a lawyer," Garvin said.

"It was my dream for a long time, but I put it aside. I'm proud that you're following through."

"Proud?"

"Proud."

"You wanted to be a lawyer?"

"I didn't trust law—I had an idea to make it right. But the same pressures that squeezed Reggie Salmon squeezed me. I knew before I made right I had to make money, or it was all over for the Prells. We took different routes, Reggie and I. He strapped himself to land. I took on the real world. Who do you think won, Garvin?"

The question caught Garvin by surprise. "You won," he said, not quite convinced, so he sounded the theme again in different words. "We won—the Prells won."

"As we went, so went the country. Or perhaps the other way around. Business is a tide, my boy, drawing in, retreating."

Garvin, a little spun off by E.H.'s not-quite-apt metaphor, said, "Now we have the rewards."

"That's correct, yes, but I'll tell you this: the game never ends. At the present time, we—that is, you—have a new adversary, although one not so worthy as the Squire."

"Monet."

"Where do we stand with him?" E.H. asked, and for once Garvin did not resent such a question.

"We have him in court, and he has us in court," Garvin said. "It's a standoff, but he can't win going that route unless he has more in the bank than I think he has."

"Ah, sooooo," E.H. said, like some grand Oriental philosopher.

Garvin recognized that familiar but alien voice now. It was E.H., twenty years ago. It was the voice of the man who had taught him everything. It was the voice of his true father.

"I'll bring you up to date," Garvin said. He hadn't planned on telling E.H. about the caretaker's plan. There was a certain illogic about it that E.H. was sure to spot. But now, with the mood he and his father were in, Garvin told E.H. all. He awaited the inevitable criticism.

"Provocative idea." E.H. spooned out his words. "I am sure that it is not lost upon you that Monet Salmon considers himself the de facto caretaker of his brother's lands. Perhaps Monet will make a fool of himself at this upcoming meeting of the Trust, especially in view of his recent political defeat, and cut himself off entirely from Lilith. If that should be the case, we will have gained indeed, because then you can count on Lilith's vote on the Trust board ad infinitum. At any rate, the caretaker move will frustrate Monet for the time being."

"It may even drive him out in the open," Garvin said, confident now that he wasn't going to be cut down, "because for all the world I cannot fathom what Monet wants out of the Trust lands."

"He wants his brother's soul," E.H. said. "I know because I wanted it, too. So far, Monet has won all the battles with his stalling tactics in court. Is your confidence shaken?"

And there it was: the slap in the face that Garvin had expected, steeled himself to accept, and then, in belief that it was not forthcoming, lowered his guard against.

"No, it has not shaken my confidence," Garvin said coldly.

And again E.H. surprised him by his kindness and sensitivity. E.H. took his hand in his own and said, "I'm sorry, son. I was merely making an inquiry. I sense that Monet is reaching the end of his line of cash. In the long run, Monet cannot win in court, because we can outspend him. After all the court battles have been waged, our position will be more solidified than ever. But I ask you, why not abbreviate the difficulties by giving him what he wants?"

"Give him what he wants? We can't give him the Trust, because he'll have it and we won't."

"Give him the ledges. They're worthless to us; he can act out his brother's fantasy in that realm. And we can go to work and bring the rest of the property into productivity."

"I don't want to give him anything, Father," Garvin said, again expecting insult.

But E.H. continued his gentle ways. "All right, then. He can't last forever. Eventually, something will happen. He'll fly apart."

After a pause, E.H. said, "What worries me is the infant."

It took Garvin a moment to realize E.H. was talking about the child Lilith was expecting.

"How so?" Garvin asked.

"I'm not sure at this point in time . . . just what point in time . . . point in time," E.H. said, and he rocked backward for a moment, as if he'd lost his balance.

"Is something wrong?" Garvin was alarmed.

"No, I just lost track of things for a second. Just lost track. I'm all right now." His voice was steady, even confident, and Garvin relaxed.

The waiter was back. Garvin ordered the house luncheon specialty—Full and Trim, half a chicken sandwich, a cup of soup, and a small salad with the creamy-garlic house dressing. E.H. ordered a huge meal, breakfast really—pancakes, eggs, bacon, sausage, fried potatoes, and another martini.

They were in the middle of the meal when Lawrence Dracut and the Reverend Spofford Hall appeared. "Isn't that our new selectman?" E.H. asked.

"One and the same."

"In Crabb we had a friend in the town government. Have you sounded out the new bird?"

"He favors schools, but says he's a fiscal conservative," Garvin said. "He's rabidly against Monet, but claims to be pro-environment and hasn't taken a stand on our development. I don't know what he wants, or who he is. Nobody does. We'll just have to wait and see."

"I don't have time to wait, so I think I'll see for myself." E.H. rose to his feet and moved toward Dracut and Hall. The old man walked with the stiff grace of an experienced drinker taking a policeman's coordination test for DWI. Garvin followed.

E.H. introduced himself, shook Dracut's hand, holding on to it just a tad too long. Garvin felt mildly embarrassed and a little unnerved by Dracut's coolness, which was odd, because he himself cultivated coolness, was usually comfortable with coolness, which protected a man without declaring hostilities against other men. The Reverend Hall was all over himself explaining to Dracut E.H.'s position in the community.

Back at their table, E.H. said, "Dracut's a smoothy."

A few minutes later, Marcia Pascal came in with Noreen Cook.

"The town pump pregnant, and with a beautiful woman and in a restaurant out of her league—something's going on," E.H. said.

Garvin smiled. "The dark beauty is Monet Salmon's new wife."

"This is a recent development?"

"When you were ill. As for Noreen Cook, your guess is as good as mine. There has been, how shall I say, a good deal of speculation about the issue of Monet, his wife, and Noreen."

"The new wife appears to be something out of Monet's Colombian connection."

"There's no direct evidence of that," Garvin said.

"You looked into it?"

"The state attorney general's office is investigating Monet, but so far has turned up nothing conclusive. We know this: the wife goes by the name of Marcia Pascal, and she is a legitimate scientist. Ph.D. in zoology."

"I look at her and I say, I wish . . . I wish . . ." E.H.'s skin seemed to radiate light from the sun, its sheen an embodiment of the afternoon light that poured in through the windows.

Several more local people came by to say hello. It was almost 2:00 P.M. when Garvin paid the check. They were sipping coffee, and Garvin was thinking that in another few minutes they'd be on the way home. He'd say goodbye to E.H., then head over to the Salmon house. At that point, E.H. said in a barely audible whisper, "Come close to me."

"What?" Garvin did not understand.

"Lean your head close to me, as if I was telling you a secret," E.H. said, his voice soft, controlled, and yet oddly metallic.

Garvin leaned toward his father so that the two men were almost touching. E.H.'s breath smelled like dead leaves.

"Garvin, I believe I am having a heart attack at this moment," E.H. said in that soft, soft voice.

Garvin jerked his head away.

"No quick movements . . ." E.H. said.

"I'll call a doctor."

"Not yet, not now—you have to get me out of here first," E.H. whispered.

Garvin noticed now that his father's face was wet with perspiration, and his color was bad. "Father, I have to bring you to a hospital," Garvin said.

E.H. took his hand, as he had earlier. "No, my son. These people have come to see the ChaMadonnan. I won't be lugged out of here on a stretcher." E.H. stood, then managed to raise his voice so that he sounded jocular. "Ah, my boy!" he said. "I want them to remember me . . . remember me . . ." His words died in a whisper.

Garvin and his father made their way to the door. Sanborn

House stopped to say a word to E.H. He grinned crazily at him, took his hand, squeezed it too hard because House seemed to run away. "They mustn't see me down," E.H. said. "I am the ChaMadonnan." He was gasping for breath now.

The two men walked arm in arm, appearing like drunken buddies, the younger man half holding up the older man. Just before they reached the door, E.H. collapsed in Garvin's arms. No one was around. E.H. whispered, "Don't let them see me." His face was blue.

They were right by the men's room. Garvin threw open the door, and dragged his father in. He locked the door behind him, and laid E.H. supine on the floor. He cupped his hands and pressed on his chest. He tried to remember how to give CPR.

6

Death and Taxes

Frederick and Lilith wore their best for the funeral of E. H. Prell. Lilith bought a maternity dress for the occasion. Frederick put on a jacket and a tie. (He owned one of the former, two of the latter.) As they were about to get into the pickup, Frederick noted the morning. Cool, damp air lifting off the melting snows flowed through sun-heated air like a river coursing off its delta through the depths of an ocean. The breeze whispered the vague promises of the spring thaw. To Frederick, such a day spoke of hope and home, the Trust, the caretaker's job, the new work—the new life.

They hadn't gotten out of the driveway when Lilith asked a question: "What's that noise?"

"Hole in the pipe between the manifold and the muffler," he said.

"It's getting a little loud, isn't it?"

"Does seem to bite a little more than yesterday. I'll bring the truck down to my father's barn pit by and by, and we'll fix it."

"You wait until the last minute for everything." She was trying to tell him that he had to grow up soon, that he had obligations now. Persephone had her Saab shipped to Australia, so Frederick's truck was their only vehicle.

"Right again," he said. The words and the tone got across his point: he didn't like her nagging.

338

As they drove, Frederick fell into a reverie on the caretaker's job. Mentally, he was already in the woods—patrolling, mapping, making plans. He knew how to stop the poaching and how to bother the trespassers. Keep on top of them. Poachers would be hard to find in the woods, true, but they had to arrive in registered highway vehicles. He'd set up an intelligence network, make some kind of deal with Mrs. McCurtin. He'd find the poachers' vehicles. He'd wait for them to return, then put it to 'em with Elman bluff, explain politely that there were a lot of crazy people around here that might damage a vehicle that was left untended. That was the language those people understood; it was the language *he* understood. He'd have to arm himself, of course. He had a rifle, a .308, but he needed a pistol. Nothing like a gun belt strapped to a man's waist to make another man stop and think. He'd reduce the joy-riding four-wheelers and other trespassers just by being around and by giving them a hard time when he ran across them. The word would get out.

Oh, he wanted this job. But, from the vantage point of that want, he saw a prison. A man with no hope and no home was free; a man with hope and home was fettered. Normally, he would have talked to Lilith about his concerns. Well, not talked. He would have carried on theatrically, hooting and hollering, imitating (and badly) his father. Now, all of a sudden, he found himself cautious, trying to be a politician, and the result was, he expressed his frustrations roundaboutly instead of directly. He was becoming civilized, and he didn't like the feeling—snippy, a scaredy-cat. His old fears of losing himself in her money and status were being realized. Frederick buried his worries in thoughts about the pistol he would buy.

"When I go back to school, I think I'll major in forest management," he said.

"I wish you would." She could see him struggling to find a new self. He was a year or two away. If they could just hang on until he was ready. As an afterthought, she reached out a hand and touched his shoulder as he drove.

The touch surprised him, shocked him. She'd been distant and erratic lately, or perhaps only distracted. Something was wrong. The baby? One minute Lilith was here, with him, and the next minute she was in her own world, sequestered in her greenhouse, or in his presence but like an island in which the air between them was thick with black flies and he could not approach her. No matter how much she showed him, she seemed to be hiding so much more, but what? Now this—affection coming out of nowhere. He didn't like it; he didn't trust it.

"Lilith, I love you," he said; the love felt like a craving for a drug.

"I know."

"Maybe it's the baby, but I feel as though you've been off somewhere, and I'm not along." They were on Route 21 now, approaching the auction barn.

"It's nothing like that," she said.

"So?"

"I don't know. Forget it."

It was at this point that the muffler fell off. There was a klunk! followed by raw engine noise pouring out of the manifold, then the drag sound of the muffler being pulled along the road.

"Well, that's interesting," Frederick said, with deliberate understatement. He was thinking that maybe this would get him out of going to the funeral. He pulled the truck off the road into the auction barn's parking lot.

"How are we going to get to the funeral?" Lilith said.

"I don't know." He fertilized his words with a tone of understatement. It was what a workingman did when the going got tough.

The auction barn was crowded, as usual, but only a couple

340

cars were parked in front of the Kwick Stop. Beyond, a backhoe scooped out still-frozen dirt, which broke off in brown crystals as the machine dumped its load.

"Some kind of construction project," Frederick said, as he and Lilith got out of the truck.

"They talked about it at the town meeting," Lilith said, watching Frederick crawl under the truck. "Critter Jordan is building a recreation center—bowling alleys, arcade, video parlor."

"Uh-huh." Frederick understood. The new venture was Critter's response to a loss of business to Joe Ancharsky's store. From underneath the pickup, he saw only her black, medium-high heels and ankles in sheer nylon stockings. He shouted at the ankles. "Gimme a coat hanger from the camper." The ankles went away. The truck jounced a bit as she rummaged about above him. This was what family life was going to be like. A minute later, the ankles reappeared, then a hand. He took the coat hanger and wrapped it around the rotted end of the exhaust pipe and the old coupling. It wasn't difficult work, but the muffler was hot and he burned his arm slightly, yelling ee-youch! He was proud of the work, proud of his wound. But when he slid from under the truck, Lilith gave out a sound of her own, a yelp of startled, restrained dejection, as one might utter at the sudden sight of an old friend with a dread disease.

"What's-a-matter?" Frederick stood.

"You're dirty, just filthy."

He understood now. She didn't want to be seen with him at the funeral. Well, he was going to go, goddamn it. They drove to the church in silence.

The parking lot at the Unified Church of Christ had long been full when they arrived, and cars lined the side of the road for hundreds of feet, but a narrow space remained almost in front of the church. Frederick, whipping along as if going on to Kingdom Come, jammed on the brakes, and the truck screeched to a halt. He parallel-parked without looking. The breath of risk relaxed him, tightened Lilith. They walked by the side of the road—Lilith first, along the edge of rotted snow-banks pushed up by the plow; Frederick lagging behind and on the blacktop. Just before they reached the church, Lilith unsuccessfully attempted to brush dirt from Frederick's shirt collar.

They had just turned to go into the church when Lilith caught the eye of Lawrence Dracut and his family. They, too, had arrived at the last minute, and apparently had witnessed Frederick's speedy entry, heard the muffler, seen the Squire's daughter tidying up her trash man. Mrs. Dracut had a Florida tan and a blond page-boy hairstyle; the boy was tall, about sixteen; the girl younger and very blond. Lilith saw that rueful, slightly amused, slightly pitying, slightly contemptuous smile that she had seen on the face of Dracut that day at the cemetery when he had sized up her father's Bronco, but now she saw the smile not only on the face of the man but on the faces of his wife and children.

The seats were all taken, and Frederick and Lilith had to stand in the back. The church—painted white inside and out, no pictures on the walls, barren, the kind of place any animal would avoid—seemed to Frederick designed more to drive away a God than to invite one in. The mourners were like himself, he thought, vaguely uncomfortable, vaguely bored, but duty-bound. Unlike himself, they were well dressed, un-soiled, and inconspicuous. The air in the church was respect-ful, but unsweetened by the incense of grief. Indeed, the issues of God and grief did not seem to matter. Everything was for show. Maybe formal occasions were for show because people could not stand the real thing.

Frederick resisted an urge to swear or fart. If he had one thing in common with his father, it was an attitude toward the Creator. Elenore was a hybrid Catholic; Howard and himself were hybrid atheists, men who didn't so much disbelieve in God as in the invention of God. If there was such an entity, what would be the point of worshipping Him? Her? It? Why would this entity, Creator of the universe, need a bunch of people to tell Him he was great? As for God's own people, those chosen ones, Frederick couldn't deny that many of them had peace of mind. He respected their power and feared their secret motives as they themselves feared their God and His secret motives. People who could build solid foundations in the vapors of a fantasy were fearsome indeed.

Of all the churches Frederick Elman had been in—not many—he liked this one the least. His mother had taken him into a Catholic church when she'd converted to the faith, and he found the atmosphere tolerable, if a little gaudy. But this church, the Unified Church of Christ in Darby, was stark and cold and critical. It seemed to pay homage to a deity whose message was "Live free and die."

Frederick and Lilith were only in the church a minute or so before former Selectman Arthur Crabb—back from a long Florida vacation—rose from his end pew in the rear, slowly approached them as if to pass by, then stopped, bowed slightly before Lilith, and took her hand. Lilith obeyed the old man's silent command as one hypnotized. Without a word he led her to his seat. Beside the tall, strong young woman, magnificent with child, the old man appeared even more bent and shriveled than he was, so that the people who saw them together at this moment did not later remember his courtesy to her or her compliance to him; they remembered a change in Crabb's appearance. As Mrs. McCurtin later said, "Have you noticed how Arthur Crabb has aged? Overnight—these retired people get old . . . overnight."

After Lilith had sat down beside Mrs. Crabb, Mr. Crabb took the standing position beside Frederick that Lilith had vacated, so that a camera might have scored the former selectman and the current trash collector as a New England–hills odd couple. In fact, while the two took note of one another, they never made eye contact. Crabb was only dimly aware that a young man stood with him. Frederick, getting a whiff from Crabb's shoes (he'd helped his son with the cows that morning), smelled the dung of his own indefensible hostility toward the old farmer and his kind.

Mrs. Crabb wondered only fleetingly what her husband was up to when he rose from his seat, because she was preoccupied with deciphering the meaning of the facial expressions of certain mourners. At the moment, she scrutinized Dr. Marcia Pascal, the woman who had married Monet Salmon. A cool customer, thought Mrs. Crabb. And then she found herself looking at Lilith Salmon on Arthur's arm, as he was escorting her to his seat.

The expression on Mrs. Crabb's face—startled anger—struck Lilith as revealing of motives and character, the kind of payoff that Mrs. Crabb herself sought from her own observations. Lilith believed that Mrs. Crabb regarded her as an interloper. And perhaps it was so; perhaps her attempts to take over the Salmon house against the will of Darby constituted an invasion that carried over from the Salmon property into the kitchens of farmers' wives. Lilith could not bear the contempt which she believed Mrs. Crabb felt for her, so she turned her eyes away. As a result, she did not see the following flicker of compassion in Mrs. Crabb's eyes, for the old woman had read something in Lilith's response to her own jolt of surprise: fear and desperation. In that instant, Mrs. Crabb knew that she and Arthur had made the right decision to sell their remaining interest in the farm and move to Florida for good.

It took a while for Frederick to realize that four of the six pallbearers bringing the casket to the front of the church were the sons of E. H. Prell. Except for Garvin, the Prell children had long ago left Upper Darby, but they had flown in for the funeral. It glanced off Frederick that Garvin Prell, like himself, was the youngest male of his clan. The pallbearers left the casket, unopened, at the head of the aisle. Above stood the Reverend Hall in a gray suit and a black shirt. The Prell men took seats with their sister in the front-row pew. These people sat down on the fifty-yard line of life, Frederick thought, while he resided in the bleachers. (It didn't occur to Frederick that the Prell children had "good seats" for the simple reason that they'd lost a parent.) He couldn't think of them as real human beings. They were, he thought with a tiny thrill, duckpins: the chosen duckpins, chosen to operate the businesses, run the armies, write the laws, design the products, set the standards, create the future; God's chosen duckpins for Planet Earth. Frederick Elman did not number himself among them.

The Reverend Hall prepared to give the eulogy. Hall was a tall, heavyset man who managed to appear neither fat nor muscular, but merely oversized. In this respect, he resembled Lilith's father. But, unlike the Squire, the reverend did not carry himself like a big man but, rather, like a large, successful child. Hall spoke slowly and without gestures or obvious intonations of voice, and with only a trace of a Southern accent. The reverend was not callous or uncaring; he was by temperament uninterested in people, disinterested in divinity. Yet his very lack of emotional involvement elicited interest, even respect, from the more thoughtful members of his church. His congregation wondered about his convictions the way one wonders whether cats think about art, or dogs about friendship, or parrots about language. Like those people who have such thoughts about their pets, the congregation, in the end, believed in their rector. Perhaps that was why he had come here. He really didn't have enough personality to make it as a minister anywhere else but New England.

"His name was Edward Hazard Prell," the Reverend Hall eulogized, "but to all of us who knew him he was E.H., the

345

foremost citizen of Upper Darby." (Not true, thought Lilith.) "E.H. was chairman of the board of the Granite Bank in Tuckerman. He was chairman of the board of Prell Enterprises Inc. And so forth. But to his friends, he was more than the chairman of boards, he was a friend—er, ah—indeed; to his children, he was more than the chairman of boards, he was their father. Like our Father in heaven, he was stern but loving. . . ." (A lie—it made Lilith think of her own lie. The lie of the money. With the lie, she was who she was. Without the lie, she was a shadow.) "As, in the end, all of us cry out, E.H. cried out, 'You? To whom shall I go? You, You, You, who have the message of eternal life."

After the eulogy, the Reverend Hall led the congregation in the singing of "Gone Are the Days," and then the congregation filed out. Frederick and Lilith did not attend the graveside ceremony for the family. They drove on into the village, to buy a few things at the general store and to pick up the mail. At the post office, Lilith had to sign for a registered letter from the town selectmen. She opened the letter on the drive back to Upper Darby.

"Well?" Frederick said.

She hesitated for a moment, as if trying to find a way to deny him access to the letter and also to blunt his curiosity about it. Finally, she handed him the letter, and he scanned it as he drove. The notice was stamped with the official town seal. The taxes on the Salmon property had not been paid in three years. The town threatened to put the property up for auction if the money was not forthcoming within six weeks. The letter was signed by the three Darby selectmen. Lawrence Dracut's signature was at the top.

"This is Dracut's way of getting back at Upper Darby for supporting Monet in the election," Frederick said. "But, Lilith, why didn't you pay your taxes? Why?"

"It was an oversight," Lilith lied. "My father was sick for a

346

year, and then he died, and my mother . . . Well, she just let things slide. I'm afraid I did the same."

"My father would never do that. My father might burn down his house for the insurance money. He might declare war on Darby. But he'd pay his taxes, or die from shame."

"Shame? Shame is peculiar," Lilith said.

"You don't have any shame here in Upper Darby?"

"No—we have guilt instead." Of course she didn't mean any of this. Couldn't he see? Why was he so stupid?

Frederick could almost feel her ferocity. Typical Elman, he returned fire with fire. "And nobody in Upper Darby pays for anything unless they have to—right?" he said.

"Right."

"Secrets of the rich," Frederick said.

"Why do I have to defend Upper Darby? I'm alone in my world."

"Alone? You've got me."

"You can see your mother anytime you want. Mine's gone. You could reconcile with your father anytime you want. Mine's gone."

Frederick felt defeated. It seemed to him that Lilith was toying with him, and that, furthermore, he deserved to be toyed with. But, as usual, he misread her, as even he could see a moment later. Lilith withdrew into herself. Her anger had vanished, and she was trembling. Something dawned in Frederick now. He visualized the Hearth Room. Was it possible that Lilith could not afford to pay the taxes? "Lilith, do you have the money?"

Lilith uncoiled. "It's none of your business."

"Like everybody else, I always assumed . . . But I think about your place. . . . It needs work. I don't see anything new. Your father's Bronco was ancient, and you never replaced it when you cracked it up."

This was the time to tell Frederick the truth, and yet she

could not. "I like the house the way it is." She waved at him with a hand, as if shooing a fly. "I do need a car, yes. I need my own car. I can afford it—why shouldn't I have my own car?"

Frederick glanced at Lilith. There was something unreal about this conversation, something unreal about her. "Is everything all right?" Frederick asked.

"Everything's fine," Lilith said with exaggerated good cheer. "You're right, you're right about the taxes and the car. So, let's take care of all this today—now. Drive me to Mrs. McCurtin's house."

"Mrs. McCurtin? Now?"

"Yes—turn around. She's the town clerk. I'll give her the money personally." She reached in her handbag for her checkbook. "I want the word to get around that Lilith Salmon pays her debts, and then we'll go to Tuckerman and shop for a car."

"This is crazy," Frederick said, half in horror, half in amusement.

"It's long overdue," Lilith said. In her dead certainty, in the curious deadness of spirit of that animated certainty, Lilith reminded Frederick of Persephone Salmon.

7

Washing

Every day the trash route was harder to do for Frederick. It wasn't the labor that wore him down; it was the constant sameness. Howard had cooked up a system, and it worked slick. Nothing new to learn, no room for individual enterprise. If only Cooty had been around to keep him honest, throw him off balance with his quirky ideas. As it was, all he had for company was his own ideas, which were not so good. He thought: I think too much about myself. He brooded on this matter just long enough to realize he was going around in a mental circle. Trash man, trash brain. Put the brain in the back of the truck, and bring it to the landfill for burial.

He was on Route 21, driving about sixty, when a car from the rear gave him the horn and rocketed by. Before he saw it pull into the headlight beams of the Honeywagon, he recognized the horn toots—three short and a long, Beethoven's Fifth. It was Lilith in her red car, taking her evening drive. He sounded the Honeywagon's horn in a return greeting, but by the time he'd rolled down the window to give her a wave, she'd disappeared around a corner.

She'd bought a licking red flame of a car, at once advertising danger and availability, the fantasy of a college girl, and, pregnant, she looked ridiculous behind the wheel of it. He himself was uncomfortable in the passenger seat of the red car. He was constantly moving his shoulders as if to steer, and he could feel his right foot wanting to step on the brake. He wished she'd bought a station wagon or a four-door sedan or another Bronco, anything but a sports car. Goddamn it, he wanted to criticize her judgment, but at the same time he was held back from doing so because, well, he had no cause. It was her money. She could do what she wanted with it. He had even told her she ought to have her own car. But now that she'd actually bought one, all suddenlike—jeez! twenty minutes to complete the sale—well, he didn't approve of the way she'd gone about the business. A red sports car! The thing insulted the likes of him and his Live Free or Die pickup, and it troubled him that she so unabashedly enjoyed showing it off around town.

However, he had approved the way she'd laid down that tax check in front of Mrs. McCurtin, plopped it right on her lap. Reduced the town gossip to a-ba-ba-ba. Remembering the look on Mrs. McCurtin's face made him smile. He tried now to visualize Lilith up ahead, cutting into the corners, just a little too fast. He wished he was with her. They had in common a pleasure in speed.

Lilith's attention was on car/self, and she hardly gave Frederick a thought as she barreled past him. For the moment, she was indifferent to him, just as at other moments she might be indifferent to her mother or the weather or her money. Yes, even the money. No, Lilith, you are never far away from the truncheon of money. The thought passed by like scenery. Her mind was like her car, a speed demon, all for show. And then a word-thought came back—"indifference." It would be so sweet to be indifferent to everyone and everything. Indifference—sweet indifference—you put it on your soul as you put sugar on your grapefruit to smooth out the sour taste.

She moved slightly, and her belly rubbed the steering wheel. Who are you? What are you? In your baby brain, do you know me? I doubt it. Like all of them out there, you make me up. Then I'll make you up. We'll start over, making each other up. What do I say to you? How do I teach you when I know nothing? Perhaps we'll hide together. I'll take you into the rocks, and like a she-wolf I'll raise you. When you're ready, I'll bring you down from the ledges into the town.

Never mind what they call you—you'll be a Salmon. We'll enter a float in the Old Home Day parade. We'll put the Salmon house on wheels. Frederick, you can drive. You and I, my child, will stand at the peak as we pass in review. Wave to the people, smile, throw doubloons. Thank them for their applause by showering them with your radiance. Never mind your secret heart. After a while, you won't know you have one. . . . It wouldn't be like this if we had money. No, it's not the money— it's the lie of the money. It's not even our lie. We are merely its conveyors. Conveyors of the family lie, conveyances for the town's dreams.

School bus up ahead! Slow down. Lilith snapped back to reality. If only Frederick could see through her, understand her, break her lie, understand her . . . understand . . . understand, then maybe this strange, alienated being that guided her soul would fall away like a scab on a wound. Frederick, see me, recognize me, so I can see myself in reflection. I don't care. Why should I care? Here in the car, I'm almost myself, almost real. Here I dare anything; I cry; I cry out. She felt the baby kick—I am not your child. You are only carrying me for someone else—Who? Tell me who?

She had tried to broach the subject of her confused feelings about self and child with Frederick.

"We won't know how to raise the baby," she had said. "The Upper Darby way can't work anymore—maybe it never did. The Center Darby way is worse, always was. Neither one of us knows how to prepare our child for the world. What are we going to do?"

She had seen that she scared him; he'd thrown out some meaningless words. "We'll read books, we'll make it up," he had said.

His ideas about the baby were indefinite as the thin morning fog over the snow fields; the ideas had come from movies he had seen, proclamations from elders, and romantic notions he'd conjured up in place of real knowledge. If it was a boy, he'd play ball with him; if it was a girl, he'd bounce her on his lap. After that—nothing. He had even less of a sense for bringing up a child than she had, and yet she was looking to him for leadership.

A figure on the side of the highway. Not hitchhiking, just stumbling along. Lilith hit the brakes. She skidded to a stop a couple hundred feet beyond the figure, rolled the window down, and looked back. For a few seconds she saw no one. Why had she stopped? As her mother had pointed out a number of times, it was not prudent for a woman alone to give a ride to a stranger. The figure appeared in the darkness, coming slowly toward her. She couldn't make out whether it was a man, a woman, or a child. He or she did not change pace at the sight of the car. Now she saw it was a man, probably an older man. "Hello," she called. No answer. She was revving the engine, about to put it in launch, when she heard a little laugh. Again she looked out through the window. She recognized Frederick's old partner on the Honeywagon, Cooty Patterson.

Lilith leaned toward the passenger side of the red car and rolled down the window. "Need a ride?"

"Why, I'm not sure. Do I need a ride: what a great question." He stopped to consider, as if contemplating a tricky problem. Then he said, "I always take a ride," and he got into the red car.

"Where are you headed?" Lilith asked.

"I was walking down this road, and I knew something would happen," he said.

"I probably should take you to your cabin," she said.

"Oh, yes. That would be wonderful," Cooty said, as if, finally, someone had put into logical form a confusing idea.

Lilith started driving toward Donaldson. She had never been to Cooty's cabin, but from Frederick's description she had a pretty good idea where it was. The old man put his hands on his knees, and slouched forward. It was obvious he had walked a long ways and he was exhausted. Yet he did not seem upset, merely worn out. His sweat smelled strange, kind of sweet, as if he'd been rolling in a field of wild flowers.

"It's six miles to Donaldson," Lilith said. "Were you planning on walking home?"

"I don't know," he said, and she could see that the word "plan" held little meaning for him.

Cooty bowed his head and began to doze. In the presence of this daffy old man, Lilith found herself unaccountably relaxed, whole, and in touch. All of a sudden, her problems, her confusion, seemed unimportant. What was important was the moment, the only goal delivering Cooty to his home.

When they reached the cabin, Lilith helped the old man out and walked him to the door, using the flashlight from her utility box to guide them. He was so tired he was almost asleep on his feet. The door was unlocked. The place was cold and smelled musty. Cooty stumbled to his bunk and lay on his back. His mouth dropped open, and he shut his eyes. Lilith shone her beam around the cabin. The walls were littered with paper and sticks, things of no account. On a table she found some candles in holders. She lit the candles and doused her flashlight. She started a fire in the wood stove. She covered the old man with a blanket, and she was about to leave when she held the candle up to Cooty's face. It was as serene in sleep as it had been in wakefulness, but it was also dirty. She went outside to the dug well and pulled up a bucket of water and brought it inside. She sat by the side of the bunk and with her handkerchief she washed the old man's face.

While Lilith wiped away the grime, Cooty, half awake, half asleep, began talking. It was during this moment that he revealed to Lilith the truth about the white bear, but since the information held little importance to her, she didn't think to mention it to anyone.

The thaw continued right into the day of the meeting of the board of governors of the Raphael Salmon II Memorial Trust Lands. The snow was almost gone, remaining only in dismal banks on the sides of roads and the edges of parking lots and in forest shade, where the isolated patches resembled forgotten winter coats shed by children. It was, Frederick said, perfect weather for making love; it was, Lilith said, perfect weather for washing the car. On the grass of the Salmon grounds, feeling the day on her shoulders like soft, grandmotherly hands, she squirted liquid soap into a bucket. The car was parked on the lawn. Road salt, kicked up around the fenders and rocker panels, had dirtied the brilliant red finish.

"Wash the car?" Frederick questioned this practice, as if in wonder at hearing tell of a bizarre rite. "In all the years I lived in my father's house, I never saw him wash a car. And, frankly, it never occurred to me either. Haven't you ever heard of rain?"

"I pity you and your father both. Get me some water." Lilith spoke in a parentally assertive tone designed to tweak Frederick's nose. The garden hose lay on the ground, water drooling from its metal lips. Frederick handed the hose to Lilith, walked to the side of the house, where a faucet stuck out like some demure sex organ. Lilith pointed the hose nozzle at the bucket bottom. Frederick turned up the corners of his mouth and waited until the moment Lilith took note of the mischief in his eyes before he cranked the handle—full-blast. For a second or two—nothing. Then a hiccup in the hose. Then a dawning in Lilith. Then, before she had time to adjust, a jet of water knocking the bucket over. Then Lilith whipping the stream at Frederick and catching him with spray as he dived to the ground and rolled with the slope of the lawn, a laughing log tumbling down a hill.

Frederick rose, brushed off a few dried-grass clippings from last year's mowing, returned to the faucet, and adjusted the flow. Lilith filled the bucket. The icy water struggled to make suds in the liquid soap. Lilith wet down the car, then rubbed the finish with the soapy sponge. Frederick raked a few dead leaves, paced about the yard, kicked at a sagging snowbank, and spoke. "Great mountains of snow reduced to the scale of the New England hills." Frederick threw down the rake. "I'm going to lie on the grass and watch you work." He fetched a blanket from his pickup, spread it out on the lawn, and flopped down on his back, knees up, hands folded across his chest.

Lilith felt him watching her through half-closed eyes. "I thought you were going to help around the yard," she said.

The sun was so strong it was already beginning to brown Lilith's arms. Frederick thought how much he loved her, more than freedom itself. "Noooo, I think I'll just philosophize— men's work, you understand," he said. "In ancient days, that's how it went. The women gathered the firewood, cooked the meals, raised the young. The men made war, hunted, and schemed. My gosh, but you're big as a whale."

"I am a whale," Lilith said.

Frederick chuckled.

"It's true," she said. "I used to be a whale. I used to eat; it was my hobby, and I was fat. I was glad to be fat. Somebody in the family had to be ugly, so it was me, and it was all right. Everybody was happy. As long as I was ugly and fat, everything was all right."

"I'm glad you're not a whale anymore," Frederick said.

"What's wrong with whales?" Lilith's red car frothed with soap suds.

"Endangered species," Frederick said.

"Not just them, but you and me." Lilith's words struck softly and deeply as a dagger sliding into flesh.

"Sometimes I think you live in a bubble, and sometimes I think you know everything. But I don't know who you are, Lilith."

"I don't want you to understand me. I want you to love me." She was thinking that her words were not true at all. She wanted him to discover her.

Not another word passed between them for several minutes. Frederick's attention drifted from Lilith and her car to the world around him. The crocuses were in bloom. Other green things pushed up through the drab mat of plant debris, and yet, despite these evidences of spring, despite the summerlike weather, it really wasn't spring in New Hampshire. Frederick smiled, remembering his father grumbling yesterday about the thaw: "Something wrong . . . something's going wrong. . . . The weather's too kindly. . . . Jeez, but I hate an early spring."

Frederick laid his head back and looked at the sky. Thinking about his father provoked him into thinking about his aspirations for the future. The only tricky part of taking the care-taker's job was going to be telling Howard he was leaving the trash-collection business. He had insinuated that he considered himself a short-timer, but Howard didn't get the hints, and Frederick couldn't seem to come right out and talk about his plans, his dreams, his desires—himself. As long as he was connected with Honeywagon Inc. and its proprietor, anything that belonged to him was not only out of his grasp, but out of the grasp of his reason and actions. In other words, Frederick treated his father just as he would any other employer, because he perceived himself as one treated like an employee. Fred-

erick's contemplation melted into mere contemplative mood-
iness when big, white, friendly clouds captured his attention.
He didn't see Lilith sneak up behind him. He sensed her
presence, and erroneously concluded that a cloud was passing
under the sun and he was in its shadow. A second later, he
felt water tickle his nose. Lilith stood over him, squeezing the
sponge.

Frederick popped to a sitting position, and Lilith jumped
away. "Got me," Frederick said. The car caught his eye; it
gleamed in the sunlight. Tiny clear droplets of water sparkled
in prismatic colors on the finish.

"It's clean—I must have dozed off."

"Yes. You were snoring. Did you dream a poem?"

"I wasn't snoring."

"That's true—you weren't snoring. Did you dream?"

"You were right: I was dreaming a poem, but I don't know
what it's going to be yet—except that it's about you. Meanwhile, I've got spring fever—feel sleepy. You?"

"No, I'm full of energy." Lilith knelt beside Frederick. There
was a tiny hole in his T-shirt, and Lilith squeezed a drop of
water through it onto his chest. Frederick grabbed at the shirt
with both his hands and in a single pull ripped it open. Lilith
moved the sponge in circles on his skin.

"How do you wash?" she asked.

"Why do you want to know that?" Frederick shut his eyes.
He could smell her essence, sweat from the sun mingled with
her perfume.

"I'm curious. You come from work and the first thing you
do is clean up. Tell me how you wash."

"I shower, I scrub everything—I don't think much. Before,
it's not like I'm dirty. It's like I'm contaminated, and I'm washing to save my life."

Lilith sponged Frederick's shoulders. She nudged his side
with her knee and he turned over on his stomach. "We washed

in separate bathrooms in our house," Lilith said. "My father showered when he got up in the morning—five A.M. I never saw him rumpled from sleep. He wouldn't allow anyone to see him like that. Persephone liked tub baths and mystery novels. Half her books bulged in the middle from getting wet and drying out."

"My mother is a little bit like your father was." Frederick talked to the damp, cool grass. "She washes in secret. Late at night. Or when nobody's around. Howard reminds me of your mother. Likes the tub—when he bathes, that is. Howard is not one of your gotta-take-a-shower-every-day people. He's public about his bathing, though. Bathroom door open, hollering for a beer. He'll drink two or three in an hour bath. Likes to smoke, drink, and complain about the government, while he reads *Time* magazine in the bathtub."

Frederick turned over on his back again. Lilith knelt at his feet, unlaced his boots, jerked them free, and tossed them away like so much debris being cleared from a wreck. Then she straddled his hips, her great belly looming over him; she unfastened his belt, unzipped his fly, and drew down his pants. He lay naked at half-mast. "You're such a big, ugly bear," she said, and dripped sponge water onto his loins.

The sun was warm on his body, and the water was cool. Lilith sponged him from top to bottom, from stem to stern. She took her time, rubbing the sponge delicately in his intimate places. Then, at the right moment, she grabbed his cock and with two jerks spurted semen onto his belly. She sponged him clean, then pushed him off onto the grass and lay down on the blanket.

Now it was his turn to wash her. He unbuttoned her blouse. Her nipples were thick and stiff; over the months of her pregnancy, their pinkness had deepened to burnt sienna. He rubbed them with the sponge.

He stripped her, and leaned back on his knees to take her

in with his eyes. He'd never seen anything or anybody so magnificent—beautiful, perfect, complete with his child. How could he be worthy of her? As she had done him, he washed her, slowly and deliberately and thoroughly and entirely. Then he opened her legs and lay his head between them. Her clitoris was swollen and thick. By the time she had her orgasm, he was erect again. She lay on the blanket on her side, and he sidled up to her from behind. In this position, the Squire's daughter and the trash man's son made love for the last time.

8

The Emergency

Agenda for the annual meeting of the board of governors of the Raphael Salmon II Memorial Trust Lands:

- Proposal by board member Garvin Prell to set aside a certain portion of the Trust as a memorial to the late Raphael Salmon and his son.
- Proposal by board member Garvin Prell, endorsed by the town selectmen, to establish zones in the Trust: profit zones for logging; recreational zones open to the public; and no-trespass zones to preserve the original intention of the founder.
- Proposal by board member Lilith Salmon to hire a permanent caretaker for the Trust, the salary of which would be paid for from logging revenues.
- Proposal by board member Monet Salmon to establish the entire Trust as a no-trespass zone.

It was now hot outdoors, but the Salmon house held its own weather, and the temperature in the Hearth Room was only warm. Frederick heard through the open windows the familiar, subdued sputter of Arthur Crabb's pickup truck. Highway vehicles all sounded the same for the first hundred thousand miles, and after that they began to sound like their owners.

360

"Crabb. What's he doing here?" Frederick watched the old farmer park on the blacktop in the space formerly reserved for the Bronco.

"The meetings of the Trust board are open to the public," Lilith said. "In fact, the town appoints a nonvoting member to the board."

"I don't understand enough of this," Frederick said. "If I'm going to be the caretaker, I should . . ."

"Talk to Garvin. He'll explain everything."

"Yah, I bet."

"Frederick, when you become the caretaker, Garvin, Monet, and I will be your bosses. You'll have to get used to dealing with us."

"Us." Frederick thought about that one for a moment. Lilith had said "us," not "them." She had excluded him; he was on the outside of the lives of the people of Upper Darby. The idea that he would be caretaker of a great expanse of land had led him to imagine he would be his own boss. Now he realized that he would be subject to scrutiny by overseers. "Us" to Lilith equaled "them" to him. Working for his father had set a fire of rebellion under him; what was working for his woman going to be like? Why did the roads of human existence feature so many head-on collisions between desires and facts of life?

Lilith greeted Crabb at the door, and led him to a seat in the Hearth Room as, two days earlier, he had led her to a seat in the Unified Church of Christ.

"Can I get you some coffee or tea?" Lilith asked.

"Sanka," Crabb said.

"Decaf?"

"That's right—Sanka. Got 'ny?"

"Of course, make yourself comfortable. I'll be right back." Lilith signaled Frederick with her eyes, and he met her in the hall, outside Crabb's view.

"You entertain him while I make his coffee," she said.

"You want me to juggle or something?" Frederick said.

Lilith answered Frederick's humor with silence. He watched her lumber delicately into the kitchen.

Frederick knew Lilith would serve Selectman Crabb caffeinated coffee, because that was all they had in the house. She changed personalities with such ease. A moment earlier, as maid in her own house, she had been nervous, irritable, honest; now, in her role as hostess, she was calm, gracious, deceitful. The difference between himself and herself now seemed like the difference between his kind and her kind. His kind behaved according to the likes and habits of the individual; his kind lied out of generalized fear or for petty, personal profit. Her kind behaved according to the demands and rites of society; her kind lied to maintain decorum or for the general good or for big money. To his kind, a person's behavior expressed himself; to her kind, a person's behavior expressed his place in the world. His kind cheated and stole for bread; her kind cheated and stole to build bread factories. In the end, his kind lost; her kind won.

Frederick followed orders and made small talk with Crabb. Farmers naturally felt superior to but not threatened by the likes of the Elmans, so Crabb was relaxed in Frederick's presence. The old man rambled on about politics and weather, carpentry and accounting, practical arts and crafty philosophy. Farmers by necessity knew more about every little thing than anybody. Frederick found himself wishing that he could get a piece of the old man, a keystone for his future.

"You are the town's representative on the Trust board?" Frederick posed a question.

"Used to be. Dracut's the man now," Crabb said, then immediately answered Frederick's questioning stare. "No, I don't need to come to this event. I come out of, I don't know . . ." He paused.

"What?"

"This hunk of land . . . this Trust, as they call it . . ."

"Yah?"

"It's goddamn important to the town of Darby."

"You think so."

"I figure it's time for somebody to come out the winner in these legal battles, so we can build our school, grow and change. We've been the same too long. The Upper Darby pissing match between Monet and Garvin, the Trust, the little girl trying to run this house, the town stuck in second gear— it all fits in; you understand?"

"Why would you care? I heard you were leaving," Frederick said, typically Elman in style, aggressiveness without assertiveness.

Crabb answered in his own style, assertion without aggression. "Lay it to habit," he said. "Or maybe spite. Maybe I figure somebody in Upper Darby is going to get his, and I've come to see it happen, and then everything will work itself out and a piece of me can go to Florida for a peaceful climate and peace of mind."

There was a lull between the arrival of Crabb and the others; then everyone seemed to show up at once. Garvin was decked out with a white shirt and a tie. Why is he in a suit? Frederick asked himself, and then answered his own question: Because he's a businessman and a lawyer; because he's a serious person. In his blue jeans and Jack Kerouac T-shirt, Frederick suddenly felt childish and out of place. He wasn't as pathetic as Monet, though. The Pocket Squire was outfitted in one of his brother's dowdy tweed jackets and corduroy trousers, and he was sweating. Frederick had heard from Elenore that Monet had had Reggie's entire wardrobe altered to fit his body. Nevertheless, the clothes didn't look right on him. Clothes, supposed to make a man, in Monet's case mocked him. He didn't look ridiculous so much as nameless. There was something odd, too, about Monet's entry—with an entourage of his

363

wife, Dr. Marcia Pascal; his attorney, Charles Barnum, carrying a slide projector and briefcase; and, amazingly, two town bums, the queer Jordan and his Asian companion, who had followed Monet in on a Jeep. Monet was carrying a long object, wrapped in paper. If he didn't know better, Frederick would have sworn it was a shotgun in a case. Monet set up the slide projector on the table. Because Frederick had never been to a meeting of the Trust board, all this registered as peculiar but not untypical.

Across the room, at the head table, Garvin Prell had a different impression, colored by his experience. Monet hadn't brought his lawyer to this meeting for nothing. Monet had his own agenda. What was he going to do now? Garvin was edgy.

Selectman Lawrence Dracut arrived, accompanied by Town Clerk Dorothy McCurtin. Dracut, like Garvin and Barnum, wore a suit. Three lawyers in the room: the fact gave Frederick pause. He looked to Lilith for some recognition of his own existence, but he couldn't catch her eye. She wore a gray cotton maternity dress. She hadn't bought too many clothes since she was pregnant. The dress was plain as nun's garb, but she'd put on makeup and jewelry, and her hair was down and flowed bright and clean as spring runoff, so that one's attention was drawn away from her body to her face. He admired her skill and cunning. In Frederick's view, women who prevailed lied, as animals lied, with coats to match the season. He winced when he saw her smile at Garvin.

Frederick watched the spectators search for positions. Abnaki and Whack Two sat in straight-back chairs near the hallway. They were quiet, respectful, and full of hidden enthusiasm, like witnesses to an execution. Marcia Pascal sat in a huge easy chair, never used by Frederick and Lilith. It had been Reggie's reading chair, perhaps the place where he composed his notes. She had good legs. Crabb appeared a little bit lost, which didn't make any sense to Frederick. (In fact, the former selectman had always sat at the meeting table, had always been more or less part of the proceedings. Now he was an observer, and he didn't quite know where to put himself. So he stood by the hall entry, arms folded.) Barnum positioned himself near the former selectman, as if to partake of his prestige. Frederick respected Barnum, not knowing why exactly. The lawyer's briefcase was on the floor beside him, a sentry to a shinbone. After everyone was settled, Frederick got out of the way, so to speak, by sitting in one of the red velvet chairs that straddled the fireplace hearth. Here he relaxed, waiting for his name to be called, caretaker of the Salmon Trust lands. He wondered if they'd ask him to take an oath. I do solemnly swear to uphold the blah-blah-blah of the blah-blah-blah.

Monet and Garvin sat opposite one another at the corners of the great cherrywood meeting table of the Hearth Room, with Mrs. McCurtin beside Monet, and Selectman Dracut beside Garvin. Lilith sat at the head, where before her mother and father had held forth. To Frederick, she looked like somebody he didn't know. Somebody he didn't want to know.

Lilith was thinking that last year, when she had come of age, she had been under the thumb of her mother, distracted and upset by the unfinished business of burying her father. Perhaps that was all behind her now. Her pregnancy made her feel less like a girl, more like a woman. This seat gave her what she'd never had before—power. The eyes of the town (Mrs. McCurtin) were on her, not only because of who she was but because of what she could do. She had one vote, no more, no less than Garvin and Monet. Because Monet and Garvin were at war, it wasn't lost upon her that her vote was precious to them. Her mother had talked about "standing between them." Couldn't she do more? Why not lead them? What she lacked was experience and her own vision. Vision would come with experience. Her vision would be as meaningful as any Prell's, and less cockeyed than her uncle's. But what would that vision encompass? What?

Before the meeting, Dracut made an announcement. The town selectmen were going to form a committee to study the feasibility of creating a master plan for the town.

"So that's his game—zoning," Crabb mumbled under his breath.

The official meeting started with Mrs. McCurtin reading the minutes from the last meeting and reporting the finances. Then she read the agenda. As she droned on, Frederick could hear Monet drumming his fingers on the table. Something told him the gesture meant something, but he had no idea what. Garvin Prell knew—trouble. The moment Mrs. McCurtin finished, Monet took the floor. "I have an item under the emergency-provision section of the charter."

After some debate over parliamentary rules, Garvin said, "I'd like to know the subject matter."

When Monet smiled and said gently, "Of course," Garvin heard the whisper of artillery before the shell hits.

Unaccustomed as he was to public meetings, Frederick did not grasp the meaning of this early sparring session between Monet and Garvin. The tone of the conversation was so polite— even friendly—that it didn't dawn on him that the two men were in the midst of a struggle. It went right by him that Monet's purpose in introducing his "emergency" issue was to derail Garvin's proposals for developing the Trust and Lilith's proposal for establishing a caretaker.

In contrast to Frederick, former Selectman Crabb easily kept up with the proceedings; he smelled a change coming in Upper Darby weather.

Monet? He was only trying to save himself. He could see that Marcia Pascal was beginning to wonder about him. She knew he wasn't the man he wanted to be; the man he wanted to be was gone. She was watching him, measuring him, evaluating him.

"Perhaps we should postpone the meeting to a later date." Garvin hoped that a delay would give him time to regroup, find out what was going on with Monet, plan a counteroffensive.

"Point of information: The charter sets the date for the meeting," Barnum snapped, lethargically as an old dog at a fly.

Garvin signaled his surrender with a subdued baseball "safe" sign.

Monet, with Abnaki and Whack Two beside him, spoke. "What I am about to say is difficult, shocking. Attorney Barnum, would you dim the lights?"

Barnum couldn't find the light switches, so Frederick helped him out. Humming and grumbling, Monet fiddled with the slide projector. Click! White light. Click! Colored light, picture. Frederick Elman felt the first dread in his stomach as a doughy lump. The picture, in color, showed craggy cliffs and refuse. It was the quarry where he and Lilith had been.

"Someone has been using the Trust as a private dump." Monet let the words fall. Click! Same scene, same refuse, different views. Frederick could almost imagine the photographer (probably Monet himself) stumbling around in the gorge for different vantage points from which to snap pictures.

"As is plainly evident, this is not an example of a random drop of plastic garbage bags by somebody in a station wagon. This is systematic dumping." Click!

"The person who did this knew trash and he knew the Trust." Click! Truck-tire tracks in mud. Frederick recognized the design of the tread.

Barnum snapped on the lights.

"My purpose in bringing this matter before the board," Monet said, "is that we know who the culprit is, and I'm looking for a unanimous vote from the board members that we prosecute. Abnaki, would you step forward?"

Abnaki grinned at the board members, strings of meat hanging from his yellow teeth. Whack Two stood behind, looking around the room with the awe of someone discovering one of those vast, limestone caverns that go on for miles under the surface of the earth.

Monet sat down, and Barnum stepped forward. He folded his hands in front of him. "Mr. Jordan, you and your friend like to go into the woods, do you not?" Barnum said.

"That's correct, sir." Abnaki spoke in the peculiar diction of a thug coached by a lawyer.

"And the weather's been nice lately, has it not?"

"That's correct, sir. No black flies yet."

"Sometimes you wander onto the lands known as the Trust, isn't that correct?"

"Yes, sir. That's correct. Sometimes we get so carried away that we don't notice we're trespassing."

"Earlier this week, you happened to be on the Trust lands, and you were in this area here." Barnum whipped out a map from his briefcase and pointed to a spot on it.

Abnaki nodded. "That's where we seen the Honeywagon make a delivery."

"Tell the board what you mean by 'Honeywagon.' "

"Well, a honeywagon is a honeywagon, sir," Abnaki said.

Barnum was only slightly thrown off course by Abnaki's failure to regurgitate the words he had fed him earlier. "Did the operator of the Honeywagon leave his vehicle?" Barnum asked.

"He did. He exited the vehicle after he dumped the load, and he looked over the banking, and then he got back in and drove away."

"So you had a good look at him."

368

"That's correct."

"Did you recognize him?"

"I did, sir."

"And who was the man?"

"It was Howie Elman."

Barnum turned to Whack Two. "You saw Howard Elman, too, did you not?"

Whack Two nodded vigorously, but he did not speak.

"Thank you, gentlemen. You may go now," Barnum said. Abnaki and Whack Two left the house, and drove off in their Jeep.

Meanwhile, Monet grabbed center stage again. He opened the package he'd come into the room with. "I found this, going through the trash," he said.

Frederick recognized his father's homemade crutch.

"If we are going to preserve the integrity of the Trust, we must prosecute," Monet said.

Garvin Prell took Lilith's hand in his own. "I'm afraid Monet is right," he said.

Frederick didn't hear Lilith's answer, but he heard Monet's victorious proclamation. "It's unanimous. The board votes to prosecute Howard Elman."

So that was the way they did things in Upper Darby, Frederick thought. They brought you up, then let you down. He should have known.

The next minute or so reminded Lilith of swimming underwater—things interesting but indistinct, sounds seeming to come from everywhere and nowhere. Then Mrs. McCurtin's grating voice brought her into the air again.

"What about the agenda?" Mrs. McCurtin asked.

"I propose we adjourn the meeting for a couple of days," Garvin said.

"We do have an agenda." Monet was still feeling his power.

Lilith stood suddenly, awkwardly pushing her chair out of

the way. The noise jolted everyone to attention. "I've had enough for now." She spoke almost in a whisper, and walked away from the table. She went into the hall, and Frederick stomped after her.

At the meeting table, it was now Monet's turn to yield. "Okay, I guess that's it—we'll adjourn," he said.

In the hall, striding toward Lilith, Frederick managed to appear intent and distracted at the same time, so that for a second Lilith thought he didn't actually see her.

"I don't think I want to spend the night in this house," he said, trying unsuccessfully to sound nonchalant.

"All right—I don't think I want you here," Lilith said, but thinking no such thing, thinking that he should insist on staying, insist on talking to her, insist on working things out.

They stared at each other, both feeling blank and stupid and desperate, yet the looks they gave conveyed only the background anger of one class for another.

"I'm sorry," Lilith said perfunctorily.

"Yah." He turned his back on her and started toward the door.

And so, they parted, guilty and confused creatures both.

A few minutes later, back in the Hearth Room, Lilith stood alone at the head of the meeting table. She looked out the window as Crabb drove off in his cranky pickup. Frederick had already left. Monet and company chugged away in Monet's new Bronco II. Lilith looked for Dracut's station wagon, but it was gone. She felt the quiet then, warm and soothing as the thawy air. She was oddly at peace, on an island between the troubled waters of the past and the troubled waters of the future. The problem was them, loved ones, dead or alive. Alone, in the quiet and warmth of the afternoon, she could simply be.

"Is he gone?" It was Garvin.

"Frederick? Yes—gone."

370

"We have to talk," Garvin said.

"I think I want to be alone," Lilith said, but Garvin ignored her plea and she did not push it, and before she could think clearly they were back at the meeting table, only this time Garvin was at the head.

"Lilith, listen to me. You must, please?" Garvin said, then plunged on. "When my father died I was in shock, and then . . . and then . . . Lilith, I was glad he died—relieved, even happy. During the funeral and when my brothers and sister were here, it was all I could do to contain myself from bursting into laughter. Mad laughter—okay? And then I did something completely out of character for a Prell." Garvin paused for Lilith to respond, and when she said nothing he continued. "Critter Jordan came to E.H., asked for a loan to expand his business. E.H. would no more back a Jordan then vote for a socialist. Lilith, I lent him the money." Garvin laughed, as one might laugh at one's own recently amputated limb. "Lilith, you understand what I'm saying?"

"You're talking about your freedom."

"Yes, yes—you know everything about me, and I know everything about you." Garvin reached for Lilith's hand, but she drew it away, and he turned slightly as if to indicate that he had never meant to touch her. She knew he was referring to the money.

Lilith watched a moth that had found its way in the house when the guests had left.

"Lilith, I want to marry you."

"You want to what?" Lilith didn't know whether to laugh or to cry.

"Don't say anything yet. Let me make my case. Lilith, if you marry me, your child will have a legitimate name."

"Prell," Lilith said.

"Yes."

"A Prell will inherit the Salmon house."

371

"It's the only chance you have, Lilith."

It was clear to Lilith that Garvin sought not only her hand in marriage but her property. Yet she was touched. Acquisition, and an appreciation of acquisition, was Garvin's way of showing love. If she married Garvin, they would spend a lifetime measuring gain and loss in the relationship.

"I have to talk to Frederick," she said.

"Do you really think he'll want to deal with you after you voted to bring his father to court?"

"I don't know."

"I can wait," Garvin said.

9

In the Pit

Darby Constable Godfrey Perkins came that night to serve Howard Elman the papers. Frederick and his parents were at the kitchen table when the knock came. Howard answered the door, planting himself in front of it, not allowing the policeman actually to enter his domain. Frederick stood by with Elenore. Frederick was ready to jump Howard in case he gave the constable some trouble. The last thing he wanted was his father in the slammer on a murder rap. But Howard took the news calmly, even with a touch of humor.

After Perkins had left, Elenore said, "Well?"

"I have to go to court Monday," Howard said in an even voice as he peered at the paper.

They settled down again at the kitchen table.

"You want a beer?" Howard offered. Frederick accepted, and Howard fetched a Schaefer for Frederick, but not for himself. Strange behavior for Howard. It seemed to Frederick that his father was acting deliberately opaque.

"Howie, why did you dump your load on the Salmon Trust lands?" Frederick asked.

"Convenience," Howard said.

"Spite," said Elenore.

Howard folded his hands, put them behind his head, cradled

his neck in his palms, and leaned back in his chair. "As usual, your mother is correct."

Frederick suddenly saw the light. "You don't care about going to court, paying a fine. You wanted to be caught. You wanted to stick their noses in it."

Howard chuckled.

Elenore wagged her judgment finger at Howard. "Bad man; bad, bad man. Your pride and your sense of humor is going to bring down this house."

Howard's chuckle erupted into har-har laughter.

When he stopped, Elenore said, "When are you going to talk to your son about you-know-what?"

Frederick was suddenly alarmed. When his mother used that phrase—"you-know-what"—it meant danger. There was something he didn't know, something important. "What's going on?" he asked.

"Tomorrow," Howard said to Elenore as if Frederick was not in the room.

"What?" Frederick shouted, helpless and exasperated as an animal with a foot in a trap.

Howard ripped off his hearing aid and yelled at Frederick. "About time you replaced that muffler, isn't it."

"What's it to you, Howie?" Frederick was almost grateful for this familiar noise directed at him.

"I picked up a muffler a while ago, fits that son-of-a-bitch Ford of yours. We'll put it on first thing in the morning." Howard faced Elenore. "You going to bed?"

"I'm going to bed," Elenore said.

"I'm going to bed," Howard said, as if dramatizing a momentous announcement.

Howard went to bed, and Elenore went to bed, and Frederick sat alone with his beer.

Howard might holler, but he couldn't really talk about serious matters unless his hands were busy and he didn't have to look at you. So, when Howard summoned Frederick to the pit, Frederick knew Howard had something of consequence to say to him. But what? Something to do with himself and Lilith? Had to be. Nothing else of much importance to discuss. Were his parents going to insist he marry her? Did he want to marry her? Should he marry her if he didn't want to? Did she want to marry him? What about the baby? The baby! Jeez! He hated to think about it. And her! What about her? Lilith had shown her true colors. Upper Darby all the way. And yet, given the circumstances, what else could she have done but turn Howard in? Even though he understood, Frederick couldn't help feeling a coldness toward her. *Coldness*—he'd gotten it from her; she'd done her job on Howard cold. Maybe that was what bothered him and, now, chilled him. He was a hothead; these Upper Darby people lived at twenty below zero in their souls. Frederick warmed himself with two more beers, drunk very quickly, and then he went outside, crawled into the bunk in the Live Free or Die, and went to sleep.

The next morning, Frederick did not eat breakfast in his mother's kitchen. He drove to Ancharsky's Store, bought one of yesterday's grinders and a cup of coffee, ate in his truck, and listened to the radio. Willie Nelson sang "On the Road Again." Frederick returned to his parents' place.

His father met him at the door, barring his entry, as the night before he had barred Constable Perkins' entry. "Where the hell you been?" Howard boomed.

"What do you care? I'm here."

"Okay, let's go." Howard barged past him and headed for the barn.

Frederick tried to catch his mother's eye, but she remained bent over the kitchen sink. A portion of her back seemed to want to sneak up over her shoulder blade. Old-and-stooped was one of her fears, he knew. She was getting there. Frederick hopped into the Live Free or Die and drove it over the pit, then descended with Howard, walking down crude plank steps into the hole. Light came from two directions in two colors, white from the outside and yellow from the droplight shining up into the undersides of his truck. Years ago, before Frederick was born, Howard had dug out the pit to work on cars, shovelful by shovelful. The smells were generations old—motor oil, man-sweat, and earth. He felt as if he were a boy again.

As Howard inspected Frederick's truck, he made small talk about the weather—"disgustingly warm for the time of year."

Frederick, not exactly attempting to continue the small talk, but close, asked Howard about his upcoming court appearance.

"Don't mean nothing to me," Howard said. "I'll plead guilty, and they'll fine me a couple million dollars, and that'll be that." When Howard spoke in superlatives, talking about millions when he meant hundreds, Frederick felt airy and uplifted and curiously empty, as one who, having been entertained by a skillful musician, goes home and thinks about the meaning of what he has seen.

"This place hasn't changed since I was a kid," Frederick said.

Howard answered with a grunt as he turned a nut with a ratchet wrench. Frederick felt the same discomfort he had as a boy, watching his father work but not allowed to do anything himself, so that his hands seemed useless.

"Your old pig Ford is in pretty good shape," Howard said, rubbing his fingers along the dark underbelly of the Live Free or Die.

"It's only spent this one winter in New Hampshire," Frederick said.

"No road salt—good; road salt decays your metal body. Decays, you understand?" Howard said.

"Sure, Pop."

"Decay—I hate it, I love it. Decay is my living," Howard said.

Frederick was becoming more and more annoyed by this dreary chatter. "So, what do you want to talk to me about, Howie?" Frederick machine-gunned the words.

Howard didn't answer for a minute, pretending to be preoccupied with pulling off the old muffler. When it finally came loose, he let it drop onto the earthen floor of the pit. Frederick smelled the petroleum-perfumed dust of the muffler. He felt closed in, as one wedged between rocks in a cave. "Couple things," Howard finally said. "First off, I got the bank loan for the new Honeywagon."

"Congratulations." Frederick felt sick, hot, confined.

"Yah, I feel pretty sweet about it," Howard said.

Another empty moment.

"You don't really want that Honeywagon, do you?" Howard said.

"Well, I, ah . . . not really."

"Never did like the trash-collection business, did you?"

"Not really. No, never. I hated it." Frederick felt a little better now; honesty was making him strong.

"I knew it all along. Too stubborn to admit it. I guess you'd say that Howard Elman is a little bit on the stubborn side."

Frederick thought for a moment, and then he said, "You're a horse's ass, Howie."

Father and son broke into laughter. "Horse's ass" was Cooty Patterson's term for the both of them.

"Old Cooty's kinda weak now, but he'll get his strength back," Howard said. "I got a good man in Pitchfork. He'll get the new Honeywagon and his own crew. I'm going to hire some more men. Guys like Abnaki Jordan. Let them do the shit work while I stay home and figure what's what on the computer."

"You're good at that, Howie," Frederick said.

377

"And you, you're going to be somebody. You're going to get away from here, body and soul, and be the Elman for the world." Howard lifted the new muffler. "You want to give me a hand with this?"

Father and son installed the muffler. Cooty was their common ground. By both expressing love for the old man, they could express love for one another without actually voicing words or touching skin or looking into eyes.

And when the work was over, the intimacy was over. Howard shut off the droplight and they stood in the relative darkness of the pit, and then he lowered the boom on his son.

"What are your plans?" Howard began.

"I want another go at college."

"And the girl up on the hill?"

"I know she wronged you, Howie, but I'm going to go back to her, if she'll take me."

"That brings me to the other reason I wanted to talk to you. About the girl—Lily?"

"Lilith." Frederick was aware now that, with the droplight out, he could not see Howard's features, only his silhouette, a disheveled hulk, the human equivalent of a junked car left in a field, taking up space, wrong to be there, wrong to be anywhere, a fixture by accident. And I, Frederick thought, I am the son of that.

"Baby she's carrying?" Howard said.

"The baby? What about it?"

"It ain't yours, Freddy."

Frederick flashed inside with anger, then fear.

"Your mother found out," Howard said. "She heard some tales from Mrs. McCurtin. Your rich girl was seen with somebody else."

"Cheap gossip."

"Always something to gossip: rule of life. She overheard things other places. Cleaning house at the Pocket Squire's,

378

they was talking about it. Strange baby. Not nobody's. Who's going to raise it. They was saying what everybody in town is saying: the rich girl is playing the poor boy for the fool again. Another fella put the seed in, they say."

Frederick sweltered in the closed space of the pit. He felt on the verge of hysteria. This place, so tight, so confined in space and smell and time, was going to suffocate him.

"Who?" he asked.

Howard droned on, "Prell, the counselor."

"The guy with the bicycle." Frederick laughed humorlessly. "I don't believe it."

"Believe it. He went out with her. They was seen. I imagine they had a fight, and so she took up with you to piss him off. Found herself knocked up. So all these months she's in a bind, trying to figure out what to do. In the end, she's going to hold him up or hold you up. Or both. Who knows why rich people do things? But I know one thing for sure. You thought you was screwing her, but she was screwing you."

"I have to get out of here." Frederick remembered the night he'd seen Lilith with Prell at the Inn. He pushed by his father and scurried out of the pit. The harsh white light pouring in through the open barn doors hit him like an ocean wave. He blinked. His father followed him out of the pit, and stood beside him. Frederick could hear him breathing.

"I'm going up the Salmon house," Frederick said.

"I know," Howard said.

Frederick mounted the Live Free or Die, ripped backward down the dirt driveway into the town road, jammed the truck into first gear, and burned rubber peeling out for Upper Darby.

There was something about the way the truck tore into the drive, something in Frederick's stride, something in his voice when he barged into her house—*her house!*—that strangely frightened Lilith, not because she was afraid he would hurt

379

her but because she was afraid he was somebody else, some-body other than the young man she'd fallen in love with.

They bumped in the hallway.

"What the hell's going on?" Frederick shouted his vague, useless question at her.

"I don't know what you want." Lilith backed toward the stairs, turned, and skipped upward a few steps. Frederick lurched toward her. Lilith started upward again, stopped at the head of the stairs. Frederick halted two stairs down. He glared at her.

As one offering a bauble to a savage, Lilith said, "I'm sorry about your father."

Frederick felt like an idiot. He wished he could leave and start all over again, more polite this time, more reasonable. Instead he screamed, "Fuck him! Fuck the Squire! Fuck all the fathers. And fuck you!"

Lilith was not used to naked anger. In her world, anger came dressed as criticism or spite or malice or jealousy or even tense friendliness, and always accompanied by reason as an accessory, like a bright scarf that threatened to choke. Fred-erick's anger, the real thing—ugly, stupid, dangerous, naked—seemed inhuman, animalistic.

The telephone rang in their bedroom. And the young people froze for a couple of seconds.

Frederick, more under control and therefore meaner, said, "Better get that, it might be Garvin."

It was Lilith's turn to be angry. How dare Frederick come into her house full of indignation and sarcasm? "Funny you should mention his name," she said.

"Yah, it's a riot."

"Garvin has asked me to marry him," Lilith said.

"So answer the phone."

Lilith remained still. The phone continued to ring.

"You'll make a great couple." Frederick bulled past Lilith, and now she was following him as he started down the hall.

"At least I know who he is. I don't know who you are," she said.

With those words, it was Frederick's turn to be puzzled. He stopped dead at the open door of the bedroom where they had slept, and whipped around. "Why didn't you just run off with him to begin with?"

"What do you think?" Lilith raised her voice.

"I think you had some fun with me, and you're still having it—jerking me around."

Lilith stood staring hopelessly and without understanding. It flitted through her mind that the phone had stopped ringing, and then she reflected that Frederick had put his own stamp of slovenliness on her bedroom. She began to straighten it up. Frederick held his territory in the doorway. She gathered a pair of his dirty socks on the floor along with a shirt and his headband and tossed the laundry at his feet.

Frederick saw just a shadow of her bewilderment. "I mean, if it was his kid . . ."

Lilith cut him off. "His? Garvin's?"

"What was the point of nailing it on me? Can you just explain what you had in mind, because I don't get it?"

Now Lilith understood why Frederick was angry, but she did not understand why he believed this crazy story about her. "Is that what you think?" she asked.

"I didn't believe it at first; now—I don't know."

Her anger flashed. "So it all comes to that, the baby—who it belongs to. Well, it's mine. Mine! And I couldn't care less who provided the squiggle."

Frederick doubled his fists, holding his arms tightly against his sides because of a fear he would strike her. "Then you don't deny it."

"What difference does it make what I say?"

"None—absolutely none. Because I can't believe you, can I?"

"No, you can't. You'll never understand me. You're too stupid. Go away. Stupid! Trash man! Trash! Go!"

Frederick kicked the headband back to her and stormed out.

Lilith remained motionless until she heard Frederick's truck rev and roar off; then she shoved the headband in the wastebasket and continued to clean the room, working automatically and mindlessly. A picture popped into her mind of those maids of old that kept the house clean and tidy. When there was no more to do, she felt adrift and afraid. She needed to cry but could not. She thought about the maids again, and that led her to one of the little-used stairwells.

She went up the stairs, and she wandered from room to room. Some were crammed with stuff—trunks full of old clothes fit for a stage play, stacks of magazines, leather ski-boots, wire coat-hangers, half-finished oil paintings, the same kind of junk that was on the shelves of the Hearth Room except a generation older. But most of the rooms were empty, and it was in one of these, a room with two half-dormer windows and a sharply sloping ceiling, that she rested, planting herself in a corner, sitting curled on her side. She cupped her front in her hands, and took in the place: faded yellow wallpaper that even when it was new had been drab; a foot-worn hardwood floor needing a finish; an atmosphere shocking with light blasting through the dormered windows and reverberating off slanted ceilings like the visual embodiment of an echo. Between hard shafts of light lay hard shadows, appearing three-dimensional as rocks. The smell of musty air made her feel as if she were in a mausoleum. This part of her house she had avoided all these years began to take on a magical quality.

The sounds, the creaks and groans, of the house were more personal up here than downstairs. She imagined she heard voices from long ago. She couldn't understand the words, but she caught the tone of the place—busy; strangers moving to and fro as in an airport or a train station. But such places were like cathedrals or space platforms, lonely and alien in their immensity, while this room was a sanctuary. The room was all corners, and in every corner dangled cobwebs. She watched the spiders, thinkers trapped in the webs of their own ideas. Moth pupae lay stuck against the wall, waiting for moments of transformation.

10

Live Free or Die

Bare Essentials

Cash to pay my way, wheels to carry me.
In place of a destination a direction: West.
All day and into the night—West.
Across the land—West.
Across the waters—West.
Butterfly stroke to Hawaii—West.
Breast stroke to Japan—West.
No, now East.
Is it any wonder I'm so screwed up?
The world is round.
Faster I run, faster I'm back where I started from.
North, freeze, becomes South, fry;
West, freedom, becomes East, creation.
To hell with these laws,
I'll live by my law: West forever.
Straight to the end of everything.
Live Free or Die
you're all I got for home.

The next morning, in the Elman kitchen, Frederick declined his mother's invitation for breakfast. His parents could tell something was up.

Howard said, "Listen, those bankers were dumb enough to give me the loan. The new Honeywagon's going to be delivered this morning. You wouldn't want to make a test run with me? We'll go see Cooty."

"I made my last run in the Honeywagon last night. Anyway, I don't figure you need me anymore, Howie."

Howard looked at Elenore. Her eyes brightened with tears. Frederick kissed her goodbye, but he and his father never touched. Howard had an aversion to embraces of any kind, including handshakes.

"See you later," Howard said.

"Yah," Frederick said, and was gone.

Frederick drove his pickup to Cooty's cabin. He had a notion to ferry off the old man to Las Vegas, where the two of them would live as dumpster rats. Vegas had to be a place of phantasmagorical trash. Cooty was dead asleep. He'd slept almost around the clock since coming back to Darby. Frederick didn't wake him, but slipped away. It's over, he thought. Nothing new to learn from the elders. Nothing there to begin with.

He gassed up at Ancharsky's Store and said a farewell to Joe, who, unlike Howard, was happy to shake hands. Big, soft storekeeper's hands.

It was 10:30 A.M.

Lilith awakened earlier than usual that Friday morning, alert, full of energy, and, considering what had happened the day before, mysteriously optimistic. Furthermore, she was possessed by a directive to do some work around the house. She tidied the Hearth Room, she washed the kitchen floor, she puttered in the greenhouse, and it was there, her hands in the dirt, that her directive was translated into a desire for a hedge of lilac bushes.

Outside, the Salmon spread was landscaped with trees and shrubs from all over the world. The only important plant that

385

had been left out of the scheme was the purple lilac, the state flower of New Hampshire. When she was a child, Lilith had asked her father why no lilacs. He had answered, "The lilac is a weed; I myself do not believe in the concept of weeds." It was a typical remark from the Squire. Take it the way you want, because no explanation would be forthcoming. I am a weed, Lilith had thought, and with that a secret desire to grow lilacs had grown within her. She pretended that her name, which came from her grandmother Salmon, was really meant to be Lilac. The lilac dream, like most of her girlhood dreams, was lost in the haze of school, friends, and changing self. Now it was back.

Lilith went outside and scanned the area. Her mother had talked about a hedge in the rear, to box in the flower garden and block the winter wind. And therefore Lilith would plant her hedge in the front, along the driveway. Lilacs would be her welcome and her farewell to guests. Lilith used Reggie's board-foot measure to determine the distance. In *The Complete Book of Composting* by J. I. Rodale and staff, she learned that lilacs need plenty of sunshine and well-drained soil. The book said, "A lilac should never have wet feet." It didn't say how far apart to plant the young bushes. She would put them close together, let them crowd in with growth, a fragrant purple wall.

It was 7:30 A.M., and the River Swell Nursery in Tuckerman had just opened for business when Lilith telephoned for young lilac plants. Jacob the nursery man said they could be delivered the following Monday. This was the biggest weekend of the year for flowers, and Jacob was pretty busy. Lilith said right now or no deal. Jacob said, "Er-ah." Lilith's maternal power charged through the telephone lines. The lilacs arrived an hour later, eighty shrubs about three feet high sunk in gallon-sized black plastic pots. Jacob himself drove the flatbed, one-ton truck.

A sullen helper with long graying hair unloaded the pots, placing them in ranks on the lawn in between the house and the driveway. "He was in 'Nam," Jacob whispered to Lilith, then in a normal voice asked for a glass of water to wash down a back-pain pill. Jacob made a point of talking about his bad back, attempting in his own way to communicate to Lilith an excuse for avoiding work and a scolding for rushing him out here. Lilith gave Jacob a check and the men drove off.

Using a wheelbarrow, Lilith laid out the pots along the drive. She was a little tired now, and hungry, because she hadn't had breakfast yet. But she was anxious to see one of the bushes in the ground, so she kept working. She didn't have the right shoes on for digging with a long-handled shovel; still, she managed to excavate enough of the stony soil to plant the first bush. It was lovely, the main stem curving upward, outward, and down like the neck of a swan.

Seventy-nine more bushes to put in the ground. Not a chore for a pregnant woman, but for the man of that woman. Frederick was strong, he knew how to work. He should plant her lilacs. Where was he anyway? So she'd wronged him—he'd wronged her! She mentally reran the fight they'd had several times, altering the events in her mind to suit her needs. Surely by now he had figured out that she hadn't really meant for him to believe that his child was Garvin's. He'd had his tantrum. He should return to her side. She needed him.

Another time, she would have waited. But today, in this rambunctious mood, she'd go to him. She'd say, "Come home and plant some lilacs for me." That would be that. There would be no need for apologies. She was confident that she would find him. She would search for his pickup truck. A man could hide, his vehicle could not. Once she located it, she would camp inside until he returned.

In the house, she washed, put on a loose dress and track

shoes (she hated maternity outfits), squeezed in behind the steering wheel of the red car, and drove off.

It was 10:30 A.M.

When Lilith reached the village, an old woman on the town common caught her eye. Lilith recognized her as one of the residents of the nursing home. She wore a plain cotton dress and canvas sneakers, and her gray hair was pushed halfheartedly around her head, as if she had made an attempt to put it up and failed. She looked lost. Lilith pulled over, shouting from the rolled-down window of the red car, "Can I help you?"

"Green's no green," the old woman said.

"Oh, yes, of course," Lilith humored the old lady.

"Take me home—I want to go home," the old woman said.

"Hop in," Lilith said, but the woman seemed suddenly suspicious of the red car, of Lilith, of everything. "Where's home?" Lilith tried to hold her attention.

"It's . . . there." She turned and walked into that immeasurable distance.

It wasn't until the old woman had disappeared from view that Lilith understood what she'd meant—"Green's no green." The grass on the town common, which now was being called "the green" because of the influence of the Inn at Darby Green, was not at this time of year green, but the color of hoof-trodden hay. All of Northern New England was drab and colorless. It was neither spring nor winter. The air had warmed, the human blood had warmed, but the earth was still cold. It was a between time. She was a between woman; Frederick was a between man; their child would be a between person. Maybe the whole country was full of between people, homeless hearts in a land constituted for nomads. Where are you, Frederick? Help me.

She stepped out of the car and walked across the street to Ancharsky's store. Lawrence Dracut and his children were just coming down the steps. Dracut smiled at her graciously, looked her over with gray eyes, and moved on, tall, reserved, fragrant with aftershave lotion. She found herself vaguely attracted to him. The children were guardedly civil. Lilith sensed they lived their public lives with those guards up.

In the store, she asked Joe whether he had seen any sign of Frederick Elman.

"Left town, *dih'nee?*" Joe said, as if repeating the weather forecast. Then he read the look on her face, and tried to soften his message. "You never know. A fella can change his mind."

"It's just gossip," Lilith said.

"That's right—gossip. Cheap gossip." Joe tried to make things right.

Lilith hurried away. Stupid gossip. Mean gossip. Vicious gossip. Gossip had been the source of her quarrel with Frederick. Gossip was always in error. Gossip found a way to make lies out of facts and, worse, facts out of lies.

Outside again, Lilith thought about the Dracut children. She wanted to run to them, embrace them, tell them everything was going to be all right, for the very reason that she believed everything was not going to be all right. She remembered herself as a child, fat, despised, secure if not comfortable with that depressing evaluation of self. She'd half concocted a theory that it was her duty to be ugly so that others could be beautiful. The idea made her feel noble and tragic. Then one day she wasn't fat anymore. She didn't deliberately set out to lose weight. It just happened. Now, pregnant, she was big and unwieldy again. It was as if she'd been loaned a new body to try out and had been found unworthy of it, and so it had been taken away.

Lilith headed down Center Darby Road. She had to find out the truth. A new garbage truck, driven by Frederick's father, whipped by her like a big, bad idea. She thought now about Elenore, who was a wife and mother and who might recognize her need, and she drove her red car into the Elman yard. She was intimidated by the junk cars and other crap littering the field, the ugliness, the violation of her standards of beauty, as if the Elmans were deliberately attempting to wound her. She resisted the desire to turn around; she stepped out of the car and approached the mobile home. Between the driveway ruts, tan grass tufts poked up like upside-down octopi.

In the shanty entry to the trailer, a dozen Honeywagon Inc. uniforms hung on wooden pegs against plywood sheeting. No change since the last time she'd been here, at Christmastime. The place felt as alien to her as if she were in another country.

She knocked, waited, and knocked again. She was about to leave when Elenore Elman answered. The hardness in Elenore's eyes told Lilith she'd made a mistake coming here.

"Something I can do for you?" Elenore spoke harshly.

"I am looking for Frederick." Lilith forced herself to sound businesslike.

"You want my son." Elenore, as if following the lead of the Squire's daughter, responded coolly.

"Yes." Lilith—cool.

"Gone." Elenore—cool.

"That's what I heard. I wanted to know if it was true." Lilith—cool.

"She wants to know if it's true. Took off in his truck." Elenore—cool.

"Where?" Lilith—cool.

"Who knows?" Elenore—suddenly hot. "They don't tell the women *nothn'*. *Nothn'*. Gone. Gone for good. Never coming back. You follow me?"

Elenore's anger—that maternal anger—flared up in front of Lilith. For a moment, she thrilled to its heat and brightness. It was as if she'd been lost in some wintry place, and fire suddenly flashed from the earth. But how to warm a body by a blaze? It could not be done. She stood naked between terrible

390

cold and terrible heat. Lilith took a step backward, then halted, hoping for a way to capture the warmth.

In the doorway, Elenore seemed to come to. She looked at Lilith, really looked at her, and what she saw she could not cope with. She shut the door. Alone now, in the confines of home again, listening to the groan of the refrigerator, Elenore understood something: that girl was in trouble. What to do? Elenore's only answer was to pray.

Howard headed for Donaldson in the new Honeywagon. It handled nice, lot of power, no slipping clutch, but it didn't smell very broken in.

He stopped along the way to buy stew beef, potatoes, carrots, onions, and a couple of oranges. At Cooty's cabin, he stoked up the wood stove, cleaned out the stew pot—wretched with goop but beyond stink—and dumped in the fresh meat and vegetables with some water.

"Time to start a new stew, Cooty," Howard said.

The old man lay on his bunk, hands shading his eyes from an imaginary sun. "I followed her, and she knew I was on to her, but she didn't care. She knew I wasn't going to hurt her, and she didn't want to hurt me. I wasn't worth bothering with. She roamed. They don't roam, black bears. They stay in one place, but this bear—she roamed. We went . . . I don't know where. We went . . . we went."

After Howard had gotten the fire going and started the stew, he sat down beside Cooty's cot, peeled the orange, and laid the wedges out in his own lap. He pulled the old man up to a sitting position and made him eat a wedge of orange. Cooty had eaten half the orange when he recognized his benefactor. "It's Howie, you horse's ass," he said.

"Shut up and eat your vitamin C, you crazy old hermit," Howard said.

Howard fed the wedges to Cooty with the solemnity of a priest dispensing communion wafers.

When he'd finished the orange, Cooty began to speak again, not talking to Howard exactly, but to the ages. "She was going to mate, and I wanted to see. I had carnal on my mind from the start. I never had no carnal before. Not strictly anyway."

"What color was she?" Howard broke in with his question.

"She was a black bear—black, the way I like 'em," Cooty said.

Howard laughed. "You get what you wanted from that sow? You get your rocks off?"

"I was as satisfied as her boar."

"Good for you, old man. Now, you tell Howie about that boar." Howard hoped to gather some information about the great white bear that was the talk of all the hunters in Tuckerman County.

"She kept on the move," Cooty said. "We seen bear sign, but she wasn't interested. She knew where she was going; she wanted a particular boar. I'd lose her for two or three days, then pick up her trail again. She was moving north, always north. We went up there, way up there, past the White Mountains and Connecticut Lakes, maybe up in Canada—I don't know—when I seen him, biggest, strangest bear I ever heard of. I watched 'em mate. Thirty, forty times a day for a week and then done till next year. Boar, he took off northerly, and my sow, she headed south."

Howard stopped the old man's reverie by grasping his shoulder.

"You know who I am?" he said gruffly.

"'Cohas I do, Howie."

"You say that boar was strange?" Howard interrogated.

"Nothing like any bear I ever seen before."

"Strange in color, I bet."

Cooty laughed, a weepy laugh.

Howard shook the old man gently. "Tell me," he said. "Tell me the color of that big boar."

Cooty put his hand on Howard's cheek and whispered something.

"What?" Howard turned up the volume on his hearing aid.

Cooty pushed away from Howard and stood, stretching out. "I don't remember," Cooty said.

"You don't remember?" Howard's mind cranked back to an old television show: *What a revolting development this is.*

"I knew, once I knew and I told somebody, when I was half asleep, the girl—Freddy's girl. She give me a ride, brought me back, and I shut my eyes, and everything was bright. I was seeing my sow, my darling sow. And I was seeing her boar. The girl, you understand, made my dreams bright. So I told her about the sow and the boar, leaving out the carnal, naturally. I knew the color then, and I told her. And it was like, I don't have to carry this around no more, and I forgot. It just went away."

"That's okay; I think I heard when you whispered." Howard wasn't going to let Cooty's forgetfulness get in the way of his own deeply held beliefs. That bear was white, and one fine day Howie Elman was going to hunt him down, skin his hide, and show that whiteness to the world.

"I lost her on the way back," Cooty said, "I lost my own self, but I figure she made it to Darby in the fall of the year. She musta had her cub this winter."

"Little tiny blind critter," Howard said. "Beast mothers have their young alone, lest the fathers eat 'em."

"I was lost for so long, Howie. I didn't know where I was or who I was. But I wanted to come back, wondering, you know, wondering. . . . Howie, do you know me? Does anybody know me? Howie, I'm back, ain't I? Ain't I?"

Persephone Butterworth Salmon Blue, flying home from the underbelly of the world, sat with her daughter's last letter in her lap. Lilith had discovered the greenhouse, which she'd transformed into "a place like my mind," a phrase that mystified her mother. College seemed far away, Lilith wrote. She'd talked to Harriet on the telephone just before she left for London to attend plays and study theater. Harriet was getting married in June. Like all of Lilith's letters, this one was full of chatter, close to the surface, but it also contained a reference to her unborn child that Persephone found disturbing. "I always thought that as a Salmon I had been given a great heritage, not to mention material wealth and property. I was not given quite what I expected. Now it's my turn to pass on something of myself to my own, and I find even less to give. What if all I have to give is the Salmon blood?"

Persephone folded the letter and put it back in the travel bag. She had written Lilith a couple of letters, the sum total of which said that she was healing herself and soon would return to Darby. She hadn't mentioned Hadly. Their relationship was private, hard to explain to one so young. How could she say, "We have a part-time marriage based on the principle of the semester." So she had said nothing. Indeed, she had skirted the whole issue of her own feelings. She'd meant to protect Lilith. Or maybe she had been too preoccupied with her own problems to deal with a daughter. She had neglected Lilith and now was returning to Upper Darby to set things right. Guilt no longer mattered; self no longer mattered. Only mothering mattered. That was always the way with a woman; everything came after mothering.

She had written Lilith to tell her she was coming home but not when. Persephone might feel spiritually and physically renewed (her arthritis was in remission), but her habits had not changed. She didn't want the word to get around Darby that she was back until she had actually arrived. Keep them off balance: that was her theory. She certainly couldn't trust Lilith to keep her mouth shut, so she had decided to surprise her. Persephone listened to the drone of the plane. *Spirit off the daughter. Leave Darby stunned and wondering. Raise the child. Teach the child. Prepare the child. Devise a way for the child to come back. Swoop down on Darby. Retake Darby.* She came out of the reverie, and shook away these terrible images—she hadn't had thoughts like this since she'd left America. Darby was a dangerous place, a trap; that young man from Center Darby, the Salmon house, the Trust—all traps. One problem was history—too much; another was money—not enough. She had to get Lilith out of there. After a long abstinence from tobacco, Persephone found herself wanting a cigarette.

The tires of the red car spun, kicking up dirt as Lilith tore out of the Elman yard. She drove home very fast on automatic pilot. As she pulled into the drive, the lilac bushes in their pots seemed scraggly, pathetic, drying out, dying. She ran to the barn, hauled out the shovel, dug a hole, planted a bush, dug another hole, planted a bush. After an hour, she'd planted nine bushes. She heard the telephone ring inside the house, and she dropped the shovel and ran for the door. The phone stopped ringing before she could get to it. Who had called—Frederick? Maybe he hadn't really left her. Maybe he'd changed his mind and was coming back. She waited by the phone. A minute passed. Another. Another. If it was Frederick, what would she say? Come on home, you bum! The phone rang. She twisted inside, but waited until the second ring to pick up the receiver.

The caller was Jacob the nursery man. Her check had bounced. Without any conscious cunning, Lilith lapsed into that peculiar role of the Squire's daughter in which she was self-conscious but unfeeling, carried along by habit and form. She soon persuaded Jacob that there'd been a financial mix-up with a couple different accounts. All would be set straight in a day or so. If Jacob doubted her word, perhaps he should return to the Salmon property and take back his plants. She could always buy lilacs elsewhere. "No problem," Jacob said, and apologized for troubling her. Lilith accepted the apology.

At the instant she hung up the phone, she was her true self again—desperate, confused, alone. It had been months since she'd checked her bank balance. But I have plenty of money. The Salmons are rich. Her grandmother would say, "See no evil, do no evil." She put her hands on the hard ball of her front. Who knows me? Her father used to say, "In the end, our own people save us or doom us." Perhaps that was the answer to her need—she would turn to her own people.

Praise the Road

> I stay on back roads to avoid police,
> real and imaginary.
> I listen to the Christian minister on the radio
> and look at the scenery.
> A wood-frame schoolhouse
> has been converted into a chiropractic center.
> Praise the Lord.
>
>
> Aching backs, arthritic joints, venereal sores,
> cancerous tumors, AIDS kisses, broken hearts,
> busted humps—pain and mortality—why, yes,
> I understand now what it's all about,
> the world not round but inside out,
> a Mobius strip dangling like a decoration
> in the waiting room of a chiropractic center.
> Praise the Lord.

If I ain't good at living,
what's the point of living?
If I'm no good to me and thee
what's the Good?
They'll say he drove too fast.
They'll say he jumped the rail,
At road's end, they'll say, man and vehicle
took holy communion with a telephone pole.
Praise the Lord.

Frederick stopped at a diner almost at the New York border. Dying restaurant, dying world. A McDonald's he'd passed down the road had siphoned off the business. A sign warned lone customers they might be asked to move from booth to counter if business picked up, an unlikely event, judging from the look of the place, but he took a seat at the counter anyway, because he liked the silver-based, red-topped bar stools. He scanned a public bulletin board cluttered with papers and cards. "Baby-sitting, in my house . . . Chevy pickup, runs good . . . Roofing, free estimates." And so forth.

He'd brought his map in and gazed at it absent-mindedly. The map gave him something to focus on and announced to the natives that he was a traveler, harmless to them, immaterial in their world. Perfect. The waitress was dumpy and sixty, and she wore a pink apron over blue jeans. She made him think of his mother. It was past lunchtime, and to celebrate his inverted view of the world he ordered breakfast—blueberry pancakes, sausage, orange juice, and coffee.

With the traveler's twenty-twenty vision for detail, he watched the short-order cook working at the grill. From the smooth, swift, but thorough way he squeegeed the grease from the grill, it was clear he was good at his trade. The man was ruggedly built, with a pockmarked face and worn eagle tattoos on his shoulders. He looked more like a Jack London–type seaman than a cook. (Frederick had read London from the library of Reggie Salmon.) The cook was skillful, precise, and even fussy. He poured the pancake batter from a recycled quart can of A&P tomatoes. He measured the amount by eye, but each cake was exactly the same size. He tossed the already partially cooked link sausage on the grill. He spooned exactly one tablespoon of blueberries onto each pancake. When the batter began to bubble, he flipped the pancakes over deftly as a fisher cat turning a hedgehog belly-up for supper.

"You do good work," Frederick said.

The cook eyed him suspiciously. Nobody talked to the cook, it wasn't done. "I never think about it," the cook said.

Garvin was surprised when Lilith arrived at his office and a little shocked by her appearance. The other night, when he had proposed marriage, all he'd really seen were parts of her— eyes, hair, glowing skin, full breasts. Now, as he greeted her at the door, he was painfully aware she was taller than he and, in this condition of pregnancy, heavier.

"You're . . . you're . . . so big," he said.

"The baby's dropped," Lilith said.

"Sit down, rest—please." Garvin led her to the leather-upholstered chair in front of his desk where he seated his clients.

Lilith hesitated but took the seat. She would tell him: I have no money—you know that. Frederick's left me. I'll marry you, Garvin. I'll do my best to be a good wife. "I just had to see you," she said.

"You must have found out about Dracut," Garvin said. It pained him to look directly at her swollen body, and so he looked half at her face and half at the door.

"Dracut?"

"Is pushing the state legislature for a law that would tax the Trust at the same rate as any other property."

"Well, isn't that just fair?"

"Fair? Lilith, the point is, this changes the whole picture. Limited development of the Trust won't be enough to pay the taxes that the town will be able to levy because of the change in the law. For the town, it means—basically—outside money coming in. We'll lose Darby. Monet and I are dropping our court suits to fight Dracut." Garvin's voice was full of war fury.

Lilith tried and failed to gather her thoughts. She remained in place, trembling and mute.

To fill the silence, Garvin asked, just as easily as if he were commenting on the weather, "So, is Frederick around?"

The question jarred Lilith out of her anguish. Garvin was probing.

When Lilith did not respond, Garvin added, "I heard that his pickup wasn't parked in your drive last night. Maybe he's having it repaired?"

As easily as Garvin had spoken, she said, "He went up to the mountains to hike for a couple of days. I mean, the baby's not due for a week."

Garvin dropped his jaw and raised an eyebrow in appreciation of her blatant lie.

They yammered amiably. Garvin talked about fitness. Fit people looked better, lived longer, and, according to mounting evidence, thought better, because more blood flowed to their brains. In response, Lilith made a pitch for gardening. Not only did you get the exercise you needed, but you improved the appearance of the world. Not by her father's standards, Garvin countered. Lilith reminded Garvin that he'd drifted far afield from the issue he had raised—fitness. Garvin's comeback to that one was that it was she who had established the subject matter for the discussion, not fitness but hiking.

Through all this, Lilith skated into an ether. At the bottom of everything between herself and Garvin was deception. She remembered childhood games: Takes one to know one. She was touched. Lies were the best Garvin could do by way of intimacy. If she married him, they would spend a lifetime deceiving one another and forgiving one another for the deception. Marriage with Garvin would be sporting. Perhaps they would be happy. Too bad Garvin was not the father of her child. Too bad Garvin was not the man she loved.

Then, not deliberately, out of the blue, Lilith knocked Garvin off balance. She wondered for a moment about his inner life, the life beyond his possessions, beyond his rebellion against his father, beyond his lies. "Garvin," she said, "do you think about happiness?"

"Why do you ask that?" He was slightly annoyed with her now.

"I just want to hear what you have to say. It's important—happiness is important, isn't it?" she said.

They both sensed the atmosphere between them thickening.

Garvin sought to regain the offensive. "Do *you* think about happiness?"

"I can't say I've ever been truly happy—never."

"I think about . . . I think about . . ." Garvin paused, deciding between making light of this or being serious and revealing himself. He chose a middle course. "Be happy—of course that's what it's all about. But what is happiness? Money? Love? Contentment? Keeping busy? Who knows? Why think about something you can't define?"

The intercom system on Garvin's desk honked. "Mr. Horace Debussey Jones here." The receptionist sounded as if she were shouting through a culvert. Lilith thought about kids talking through cans on taut strings.

Garvin addressed the intercom—"Ask him to wait a minute"—then turned to Lilith. "This is really not a good time. I have appointments."

"Oh, of course." She didn't belong here. She didn't belong with Garvin and his ideas and his life.

"Listen, when I talked to Monet, we agreed to meet at the Salmon house tonight to work something out—okay?"

"Yes, a meeting," Lilith said. Face them, smile at them, serve them drinks and crackers and cheese, and then tell them you have nothing to say . . . nothing . . . nothing.

She was almost outside, in the nether zone between office and waiting room, and Garvin was pulling away from her, when she blurted out, "Garvin, I planted some lilacs." Humiliation flooded over her the moment the words escaped from her mouth.

"That's great, really great," Garvin said with a private little laugh, as if filing away this story to tell to his friends.

Lilith headed for her uncle Monet's place. He was the only family she had left in Darby. Perhaps he would help her. Perhaps she would accept his offer to buy her house. But how to ask for help? How to take a hand reaching out?

When Howard returned home from Cooty's place, he found Elenore kneeling at the feet of the concrete Virgin.

"You went to church already—this one of those twofers-for-Jesus days?" he said.

Elenore usually answered Howard's jests with one of her own, but this time she did not speak, nor look up. Her eyes remained fixed on the Virgin.

"Isn't once enough?" Howard barked out his questions. Things didn't look right or feel right.

"I've sinned," Elenore said.

"Sinned? You ain't sinned in your whole life. I'm the sinner." Howard was bragging.

"I have . . . sinned." Elenore spoke to the Virgin.

"Well, what did you do?" Howard squatted beside Elenore. A pain shot from his bad leg right into his buttocks, driving him to his knees. He suppressed the voice of the pain, and remained in the kneeling position because it was more comfortable than squatting. The doctor had told him the leg would be tender now and again when he least expected it.

"I ain't sure," Elenore said. "Something about that girl. Something."

"I wish I knew what you were talking about."

"I wish I knew."

"Damn-fool woman," Howard said.

"Pray with me," Elenore said.

"All righty, what the hell."

In Monet's Butterworth house, Lilith followed her uncle through the hallway. She had been surprised by his greeting— somber, distracted, so unlike him.

"You haven't been here since . . . Marcia, have you?" he said.

"No," Lilith said.

"Let me show you the carnage," he said, and with that disturbing remark led her to the room that had been designed as dining hall, library, meeting room, the Ball Room, as the Butterworths had called it. When Monet opened the big oak door, Lilith was startled by the sight of a human skeleton dangling from wires. A second later, she smelled something that reminded her a little of a college biology lab. But there was another smell, not a chemical smell so much as a musty, organic smell.

Now Lilith noticed a lab table. On the edge was an open bottle of Mexican beer; in the center, an animal skewed on a stand. It was pink and filmy and dissected to the point where Lilith couldn't tell what it had been when whole. This creature, its identity unknown to her, its body parts laid out on a table for identification—what to think of it? She remembered now that last year she'd decided to switch her major in school from music to premed. "What is it?" she asked.

"A thing that lived and never lived." Monet smiled slyly and drank from the bottle of beer.

Lilith frowned.

"It's a fetus, female. I found her on the Trust lands all wrapped in her mother's slimy gauze. The doe had been run down by coyotes, or maybe pack dogs. She got away, but she'd dropped her fawn."

"I wonder if the fawn was happy. Did she think? Did she feel? She had to dream. In your mother's womb—that's where you must learn to dream."

"Lilith, you're such a Salmon—a romantic at heart." Monet's voice was full of pride.

She sensed that now, now was the time to plead her case. But she hesitated, not knowing why. She saw something on a paper towel. "The heart?" She pointed.

"Yes," Monet said.

Lilith bent by the table and stared at the fetal deer. She felt no revulsion, no curiosity as such, but a yearning whose meaning she could not grasp.

"Come with me," Monet said.

Lilith followed him to another room, and the sight of it turned her upside down for a moment. Monet had constructed a replica of Reggie's study.

"Do you like it?" Monet read the awe on her face.

"I don't know," Lilith said.

"Sit down, Lilith. I have something to tell you." He stood behind a chair, and Lilith took a seat. Lilith watched her uncle pace the floor, so like her father and so completely opposite. She felt a coldness toward him, perhaps something like her mother's coldness toward Reggie. These Salmon men were so ridiculous and destructive with their dreams. How to ask such a man for something without losing everything to him?

"Marcia has left me," Monet said. "She took Noreen with

her. Noreen was carrying our child. Marcia could not bear a child. I've lost everything. My wife, my child, my ideas, my pride. We were going to change the world. Look what it came to—nothing. I'll be honest, Lilith. I thought you would crack eventually and sell me the house. My son would have inherited it. The Trust would have been his domain. That can't happen now. I spent most of my money on legal fees fighting the Prells. All I want to do now is build a little cabin in the Trust, live out my days in solitude." Lilith said nothing, and Monet had to continue talking to fill the void. "Right from the start, I think Marcia and Noreen were having . . . a relationship."

Lilith was barely listening. She was starting her ascent to a sacred place.

Nowhere

> Whip off the main road
> onto a road without a name sign or number
> then off onto another road.
> Lose yourself.
> Go nowhere, sleep nowhere, wake nowhere.
> In the morning, drive away from the sun.

The road went up over a mountain, wound down, then followed a river. He stopped at a fisherman's pull-off, shutting down the engine and listening to the whisper of the river. The water hurried over rocks with an apparent purposefulness that made his own travels seem frivolous. Not a house in sight. Hardwoods, bare of leaves but colored maroon with buds. On the steep hillside, beyond a bend in the river, the shadow of a bridge. He walked a couple hundred yards to the bend, where the bridge suddenly came into view as he turned. It was an old railroad trestle, straddling the river gorge. He walked until the bridge was dead above him, blocking out part of the sky,

404

like the weight of an old crime blocking out a man's peace of mind.

The bridge impressed Frederick, looming over him, a black belly and gridwork hanging like entrails. And what gridwork! Hundreds of upside-down metal arches supported the rail bed. Must have been an architectural wonder of its time. The bridge hadn't been painted in years, and likely never would be painted again. Exempt rail line. Some day maybe they'd dynamite the carcass of this old dragon. He'd always wanted to see a bridge come down. Some day.

He was about to leave when he spotted a slash of color high up in the gridwork, bright red in a mass of black. Didn't make sense. He walked back to the truck and hauled out his binoculars. He could see that somebody had spray-painted some words, but he couldn't read them. Frederick put the binoculars away and drove off, but after a minute or so he began to wonder about those words. Who would want to risk life and limb to write a message no one could read except someone else crazy enough to climb up? What words could mean so much? A name? An insult? A curse? Some personal expression deliberately left in that limbo between earth and sky? Frederick turned the truck around and returned to the bridge. He had to wade into the stream and climb up a pyramidal stone-block base before he reached the gridwork.

The climb went more easily than he'd expected, because there were no big pieces to get around. He was constantly in a network of metal. He felt safe and secure, but the grid obscured the vision of his destination. He'd get a glimpse of the graffito, and then it would disappear as he climbed. He'd go up, and then he'd have to go down, following the arch of the metal. Meanwhile, he'd lose his bearings, so that, when he looked for the message, it wouldn't be where it was supposed to be. He found himself having constantly to double back and try again. The easier the climb was, the farther away he seemed to be from his destination. When, finally, he began to draw closer, the grid seemed to thicken, so that he could never get a clear view of the graffito. He'd see a touch of red, he'd move, and black steel would be in his way.

Eventually, he lost sight of the graffito altogether. He began to think he'd dreamed it up. He climbed some more, then decided to rest, cradling himself in a network of steel. The sun had warmed the metal. This was not a bridge that he would want to paint. It was just too complicated. It would drive him nuts—maybe he was already nuts.

He pondered himself. He was a failure, utterly and without redemption. He had failed all his loved ones and he had failed himself. He had rejected honorable work because he was, in his own way, more of a snoot than any of those Upper Darby people. Maybe he had never actually loved Lilith Salmon; maybe he just liked the idea of being seen with her, liked the idea of people gossiping about them, liked the idea that his presence demeaned her, brought her down to his level. She was certainly better off without him, as was the baby. Who did it belong to? At the moment, he was relieved that he wouldn't have to take care of it or act as a good example for it, and probably it wasn't his anyway. His life was over. He had nothing—no job, no lover, no past, no future, no hope, no ambitions; nothing but his freedom. Maybe the best thing to do was just drop off, enjoy the ride down, and let the sudden stop take care of everything.

From Monet's, Lilith returned to her own house. She was changing again on the inside. She didn't feel pain so much as an intimation of pain. The feeling was accompanied by a sense of danger, nameless, featureless, thoughtless, but pervasive: the air of Upper Darby, more dense in her house than anywhere. Soon Garvin and Monet would arrive to lay their plans. They sought neither peace nor resolution, but a continuation of fighting. They had competed not strictly out of greed or a desire for security, or even for personal gain, but for the sake of competition. Combat, fought under the rules of engagement prescribed by the principles of law and business and heritage, was their drug, their god, their romance, their beginning, and their end. Now they were allies, conspiring to face a common threat—Dracut. Next week, next month, next year, it would be somebody else, some other idea. No end to it. Her house was no longer hers. It belonged to them, confiscated in behalf of the war effort. Everything belonged to them. War kept her people intact, busy, and engaged, but a war without casualties was no war at all. Her place in this scheme of things was to be the casualty. She feared not for herself but for her unborn child; she feared the radiation of war lust.

It was the secondary feeling of danger that Lilith acted upon. Had she known how imminent her time was, she might have driven to the hospital in Tuckerman, but, like many first-time mothers, she did not recognize the early stages of labor. Perhaps, if she had not misread the signs, she might have fled to the Trust anyway. Her impulse now was to hide in that private place that was both a physical locale and a state of mind. Another woman might have questioned herself, but in Lilith's life only impulsiveness and spontaneity had allowed her to do anything. When she thought things out, or consulted with others regarding her desires, she would find herself blocked from action. Now she was moved to act not by mind but by blood.

She made a couple of tuna sandwiches and stuffed them in her backpack over a blanket. Outside again, she found a belt ax and a bow saw in the barn, things belonging to her father that Monet had overlooked in his raid months earlier. She started walking.

When she reached the ledges, she built a rough lean-to of hemlock boughs, and then she made a fire. She had finished the work, and the fire was going, when the labor pains started getting closer together and more intense, and she realized what was happening. It was too late to go back, and anyway she didn't want to. She'd await her hour like those Indian women of old. She began to lose track of time, of people, and soon even of place.

Frederick was flirting with the idea of jumping when he slipped off the beam. In that split second when he might have fallen, he realized how self-pitying and false were his claims against the fear of death, the promise of life. He caught himself, but his body pitched forward just enough so that he had a revised view through the grid. And there was the message, not above but below him, just as clear as if he'd written it himself moments earlier, red spray paint shaping the ancient declaration of one soul to another: I LOVE YOU.

He hoisted himself up to a sitting position in the net of metal. I LOVE YOU. Of course. He loved Lilith, and she loved him. Or maybe she didn't love him. That didn't matter right now. Lilith needed a father for her child; she needed a hand to do things around the house, a shoulder to rest her head upon; whether she loved him or not, it was his care she needed. What's more, he owed her; she had saved him. He wasn't going to kill himself; he wasn't going to drift around the country forever. He was going to go back to school, and this time he'd succeed. He was going to make his contribution to the world, and he had Lilith to thank.

His past life seemed narrow to him now, his travels nothing. He'd go here, he'd go there, but whether he was in New Hampshire or Louisiana or Texas or Colorado, he'd find himself in the world of the Honeywagons and the Howard Elmans. Lilith had shown him one of these other worlds, not better or worse than his own, but different, messed up in a different way. Maybe, now that he knew that, he could be a little more compassionate. Anger came easily—fear came easily—passion came easily—opinion came easily; compassion came hard. He would never belong to her world, but he could never go back to his father's world. He belonged on bridges. Perhaps some day he himself would be a bridge.

And the baby? What difference did it make who the biological father was? It belonged to Lilith; it belonged to Darby; it belonged to everybody. Everybody belonged to everybody else. Now he understood about the bridge. A man had to be a bridge for the children of the earth. The old duty, the common duty, the noble duty of parenthood was still the most important duty. It was time to point the Live Free or Die East toward creation.

It was getting dark when Garvin and Monet, comrades at last, just happened to arrive at the same time at the Salmon house, Monet in his Bronco II, Garvin on his bicycle. They talked outside for a while, then drifted into the Hearth Room.

"Lilith?" Garvin called.

No answer.

"Her car's in the yard. She must be in the greenhouse, or out in the garden," Monet said.

The men took positions at opposite ends of the couch in the Hearth Room. Here Garvin had sat with Reggie Salmon to discuss the legal details of the Trust. Here Monet had slept off his first drunks as a teenager. To seal their alliance, Monet agreed to support Garvin's plans for limited development of the Trust; Garvin agreed that Monet should be made the official and permanent caretaker of the Trust lands. In the next town election for selectman, they'd both throw their support to Critter Jordan in an effort to move Dracut out.

Their conversation was interrupted by a sound outside. Car coming. Monet went to the window, watched the headlights wind down the driveway. He turned to Garvin. "It's a taxi cab."

On the Trust, the weather was turning. The wind had shifted from the south to the north. The temperature had started dropping. Lilith was aware of none of this. She was in hard labor, and between the contractions she could only think about the next pain. She had become her effort.

Speeding back to Darby, Frederick had a premonition of danger in the form of images tumbling about in his mind. A hunter. A deer, full with a fawn. A pack of dogs. Crusty snows. He didn't know what to make of these mental pictures, constituted of dreams, memories, desires. They had something to do with Lilith, he knew that. He tried to call her from a pay phone. No answer. Could he trust his sense of foreboding? Perhaps he was wasting his time. Perhaps she'd already forgotten him, and was making plans to marry Garvin Prell. Didn't matter. He had to go on. All the hours he drove, he couldn't shake the feeling that something was terribly wrong. Wrong? Who—what—was wrong? He'd been wrong to leave her, that much was certain. But there was a greater wrong, a wrong outside himself and herself, that had divided them. Their world? Just the way they were made? He didn't know. He drove on, carried forward by machine, by habit, and by these disturbing pictures in his mind.

It was night when he arrived in Darby. He didn't bother stopping anywhere in town, but drove right to the Salmon house. A light was on inside, Lilith's red car was in its place, all seemed to be normal. He relaxed a little. He wondered now what he'd say to her. Maybe they were even. No reason to say anything. He made a conscious decision to revert to family type—walk into the house as if nothing had happened. He did just that, barging in as if the place was his own, and announcing, "I'm home!" No response to his arrogant shout. No music from the stereo system. And the place didn't smell right. In the Hearth Room, a True Blue burned in an ashtray. Empty drink glasses littered the meeting table.

"Lilith!" he bellowed.

"She's not here."

Frederick whipped around at the sound of the voice. Persephone Salmon stood in the doorway. "We were talking, we were planning the future of Upper Darby."

Frederick was stunned. When Persephone had left for Australia, she'd seemed on the verge of some terrible illness. Her skin was red and rough, her voice raspy, her breath offensive, her body bent, and her hands like claws. Now it was as if he were looking at the same woman twenty years ago, before illness and age had caught up with her. Persephone was beautiful, her skin tanned and smooth, body carriage straight.

She walked slowly toward him, and there was a kind of hypnotic, snake-slither menace in her movement. She came close, not a foot away, before she stopped. Her breath was sweet and acidly perfumed as an allergen; it made his eyes burn. "The plans we made—I've never felt so alive."

"Where's Lilith?" Frederick was angry now.

"We don't know," she said, and a change in her voice, vulnerable and frightened, washed away his anger, and Frederick realized that he too was frightened.

Persephone led Frederick to the greenhouse while she told him what had happened. "The men were restless. They wanted someone to bring them drinks. I'm past the age where they can make such demands on me. They—we—looked for Lilith."

Frederick understood. It was Lilith's job to serve. Youth's place was to serve the elders their intoxicants. Send the boys to fight the wars of the old men. Marry off the girls to the sons of allies. Subvert the idealism of the young to their own. Prey on their idealism. Crush their idealism. Frederick resisted an urge to hurt Persephone, to dirty her up.

411

"She's missing," Persephone said. "Monet and Garvin went outside, screaming like idiots. We examined every corner of the house, even the top floor, where we found her footprints in the dust, but no Lilith."

Persephone had just called Constable Perkins, who was organizing a search party. Meanwhile, Garvin and Monet were looking for Lilith by their own lights. Monet supposed she'd head for the old cemetery, where Reggie had once been buried. He had left in his Bronco II to check out that possibility. Garvin had taken off on his bicycle, believing he'd find Lilith at the Prell development down the road.

While all this was sinking in, Frederick wasn't thinking clearly. He was under the spell of this strange woman, his bastard mother-in-law. She took him to the greenhouse. After Monet and Garvin had left, something had told her to go there. Persephone hadn't stepped foot in the place since she'd cleaned it out almost a year ago, so she was shocked when she'd seen it tonight—just as Frederick was shocked.

He couldn't have named the plants, but he could feel their effect on him—he was in paradise. All those hours when he was at work, Lilith had been toiling in the greenhouse. She'd created a garden, not lush and cordial and ordered like a European garden, not spare and self-composed like a Japanese garden, but purely American—wild and self-absorbed, yet oddly fragile, as if at any moment a change in weather could destroy it. The smell of flowers made him want to weep with love for Lilith, love for the Northern New England earth, which of course is not earth at all, but stone.

Persephone lit a cigarette. "We've misjudged her—we've let her down—all of us."

"I know where she went," Frederick said.

Frederick told Persephone where to send Constable Perkins and his searchers, and then he headed out. Even on a dark night like this one, it was faster to cut through the hills on foot to get to the ledges than drive to the pond on the Trust road.

A sickle moon illuminated the field outside the Salmon house until he reached the woods beyond the stone wall, and then it was almost pitch-black, much darker than he had anticipated. But he jogged along the path, going as much by feel as by sight. He'd blunder into some branches, then veer off back into the path. Every once in a while, he'd see starlight above and the path would appear, before it vanished into the gloom.

When he reached the ledges, where the trees fell away, the sky opened and he could see quite clearly. Moonlight washed over the granite. It was getting cold. Winter was returning. He hiked over the rocks until he reached the Indian camp. Lilith was only a few feet away, curled on her side, under the cover of hemlock branches.

"Lilith?" he crawled into the lean-to. He felt the blood on his hands; he could feel it soaking into the soil. He'd seen blood like this before, from the burst arteries of deer shot with high-powered rifles.

"Frederick. Oh, Frederick." Her voice was soft as the hemlock boughs.

The baby was at her breast.

A ray of moonlight fell on the infant's face. "Beautiful," Frederick said.

"You came back. I didn't think you would. I thought—He's gone, gone forever." Her voice was soft as the sound of mist.

"I came back to take care of you." He knelt by her. He knew he was too late. The life was draining out of her.

"Frederick, I'm happy. For the first time in my life, I'm happy." She put her hand on his beard, and then it slipped away. She shut her eyes.

He slid his hand between the baby and Lilith and put it over her heart. He could feel the child's rapid, strong heartbeat and

413

Lilith's weaker, slower beat. He knew that, even at the end, dying creatures can hear clearly, so he whispered, "I love you." She opened her eyes for a long moment, and then they closed of their own accord. Each heartbeat was weaker than the last, and then there was none. The child's heartbeat continued strong and sure, and his son drew in his life from his mother's breast.

The Dogs of March

My feet sting with cold
—"His feet sting with cold,"
the choir mocks him in song—
the back of my trigger hand is numb and blue;
my nose runs, I weep.
"This is no hunter, providing food for family and tribe.
This fellow confuses police tactics with religion,
exercise with duty. He's just a man with a gun."
I listen for the crackle of disturbed leaves,
hear only the crunch of my own footfalls.
I scan the measures between trees.
I search for movement, a flash of white light.
She's there. I sense her, delicate, unaware.

Snow begins to fall,
as if it had been falling in a time before this,
I a self before this self.
The gray whitens, less a cloak,
more a sheath to protect the blade of the new season.
I cut the distance between us. Down wind,
I wait, patient, stiff;
my smell crouches in the rocks like a bad memory.
"Mocking himself, he mocks us all.
Disinter his bones and put him in the movies."

I hear her. Hoofs stroke the snow.
Soft mouth nuzzles the tips of the hemlock trees.
My neck is sopping with frigid dew,
and I am cold but do not shiver.
The rifle warms me, squares my shoulders,
drops me to one knee, until I am in perfect position.
I feel like a dancer.
My vision narrows to a point of white light.
A string tightens from a place inside me.
The noise goes slack, then comes round in echo.
I rise to my feet and follow the bullet.

Snow forms flesh on the bones of the trees.
It falls as if in a time before this,
to pay homage to a time before that.
It falls with the grace of a penitent
dropping to his knees.
The doe has no vision of coming winter,
no vision of the dogs of March,
their paws skimming along the hard rough snows
while her sharp hoofs plunge through.
A dancer, suddenly awkward, alone, pursued,
she listens to her breath:

She sees shades of gray over shades of gray.
The trails she follows are marked by their smell,
wind down into nodes,
where remembrance of sleep lies softly as fur.
Her ears are cocked like an audience's,
her nerve endings choir singers
listening for their cues.
It is then the horizon joins the earth,
and becomes moss.
Is this sharp awareness a color? Is color a curve,

like a boat and she rising to the surface to meet it,
rising to meet the horizon,
rising from the dark depths of oily waters, rising,
breaking through to the broad lake and the bucks?
Or only snow pressing against the leaves?

The bright color of flesh colors the leaves.
She begins to fall slowly to her knees,
then she rises while a part of her does not rise.
Her nerve endings jerk spasmodically.
She crashes through brush,
the strings of her body pulling all wrong and violently.

"In pursuit, he hears a pounding on the forest floor,
which is the sound of his own feet
mingled with the sound of his crazy dreams.
He hears his child bang without purpose
on an organ in an empty church."

She falls and is still. I find her.
I unsheathe my knife and open her belly,
leaving her insides steaming on new snow.
I curse, my lips crack when I try to speak
and my hands blister when I reach for her.
I drag the body across the orchard.
The falling snow gently heals the bruised earth
with its nothingness.